Nadeem Aslam was born in Pakista
He is the author of four previous n
longlisted for the Booker Prize, shortlisted for the IMPAC Prize
and DSC Prize for South Asian Literature. He has also won the
Kiriyama and Windham-Campbell Prizes and the Lannan and
Encore Awards. He is a fellow of the Royal Society of Literature.

Further praise for *The Golden Legend*:

'The setting of *The Golden Legend* may be Pakistan, but the
closing of minds and hearts it laments is universal.' *Economist*

'Aslam's crystalline prose and emotionally nuanced characters
give his novel a wide resonance ... Though unsparing in its
depiction of the brutal exercise of power, this is also a paean to
human resilience.' *Financial Times*

'Few [novels published this year] are likely to be as beautiful
... This brutal, gorgeous novel feels like an elegy to a lost ideal.'
Daily Mail

'The year certainly begins in topical fashion with the latest
book from UK based Pakistani author Nadeem Aslam, who
regularly investigates political, social and cultural issues in
tales of incredible beauty and thoughtfulness ... It is un-
doubtedly the first must-read book of the year.' *National*

'Elegant but nostalgic ... told with beautifully measured
precision ... This is legend as myth, golden like the Golden
Age, lamenting the decline from a luminous, earned multicul-
turalism to aggressive bigotry. It's a very beautiful elegy for an
ideal that died in Pakistan some time ago and won't be back
any time soon.' *Artsdesk*

'A hymn of praise to cultural mixing.' Tom Sutcliffe

'A remarkable book [and] a remarkable writer ... a grieving not just for Pakistan, what it could be and what it has been but for the whole of civilisation.' Jamila Gavin

'I can't remember a book that has had such a profound visual effect on me ... Extraordinarily moving.' Alex Preston

'What Aslam does so brilliantly is juxtapose these very beautiful images with accounts of shocking quotidian brutality.' Stephanie Merritt

'Beautifully imagined ... [Aslam] makes the unfathomable appear almost ordinary, drawing readers into his multifaceted story and making its brutality more recognizably terrible. Mr. Aslam's expansive view of history lends his writing this equanimity, as well as its stubborn sense of hope.' Sam Sacks, *Wall Street Journal*

'Stunning ... Masterful and compelling fiction, intricately layering symbols and parallels, unspooling its plot in dramatic twists until the very last sentence, and revealing the deep interconnections between the themes of power, principle, love, and loss that underlie those realities.' *Boston Globe*

'A powerful and timely comment on the precarious state of religious minorities in Pakistan, and ... an honest mirror to the Pakistani state and society.' *Washington Post*

'An aching, lyrical story of schisms and secrets ... Brooding and beautiful: a mature, assured story of the fragility of the world and of ourselves.' *Kirkus Reviews* starred review

'Exquisite ... Aslam uses lush, sensuous prose to create beauty from ugliness, calm from chaos, and love from hatred, offering hope to believers and non-believers alike. This thoughtful, thought-provoking read will enthrall lovers of international fiction.' *Library Journal* starred review

'[An] exquisite, luminous novel.' *Publishers Weekly* starred review

'[Aslam is] a brilliant novelist, one of two or three truly great writers in the world today ... *The Golden Legend* is a magical book, but also a pragmatic one, offering hope in the face of violence and tragedy, bigotry, and intolerance. Aslam's writing is lyrical and expansive, luminescent, replete with stunningly beautiful passages. His characters resist oppression, growing in strength and dignity as they refuse to bend to hateful authority.' *Counterpunch by the same author*

SEASON OF THE RAINBIRDS
MAPS FOR LOST LOVERS
THE WASTED VIGIL
THE BLIND MAN'S GARDEN

THE GOLDEN LEGEND

NADEEM ASLAM

FABER & FABER

First published in 2017
by Faber & Faber Limited
Bloomsbury House
74–77 Great Russell Street
London WC1B 3DA
This paperback edition first published in 2018

Typeset by Faber & Faber Ltd
Printed and bound by CPI Group (UK) Ltd, Croydon, CR0 4YY

A CIP record for this book
is available from the British Library

ISBN 978-0-571-33075-1

2 4 6 8 10 9 7 5 3 1

For Khayyam and Lisa

There is no greater denier of God than he
who accepts injustice instead of rebelling.

QATEEL SHIFAI

The first place of note is the Minaret Fortress. As we
approached it our convoy passed through a delightful
valley between burial mounds overgrown with lime and
plane trees. These were the graves of several thousand plague
victims. Here blossomed many-coloured flowers, born of
the infested ashes.

ALEXANDER PUSHKIN
*A Journey to Arzrum at the
Time of the 1829 Campaign*

Contents

PROLOGUE

It was a large room. There were many shelves of books, a metal helmet for a stallion from the times of the Crusades, and there were the vertebrae of a whale from a bay in Antarctica. In one alcove was the earliest known photograph of a snowflake.

The child entered the silence and stillness of the vast interior through the far door. She came past the fishing canoe resting on a long low table under the window.

She was seven years old and her name was Helen.

Two buildings stood next to each other at the centre of the room. Each was taller than the girl, was perhaps four times her height. During that early morning hour, the light still only half awake, she stood looking at them.

They appeared to be mosques, and they were beautiful – with their families of domes, semi-domes, and minarets. She thought of them as two elaborate hats or headdresses, possibly meant for djinns or a pair of giants from a fairytale. She considered taking a few additional steps and peering through one of their windows. The colours and features were so precise and assorted – the muted shine on the walls and the arcs of the domes. She reached out and touched the detail of a painted leaf.

Buildings situated within a room! Normally it was a room that existed within a building, was contained by it.

She described a circle around them now. She went past the cupboard where stood the vase of dried branches brought back from Russia. They were from the apple trees that Count Tolstoy had planted with his own hands. Four of them were still alive in his orchard.

The girl stopped when one of the buildings produced a creak, as though it were experiencing a mild earthquake. It stirred now and rose a few inches, breaking free of gravity, swaying a little. And then it ascended further, beginning to travel at a languid pace towards the ceiling. It was being pulled up by the delicate-seeming yet strong chains that were attached to the tips of its minarets. Eventually it came to a stop – up there, in the high distance.

The immense room she was in was a library and a study. A place of fertile solitude. Due to its size it was difficult to heat in the winter months. Not long ago they had had the idea of bringing in two small cabins – each just large enough to house a desk and chair, a stack of immediately necessary books and papers, and a small heater. The thinking was that from December to February a person would go into one of the cabins, close the door behind her, and work in that pocket of warmth. From ordinary cabins, however, they had become detailed models of two historic buildings – the Great Mosque of Córdoba, and the Hagia Sophia in Istanbul.

The girl had caught glimpses of them being constructed during the previous few weeks. Now they were ready, and because it was June they were being winched up, to remain suspended up there until December.

After the Hagia Sofia, she watched the Great Mosque of Córdoba being pulled up by the system of pulleys and chains.

Neither of the two buildings had a floor of its own. They would borrow the room's floor when they were down here. So when Helen looked up now she could see into the interiors. She imagined moths fluttering like trapped prayers under the miniature domes in the evenings, bumping against the coloured insides. She would always remember this handful of moments from her early years. Childhood – when minutes could feel as prolonged as hours, and the days vanished in the blink of an eye.

It was Helen's father who had carpentered the buildings. And it was he who was causing them to rise through the air, storing them out of the way. She turned and looked at him where he stood at the other end of the room, operating the various cranks and pulleys located near the corner. She liked the fact that he made one last minor adjustment to the chains, making sure both buildings were held at exactly the same height.

He was a tall bright-blooded man, and his name was Lily.

I

THE ORCHARD

1

This world is the last thing God will ever tell us.

A few hours before he was killed, Massud woke at the call to the predawn prayer. It was issuing from the loudspeakers attached to the minaret just across the lane. He imagined the worshippers approaching the eighteenth-century mosque in silence, some of them carrying lanterns. The sight of empty shoes at the thresholds of mosques had always made him think that the men had been transformed into pure spirit just before entering.

After the call ended, the smell of bread drifted to him from the house behind the mosque, where the cleric lived, the man's daughter rising at this hour to prepare a meal for him.

Massud turned his head on the pillow and looked at Nargis, asleep beside him. How long he lay there looking at her he would not have been able to say, but the amount of light was increasing softly around them, the earliest rays of the day arriving at the house. There were shadows but they were out of focus. How noisy the sun would be, Nargis had observed once, if sound could travel through space. The ceaseless firestorms. The oceans of flame.

Massud had turned fifty-five years old the previous month, and Nargis was fifty-two. They had met and married when they were in their twenties, and as he would confess to her later, he hadn't had the courage to cast a direct second glance towards her until a fortnight after the first. With her contemplative calm and beauty, she hadn't seemed like a real person at all. Much to his embarrassment, he had almost lost consciousness the first time he had taken her into his embrace.

He lay awake now, grateful for her presence beside him in life. The breeze came from the direction of the mosque again, and as he fell back asleep he remembered reading somewhere that the smell of bread instils kindness in human beings.

Numerous bird wings were hanging from nails driven into the far wall of the kitchen, lit up by lines of sunlight. They were in a range of sizes, beginning with a sunbird's two-inch pair, and ending with a single giant one that had belonged to a trumpeter swan, with dozens of species in between. The most beautiful modern building in Pakistan was said by many to be a mosque designed by Nargis and Massud. They were architects, and they lived surrounded by objects from which they might draw inspiration. Apart from the bird wings, in one corridor there was a chariot from Sindh, and there was a samurai's suit of armour that looked as though it were made out of dragon scales. The earth was not a perfect sphere. Were the oceans to be emptied, it would resemble a distorted ball, and Massud had carved that shape precisely in sandstone. It stood at the centre of the garden. Scattered on various tables and ledges around the house were small replicas of some of the world's celebrated buildings. The cross-section of Durham Cathedral. The Forbidden City. The Glass House in New Canaan, USA.

In the kitchen Nargis was preparing tea. She switched on the radio when it was time for the news.

For a few weeks now, someone had been entering the city's mosques – most often during the night – and revealing the secrets of the citizens over the minarets' loudspeakers. People's immoral acts and corruptions, some of the most securely concealed vices were now in full view. No one had been able to catch the culprit, or culprits, and the city of Zamana was experiencing a strange new dread. Perhaps inevitably, it was

8

being said that it was the voice of Allah. There were those who thought that the clerics of the mosques themselves were responsible for the distressing phenomenon, but in a number of instances the loudspeakers had exposed the profound defects and hypocrisies within a mosque itself.

Nargis became still as she listened, the newscaster telling her that a young woman had died at the hands of her brothers during the night, an hour or so after a minaret revealed her trysts with a lover.

She went to the shelf and switched off the radio.

Through the open door she could see Massud in the garden. It was still early, still the fragile hour, though the trees were woven through with sunlight. He was examining the Rangoon creeper that the hailstorms had damaged last month.

Nargis looked at the clock. This morning they would leave the house to supervise the transfer of thousands of books from one of Zamana's oldest libraries to its new premises, which had been designed and built by them.

The majority of the library's books had already been taken to the new premises. The volumes in the Islamic section were the ones that would be moved this morning. Since each one of these texts contained the names of Allah or Muhammad somewhere, it had been decided that they should be taken from one building to the other by hand. In a truck or cart the risk was too great of something coming into contact with uncleanliness. Nargis and Massud would be walking to the nearby Grand Trunk Road to be part of a human chain, and the books would travel a mile-long succession of hands.

'We should leave by seven-thirty,' Nargis said when Massud entered the kitchen. He had just watered the sunflowers, and a sequence of his wet footprints marked his passage on the floor.

He came and closed his arms at her waist from behind, his chin resting on her shoulder. 'I had the strangest of dreams,' he said. 'Someone was walking with a lit candle in his hand.'

'That's not so strange.'

'It was raining. Hard.'

'Well,' Nargis said, considering the words, 'the brain is the most complex object in the universe.' Her own sleep was always much deeper than his. She rarely dreamed.

'Helen said she will be here this morning,' Massud told her as he was setting the table for breakfast. 'She is writing an essay and wanted to consult some books in the study.'

Nargis did not react outwardly, but her silence made him look towards her.

'I know,' he said.

'We have to tell her, Massud. We have to tell both Lily and her.'

Massud nodded.

'We really mustn't delay it any further.'

And with a new note in her voice, Nargis added, 'Pakistan produces people of extraordinary bravery. But no country should ever require its citizens to be this brave.'

Helen was the daughter of the couple whom Nargis had employed as housekeepers. Lily and Grace were Christian and were both illiterate. And Helen – who was now nineteen years old – too would have grown up to be an uneducated servant in some Muslim household had Massud and Nargis not provided her with an alternative set of opportunities. They had paid for her education at Zamana's finest schools and she had been an assiduous and brilliant student until three years ago when her mother's life had come to a terrible end. There were several witnesses to the crime, but the murderer was a Muslim and this was Pakistan. The police were initially reluctant to even register a case. Eventually, however, the man was sentenced to life imprisonment – but the day before yesterday Nargis and Massud learned that Grace's killer had been released, as a reward for having memorised the entire Koran. He had served less than a year in prison.

'They are only just beginning to recover from the death,' Nargis said. The loss was detectable in the eyes of both father and daughter.

After they finished breakfast, Massud walked out into the garden again. At its other end was the largest room in the house: their study and library, where the Hagia Sophia and the Great Mosque of Córdoba were suspended from the ceiling. He told himself that he should make sure at least one of the desks in there was tidy for Helen.

Nargis and Massud had demanded that the correct legal procedures be followed. They had engaged the best lawyer, and they felt that the verdict had been a just one. Neither they nor anyone else, however, could have predicted what happened shortly afterwards. A few days after he delivered the verdict, the judge was stabbed to death as he left his house in the morning. And on several occasions over the coming weeks, men on motorcycles slowed down outside the lawyer's home to spray the exterior with bullets from machine guns, one bullet narrowly missing his young child, until he and his family went into hiding.

Beyond everything else, Nargis and Massud blamed themselves for the fates of the lawyer and the judge.

The air in the garden was noticeably warmer now. It was April and the days were already twelve hours long. Massud went towards the study, passing under the rosewood trees that were being visited by many dozens of pale butterflies. It was a wonder to him that so much activity did not produce any noise.

Helen would let herself into the house with her own key in their absence. The house was a former paper factory, and it was said that it had made the entire area smell like money when it was operational. As young architects Nargis and

Massud had visited the neighbourhood one day and decided to convert the abandoned building into a home.

Massud had always regretted not having had children – or, more precisely, a daughter – and that was what Helen had become over the years. She and Lily lived next door but she had more or less grown up in this house. She had a room of her own here. As a child she took running jumps onto Massud's back, much to her parents' embarrassment. Here he had seen her draw a cat with five legs by mistake. He still remembered the day she returned from school aged five or so, her eyes wide with indignation as she announced, 'The wolf ate Little Red Riding Hood's *grandmother*!' Massud had told her the wolf had eaten all the biscuits in the grandmother's house, but the other children had revealed the truth.

It was 7.20 when they left the house. As always at this time of the year, Massud was wearing a pale linen suit. Instead of a belt his trousers were held up by braces, and his head was protected by a straw hat purchased in London some years ago. Nargis was in a voile shalwar-kameez. Its neck had been embroidered by Grace. Their destination – the human chain stretching along the Grand Trunk Road – was a half-hour walk away.

The neighbourhood was known as Badami Bagh. As the name suggested, it was once an orchard of almond trees. It had stood on the northern outskirts of the city for almost two hundred years. In 1857 some of the leaders of the Mutiny had hidden in the orchard's thick groves, plotting their attacks; and later, once the Mutiny had been put down, the British had hanged them from the branches of the same trees.

By the 1950s – the British had left by then and Pakistan was an independent nation – the city was growing rapidly towards the orchard, and its owners were beginning to realise that the land on which the almond trees stood would be more lucrative if built upon. The orchard was owned by a single extended family, and they decided to build the smallest possible houses and rent them out mostly to Christians, who worked as servants in the houses of Zamana's Muslims, or cleaned the city's roads and sewers, and were docile and obedient.

By the time the twenty-first century began, Badami Bagh was the poorest neighbourhood in Zamana, a ghetto. The city had continued to grow and had approached, half-circled and finally swallowed it, spreading far beyond. Surrounding the enclave of Christian houses with Muslim ones on all sides.

And a single tree was all that remained of the orchard. It stood in the courtyard of Lily and Helen's house. Now and then, the ghost of a hanged Mutineer would climb down from its branches and wander about Badami Bagh, asking people to untie the noose from around his neck.

Walking towards the Grand Trunk Road, Nargis and Massud took the lane that was the only way in or out of the neighbourhood. There used to be many others but they all opened into Muslim areas, and the Muslims had objected to Christians walking past their homes, and so eventually everything except one lane was walled off. It brought Nargis and Massud to the square that marked the end of Badami Bagh. The shops and stalls that lined all four sides of the square attracted and held Nargis's attention: her pace slowed and, finally, with a glance at her wristwatch, she moved towards a glass door.

'This is new,' she said. 'Let me quickly see what they have.'

Massud remained in the open air. In the April sunlight the new red foliage on the banyan tree seemed to glow like cellophane amid the dusty older leaves. A sign in front of Hotshots Snooker Club was promising 'two games for the price of one' in honour of Prophet Muhammad's birthday next week. Outside the factory that produced ice in four-foot blocks, a woman sat like a gem cutter with a small ice pick, carefully extracting moths that had fallen into the water during the freezing process.

He stepped into the shop after ten minutes, to find Nargis paying for the various foodstuffs she had bought, along with two kilograms of river reeds to be tied into two brooms.

She was the only customer. 'Would you be kind enough to deliver all this to the blue house in front of the mosque?' she said to the shopkeeper. 'Down there in Badami Bagh.'

The man pointed to the young boy stacking shelves in the far corner and said that he would send him out within the hour.

'I wonder if Helen would hear the doorbell,' Nargis said to Massud. 'Lost as she would be in a book.'

Massud was anxious to leave. He had experienced something resembling sorrow the moment he entered and saw the floor of the shop. At their feet, here and there on the tiles, the national flags of the USA, Israel, India, France and Denmark had been painted. For customers to walk on and defile.

He was a quiet withdrawn man, and this was too loud a gesture for him. He could make himself imagine the impulse that lay behind it, of course. There was the cleric's widowed daughter in the house behind the mosque, her bread waking Massud in the predawn darkness. She had come to live with her father because her husband had been killed by a missile fired from an American drone, a year or so ago, in the faraway deserts of Waziristan.

'Will we ever learn to make our feelings known in a different manner?' he said to Nargis, indicating the floor.

It was barely above a whisper but the shopkeeper heard him.

'Forgive me, but you don't have to return if you find us uncivilised,' the man said.

14

Nargis and Massud turned towards him. His face wore an aggrieved smile.

Massud seemed at a loss. 'I apologise if I have offended you,' he said quietly.

The shopkeeper was staring at his hands and did not look up.

By the shelves, the boy had stopped working and was peering over his shoulder. Nargis motioned Massud towards the door, sensing his confusion and regret. 'Just send the things to the blue house, brother-ji,' she said. 'We are grateful. Thank you.'

Once they were outside, she touched Massud's hand to reassure him.

Massud said, 'Yesterday a shopkeeper in Moon Bazaar declined my money unless I wrote *Jihad is a Duty* or *Implement Strict Sharia Law* on it.'

As they left the square, he took out his mobile phone and sent Helen a text message, squinting at the sun-dimmed screen, telling her to expect the delivery from the shop.

Ahead of them the street they were on passed between the backs of two cinemas – Kashmir Palace and Minerva. The colourful billboards roped to the facades of both buildings were announcing five screenings instead of the usual four next Friday to mark Muhammad's birthday. After that the street widened considerably and delivered them to the Grand Trunk Road.

It was one of the planet's great sinews. According to a nineteenth-century Urdu poet, all life of Zamana could be found in the city's four crowds – the one at the Mughal Fort; the one at the Gate of Hesitation that led to the medieval pleasure district; the crowd at the Friday Mosque; and the crowd at the mausoleum of the saint Charagar. Both Nargis and Massud had often felt that the Grand Trunk Road should be added to that list.

Energy dancing with itself – the flow of rickshaws, motorcycles, bicycles, cars, horse-drawn carriages, donkey carts, trucks and buses stopped and started up again in sectioned paroxysms, the air full of hot fumes, the roar of vehicles, the sun flashing off the glass and metal. Amid all this Nargis and Massud were looking for a place to cross. Before them was a roundabout at the centre of which stood a massive fibreglass replica of the mountain under which Pakistan's nuclear bomb was tested in 1998.

Massud could see that the human chain was already forming on the footpath on the other side. A number of the city's schools had sent their pupils to participate in the task of moving the books, and it was their matching uniforms – as noticeable as groups of animals with identical markings – that had drawn Massud's attention, telling him precisely where he and Nargis needed to be in the disorder.

After they had crossed, Massud made and received several phone calls, to ensure that everything was proceeding as planned. He and Nargis positioned themselves in the chain, closer to the old library than the new building, and the first book arrived in their hands at just after 8.30. The quickness with which it was followed by others reminded them of objects rushing along on the rapids of a great river.

A ninth-century Abbasid Koran was followed by a book of Mughal paintings of which Rembrandt had made copies in seventeenth-century Holland. Next was a thirteenth-century Arabic translation of Dioscorides' *De Materia Medica*. There were verse guides for pilgrims to Mecca and Medina, and there were collections of sentences spoken by the Prophet. And there was a sorcerer's manual from Moorish Spain.

The schoolchildren were thrilled with their morning, and their thin voices were like whistles in the air. As the books continued to travel, the traffic lights changed periodically on the Grand Trunk Road: the vehicles came to a halt next to the

16

footpath and then moved on. At around nine o'clock, Nargis noticed that the driver of the car that had just stopped near her was a Westerner. A large healthily built white man, he was something of a surprising sight, and those passersby who had noticed him were looking at him with open curiosity. Almost all of them, Nargis was certain, had never seen a living white person, though some of the shop fronts and billboards around them carried images of European or North American faces.

A little boy grinned and raised his hands to wave at him. Just then a motorcycle pulled up between the Westerner's car and Nargis: both young men on the motorcycle were holding pistols, the barrels pointed at the white man's head. She saw the pillion rider's gun reach forward and it touched the window glass with a clean sound.

They had been following him. Before Nargis could react, a gun had materialised in the white man's own hand, and he had begun to fire through the car window, Nargis hearing the sound of each shot separately, distinctly.

The window shattered. Hit in the stomach and chest, the pillion man fell onto the road, the wounds bleeding thickly, smearing the tarmac with red. As the other man revved the motorcycle and was fleeing, the white man opened the car door and stepped out and, standing firmly with one foot on the pavement and the other on the road, fired several rounds into his back.

The children were screaming. Any number of books had been dropped onto the ground and were being trampled by the panic-stricken crowd. Nargis caught the smell of urine. In the coming hours it would be determined that the American man had fired approximately one hundred bullets during the incident. A mobile phone inside his car would turn out to contain numerous photographs of Pakistan's military installations, taken surreptitiously – illegally. The vehicle's number plates would turn out to be false. And with the passing of days, words

like 'espionage', 'the CIA', 'the Crusades', and 'Jihad' would begin to be spoken, connecting Massud's death with greater and
greater things, to the vast sicknesses of the world.

But for now – as the young Westerner re-entered his car
and began to make phone calls, frantically shouting into the
device, raising and pointing his gun whenever he perceived
some movement nearby to be a threat, or looking out at his
surroundings with the expression of someone who had suddenly gone blind – for now Nargis was searching for Massud
in the chaos, the full enormity of the occurrence still disguised
from her.

Massud had detached himself from the chain when one
particular book had arrived in his hands, about ten minutes
earlier. It seemed too long ago now. He had stepped away to
examine the book, happily, waving to Nargis and the others
to close the gap created by him. She could not locate him
now. They were still the first few minutes after the disaster: the
loudest sound was that of the wounded pillion rider, who was
still alive and lay exactly where he had fallen, shouting, 'Allah,
save me! O Allah, help me!' as though another outcome was
possible.

The large, magnificent book Massud had walked away with
had been written by his father, published the year Massud was
born.

It was 987 pages long, and it was an acknowledgement and
celebration of the countless ideas and thoughts that had travelled over the ages from one part of the planet to another. It
outlined and examined how disparate events in the history of
the world had influenced each other, the hidden or forgotten
contributions that one set of humans had made towards the
happiness and knowledge of another. Traditions and histories

had always mingled, and nothing in the East or the West was ever pure. Dante Alighieri had in all probability read accounts of Prophet Muhammad's miraculous journey to Paradise and Hell before he wrote *The Divine Comedy*.

Massud and Nargis's own copy of the book had gone missing more than a decade ago and they had been unable to find a replacement. The last copy they saw was at the New York Public Library the previous summer. And yet here it was this morning too, coming towards them, borne on the hands of adults and children. They had both exclaimed when they recognised it, because the library had been asked if it had the book on its shelves but the answer had been no.

Massud had opened the pages immediately and discovered that it was their own copy. His name was on the flyleaf. At some point after it was lost, someone had found it and donated it to the library.

She saw him now, in the distance. He held the base of his neck with a red hand. He was standing perfectly still amid the turmoil, the book lying at his feet, one of his knees slightly bent so that he leaned sideways. And his mouth was open. He faltered but was then upright again, as though uncertain which way to fall. He had made a sudden movement to shield a child and had been shot, she would learn later. She reached him just as he was about to sink to the ground and she eased him down, his face ashen, his forehead covered with broken beads of sweat. With his free hand he touched her face as though trying to comfort her. He had strength only for an instant of contact before the arm fell away, but his eyes remained on her as though absorbing her details for the last time. She shouted for help, looking around in desperation again and again, seeing the policemen arrive and surround the young white man's car, their weapons drawn, seeing the bleeding pillion rider being carried off the road. The dead body of the other lay beside the motorcycle in the middle of the road, a policeman running to direct the traffic away from it.

A goldfish seller had been passing by when the gunshots began. Carrying a pole to which two horizontal bars were attached near the top, like a crucifix with four arms instead of two. From these hung dozens of clear nylon bags, each three-quarters filled with water and containing a single goldfish. It had looked as though each glittering creature was held captive in a living lens. In the ensuing chaos the pole had fallen, its arms splintering as they made contact with the ground. Nargis saw the goldfish leaping nearby, the area around each one made darker by the spilt water, the plastic bags flattened where they fell. A young man came forward to pick up one of the creatures in his cupped hand and look around for the best way to proceed.

2

Helen switched on her laptop and adjusted the angle of the screen. The white glow softly lit her palms. She was in the study and the morning was perfectly silent. As she worked she looked up occasionally, to gather or refine her thoughts, or she uncapped her pen to write a sentence in the notebook that lay beside the computer. She walked to one of the shelves and consulted a book. On the side of the sofa where Massud liked to sit, there was a permanent suggestion of his cologne. She had received his message, asking her to expect delivery from the shop in the square, and had left the door of the study open to be able to hear the bell.

There were cities at her feet – models of them placed on the floor – and she loved the epithets that had been given to some of them over the ages. Rayy was 'the bridegroom of the earth', Merv 'the mother of the world', and Jerusalem was 'the Palace'.

She got up and went to stand directly under the suspended Hagia Sofia. She was looking up towards it, her head tilted back. A book she needed was resting up there on the Hagia Sofia's small windowsill. She had been searching for it for the past several days, not knowing that it had gone up with one of the buildings at the end of February. She would have to use the stepladder to retrieve it.

Lily had constructed the two models, and students from the National College of Arts in Zamana were brought in to decorate the undersized walls and ceilings, the blue and gold dome of the Córdoba Mosque, the brisk minarets of the Hagia Sophia. According to legend, when Muslims entered the Hagia Sophia in 1453, which at the time was a cathedral, the interrupted priests had taken the sacred vessels and disappeared into the building's eastern wall, through which it was said they would return one day to complete the divine service.

Helen went to the window that gave out onto the garden. Three days ago she had discovered that the man responsible for her mother's death had been released from prison. She still hadn't shared this news with her father, or with Nargis and Massud, knowing the distress and unhappiness it would bring them, remembering how difficult that period had been for them all. Twice the trial had had to be postponed because the police claimed they had lost the case files, but Nargis and Massud had insisted the paperwork be reconstructed from carbon copies and scans.

She herself had been unable to speak for almost three months after Grace's death, the mind overcome with grief, unable to see or discover a way out of loss. She had almost lost a year of education at school. And then one day she came into the study and quietly asked Massud if he knew what had become of the rings she used to wear on her thumb and index finger. She had seen a portrait of Alexander Pushkin with such rings on his right hand and had imitated him. The love of her sixteenth year. She remembered Nargis's laughter at that. 'How many girls dream of Pushkin, I wonder!'

She knew she would never really recover. It was as though her pen ran out of ink while writing a letter. She had picked up another containing ink of a different colour and continued; but even if the words and the lines of thought remained the same, something had altered.

She looked out at the garden. The tall silk-cotton tree had almost entirely shed its heavy blossoms – they were as heavy as fruit – but at a much lower height the coral tree was just coming into bloom.

From the window she could see the minaret of the mosque across the lane – the top third of its length was visible above the canopies of the garden. Perhaps it was this sight that made her think of the cleric's daughter. But then, just an hour ago, there was news that an unmanned drone – flying above Pakistan's tribal belt but operated remotely from within the USA – had assassinated yet another militant leader. How many others had been killed with him was not mentioned.

The doorbell rang at last. When she answered it she found a boy of about eleven or twelve standing in the lane, with several bags of food and a thick bushel of reeds.

'You should be at school,' she said when she brought him into the kitchen.

He did not respond. His face was beautiful and doll-like and he was looking towards the bird wings hanging on the pink wall. He had placed the bags on the dining table and was using his grimy sleeve to absorb the perspiration from his forehead and upper lip, holding his gaze on the wings. He went towards them and reached out with a finger and touched the lime green feather of an Alexandrine parakeet.

'Does the man with the straw hat live here?' he asked. 'The one with the elastic going over his shoulders.'

'They are called braces. Or galluses.'

'Gal…lu…ses.'

She held up the bottle of Rooh Afza he had brought, cracking open the seal on the cap. 'Would you like a drink of this?'

He seemed uncertain. 'I overheard the lady mention someone named Helen,' he said. 'Is that you?'

'Yes.'

'Are you an infidel?'

Helen had been looking into one of the bags. She raised her head but not her eyelids. At the beginning of high school, when she was fourteen years old, a teacher had asked her to stand up in class and 'justify taking the place of a Muslim'.

'Are you a servant here?' the boy continued. 'You don't look like one.'

When she finally glanced at him he nodded towards the Rooh Afza bottle. 'I am a Muslim, I can't accept a drink from your hand.' And he added, 'You should know that. Shouldn't you?'

At nineteen, Helen was old enough to remain unsurprised by occasions such as these. She had always known them and could not have separated them from the most basic facts of her existence. Still, sometimes she was caught off guard.

She watched him from the kitchen window as he crossed the garden at an unhurried pace and left the house, stopping twice on the semicircular path through the grass, to look up at the ripening fruit or some creature moving in the branches.

She put away the items of food, and divided and bound the river reeds into brooms. Afterwards she carried the aluminium stepladder to the study and unfolded it below the model of the Hagia Sophia. She stood there for a few moments: even from the topmost step of the ladder, the book would be too high up. She needed something to nudge it with, and she went back to the kitchen and unhooked the giant wing of the trumpeter swan and returned with it, the feathers blindingly white when she walked through the rays of the sun on the veranda, almost a detonation.

As she climbed up with the four-foot wing she thought of her mother who would use this ladder to dust the upper reaches of walls and shelves in this house. She recalled the story of her parents' first meeting. Grace had been fifteen years old at the time and was a servant in someone's house, and she had approached a passing policeman one day in a distraught state and demanded that he arrest a certain seventeen-year-old gardener's boy from a nearby house. 'I cannot stop thinking about him!' she had declared. 'Each night the thought of him keeps me awake, and all day I long for him. I demand justice!' Looking for a few moments of amusement, the policeman had followed the spirited, indignant girl as she led him to her criminal. He was entirely unaware of her, of course, and was speechless now, to find himself accused of being her incremental killer.

Helen arrived at the top step of the ladder – 'This is where the wolf lives,' Grace would say – and she stretched the wing of the swan cautiously towards the book on the small windowsill. The tip of the last feather fell just short of making contact with the book's spine, and she raised herself onto her toes to attain the extra inches. There was a dull, indistinct noise from somewhere below her at that moment, and she glanced down to see that the boy from the shop had appeared at the door to the study.

Carefully she brought her heels back down to the metal surface of the step. She had neglected to lock the door after his departure.

'Did you forget something?'

He was looking at her and the expression on his face was somewhere between a sneer and a swoon, his body partly concealed in the shadow being thrown by a shelf. As he advanced into the room Helen saw that he was in fact trembling, the sharp length of the knife in his right hand moving to and fro as he approached the ladder.

'What are you doing?' she said with shock.

But it was the walk of a sleepwalker. It was almost as though he was being pulled forward by the knife, his arm outstretched. She wished she could reach up and grab the bottom edge of the Hagia Sophia to steady herself but it was out of reach. The touch of the wing had set it swinging gently above her.

He had arrived now and placed a foot on the first step. It made her think of a gardener or a gravedigger about to break ground with the shovel. There was nowhere she could go. He was a child but he had a naked ten-inch blade and she was precariously balanced, a terrified lightness in her soles.

'What do you want?'

25

In a tranced, slightly submerged voice, he said, 'I have to see.'

'What do you have to see?'

'Christians have black blood.'

She recognised the bone-handled knife as being from the kitchen out there.

'Who told you that? It's red, just like yours.'

She could see both his determination and his fear much more clearly now.

'My mother told me. I have to see.' The metal creaked under his weight as he rose another step. If he wished he could cut her leg but he was in another place.

She was about to swipe at him with the wing when her phone rang on the desk. And it jolted them both.

He whipped his head towards the device blinking among the papers.

'You have to go,' she said. 'Right now.' He looked at her and raised the knife and she decided to lie. 'I am expecting someone. That's probably them ringing to say they're almost here. You have to go.'

For the next few moments, as the phone continued to ring, he seemed in a paralysis of will and she touched his shoulder with the outermost feather. And it was as though she had activated a mechanism. The knife made a sharp metallic sound on the marble floor when he dropped it. He stepped down and slowly walked backwards, looking abject.

She felt reality seep back into things.

Turning around at the door he vanished out of the room as suddenly as he had appeared.

She climbed down and went to the kitchen and poured herself a glass of water. She drank a few sips, her other hand resting on the surface of the table. Her limbs seemed numb, but just a few moments later she was running towards the front door. She opened it and saw that he was about to disappear

26

around the slight curve in the lane. He stopped when she called out but he did not turn around immediately. When he did look back she waved at him to make him return.

He arrived and stopped just beyond arm's reach. She opened the safety pin she had taken from a drawer in the kitchen and with it she quickly stabbed the tip of her index finger and held the drop of blood towards him.

'It's red. I want you to promise me you won't try to injure someone else.' His face was wrenched with emotion, but she said firmly, 'Look at it. You've seen now that it's not black. Look at it.'

There was a silence. When she tried to say something further, he flinched, and then he covered his face with both hands and gave way to tears quietly.

'I am sorry.'

'Promise me.'

'I promise,' he said.

She stayed with him until he had composed himself. After he left, she came back to the study where her phone was ringing again. It was Nargis, who said that she was calling from a hospital and that something had happened to Massud.

3

Nargis had fallen asleep while reading and was now woken by the weight of the book resting open on her breast. It was an old story of courage and justice. There had been a power cut in the evening and she had lit a kerosene lantern. As she slept, it had extinguished itself and the room was perfectly dark around her.

Ten days had passed since the death, and the house felt haunted by Massud.

She relit the lamp and looked about her. Somewhere she had read of a place where those left behind by the dead wore masks for a certain number of days. It was done so that the spirit would not recognise them and be tempted to remain on earth. Encouraging the soul to begin its journey for the cities of the next world.

There were decisions no one could teach anyone to make. Nargis did not know what to do with the clothes she and Massud were wearing that morning, his blood on them now.

She recollected gestures and words, everyday things that had now been made monumental. On several occasions during the previous week, she had walked around the rooms wondering what might be the last object Massud had touched. What was the one thing his gaze landed on as he left the house that morning ten days ago, the last colour he thought of, his last ever sensation?

Laments were as old as verses of love, she knew. They *were* verses of love. For the departed who will never be met again, for the burned cities.

She wished the dead were somewhere specific, but they were

nowhere. They were erased into memory.

At twilight the words of St Augustine came to her. *And I enter the fields and spacious halls of memory, where are stored as treasures the countless images . . .*

Late one morning, she answered the door to a man she assumed was an acquaintance of Massud's, someone who had arrived at the house to offer her a few comforting words.

'I am here about your husband,' he said.

When she invited him in, it was done almost mechanically. Had he turned around and gone away, she would never have been able to describe him. Her mind was elsewhere. She had no other wish than to be alone, to somehow recover her stillness, to attempt to regain her balance. She unrolled the cane blinds in the arches to keep out the rising heat and sat down with him on the veranda.

'We have to discuss the matter of your husband's death and the American man,' he said.

She looked at him, unable to understand what he meant. 'How did you know my husband?' she asked, examining his face with care.

'I didn't.'

Journalists and reporters had begun to knock on the door hours after the death but she had declined to speak to anyone.

The man seemed to read her thoughts. 'I am not a journalist.'

She noticed the intensity of his gaze now. The eyes were too large for the face, educated in watching everything.

'The American man is in custody, as I am sure you know,' he said. 'But the American government has told us that he is a diplomat and therefore has immunity. They insist he must be released.'

Nargis had begun to stand up even before he had finished speaking. 'I would like you to leave,' she said quietly, without looking in his direction.

'I can't do that,' he said. 'This matter has to be dealt with.'

Nargis shook her head to herself.

'The American government insists he is a diplomat—'

'I heard he was involved in espionage,' Nargis said, 'that he is a spy and did not have permission to be in this city.'

'Please don't interrupt me again,' the man told her with a pained expression on his face, clearly taken aback by the tone in which she had addressed him.

Nargis looked around, her eyes searching for Massud. One of the things Massud and the child Helen had loved were 'book ghosts'. It was when an image printed on the reverse of a page showed through on the other side, the ink seeping across the fibres. A horse – disproportionately large – flying faintly through the sky above a city. A palace situated inside a mountain. A car lodged in a goddess's crown.

She brought her mind back to the man, listening to him again.

'The American government insists he is a diplomat, and we have to release him.'

'I really don't care.' She knew who this man was now. He was from the intelligence agency run by the military. A soldier-spy.

'Well,' he said. 'You may not care but the people of Pakistan do. They are angry at what he has done, so we can't just release him. They will say Pakistan does what the West tells it to. And—'

'As I said, I don't care.'

Nargis was feeling all sense of comportment slipping away from her, and the man exhaled impatiently. There was a new firmness in the voice when he did speak again:

'You have to publicly forgive him. You have to declare that you want him to be free.'

Nargis tried to place her thoughts elsewhere, on to a more bearable reality. She could think of nothing.

'You are the dead man's next of kin, so the forgiveness has to come from you. The last blood relative was a sister, but she left Pakistan and is now deceased.'

'What about the families of the boys on the motorcycle?'

'Those two-bit thieves.'

There was open mockery in the tone of these words, and Nargis felt a surge of anger inside her, a sudden intensity after the sensationless days. The idea was that the boys would have to have been flawlessly virtuous for their murders to be unjust.

'We are approaching their families too,' he said. 'They too will announce that they have no wish to press charges. You will all appear in court and sign various papers.'

'I have no intention of doing any of that,' Nargis heard herself say.

Perhaps the American government would reward Pakistan's military and government for the freedom of the killer. Various deals would have been worked out.

'Let him go,' she said. 'I have no wish to get involved.'

'But you are involved.' He sat forward and looked at her through the prominent veins in his eyes. 'You have to remember that the world did not end the day your husband died. Nor did it begin that day. Many older facts and relationships have to be taken into consideration.'

Massud had once said that the Pakistani military was a curse. It had been eating Pakistan's children for decades.

'*Is* he a diplomat?'

'I will not repeat what I have already told you.' Though controlled, his hostility was visible as he pointed to her chair and said, 'Sit down and listen to me. As an educated person, you must see that—'

'I would like you to leave,' she said, fully resolved to put an end to the exchange. It was scarcely believable to her that

31

she had allowed it to continue for so long. There had been no words of sympathy, nor had he introduced himself. He was in civilian clothes but his rank must be a major – she could tell from his bearing and manner. The families of the two young men on the motorcycle would have been visited by someone lower in rank, a lieutenant or a subedar.

Despite what she had said he remained in his chair, just as she herself was still standing, regardless of his curt demand.

'You obviously know a good deal about us,' she said. 'Do you know about my husband's brother?'

There was an imperceptible shrug; he managed to restrain it just in time but Nargis registered it. 'He was a journalist, he died some time ago.'

'Twenty years and eight months ago. But who's counting,' she said, smiling at him with rage. 'He was a journalist and was found by the roadside. Tortured to death soon after he began investigating a story about the military-intelligence agency.'

'I would strongly advise you not to repeat that in my presence.'

'What about in your absence?'

She had seen paintings of St Anthony bringing a dead man to life, so he could reveal the name of his murderer.

She could hear her agitated breath, feel the stiff smile on her face. There was a tearfulness, held back. 'Why don't you have me killed?' she said in as clear a voice as she was capable. 'Massud would have no next of kin then.'

They stared at each other without saying anything. One evening Massud's brother was sitting at the kitchen table, singing a ghazal for them all, everyone a little drunk after dinner, on wine and jasmine vodka. The candlelight was flickering and there were the blue bones of fish on the plates, the laughter of friends and family, and he got up to answer the doorbell and never returned. They were all in their twenties and early thirties then, a small nation of love. Someone was eating a rose petal from the vase. At first they thought he had gone to the crossroads for a packet of cigarettes. The mutilated body was found a week later.

The first sentence in all of his notebooks had been, *War will drown in the writer's inkwell.*

She stood looking at him. She needed Massud's guidance and aid, and for a moment it confused her that he was absent from the aftermath of his death.

She entered the study and set the lantern on the table. On certain nights the moon wandered through the house but tonight it was absent. The lantern's yellow light was too weak to reach the edges of the vast space. Nothing but a pale sphere was illuminated around her as she stood breathing in the night air. Everything else was lost. The suspended Hagia Sophia with the small carved bird on one of its domes, and the Mosque of Córdoba with its arches resembling the fronds of date palms. Within the sphere of light, surrounded by the darkness, there was a sense of safety, of being in a chamber which she had made smaller by pulling the walls in and in. They had once calculated that the house contained upwards of fifteen thousand books, a large proportion of them in this study.

The man had gone away with the promise – the warning – that he would return in a few days. She had remained on her feet, and had not moved to show him out. She could see that she had insulted him, but it was done more out of a sudden sense of exhaustion than any feeling she had towards him and what he represented.

She opened the large heavy book written by Massud's father, the book Massud had walked away with on the morning of his death. It had been sent to the house with his belongings, a mistake she hoped to correct soon.

Its title was *That They Might Know Each Other*, words inspired by a verse in the Koran. A meditation on how pilgrimage, wars, trades, and curiosity had led to contact between cultures. Tracing the umbilical connections between places. Nargis turned the pages now, stopping occasionally to read a few lines, to look at the images, vivid even in this light.

The volume was organised in twenty-one sections. The Book of Earth. The Book of Water and Other Mirrors. The Book of Stars. The Book of Fairytales. The Book of Colours. The Book of Motion. The Book of Numbers. The Books of Animals and Birds. The Book of Love. The Book of Memory. The Book of Philosophy. The Book of Maps. The Book of Ghosts. The Book of Utopias. The Book of Light and Geometry.

The Book of Architecture. *The Turkish rulers of Athens converted the Parthenon into a mosque in the 1460s. At the time it had been a Christian church, and before that a pagan temple. A minaret and dome were now constructed. This Muslim place of worship was surrounded by the Greek friezes of humans and animals, immodestly apparelled gods and goddesses. Some of these marble figures had been destroyed earlier by Christians as idols. A traveller had described it as the 'finest mosque in the world'* . . .

The Book of Names and Languages. *The town named Saracinesco in Italy was founded by a group of Arab raiders, known to medieval Italians as Saracens. These raiders had been cut off from the main Muslim force following the Arab attack against Rome in the year 846. The trapped men took refuge on top of the rocky outcrop that would eventually become Saracinesco. As a condition of surrender, they agreed to convert to Christianity. Their modern-day descendants in Saracinesco had names like Giuseppe Dell'Ali* . . .

The Book of Flowers. *Cotton had emerged as a crop more than 5,000 years ago here in the Indus Valley of what is now Pakistan. Medieval Europeans knew of it only from travellers' accounts. It was sometimes referred to as 'vegetable lamb'* . . .

The Book of Music. *In 1930s Harlem, Bahadour Ali, the son of a Bengali man and an African American woman, had made a splendid name for himself as an emcee. He was hired by Harlem's leading jazz bandleader Chick Webb and was often credited with introducing Webb to a young Ella Fitzgerald, insisting he hire her as a singer . . .*

The Book of Books. *Thomas Jefferson had purchased a copy of the Koran in 1765. He had inscribed his initials at the bottom of page 113, under the verses of the fourth chapter that emphasised the importance of fighting 'in the path of God'. In the election of 1800, President John Adams's campaign against Jefferson had included the accusation that he was 'an infidel'. . .*

The call for the predawn prayer sounded from the mosque across the lane, and Nargis realised that she had been turning the pages of the book for more than an hour. In a while, with first light, there would come the sound of a neighbourhood man leading his high-eared horse to the river, both up to their knees in water as he made a scoop with his hands and bathed the chestnut-coloured animal.

She ran her hand over a page, feeling the texture of the paper against the skin. She heard the binding creak when she closed it. In a tired dreamlike state, she imagined The Book of Water and Other Mirrors to be printed on paper that undulated, the words floating as though on a pool, flowing off the edges. Imagining the section known as The Book of Stars, she saw constellations stretched in the air between two pages like fine cats' cradles.

She raised the kerosene lantern and looked around in the light. The study was one of their own additions to the original paper factory, and it was Nargis who had designed it, minutely considering what shadows the sun would cast where as it rose on Massud's birthday. On spring evenings great long rays of light entered deep into the house through windows she had introduced. The place seemed to fill up with glowing three-dimensional kites, softly on fire.

From the back of a drawer Nargis took out an old envelope, and from it she retrieved a photograph. There was a much-read letter too but she let it remain folded inside. The photograph was four inches square and its edges had been trimmed with zigzag scissors. It depicted a man in his thirties with two children beside him. At the back was the circular stamp of the photographer's studio in violet ink, and there were seven words in Nargis's own childhood writing. *Me and my sister and my uncle*. She remembered walking to the studio with the two of them to have the picture taken. She remembered the colour of her frock, the colour of the ribbons in her sister's hair. Their uncle's moustache was like two strokes of Urdu calligraphy, and he would raise both his hands symmetrically to smooth back the hair on his head. All of it a lifetime ago.

Last year she and Massud had built a house for a client but the man's grandmother hadn't wished to move to the new place. She said she had too many memories associated with the old one. Now angry, now sorrowful, the old lady sat in a room muttering to herself. It aggrieved her that her wishes were being ignored, that she was being disobeyed and contradicted. Nargis had overheard one sentence from her mouth and it had astonished her. Still today it had the ability to amaze. She was in her mid-nineties, and yet she had said:

'If my mother was alive, I would have left you all and gone back to her.'

It had shaken Nargis, the significance and power in those two or three early bonds.

Now she sat with the envelope in her hand. Her sister was no longer alive and the ties with her uncle were severed. She had nowhere to go, to punish the world for what it had done to her.

4

Helen appeared out of the afternoon sun and found Nargis asleep at the kitchen table. Her head was resting on folded arms. Two white wings hung at an angle from the back of the chair next to hers, the strong lengthy feathers at the tip curving against the floor. She was about to withdraw but Nargis heard her and opened her eyes. She pushed the chair back but did not get up.

'I came to see how you were.'

The girl went forward and lowered herself onto the cool floor, eventually resting her head in Nargis's lap.

She was too old for this, but both of them found calm in each other's nearness and presence.

She looked up and smiled at Nargis. As with most people in middle age who had someone young in their life, Nargis had on occasion told Helen how beautiful she was. It embarrassed the girl but it was scarcely believable to Nargis, the loveliness. It certainly seemed impossible that Nargis herself had been as perfect when she was Helen's age.

'Did he come again, that man?' Helen asked.

The military-intelligence agency inspired such fear that people did not dare to utter its name.

'No,' Nargis said. 'He will, but I don't want you to be concerned about him.'

They continued to sit in silence, and then Helen began to speak in a low voice.

'Remember how I stopped speaking after my mother's death?'

Nargis gave a nod without looking at her.

'At the time I didn't really know why I did that, but I think I do now. I have thought about it since.'

'You didn't want it to become real,' Nargis said.

'Yes. That's it. Speaking about it to others would have made it real. It would have become a fact. Their reaction, their responses, their words – it would all tell me that the terrible thing *had* happened. That I wasn't just imagining it.'

In the evening as she tried to sleep, Nargis thought about one of Helen's comments. Referring to the man from military intelligence, she had said, 'Sometimes I think I don't know the first thing about how the world works.'

Nargis recalled that there was a stage of development that a child's mind went through between the ages of five and six. If an apple was placed in front of the child and she was told to draw what she saw, the child drew an apple to the best of her abilities. A circle, perhaps with a little dent at the top, maybe a stalk emerging from it. If a pencil was then pushed through the apple, so that an inch or so of the tip peeked out of the other side, and the child was told once again to draw what she saw, the child would make a circle as before, and then draw a line going *all* the way through it. 'Is this what you see?' You could ask the child this question a hundred times, and she would be adamant that that was what she was seeing. Of course she couldn't see the bit of the pencil hidden inside the fruit. But at that stage of development, the child *knew* the pencil was there, so she *saw* it. There was no difference between knowing and seeing. As the weeks and months went by, the mind slowly learned to leave out the section of the pencil that was not visible.

But Nargis sometimes thought that perhaps humans needed to hold onto that earlier stage, the stage when they 'saw' what had been hidden.

39

Sometimes I think I don't know the first thing about how the world works. Nargis looked towards the window, the country outside it and the world beyond. The hidden lines of force moving through the room, through her body. Everything this land and others like it were going through was about power and influence. All of it. And these struggles of Pakistanis were not just about Pakistan, they were about the survival of the entire human race. They were about the whole planet.

5

Helen was making breakfast for her father. The last of the orchard's almond trees spread its branches above the small house, and Lily was in the courtyard, repairing the light above the front wheel of the rickshaw he drove for a living. It was Nargis and Massud who had given him money some years ago to purchase the three-wheeled vehicle.

Lily's last passenger yesterday was a man with a dancing bear, the creature sitting obediently with its head against the ceiling on the back seat of the rickshaw, next to the trainer. The necklace of bells had sounded every time the bear made a movement, every time there was an unevenness in the road, and at the other end of the journey the bear had taken Lily's hand in its paw and shaken it. This morning Helen and Lily had spent about an hour eradicating the traces of the animal's odour from the rickshaw's interior, the secretions of the glands and the thick dusty fur.

'I wonder if I should visit Nargis-*apa* before starting work,' Lily said. 'To see if she needs anything.'

Helen answered him through the kitchen window. 'Do it quietly, in case she is asleep, but I'll go to her in about an hour anyway.'

He was grimacing as he stripped the rubber casing from a wire. 'I'll visit her when I come back for lunch,' he said. He was thirty-eight years old and there was a quick sureness to his manner. Like his daughter he had a deep brown complexion and heavy waxy hair that retained the grooves of the comb. The crucifix he wore around his neck was on a chain just long enough not to be visible above the open neck of his shirts. At times it was considered a provocation by Muslims. He was often mischievous but there was a certain innocence to him too. He used to derive more pleasure from Helen's toys than she herself did, and as she grew older he would ask her to read out the jokes from the children's magazine she was reading, her wild wild father who had taught her to swear as a child, promising her a rupee each time she repeated an obscenity without knowing its vileness, Grace looking on aghast while he grinned and kissed the child. As a teenager he had smoked cigarettes with gunpowder in them. 'I was mad back then,' he had told Helen. 'But I didn't want to break any laws, I just wanted to obey better ones.'

'What do you think will happen to the American man?' Helen asked, coming to the kitchen window and resting her chin on her palm.

'America is a powerful country,' Lily said. 'One way or another it'll get what it wants. I may be almost illiterate but I know that much.' He drank from the steaming bowl of tea she had left on the rickshaw's dashboard and swallowed four pills. And after a while he said, 'But then we don't need Westerners to come in and destroy us. Look at what's happening with the minarets and the announcement of people's secrets. Right in front of my eyes there was a knifing in Soldiers' Bazaar yesterday. The loudspeaker had said something a few hours earlier and the matter got out of hand.'

Having repaired the light, he put away the pliers in the toolbox under the seat, and began to rub the tyres with an oil-soaked cloth to impart a shine. Nargis and Massud had paid 150,000 rupees for the rickshaw and he tried to return 3,000 a month, though they had never asked for any of it back. The vehicle meant no longer having to be a sweeper. The small two-roomed house was purchased with a loan from Nargis and Massud too. All that in addition to the cost of Helen's education.

At the back of the rickshaw was painted a humorous exhortation to Lily's fellow road users, chosen from the many dozens that the vehicle-decorator had read out to him from his notebook:

PLEASE USE HORN SPARINGLY
THE MASSES ARE ASLEEP

In white paint at the front was the promise that the first kilometre of the journey was free for disabled people.

He picked up the bowl of tea and went into the kitchen and settled cross-legged on the mat on the floor.

'God bless the inventor of Paracetamol,' he said. 'Sometimes you wake up in the morning and everything aches. Take a few Paracetamols and you're fine within half an hour.'

Helen brought him a plate of yogurt sprinkled thickly with sugar, the crystals becoming pale green as they absorbed whey from the yogurt. There were two eggs fried into tidy circles with lacy edges. And two parathas.

'The best cure for some aches is not drinking too much alcohol the night before,' she said.

Lily expected a gentle slap on the top of his head to accompany his daughter's words, but she just touched his hair lightly before walking away.

'Noted,' he whispered to himself.

As he ate he watched her wipe the glass of the pictures hanging on the kitchen wall. In a gold-plastic frame, there was the image of the Madonna with the Instruments of the Passion arranged before her, on an expensive-looking white cloth that preserved the square creases of storage. Beside this picture was another small print brought back from a journey to Europe by Nargis and Massud, of Christ with John the Evangelist asleep on his breast during the Last Supper. And there was a photograph of Bishop Solomon, who was Pakistan's first Roman Catholic bishop to have been born in Pakistan. A source of pride for the country's Christians.

When she finished she picked up the newspaper for a few moments but then put it down again. 'There is nothing worth reading here.'

'Maybe there is no news,' Lily said, but only a moment later he corrected himself: 'There is news, they just don't put it in the newspapers any more.'

Helen went to the back window of the kitchen. She knew well the flaw in the glass pane – how if you aligned yourself in a specific way, it doubled the number of stars.

She could see the signal tower that the mobile phone company had constructed in the rear courtyard of the house.

'What time are the engineers coming?'

'They didn't give a time,' Lily said. 'They just said this afternoon.'

'I'll be in,' she said.

About three months ago, a young man with a briefcase and clipboard had approached her out on the lane and asked if she lived nearby. When she said yes, he expressed the wish to speak to her father. She had told him that he could talk to her, and he had explained that he represented a mobile phone company that wished to erect a tower in the area. But the neighbourhood was densely populated and no vacant plot seemed available. 'Is there enough space at the back of your house?' he had asked. 'The company will pay annual rent to your family.' She had told him to return in the evening, when her father would be home, and the contract was signed a week later, Nargis and Massud having examined it carefully. Lily would be paid just over 300,000 rupees a year. All this had occurred during the last days of January – Helen remembered that there was still no red on the silk-cotton tree in Massud and Nargis's garden, and the kites had begun to emit their piercing mating cries – and the tower was becoming functional at the end of this month.

When Lily finished eating, and Helen came to take away the

44

tray, he said, 'Sit here for a minute. I have something to tell you.'

She lowered herself onto the mat beside him.

'It's about Grace,' he said. 'About the man who . . . took her life.'

Helen nodded.

'He's been released,' her father was saying.

'I know.'

'You do?'

'Yes.'

They sat together without saying anything. A silence in which she thought of Grace, as did her father, she was sure.

Why can't I wake up? she had said upon opening her eyes in bed the day after her mother's death.

'I have known for some days but wasn't sure how to tell you,' Lily said.

Something occurred to Helen and made her panic. 'You won't do anything, will you?' she asked.

'No,' he said. 'Don't worry.'

Every time Helen came home in distress, at having been mal-treated for not being a Muslim, Massud would tell her to keep her mind on her education as much as humanly possible. 'There are rocks that shatter into small pieces when struck,' he had said to her once. 'And there are rocks that withstand the blows. These are carved and worshipped as gods and goddesses.'

Helen stood up with the tray. 'Have you told Nargis-*apa*?'

'No. Not yet.'

It was not always the case that surviving a terrible experi-ence strengthened a person's character. Sometimes a bad thing left you permanently weakened.

Lily opened the metal gate at the end of the courtyard – it was just large enough for the rickshaw to pass through – and began to roll the rickshaw backwards, pushing it out as he walked alongside it.

45

As she crossed the courtyard to close the gate after him, Helen experienced a sense of foreboding. On two occasions during the course of this month, after Lily had gone out through the gate and she was sliding it shut, she had seen the silhouette of a woman appear on the high window behind the mosque.

The house where the cleric lived with his widowed daughter.

On both occasions Helen had seen Lily begin to turn his head towards the window, but he had stopped on noticing Helen.

Now as she arrived, a passerby was taking a quick sideways step to avoid being hit by the backward-rolling rickshaw. Lily's attention was on the house behind the mosque. The man let out a cry of fury.

'Babur, I am sorry,' Lily said, straightening. 'I didn't see you there.'

Babur's face was a grimace of hostility.

'You didn't see me!'

'No I didn't, Babur, and I have apologised.'

Babur turned his head to glare at Helen, and then raised his eyes to look at the phone tower rising into the sky behind her. Finally he returned his attention to Lily.

'Your head has always been a little too big for your own good.'

Lily threw up his hands.

'I am so sorry if I have offended you,' Babur said, taking a step closer. 'You think you are better than everyone else because Massud can buy you a house and a rickshaw. And now there's the promise of the money from the tower.'

Under other circumstances Lily would have just driven away, but he couldn't leave Babur here with Helen. He took a rag and began to clean the handlebars, accidentally pressing the horn. 'I don't have time for this,' he said.

Babur reached into his pocket and took out a thick bunch of keys and shook it at Lily. 'Nine out of ten houses in this neighbourhood are mine. That tower should be on one of my properties.' The houses he owned were rented out to Christians, for whom – men, women and children – he found cleaning jobs in the richer areas of the city. He had sabotaged every attempt to open a government school in the neighbourhood.

'Well, they came to my house,' Lily said.

'No they didn't,' Babur said. 'They came to one of my houses but your daughter lured them away.'

By temperament Helen avoided confrontation but she knew she had to respond now. She searched for an appropriate tone of voice. 'Forgive me, but that is not true.' Her only wish was to step back into the house and lock the gate.

'Yes it is,' Babur said, almost snapping at her. 'Many people saw you talking to that man. You must have asked him to come to your house and not go to any of the others.'

'The man just stopped me and asked,' Helen said. 'I didn't know until later that he had knocked on other doors and got no response.'

'Well, most women don't like to show themselves at the door or wander around the lane like . . .'

Now it was Lily who took a step towards Babur. 'Hey!' he shouted. 'Don't talk to my girl like that. You heard what she said, and you've heard her say it before. How many times do you think you need to talk to us about this thing?'

As he stood there Babur nodded to himself several times, holding Lily's eye. During a previous argument about the tower he had said, 'You think you'll climb that tower all the way to Paradise?' Now he gave a small laugh:

'Sweeping and cleaning is too lowly a job for you. Mr Bigshot Rickshaw Driver is leaving for work in the morning, with the smell of eggs and parathas spilling out of his house.' He extended his arm along the length of the lane. 'Don't let me stop you.'

He turned and walked away and Lily brought the rickshaw to the side of the lane and went to Helen.

'Are you all right?' he asked when they had both walked back into the house.

'Yes,' Helen said, placing a hand on his wrist. 'You go to work.'

'Are you sure?'

'Yes.'

Helen wished to busy herself with a task. A square of sunlight had reached the courtyard. She would wash the breakfast dishes and carry them out in the wire basket, to dry in the square that would soon lengthen to a rectangle. She had broken out in sweat and she wanted the cool air of the fan but there was no electricity. It was still only April but yesterday the current was absent for almost five hours. At the height of summer it would be gone for twelve hours each day.

Even during an argument Lily could be made to smile in a fraction of a second, but now he walked towards the gate and stood looking in the direction Babur had gone.

'These rich people think they own us,' he said, his furious expression unaltered. 'But just watch. When the money from the tower begins to come in, I will buy another rickshaw, and then another and another. The men he thinks are only good enough to stand up to their necks in excrement in the sewers will soon be driving on the roads.' He looked at Helen. 'And I want a school.'

Some years ago Babur had had an accident and had spent a month in hospital. When he was discharged the first thing he did was to destroy with a sledgehammer both his car and the wall it had hit, to recover his sense of self.

When she spoke, Helen was aware that she was referring as much to Babur as to the silhouette on the curtain behind the mosque. The woman had appeared when Lily pressed the horn. 'Be careful,' she said. 'You can't fight a tiger.'

He answered her just as he stepped out of the house.

'Yes you can,' he said. 'You can if you are a tiger yourself.'

II

THE SECULAR WORLD

6

As the sun climbed higher, the morning light slowly moved down the walls of the city.

Nargis was walking along the Grand Trunk Road. It was still early but she had left the house on a vague impulse.

She stopped and spoke to a man who was opening up his shop, and having received directions she walked a little farther and entered a side lane. The shopkeeper was the fifth or sixth person she had spoken to during the previous hour, asking for guidance.

A man was sweeping at the other end of the lane she had entered, and dragon-like shapes of smoke were rising from the fire in which he was burning what he collected. She consulted him and thanked him before moving towards where his finger pointed.

This small house was constructed from naked bricks. She knocked on the door and was told that the young man she wished to see was in the back courtyard. She was invited in and went along the wraparound veranda. Arriving at the rear, she looked up and saw the hundreds of small fish swimming against the sky. They were suspended in the air, fifteen or so feet above the ground, and they were moving contentedly, each in its small plastic bag of water, brilliant in the sun.

The goldfish seller had hung the bags from thin nails driven into the branches of the tree that grew in the courtyard. He turned to look at her when she approached. It was the seventeenth day since Massud's death. Though he was no more than a bystander, she had wanted to locate him since that morning on the Grand Trunk Road. Her mind wishing to examine

53

every detail of the death for significance. To reach back and collect every moment. Later as Massud lay dying at the hospital, someone had come forward to donate the blood he had needed, and she regretted not having been able to thank him.

'Why have you done this?' She gestured towards the fish swimming up there among the foliage and the bees and the morning's other winged insects; and he – looking like a young prophet with his scant beard and threadbare clothes – smiled shyly and invited her to the roof of the house. Up there, her eyes were level with the canopy of the tree, overlooking the lanes and streets of this part of the city.

'Sometimes I hang them in the tree for a few hours,' he said. 'It is a kind of atonement.'

She still did not understand and so he pointed through the branches of the tree. 'From up here, they can see the river. Look, it's over there.'

On the way home she bought the morning newspapers, sitting with them in the study. She wondered when the man from military intelligence would reappear, hearing the precise ticking of the clock on the wall.

All his life Massud had resisted having anything to do with those who wielded power. She had never seen him bow towards authority, those who demanded respect instead of earning it. It was in his blood.

In 1913 in the American city of Astoria, Oregon, his grandfather had been present at the founding of the Ghadar Party. He had gone to the USA a few years earlier, landing in California with thousands of other Punjabis – from Ludhiana, Jalandhar, Heer, Amritsar and Zamana. Stories of the gold rush were being printed in *The Civil and Military Gazette* of Zamana, but he had not boarded the ship at Calcutta because of that lure.

He was escaping: he was among those who were being hunted for demanding an end to British rule. In 1913, the Ghadar Party – the Party of Rebels – was formed in Oregon, and in 1915 five ships were hired and loaded with weapons and propaganda, setting sail for India from various ports in California, to liberate their homeland from the British. Massud's grandfather returned on one of these ships. An estimated eight thousand followers of the Ghadar Party arrived by sea to assist with the revolt – but many of them were arrested on disembarking. Initially Massud's grandfather succeeded in evading capture, being among those who came in through Bombay, Colombo or Madras, instead of Calcutta. Eventually however he too was caught and executed by the British with 145 other Ghadars.

Nargis put away the newspapers and went along the corridor. On a shelf were the cloth dolls which Grace had stitched out of mismatching scraps for Helen when she was a child, but which Massud had said were too marvellous to be thrown away once the girl outgrew them.

7

There was to be an eclipse of the sun in the afternoon, and around midday the cleric from the mosque arrived to see Nargis. As always he was carrying a thick encyclopaedia of sins in his left hand, a rosary in the other.

'I wanted to come and see how you were,' he said.

He was perhaps seventy years old, his beard white, the frame of his body somewhat bent forward. The forehead of an observant Muslim was meant to touch the ground at least thirty-four times a day – when he bowed towards Mecca during the five prayers. It could add up to millions of prostrations in a lifetime, and so in the centre of the cleric's forehead was a dark bruise, a mark that spoke of his lifelong devotion. It was said that on Judgement Day this discolouration – the *mihraab* – would begin to glow, making it easier for Allah's angels to identify the devout Muslims.

'Has Massud appeared to you in a dream yet?' he asked.

Nargis had brought him into the kitchen.

She was uncertain about how to respond to his question, not quite sure what was being asked.

'Please think about it later,' said the cleric, noticing her confusion. 'If the deceased person is reciting the Koran in the dream, it means he has been admitted to Paradise.'

She murmured a 'thank you'. Massud was not religious in any sense, and nor was she. They certainly were not interested in piety and decency based on reward. Nargis believed that God was just another word for 'consolation', and Massud had told her that as a child he would sit in the mosque counting the thousands of tulips and lilies painted on the walls.

7

56

She filled a pan from the tap to make tea and placed it on the hob. It swayed from the weight of the water, then settled. The tips of the flames showed around the base, as though clamping it in place.

'You must read a chapter of the Koran every day,' the cleric said. 'It'll bring you peace.'

'Thank you, I will try. How are your daughter and her little boy?'

The cleric remained silent as though he had not heard, his head bent towards his lap.

Nargis watched him. It sometimes seemed to her that 'failure' was a term of abuse these days. To have not succeeded in the world was required to be a source of shame for a person. And yet she suspected that failure in worldly terms was the condition of the majority of the people in the world. To have been rejected, to have lacked courage, to have tried but failed. She was not religious but she was sympathetic to the idea that religion might offer a consolation to those who had been humiliated by life.

'How is your daughter?' she asked again.

'She is well, praise be to God. They are both well. Patience is a great virtue.'

His daughter was in her early thirties, and after her husband was killed, the cleric had made attempts to arrange another marriage for her, but according to her husband's brother and his militant companions, a holy martyr's widow could never remarry. She had to remain untainted, for her eventual reunion with her husband in Paradise. So her prospective husbands were warned off. One man who persisted was beaten so severely he had lost an eye. Nargis was sure that the cleric and his daughter lived in fear of her former brother-in-law, who had taken up residence at the mosque, to ensure her continued purity.

'God is watching everything,' the old man said quietly.

They both looked out at the timeworn mosque through the kitchen window. Only a handful of Muslims lived in Badami Bagh and all of them were extremely poor, so there were never enough donations for the upkeep and repairs.

Nargis opened the cupboard and took out the teapot and cups, from the set whose colour and pattern always delighted the cleric.

There was, he believed, a mark on his family. His great-grandfather had been a contractor and had collected the bricks from the hundreds of mosques that were demolished by the British after the Mutiny. He had used them to build barracks for the Empire's soldiers. He was said to have been cursed as a result and had died a pauper. Decades later, when the cleric's mother had fallen ill she had refused to consult a Western doctor, because successful treatment would have been humiliating to the pride of her fellow Muslims. She had eventually become a martyr to that loyalty.

He raised his face towards her when Nargis brought the cups and saucers to the table.

'I must admit that I have come here for a specific reason.'

'Yes?' Nargis was about to turn away but stopped.

He looked for a way to begin. 'I heard on the radio that the government will ask the relatives of the three deceased people to forgive the American killer. The spy. I have come here to ask you to refuse the offer.' He was avoiding her gaze as he spoke. 'It is my feeling that he must be put on trial here in Pakistan,' he said. 'You must show the government that, unlike them, you face Mecca when you pray, not Washington.'

In all the years Nargis had known him the cleric had never used such vocabulary. She stood there beside his chair, the scepticism apparent on her face, she was sure; were he to look. These were not his thoughts. He had been sent here by the younger men who had taken over his mosque, the brother-in-law and his companions.

'You must remember that we Muslims have mosques that are twice as old as the United States,' the cleric said. 'Three times as old.'

'Forgive me, but I don't want to think about any of this,' she said gently.

The cleric glanced towards her and then away. But then he straightened and seemed to decide to continue, delivering the message he had been sent to deliver under who knew what amount of duress. 'Our politicians and army men are very shrewd,' he declared. 'They will say that under Sharia Law the relatives of the dead can accept blood money in exchange for pardoning a murderer. And indeed they can. But I implore you in the name of Islam, in the name of Pakistan which was created in the name of Islam, to not do that. You must refuse.'

He looked at her, so Nargis smiled.

'As I said I don't want to think about it.'

The water was boiling. She returned to the counter and began to attend to the tea. In the morning she had placed the milk in the fridge just as the milk-wallah had handed it to her. Now she spread a piece of an old veil across a saucepan and strained the milk through it, to catch any chaff or impurity. Then she put it to heat to eradicate the possibility of bacteria.

Behind her the cleric was quietly beginning to clear his throat again. 'The young men are asking me to prepare a sermon for this Friday, in which I shall mention the martyrdom of your husband,' he said. 'Our people must awaken to the threat they face from the Crusaders, they who have been at war with us even before we were born.'

The information was too disturbing for Nargis. 'I must ask you not to do that,' she turned to him and said, perhaps a little too loudly.

For a few moments the cleric seemed bewildered. Finally, he said, 'I understand.' He was clutching the rosary so tightly she thought the beads would scatter.

She could see he was ashamed, that he did not wish to say the things he had been saying. She knew he felt a sense of injustice at what had happened to Massud and Nargis, but he would not articulate it the way he had just now.

'Thank you,' she said.

'It was inconsiderate of me.'

'Please think nothing of it.'

She placed cumin biscuits on a plate and carried them to him.

The group of young men all had the discolouration on their foreheads too, every one of them, even though they were only in their twenties and early thirties. They struck their heads on the floor with deliberate vehemence in order to acquire it, and they were threateningly contemptuous of men who did not do the same, whose brows were yet unmarked.

She brought the teapot to the table but the cleric had picked up the encyclopaedia of sins and begun to stand up. He seemed overwhelmed and humiliated, by the stilted sentences he had delivered. 'I must leave,' he said. He was frail and his hair was completely absent from the scalp under the turban of white muslin.

She was distressed to see tears in his eyes.

'You mustn't feel bad,' she said. 'I understand.' Perhaps his despair was connected to his own circumstances – losing control of his beloved mosque, the long years of loneliness to which his daughter seemed condemned, the little grandson maimed by the American missile.

There was a lens – no bigger than a sequin – fitted into the largest bead of his rosary. The bead was hollow, and by closing one eye and putting the other to the lens, you could see the tiny picture of the Great Mosque at Mecca it contained. She had seen children – Muslim as well as Christian – running after the cleric asking to 'go on the pilgrimage', had seen him standing in the street with his rosary attached to a grinning child's face.

Now as she walked out with him through her garden, he advised her to read the 'Rehman' chapter of the Koran while standing under the mango tree, to invite Allah's blessing and increase its yield. She deliberately lingered with him among the veronicas, that were at their best this month. There was some calmness in his face eventually, the return of clarity in the eyes. She told him that last summer they had stopped at a thousand when they were counting the number of mangoes the tree had given. Though it would be fewer this year because it needed to recover its carbohydrates.

'They wanted to come themselves but I prevented that,' he confessed just before he left. 'I was afraid they might be disrespectful towards you.'

She sat looking out at the mosque through the window.

There were days when Nargis felt that she contained another self – a ghost.

She was born a Christian and was fourteen years old when she pretended to be a Muslim for the first time. It was a brief deception, lasting a period of a few days. Little more than a child's thrill.

Her real name was Margaret – the name she had been given at birth, in the city of Lyallpur.

At the age of eighteen, when she arrived from Lyallpur to Zamana to attend college, she decided to present herself as Nargis from the beginning.

She did not know that she would meet Massud in a few years, that she would have to carry that deception into her love and eventual marriage with him. And it could be argued that everything around her was based on a dangerous lie.

And that good man had died without knowing the truth.

A few days ago Helen had said that speaking about her

mother's death to others would have accorded reality to that death, would have made it a fact. That was why Helen had not uttered a word to anyone for some months. And perhaps Nargis had concealed her early self from Massud for similar reasons. At least initially she had – when she had only just met him. His response would have confirmed to her that the terrible things in her past *had* happened, that she wasn't just imagining them.

She slept through the eclipse, waking up only at dusk. She was on the bed in the study and she reached out and lit the kerosene lamp. On one of the tables was a pair of binoculars, which Massud – with his weak eyesight – found useful to search for books on the high shelves. Beside it was his father's book, *That They Might Know Each Other*. The story of the founding of the Ghadar Party in Oregon was in its pages.

She opened it at random and looked at the reproduction of Raphael's fresco *The School of Athens*. It was at the Apostolic Palace in the Vatican – she had seen it some years ago – and among the ancient Greek philosophers gathered under the great arch was a moustached figure in a green tunic, on the lower left corner. It was Ibn-e-Rushd, or Averroes in medieval Latin, one of the most potent forces of the Renaissance.

The flame inside the lamp's globe began to falter and she turned her attention to it. The fuel was housed in the base of the lamp, and she raised it to her ear and gently shook it to ascertain the amount it contained. She went out and crossed the garden towards the kitchen, the dying light in her hands.

When she returned to the study with the refilled lamp, the man from the military-intelligence agency was sitting in one of the armchairs.

'How did you get in?'

'I am here to inform you of the latest developments.'

The sense of entitlement in the voice was unmistakable. The serene disdain.

Nargis turned the wheel under the glass globe of the lamp to increase the light. She moved towards the open book on the table.

'I asked you a question,' she said. 'How did you get in?'

'The US government is offering money for the man to be pardoned.'

'I don't want it.' She did not raise her eyes from the pages she was turning slowly. She was standing above the book, looking down, and he was in the striped chair ten feet away, facing her.

'You, and the families of the two thieves, will each receive one million dollars as compensation. As blood money, if you like. We negotiated the deal.'

'And what are you getting in return?'

'That should not concern you. All you need to know is that you will appear in court one day soon and declare that it is your free, definitive, and true wish to pardon the American man.'

She stopped turning the pages and looked towards where he sat. His large eyes glinting, the legs crossed comfortably.

'I have no desire to offer you a huckster's sincerity,' he said. 'These are practical matters. I am sure you know that the mother of one of the dead thieves has swallowed battery acid and is now in intensive care. Some of the newspapers are saying that it's because she is being threatened to forgive the American killer. But we all know what kind of family they are. They just want to increase the compensation money with these theatrics.' He released a snort of derision. 'As if that woman wouldn't have killed her son with her bare hands for a tenth of a million dollars.'

Nargis remembered how Massud, when disappointed or hurt by someone, would find it unbearable to even think about

63

that person, to even see the name written down, or be in the same room with him. He needed time to reflect, and during that time he shut out the offence-giver completely. The length of the shutting out depended on the severity of the offence. He would 'sentence' people for precise periods – not seeing a betrayer or deceiver or liar for four weeks, or two months or – in one instance – an entire year. A time during which he recovered from the confusion and pain and slowly began to understand what had occurred. The isolation was needed because he was afraid of coming to the wrong, swift conclusion, while his judgement was impaired due to suffering.

'I would like you to leave,' she said quietly.

After perhaps half a minute had passed with her head still bent towards the pages, she saw the man's hand enter her field of vision and take the book away. She looked up: he was carrying it carefully, almost reverently, as if he were handling a sacred relic. He settled back in the armchair and she watched him produce a blade from somewhere upon his person, a scalpel. The book was open on a page depicting a painting from sixteenth-century Tabriz.

The pointed tip of the blade reached down towards the angel Gabriel's face.

He was holding her eye now – the always present threat of conscienceless temper – and she looked at him in mute appeal against what was about to occur.

The angel was looking out of the page and into the room, infinitely aware.

He perforated the face with the steel tip, and then the blade continued upwards through the angel's headdress, the various ribbons and gems. Continuing, it cut into the sky full of gold stars. Half of the page had been incised now. Never once did he lose the sense of ceremony. He brought the blade back to Gabriel's cheek – where the cut had originated – and this time the blade cut downwards. It was a swift clean stroke that sliced the page completely in half. The detached length of paper fell to the floor and lay there brilliant against the tiles of grey stone.

The soldier-spy opened the book at another page. The scalpel made contact with the paper but remained motionless, and with that frozen gesture he looked up at Nargis. Then he put away the blade, and closed the book and got up and placed it on the table before her.

She remembered the body of Massud's brother, its countless wounds. Upon seeing it she had wondered what the many burn marks meant. It was as though they had flung matches at him to pass the time.

'How long do you intend to stand there?' he said, and it was a few moments before Nargis realised the question was not directed at her. He was looking towards the door that opened into the half-dark corridor. With a certain speed he left the room and she heard him say, 'Who are you?' from out there.

'Nargis-*apa*?' Helen said. 'I came to see how you were.'

Nargis was walking around the table, to go out to the corridor, when she heard the girl release a small cry. She arrived to see that he had gripped her at the upper arm, clearly with some strength because Helen's face was distorted in pain.

'Let go of her,' Nargis said.

'How long have you been standing out here?' he asked Helen with a shake, and Helen was struggling to free herself, on the verge of furious, shocked tears. Of course, he had neither looked towards Nargis nor done what she had asked. 'Who are you?' he said to the girl.

'She is my family and my friend,' Nargis said, approaching with the lamp. The flame was throwing sharp swaying shadows onto the walls around them. 'Let go of her this instant.'

She had to overcome her sense of dignity and almost interpose herself between the two of them, had to extract Helen's arm from his fingers. They seemed fused in place like metal. She had set the light on the floor so all the movement in the shadows on the wall was now caused by their short-lived struggle. A minute passed before Nargis could walk out of the corridor with Helen, the girl glaring over her shoulder at the man.

'I'll speak to you tomorrow,' she told Helen at the front door. 'Go home.'

'Are you sure?'

'Yes, I am. Go home.'

'I'd rather stay until he's gone.'

'There's no need. I'll be fine.'

Returning to the study, Nargis said, 'I will not put up with this.'

The change in the room was instantaneous. The floor seemed to tilt. The force with which he struck her face sent her body against the bookshelf, her feet breaking contact with the ground at one point. Her head met the edge of something as she fell to the floor, and he grabbed the hair at her scalp and raised her head up and struck her cheek again with equal force. At the top of the bookshelf that she had disturbed, there was a terracotta replica of the minaret at Samarra. She heard it fall and crash against the floor somewhere near her. She saw the lamp she had let drop: it was rolling away from her. As she lay there she even noticed the half-second of silence as the glass globe went over the piece of paper with Gabriel's face. He was a young man, in his thirties, and he hauled her up, the strength and hardness of his body unbelievable to her, and more or less threw her into the armchair, as though she were already a corpse.

'Just who do you think you are talking to?'

Nargis leaned her head back against the chair. She discovered that her eyelids were flickering and that she was finding it hard to breathe. There was a pain in her ribs on the left side. She realised she had begun to moan.

She forced her eyes to remain open and saw that he was

calmly picking up the lamp where it had come to rest, the flame upright on the horizontal wick. He unscrewed the cap of the oil tank and came towards her and splashed the fuel onto her face and body, the flame thrashing inside the glass globe. She tried to scream but there was no voice inside her. The thought came to her that her face was exposed and she raised her hands to protect it, inhaling loudly behind the palms. Her clothes and hair felt fully doused, almost drenched in places.

'Now. Sit up and look to me. Sit up.' From the voice it was obvious that he was satisfied; he had reminded her of her place in the order of things. She uncovered her face and saw that he had stepped back, the lamp in one hand – that small bud of fire she found herself staring at with terror. 'This is what will happen,' he said. 'I will contact you within the next seven days, to tell you when you have to make your appearance in court. We don't know the exact date and other details yet. I was going to let you sign the papers here at the house and not appear in the court personally if you wished, but I won't be so considerate now. You will appear before the judge at some point before this month is out and say that you wish to forgive the American man, that he is free to leave Pakistan and go back to America. Is that clear?'

Nargis, her entire body trembling with each sob, gave a nod.

'I want to hear you say it.'

'I will forgive the American man.'

'Good,' he said, placing the lamp on the table. 'Now, I wish to leave. Get up and show me out.'

As with Christianity, there was an Annunciation in Islam. Gabriel appearing to Muhammad – just as he had appeared to Mary – and bringing a message from God. To Mary he had said that God would be made *flesh* through her body. To

Muhammad he had said he would receive a series of verses, which would be God made *word*. It was a mistake to say that the Koran was the Bible of the Muslims. If there was an equivalent of the Koran in Christianity, it was Jesus himself. One was God made flesh. The other God made word.

The image the man had cut up was of Gabriel bringing Chapter Eight of the Koran to Muhammad, written on a scroll that curved from his hands. The Prophet sitting in a meadow, his face undepicted.

Nargis emerged from the bathroom, her body dripping with water, leaving the clothes she had taken off submerged in the tub, as though they would remain eternally flammable. In the study she picked up the cut section of the page from the floor and carefully returned it to the book, nestling it there, and she made a pile of the pieces of broken Samarra minaret on the floor. She went to her room and climbed into bed and slowly pulled a sheet over her body, inch by inch on all sides, a kind of self-burial. One day during their childhood her uncle had asked her and her sister to be still and listen to the song of a bird, the rings of sound that were spreading from a nearby tree, waking up her awareness. 'Force has no meaning in the world,' he had said to them, and holding his thumb and forefinger an inch apart to indicate the smallness of the bird, had added, 'God speaks through the least of His creatures.'

Even a deformed rose had perfume.

At 1 a.m. she was still awake. Then 2 a.m.

She had fastened all the doors and windows carefully, returning to each several times for certainty. The upper portion of her head felt tender when it came into contact with the pillow, so she lay on her stomach, her face positioned sideways. Her cheeks burned, though there were no marks. In fact the entire surface of her body was generating a strong heat. Just after three, she went to the kitchen and thirstily drank two glasses of water. There were stars in the sky above the garden.

There was no moon – that billion-year-old desert suspended above the earth, as Massud's brother had once described it. On her way back to the bedroom something made her turn into the corridor that led to the study, some instinct or awareness.

There was electricity now and so she switched on the light.

The book lay on the table where she had left it and she saw that now all of its pages had been shredded. Some of the fragments were sticking out beyond the edges of the covers, every which way, while others lay scattered on the floor.

8

Eight very long bazaars spread out in all directions from a clock tower at the centre. It was said that the British had designed this area of Zamana to resemble the Union Jack. Lily was sitting in his rickshaw under the clock tower, looking to his left. Twenty yards from him, next to a shop that sold plastic flowers imported from China, to be used at weddings and other celebratory occasions, there was a lane. The man who had taken Grace's life lived in a house situated there.

Again and again over the past few days Lily had found himself bringing the rickshaw to this precise location under the clock tower, from where he could see the entrance to the lane.

He watched as a municipal bus went by, a pair of bulbuls sitting on the metal ladder welded to its back. It was not an unusual sight. Sometimes while the bus was stationary at the depot, the birds would begin to build their nest in it somewhere, in a gap inside the layers of the roof, or a dead light fitting. And for the rest of the breeding season they trailed the bus, flying alongside it, entering and exiting through the windows as the vehicle travelled through Zamana's neighbourhoods. They returned with it to the depot at night, raising entire broods that way.

Lily sat and watched. When he was a teenager, angry at the daily – sometimes hourly – humiliations he had to endure at the hands of Muslims, he had often felt that if Pakistan were a person he would kill it. Tired of being a non-citizen – a half-citizen at best. But then there were times, especially when he was drinking vodka at the No Tension bar – where the word for alcohol became more and more poetic the drunker everyone became, moving from vodka or beer to *sharab* to *mai* to *jaam* to *paimana* to *saghir* – he would also love everything about his life and his country, glad to be part of the beautiful mess.

Two young clerics emerged from the Metal Bazaar, carrying a six-foot brass finial that would be fitted to the dome of a mosque, and asked him to take them to Civil Lines. The very tip of the shiny object protruded from the rickshaw door during the journey but he manoeuvred himself carefully. At Civil Lines, without much wait, he was able to pick up a young couple who wished to be taken to the train station. When they got out at the station, they were both smiling.

'We've never had a driver who sang to himself throughout the journey,' said the young woman.

'Did I?' Lily asked.

'*Throughout.*'

The young man, lifting his suitcase out of the vehicle, laughed and said, 'Yes, indeed.' He put his arm around Lily's shoulder and briefly drew him to his breast. Grinning towards the woman, he said:

'My brother here is like me, a romantic.'

He watched them disappear into one of the twelve sandstone arches that formed the facade of the station. Whenever he observed couples, he felt visited by Aysha, though at this moment she was several miles away at her father's house, behind the mosque in Badami Bagh. There was a peculiar restlessness in him these days – the strange joy of new love. Tonight at midnight, after the lights had been switched off and the doors locked, he would visit Aysha at home. He had done it once before, climbing the balcony of the mosque and dropping down into the mosque's garden first. His rickshaw took him to every corner of Zamana with every kind of person sitting in the back, and he knew how people created opportunities for hidden happiness.

Helen had told him she would be sleeping at Nargis's house tonight. All but one of his previous meetings with Aysha had been out of doors, Lily making sure to be present with his rickshaw wherever she said she would be, everything arranged on the mobile phones. These years after Grace's death he was beginning to feel a sustained desire for someone again, getting closer and closer to the thing that made a human being live. He had never entered a mosque as an adult, was not absolutely sure if Christians were allowed into neighbourhood mosques, but one night last month he had found himself on that balcony, suddenly desperate, in a state of near delirium, because Aysha had been unable to meet him elsewhere during the previous two weeks.

The next passenger wished to be taken to the hotel where the current American president's mother had lived for five years, from 1987 to 1992, when she worked in Pakistan for an agricultural bank.

From there Lily took a woman to the Charagar mausoleum. When he got there and the passenger disembarked, Lily got out and stretched out on the riverbank. Spirals of insects were dancing above the water. Many channels of the Vela River flowed through the city, the roads suddenly becoming bridges, and this particular stretch of water had a reputation for healing, was connected to the memory of the Sufi saint whose tomb was located on the bank. The pilgrims were beginning to gather on the wide staircase of the building now that it was late afternoon. He refused the next two passengers, preferring to doze in the grass. He sat up and accepted the third only when the man said he wished to go to the Eight Bazaar clock tower.

He arrived and parked, and once again found himself looking towards the entrance to the lane. A grandmother sat on the front step of a house, fanning herself in the heat, a baby asleep in her lap. A little boy was trying to reach up to ring the bell of a bicycle leaning against a wall.

As he got older and Grace and Helen arrived in his life, he had lost most of the fury of his teenage years. It was a new Zamana, a new Vela. He painted anew the walls and buildings and roads of the city, with colour given to him by his wife and daughter. But the rage of his youth had returned a few weeks after Grace's death. Every time he thought of the man who had taken Grace's life, it was followed in his mind by pictures of great brutality. Guns, blades, hammers, hands that somehow acquired the strength of claws – he was shocked at how instantaneously the savagery appeared in his head, and how complete it was, and how satisfying. As the months went by, he realised that it wasn't really the killer he was trying to kill in his thoughts: he was trying to eradicate the fact that Grace was gone. The man represented that fact. Lily wasn't sure how he would feel about the killer if ever he met him in person and was alone with him, but he certainly knew he wanted to erase the calamitous situation he had put him in. By killing the man, he was trying to unkill Grace.

Sitting under the clock tower with his eyes fixed on the lane, he shook his head when a passenger approached and he waved away the next one too, finding himself unwilling to depart. The day was almost over. The sun in the windscreen was setting fast, changing its position by the second, an orb that was yellow above and dusty pink towards the bottom. And grey clouds were approaching from the east, the edges drenched with white light. He was looking at the lane, his head turned to his left, when the rickshaw swayed gently because a passenger had let himself in at the back, having approached from the right.

'Where to?' Lily said, half-turning in his seat.

'Firdaus. How much?'

It was him. The killer.

The sun, almost gone, had suddenly become as hot as noon on Lily's skin.

'Whatever seems appropriate to you,' he said. When he was a child he used to think he disappeared from the world when he closed his eyes. Now he wished he could fall asleep and be transported into nothingness. Slowly, he reached down to grab the lever that started the engine.

His passenger suggested an amount he didn't hear over the ignition, over the howling in his ear. 'That's fine,' he heard himself reply, staring directly ahead.

On the way to Firdaus the rickshaw would have to drive past that cardboard prison they'd put him in. Lily had seen him on several occasions during the trial, and he was sure he knew who Lily was, what Lily looked like – but for the time being he was distracted, settling himself on the seat, one eye on the mobile phone that filled the air of the interior around him with a ghost-like glow.

The rickshaw lurched forward and began its journey and Lily's eyes entered the rear-view mirror again and again, watching him. A man older than him, a scattering of grey in his hair but thick patches of it at the temples. He had a splintered matchstick between his teeth, and he moved it from one side of the mouth to the other without touching it. Lily felt disorientated on the roads that were entirely familiar to him, his intrepid sense of belonging slipping away from him. With a part of his mind he was rifling through the toolbox under the seat. The screwdriver, the monkey wrench, a length of cord.

His crucifix was swaying gently between his shirt and his breastbone, touching the skin in a rhythm not dissimilar to heartbeat. When he had found himself in trouble repeatedly during his youth, a priest had said to him, 'Sometimes a man has to be great enough to know how insignificant he is.'

The passenger was sitting back against the seat now, his eyes closed, listening to a recording on the phone, a piercing love song from an Indian film.

'They think we see fewer stars when we look at the sky,'

Grace had said once after an incident of humiliation at the hands of Muslims. 'Or no stars at all.'

Instead of turning into Ghazi Ilm Deen Road – halfway along which the Firdaus cinema was located – Lily went down the pitted street that he knew led to a secluded dead end, the rear of factories that manufactured washing machines, chipboard, and the pulling mechanisms of wheeled suitcases.

Which side was God on? And which God?

He reached under his shirt and took hold of the crucifix and pulled at it, sensing the chain grow taut, begin to dig into the skin at the back of his neck. He persisted until it broke. He brought out the crucifix and the chain from under the shirt and carefully put them in his breast pocket.

The priest had said, enraging him further, 'I suspect you are too weak to accept the world as it is.'

He cut off the engine and brought the rickshaw to a halt, letting it roll into a gentle curve for the last two metres. The sky was dark already.

'Why have we stopped?' the passenger asked, sitting forward. 'Something wrong?'

'Nothing to worry about,' he said. He had climbed out and was bending down to take out the toolbox and now he straightened with the tyre iron in his hand.

'Come out,' he said. He could hear the water of the Vela flowing behind the nearby clumps of reeds, the egrets flapping their wings.

Slowly the man climbed out and extended his mobile phone towards Lily. 'Take it,' he said. The recording was still active, the song issuing into the evening air. 'Take it.'

The light fell on Lily's face, and – only now, at last – he recognised him. 'O Allah!' he said, stepping back towards the rickshaw.

With a fierce swipe Lily sent the proffered phone flying twenty feet away into the reeds, where it was caught still glowing but silent. The metal had connected with the man's fingers and he let out a yelp. He was creeping away along the rickshaw, the injured hand held in the intact one. Lily stared at him. He tried to raise the tyre iron but his arm felt loath to. His face and chest had gone numb and his pulse was erratic, indecisive. His mouth was dry, and then he heard himself whisper through a sob-like catch in his throat, 'Run.'

The man seemed puzzled, then said:

'Stay away from me or I'll tell the police you swore at the Prophet.'

Lily would remember this only in the coming days. For now, managing to find his voice, he repeated the one word he had spoken earlier, loudly this time, as an order would be given. 'Run!' And he dropped the iron as though it were the heaviest object in the world, which it was.

'What?'

Lily shook his head. He lowered himself onto the driver seat of the rickshaw, aware of holding his body very still, his head bent almost in a faint. He wondered if he was having a heart attack. He was not sure if his passenger had left. Eventually the chill on his skin receded and the strength came back to his limbs and hands.

A little later he reached up and switched on the overhead light. He took out the crucifix and looked for the two broken ends of the chain. With his teeth, he eased open the last link at one of these ends. Into this tiny open half-circle, he fed the very last link from the chain's other end. Then carefully he pinched shut the circle, making the chain whole.

Outside it had begun to rain, the first sparsely distributed drops followed quickly by others that filled up the spaces in between. A cloth spread out by a beggar filling up with coins. For a while he sat listening to them sounding on the rickshaw's roof. Then he took out his phone and called Helen. Sending a text message was beyond his abilities, but having to deal with money meant that he was well acquainted with numbers. He still remembered every single line of the story Helen had written when she was seven years old, having proudly committed it to memory twelve years ago. In times of stress he recited it to himself under his breath, as he was doing now, waiting for her to pick up.

The sound of hand-made drums was playing. A gigantic elephant was striding over to a huge grassy-green mountain. Riding on top of it was a young boy named Mango. He was wearing a pair of lava-coloured pants and had a small mop of black hair on his head . . .

'It's me,' he said when she answered the phone. She would correct him every time when she was younger – 'I know who it is, Baba, your name appears on the screen' – but it was his habit to say it. 'What are you doing?'

'I was working on an essay.'

He imagined her typing into her computer, sitting on a mat in the courtyard, concentrating with a placid expression on her face.

'What's the matter? You sound strange.'

'I'm fine, I'm perfectly fine,' he said. 'I'll be home in half an hour. I just wanted to hear your voice.'

He ended the call and put the phone in his pocket and started the engine. When young, Grace would always say she wanted to die in a love story.

9

Nargis removed the lid from the birch-wood box. She took out a spool of thread from among the many it contained. It was done entirely at random, her full attention on the mutilated book that lay on the table before her. Beside the book was the collection of its cut-up pages.

In the light of the lamp she saw that the thread her hand had selected was golden.

Helen was spending the night with her and was asleep in the room adjoining the study. It was her room in this house. Though Nargis couldn't recall with any accuracy, she herself hadn't slept for almost thirty hours now, her eyelids hot, an ache in her muscles.

She looked for a needle among the spools in the box. She threaded it with great difficulty, having to lean towards the lamp, and then she opened the book and examined what remained of the first page. About a third of it was missing, taken away by the blade moving at a diagonal. She searched in the coloured heap of sliced paper and after about five minutes discovered the missing section. She held it next to the bit still attached to the book, making the page whole. With the lamp making the gold thread shine around her hand, she began to stitch the two pieces together. The tip of the needle pierced the thick paper again and again, dragging the thread behind it. The stitches growing in number.

She leaned down and bit the thread when she finished the strange suture.

She examined the now whole page, the light flickering on an image of a Gujarati Muslim pilot guiding Vasco da Gama to

India in 1498, the pilot's own name lost to history.

The cut was closer to the spine on the next page. She began to look in the pile for what was missing. There were 987 pages and so the heap was about a foot in height. This new search lasted almost ten minutes – the page had been razored into three pieces. Having brought them together like a puzzle she began to stitch again.

She had seen photographs of broken Japanese bowls and plates that had been repaired with gold. She tried to recall what the word was, her mind too tired. But then it came to her. *Kintsugi*. The art of mending pottery with lacquer mixed with powdered gold. The logic was that damage and restoration were part of the story of an object, to be accepted rather than concealed. Some things were more beautiful and valuable for having been broken.

As she worked – no sound except the needle emerging from and entering the paper, the rasp of the thread being pulled tight – she was looking up occasionally at the dark window, the immense night that was still more immense without Massud.

And now the finality of death forced her to ask herself a question. Shouldn't she have told him about her childhood as Margaret?

When mobile phones appeared on the market a decade or so ago, Massud had enthusiastically bought a pair for himself and her. But only a few weeks later she had abandoned hers, having received calls from a drunk man three nights in a row, who ranted and made incoherent accusations using the names of people unknown to her. It was one of the nuisances of urban life, and it could have been dealt with in other ways, but she had become anxious because at one point the drunk had spoken of a secret in his listener's past. She put the phone in a drawer and told Massud she felt the invention to be too intrusive, that it put her at everyone's disposal at all times.

'Marriage belongs on the first page of a novel,' Massud had

once said, 'not the last.' Sometimes it did seem unbelievable to her that she had managed to conceal her early years from him. But apart from that one thing, she imagined theirs was a marriage like most others, with moments of passion and gentleness, minor irritations and insider-humour and daily routines. The appreciation of similarities, the respecting of differences. Out of these things a tender love was invented as the years passed. There was order, safety and happiness, and there were veins of leaves dried sentimentally in books; and there was one asking the other to choose something from a restaurant menu for both. The day Massud absentmindedly thanked the cash machine after withdrawing his money; the day, five years ago, she noticed the first grey hair on his forearm; the year she almost forgot their wedding anniversary, and the numerous times he forgot his own birthday – all this was their marriage, as was Massud laughingly declaring at a dinner party, 'I am the master in my house, and my wife has given me permission to say that.' And there was Massud telling her how devastated he had been to learn of Schubert's death, and when she said that Schubert had died long before Massud's birth, he had replied, 'Yes, but I didn't know that when I discovered his music.' And there she was herself, trying to recall the title of a book during a meeting with a client, touching her brow and saying, 'What is it called . . . What is it called . . . ?' and then explaining to the client: 'I am asking my husband in my head.' And, yes, they also had two friends they hoped would one day become romantically involved, and two friends the dynamics of whose marriage they could not fathom.

Nothing had ever happened to expose her own long-buried secret, and she knew that in all likelihood she had been merely lucky, if 'luck' was the correct word.

*

Helen woke at first light. She looked in and saw that Nargis was asleep in her room. Quietly closing the door, she withdrew and climbed up onto the roof and stood under the vast sky of Zamana. She could see the phone tower and the Hanged Mutineer's tree that grew in the courtyard of her house. The branches swayed in the breeze like tresses of hair under water. When the very last section of the almond orchard was cleared away in the 1970s, Massud had told her, upwards of a hundred peahens and peacocks had spread out into Zamana, suddenly homeless, to be killed by stray dogs.

She looked towards the mosque, her gaze moving to the house behind it after a few moments. She realised she was making herself imagine the movements of the cleric's daughter, Aysha, in there.

In the far distance was the hospital where Massud had spent his last moments, and all around her – in every direction, stretching to the farthest horizons – were hundreds upon hundreds of minarets, fully aware of the secrets of Zamana's citizens, the metal finials catching the sunlight.

From the balustrade she looked down into the lane, the brick wall where yesterday she had seen a man begin to paint a sign, some slogan or advertisement. He had just finished making a large white rectangle on the brickwork when she saw him, and was sitting on the ground, waiting for the paint to dry before adding the words.

Now she read what he had written, a message sponsored by the youth wing of a militant party.

BREAK RELATIONS WITH DENMARK & FRANCE
FOR BLASPHEMOUS CARTOONS,
WITH SWITZERLAND FOR BANNING MINARETS.
FREE PALESTINE. FREE KASHMIR.

She went down and entered the study where she found Massud's mutilated book. She saw that six of its pages had been stitched with gold. She stood looking at the repairs, running her fingertips on the luminous scars.

She picked up the needle and – making sure the thread was long enough, the knot at the end thick enough – began to sew the next page, pairing up the fragmented pictures and text.

The cover of the book depicted the Speaking Tree, which bore human and animal fruit, and grew on a mythical island named Waq Waq. Alexander the Great was standing before it, straining to listen to the heads peeping through the leaves, the faces of leopards, foxes, deer, rams, donkeys. The male heads warning him that he had already received his share of blessings, the female ones urging him not to give in to greed. But both predicting that the philosopher-warrior's last days were near. 'You will die in a strange land, with strangers standing by.'

10

Aysha lay awake, her eyes closed. The window was open, a freshness to the air before the day's heat began. Her son was asleep on a bed against the opposite wall. During the night Lily had spent almost an hour in the room with her, and the air still seemed to carry the sound of his voice, their faint whispers still palpable within the atmosphere. The creak of the bed was an evocation of him.

She sat up and untied a ribbon from the headboard and secured her hair. Interrupting his sleep before sunrise to lead the first prayers of the day, her father went back to bed and didn't rise again till midmorning. His room was next to Aysha's. The only direct way out of the house was through it, so Lily could not have come in to see her from the street door. The other way into the house was through the mosque. The door of her kitchen opened onto the mosque's enclosed garden; above it was the balcony that Lily had climbed. The first time he had leapt down but later she had told him about the tree-hidden set of stairs that he could use, passing under the branches that contained beautiful nests.

During the visits he spoke to her in the darkness of this room, just a few feet away from her sleeping child. Now and then he quelled her fears (and his own) at the audacity of what they had embarked upon, wishing to know more about Aysha's marriage, telling her about his brilliant daughter. When he forgot himself, his stammer came back, the affliction that could be traced back to when he had entered Zamana's sewers at the age of eight.

Aysha was a child when her mother died and an aunt had

83

taken her to live in Dera Ismael Khan, hundreds of miles away from Zamana. She had grown up there, sending letters to her father here in the mosque, visiting him every few years. When there was talk of her marriage he came to Dera Ismael Khan for the first time, made anxious by the fact that she had chosen her groom herself. Ultimately however he was satisfied, everyone reassuring him that these were modern times.

The young man was a relative of her aunt's, and both he and Aysha had developed strong feelings for each other after meeting at a family occasion. Aysha had liked his seriousness, the obvious love he felt for Pakistan. He was pure-hearted and sincere as well as mercurial and daring. He spoke with passion about the state of things in Pakistan, the politicians who were ambitious snakes, the cynically resigned rich, the arrogant military men, and the fraudulent and superstitious mullahs. These concerns were shared to varying degrees by most Pakistanis, Aysha included, but eventually he seemed to find answers in militant Islam. After the marriage he took her away to live in Waziristan, where she gradually discovered his jihadi activities, the Arab, Chechen and Uzbek fighters who visited the house, the terrifying array of weapons she caught sight of. Belt-fed machine guns, rifles, rocket-propelled grenades. One day she found thirteen pistols under her bed; once she saw four suicide jackets being carried towards a van parked in the courtyard; a jute sack as high as her waist turned out to be full of mobile phones.

Her son was born nine months after the wedding. When the boy was five her husband told her he wished to take a second wife. At dawn the next day she took some money and left the desert house with her boy. It was the most difficult journey of her life, but she succeeded in making her way to her father in Zamana, where she began to think of obtaining a divorce. But within days her husband arrived in Zamana, and told her that he was willing to grant a divorce if she wished, but that their son would live with him in Waziristan from the day of his seventh birthday. Her father had agreed: according to Sharia Law a child belonged to the father after the age of seven. There was no alternative. And so she had returned with him to the house in Waziristan, prepared to live with him as a wife again, prepared to accept his second marriage.

Less than a month later she was back in Zamana, permanently this time, her husband having died in an American missile attack on the house.

Her mobile phone vibrated on the table, bringing her out of her thoughts, and she picked it up and saw that it was Lily. She glanced towards the child. She fastened the door to the room and answered him, her voice low.

What he told her was so disconcerting that she had to lower herself onto the bed. She listened to him as he spoke, panic-stricken. After concluding the call, she sat with the phone in her hands for a few moments, but then she reacted. She stood up and began to examine the floor of the room. She lifted the pillow and looked underneath, leaned down and glanced under the bed. He said that the necklace with the crucifix pendant was missing from around his neck. He had dropped it somewhere during the night.

'The chain broke yesterday, and I thought I had mended it, but obviously I didn't mend it well enough.'

She was about to go out, to search the corridors that led to the mosque, the colonnaded passages he had passed during the night, when her son, Billu, opened his eyes on his bed. Soon it would be time for him to go to school.

'Who were you talking to?' he asked, sitting up in bed.

She came and sat down beside him and he yawned and reached forward and embraced her.

85

'Who were you talking to during the night in this room?' His voice was muffled against her clothes.

'No one.'

'I saw you.'

'It's time to get up and get ready,' she said.

'Was it the ghost of the Hanged Mutineer?'

She went to the corner where his artificial legs stood and she brought them to him. He slid forward on the bed until he was sitting with the two stumps projecting beyond the edge of the bed. She bent down and began to attach the prosthetics, undoing the Velcro straps.

'You should watch me do it, so you can slowly learn to put these on yourself.'

But he lay back and stared at the ceiling.

'The new shop in the square sells painted wooden lions,' he said, yawning again.

'You are not allowed to have a toy shaped like a lion.'

'There is also a bird.'

'You can't have a toy shaped like any living thing.'

'Can I have a whistle?'

'Yes.'

'Can I have a whistle shaped like a bird?'

'No.'

'Can I have a car?'

'Yes.'

'A helicopter?'

'Yes.'

Each leg was severed above the knee. Before attaching each prosthetic she leaned forward and smelled the healed areas, for any possible odour of sickness.

'Can I have a gun?'

'No.'

'A gun isn't a living thing.'

'It's forbidden for a different reason.'

'Can I have a mask shaped like a djinn?'

'No, and we have been through all this a hundred times before.'

'A mask shaped like an angel?'

'Our beloved Prophet Muhammad, peace be upon him, forbade us from making or owning anything that looks like a living creature.'

'Are djinns and angels living creatures?'

'It's time to get up. Is that too tight?'

'I don't want to go to school.'

'You have to. Get up.'

He was seven years old but there were days when it seemed as though he had regressed, afraid of things he had not been afraid of before and seldom speaking above a whisper. Held in his small yet definite isolation, he complained of an unceasing high-pitched noise.

She lifted him off the bed and made him stand on his feet, her hands slow to leave him in case he lost his balance, pausing, deliberating. He had had to unlearn a lot of his movements and freedoms. But now he pushed her hand away and took a step, the features of his face prepared for the effort.

'This room smells like Lily,' he said, absently. 'You smell like him.'

He was referring to petrol fumes, a trace of them always on Lily's clothes. He had made a similar statement in the bazaar last week, when they had passed a petrol station.

'His rickshaw must have gone by in the lane just now,' he said, looking towards the window. 'That's why I can smell him.'

'Come on.'

She walked with him to the bathroom and while he was washing his face she stepped out with the intention of looking for the crucifix. To spray a little rose water in her room. But just outside the door she met her brother-in-law.

The centre of his forehead was marked by the sign of

zealous prayer, and he wore a black patch over the eye he had lost in an explosion while fighting American soldiers in Afghanistan. The blast had embedded fragments of glass under his skin, and one night a few weeks ago she had heard his muffled screams of pain.

He was standing with a white shalwar-kameez in his hand.

'I would like these ironed, please,' he said, holding them towards her.

She ran a quick glance on the floor of the veranda behind him as she took the clothes.

He had followed her to Zamana when the news had reached him in Waziristan that a new marriage was being arranged for her, and he had never left, a group of his friends joining him a little later, all seven of them with the *mihraab* mark on their foreheads.

She dressed Billu who now chirped and purled like a mynah as on most mornings – details and questions and assertions – and then took him into the kitchen for breakfast.

That day in Waziristan, she had left him for a few hours and gone to a friend's house nearby. The friend was about to get married and women were gathering to stitch sequins onto the bridal clothes. Billu had been asleep in the women's part of her vast home, far enough away from the place where the missile eventually struck. But he had got up, stepped over the sleeping Amma – his grandmother – and gone into the garden and begun to dig. His father had buried his Noah's Ark there the day before, the two dozen plastic animals, in a plywood boat that looked like a giant's shoe. He was taking the boat and the creatures out of the ground when the explosion occurred. A large section of masonry had flown towards him. The eighty-five-year-old Amma died with the men: she had woken up and come to that part of the house, looking for the child.

*

88

A knock on the door announced the ten-year-old girl who lived a few houses away, with whom Billu walked to school every morning.

He clung to Aysha's legs. 'I don't want to go.'

'You have to,' she said, trying to pry him loose. He was shaking, and she observed the colour that had risen to his face.

'I don't want to go outside.'

'Come on.'

'I am sorry.'

'Don't apologise,' she said, firmly. 'It wasn't your fault. I have told you that dozens of times.'

'Can I have the lion?'

'No. I'll get you a helicopter. But you must go to school. If you won't go to school how will you become a doctor?'

The girl, Farzana, had walked in, wearing her blue and white uniform with bright red ribbons woven into the braids.

Aysha separated him from herself and wiped his face and kissed him on both cheeks. Raising his hand she placed it in Farzana's.

'I don't want to go outside.'

'You will be late and you'll make Farzana late too. She's so kind to take you to school every morning.'

Aysha's mobile phone number was written in permanent ink on both the prosthetics, and on his schoolbag, in case the teachers needed to get in touch, to ask how to reattach or loosen the limbs.

'I am not going.'

'I will make custard and jelly for when you come back.'

He was struggling to extract his hand from Farzana's but now stopped and became still, seeming to consider. A different set of thoughts were active in the mind now. She stroked him as she would a frightened animal. Under her hand, the skin was in turbulence.

'Will you put the spoon in the fridge too, so it gets chilly the way I like it?'

'Yes. But only if you hurry now.'

In the end she had to put on her burqa and walk with him to the end of the lane. That was what he insisted on; but once there he changed his mind and wanted her to accompany him to the next bend, and then still farther to the banyan tree in the square, and then to the footpath on the Grand Trunk Road.

There was no electricity so she unfolded the ironing board beside the gas cooker. Last month she had bought an old iron in Thieves' Bazaar, cut off its cable, opened it up and removed all the circuitry and wires it contained, and then screwed the empty shell back together. This was what she ironed clothes with when there was a power cut, heating it carefully by placing it on the burner of the gas cooker, inches away from the low open flame.

As she ironed the clothes she looked out of the window, towards the trees in the garden, from where she could hear the voices of her brother-in-law and his companions. They came into view and she saw that they were bringing in a large sack of flour and another of potatoes, and there were baskets and cans of other food, raw sugar, rice, vegetables and fruits. The Muslims of Badami Bagh were extremely poor, and so Aysha could not think where the men had acquired the generous amounts of produce.

He came into the kitchen carrying a round-bottomed basket of fresh white eggs. Under other circumstances she would have reacted to their beauty vocally; it would have been enough to make her gasp.

'We need to drive out these Christians,' he said, almost to himself. Because she was in here his companions had left the other things in the corridor and withdrawn. He placed the basket of eggs carefully on the shelf and stood looking at her with his one eye. He was out of breath and poured himself a glass of water and drank it in three sips, the way Muhammad had always done. 'Sometimes I find it hard to believe that this is Pakistan,' he said. 'I am surrounded by Christians. Our mosque is a stone's throw from a place that openly sells alcohol, and there is no restriction on the noise they can make with their church bell on Sunday morning.' He placed the empty glass on the sill and turned to leave. 'I'll bring in the other things in a while. Don't try to do it yourself. They're too heavy.'

She rang Lily and told him that the chain and crucifix were not in her room, but that she had yet to examine the other areas he had passed. He said he was a wall away from her, searching in the street.

She turned off the gas fire and went onto the veranda, listening carefully for other presences, her eyes on the ground. Under the dense cluster of trees the shade was dark and she leaned down to part the blades of grass at her feet. She had seen Billu like this on many occasions in the past, hunting a lost ball, a toy truck. She looked behind the climbing rose and as she scrabbled in the earth she thought of him that day, the flames appearing near him as he dug down. The fragment of masonry was the size of a dining table. She thought of his once radiant expression, and she stopped and leaned against the tree. Tears were a magnifying glass. All the world's faults were seen sharply, as well as its beauty, all the things that were meaningless in the final analysis, and all that was worth treasuring.

'Have my clothes been ironed?' Shakeel called down from the balcony. 'What are you doing out there?'

She stood up but did not look in his direction.

'Did you lose something? What are you looking for?'

She returned to the kitchen without acknowledging his questions and relit the gas fire.

To one of the trees in the garden, he had tied the cow last year. A young animal with white skin and long eyelashes. It was to be sacrificed, most of the meat distributed to the poor, some of it filling the freezer-compartment of the fridge here in the kitchen. When she heard its desperate grunts coming from the lane in front of the mosque, as unambiguous as human screams, Aysha had gone out of the house with Billu, with the idea of never returning. A tingling sensation spread from her heart to all her extremities, branching out across her body. At the place where the buses stopped on the Grand Trunk Road, she had boarded a bus without looking where it was going. At the other end she had caught another one and then another, moving further and further away from the memory of the animal being wrestled to the ground, its legs bound in rope, the blade arriving at the throat. By nightfall she was miles away on the outskirts of the city, the sweat soaking the veil that covered her face, the child exhausted, teetering on the crutches he was using at the time, the wounds still not fully healed for prosthetics to be an option. She realised she did not have the ability to leave. Where was she? During the time of the Mughals, the Garden of Thirty Thousand Trees had been planted at that faraway location. That was all the conductor told her when she got down from the bus. Beyond was a village, and when she asked someone she was told it was called Killers' Abode – a place remote enough to have been the haunt of bandits in the past.

'You always did have a temper,' her father said when she returned home hours later. She was sitting in the chair in her room, in a daze of tiredness, struggling to regulate her breathing. She realised she was unable to cry.

'Have you had anything to eat?' she asked him after a while. 'I'll make something.'

He came forward and touched her face and she looked at his own fragile and wrinkled features. There was his rosary with the pilgrim lens and his encyclopaedia of sins.

Shakeel and his men had spread an Indian flag on the ground and cut the cow's throat onto it, an ugly gesture of soaking the flag with the blood of the animal that was sacred to Hindus. They had displayed the bloody piece of cloth with delight afterwards, taking photographs, filming the entire incident on a phone, to be made viewable on the internet afterwards.

'You just stood by,' she said to her father.

'There was nothing I could have done,' he said quietly.

'I know it had to be killed for food, but why the coarseness? Must every possible thing in this life be corrupted?'

And then she saw that her father was in fact afraid of her brother-in-law and his companions. The realisation had shocked her. She was old enough to know that fathers were fallible, but religion – this mosque and the book of sins and the pilgrim rosary – had added another layer of perfection and protection to him, his authority a little more unquestionable, unquestioned. Once when he had got into a horse-drawn tonga, the driver had – with an embarrassed look – removed the strings of bells from the horse's ankles.

Of course sometimes she forgot all this herself. She had thought nothing of lashing out at her father before that evening, for sending her back to Waziristan, telling him he shared the blame for what had happened to her child.

Now she leaned against him and allowed him to hold her, and the spirit of opposition in her ensured that she had not spoken a single word to Shakeel since that night.

When she finished ironing his clothes – the starched, crisp cotton sounding like paper – she left them on the hook on the veranda, where the walking stick her father used during monsoon was hanging.

She saw Shakeel standing under the trees in the garden, looking down, perhaps trying to establish what she had been searching for.

Stranded at the edge of the city, when the day ended, she had been unable to hire a rickshaw or tonga to bring her back to Badami Bagh, the drivers telling her it was too far, that they were ready to go home. After being turned down five times, she was becoming fearful on the narrow lonely road, but then a rickshaw appeared and stopped beside her. The driver had recognised Billu.

It was Lily. She had been aware of him vaguely up until that point, the Christian man who lived across the lane, having seen him from her window. Of course he didn't know who she was because of the burqa. It was the boy who had made him realise she must be the cleric's widowed daughter. He refused to accept money when they arrived at Badami Bagh, saying he was coming home anyway. As she went into her house, she wasn't careful enough with her gaze and caught a glimpse of the dark stain that was the cow's blood on the ground.

She was putting away the ironing board and the iron when she became aware of Shakeel standing in the kitchen door. She turned and he was looking fixedly at her. She didn't know what that look meant. Her phone began to vibrate on the shelf.

'Aren't you going to answer that?' he asked, and made a move towards it. 'Shall I?'

She picked it up, saw that it was Lily, and went into her room and bolted the door.

'Why does a woman need a phone anyway?' she heard him say. 'Especially a woman in your situation.'

Lily said this man was a passenger in his rickshaw once, and had asked him – more or less immediately upon sitting down

– why he hadn't converted to Islam yet.

Aysha's husband too had thought it his religious duty to speak admonishingly to her father when he saw Christian children looking through the lens of his rosary.

During those last months she had hated her husband, and the other men in the Waziristan house, was barely able to stand the sight of him, and there was guilt in her at times, as though she had invited their deaths, had willed the American drones to arrive overhead, carrying missiles in their claws.

A few hours after the attack the area around the desert house was cordoned off by the military-intelligence agency. It was with the collusion and acceptance of Pakistan's government and intelligence agencies that such attacks were carried out by the USA. In return for who knew what reward. The corpses of her husband and the other men were buried in secret and in great hurry. She was told to say that the house was an explosives factory and there had been an accident, leading to the deaths. A journalist, who had arrived at the scene before the military-intelligence agency, had photographed fragments of the missiles, the markings and numbers identifying them as American. A fortnight after he made the photographs public his disfigured corpse was found in a sewer. His widow said in an interview that she knew who was responsible for his murder, and that in the days leading up to his death her husband had told her that he was terribly afraid. A week after she gave the interview a bomb exploded outside her house, killing her and three of the couple's four children.

In the afternoon, when the mosque was shut for a few hours, Aysha carried out a thorough search for the crucifix. Afterwards she rang Lily and told him that she had been unable to locate it.

11

Nargis was sitting still with a sheet of paper in her hands, a message she had found pushed under the front door. There was no signature and the envelope was blank. There were two brief sentences. They informed her that in fourteen days she would appear in court to grant her pardon to the American man. There was the date and the time. A car would be sent to pick her up.

She sat with the morning sun sliding along the wall beside her. She folded the paper and replaced it in the envelope. In the bedroom she lifted a suitcase onto the dresser and opened it and began to put various items inside it, carrying pieces of clothing towards it, things for personal use. The suitcase was more than half full before she stopped. For several minutes she stood without focusing on anything specific, incapable of doing anything. Eventually, and with great reluctance, her hand reached out and she began to empty the case, returning the clothes and objects to their original places. She closed the suitcase and put that away too and sat down on the bed, her back resting against the headboard.

The book lay on the pillow, beside its cut-up pages and the thread and needle. She picked up one of the paper fragments – it was shaped like a piece of a broken mirror – and began to read the text. It concerned Abraham, the common father of Judaism, Christianity and Islam. There was an image of him being prevented by the angel from killing his son at God's bidding, the angel's hand alighting on the father's wrist to stay the knife. The text told her that Abraham had read the *Epic of Gilgamesh* at the Palace Library, translated into his mother tongue by a poet.

It stirred now, the other self she contained. Margaret.

She took out the small photograph of herself as a girl, standing with her sister beside their uncle.

A human being was nothing but her memories. Seraphina, her sister, was now dead and Nargis hadn't spoken to her uncle since the day she told him she was leading the life of a Muslim in Zamana.

The sisters were orphans, brought up mostly by their uncle, and during the earliest years there was also the presence of their grandfather. She remembered how the old man's mind became confused as he aged. It had happened slowly and inconspicuously, like a knife rusting in the dark. He said he had invented a new primary colour. He claimed to remember being in Eden. And he asked, 'Where are last year's rains?' One day it was noticed that he had drawn a cross on his right hand. After being questioned repeatedly, he revealed that he feared becoming lost among the countless other people in the world. 'This way I know which one is me,' he had said, raising the hand with the mark.

She took down a book from a shelf in the study and opened it. Inside was a cutting from a newspaper, about her uncle Solomon becoming Pakistan's first native-born bishop. The bishop of Lyallpur.

As she had got older she had realised that no pain was ever new, that there were always those first hurts and bleeding edges.

He was a distant man, her uncle, and perhaps it was that aspect of him that made it a little less difficult to break away from him. Though she did remember moments of great tenderness. In a sermon he spoke not of the ferocity of love but of its fragility. He passed on to the two girls his amazement at the fact that people kept caged birds. 'Just plant a garden!' he would open his arms and say as he walked with them under the trees.

Two years into their marriage, she and Massud had taken the train to Peshawar, during the heat of July, to visit the Parthian ruins of Takht-i-Bahi. They dated from the first century BC, and were a Zoroastrian temple to begin with, converted into a Buddhist monastery when Buddhism arrived in the area.

For the journey back from Peshawar to Zamana, they had booked places in a four-person compartment, sharing the space with two strangers. Solomon did not react when he entered with his suitcase and saw her. He was the third person, the fourth had yet to appear. Massud helped him with luggage and during the journey they fell into polite conversation, the offering and refusal of foods, the requests to borrow each other's newspapers or magazines, the comments on the weather and the government. Through all this Nargis had remained silent, her eyes averted. At one point she thought she would not be able to resist her tears. She felt rage at him, at herself, at Massud. At Pakistan, Islam, Christianity. She wanted him to denounce her right there, to expose her to Massud. She deemed his lack of reaction insulting and unjust.

She remembered the feel and colour of the fabric that lined his suitcase.

As they approached Zamana and Massud decided to get out at an earlier station – he had to photograph a bridge in the small town – she was alone for twenty minutes with Solomon and the other traveller. Her anger was long gone by now and all she could remember was his gentleness. He had been no more aloof than any other guardian or father, surely. She told herself harshly that she was focusing on his remoteness in order to justify her lie, to mask her guilt from herself. And she did feel guilt, though it was entirely possible that neither Solomon nor Massud – if he ever found out – would be convinced of it. She looked in Solomon's direction but could not see him because of her tears. She and Seraphina had been allowed to scratch that huge beard of his one day and had scattered it in all directions as though a firecracker had gone off inside it. She remembered his voice in the adjoining room at night, the words and snatches of sentences guiding her into sleep.

As the train neared Zamana and she got up to pull out her suitcase from under the seat, there was a lurch and she cut herself on an exposed bit of metal. The other man did not see this but Solomon did and he remained impassive. Did not offer any help, or a word of comfort. He watched her as she wrapped her handkerchief around the shallow wound. She dragged her suitcase out into the corridor and stood at the window, looking at the approaching city.

It was the last time she saw him in close proximity.

And now Massud was gone from her life too. Her hesitance about becoming too involved with the world – rooted perhaps in fear of exposure, perhaps in her early years as a despised Christian in a Muslim land – Massud had read as self-sufficiency and confidence, as many other people did. And perhaps over the years it was transformed into that.

She had succeeded in concealing herself in the false story she had constructed.

She read the message from the military-intelligence man again. She would have dealt with him in exactly the same manner even if she did not have anything to hide. She would not have wished to see him or anyone of his kind, for what they had done to Pakistan. Massud would not have wanted her to. But increasingly there were moments when she became anxious that he would find out the truth. *A Christian who had spent her life pretending to be a Muslim.* She didn't know what the result would be. The charges of blasphemy were a possibility. And Bishop Solomon knew the truth also, had known it all along. He too could be implicated.

12

A young man had been living on the roof of the hospital on the Grand Trunk Road for some time. He disappeared into the city during the daylight hours, and returned to sleep in the space between two water tanks. It was the life of a vagrant. He was twenty-two years old and his few belongings were in a rucksack, one section of which contained nothing but hundreds of keys, some of them rusty, others pristine.

He sat with his back against a low wall and took out a creased newspaper. Unfolding it before him he began to examine the photograph of the man named Massud and his wife Nargis, carefully reading the accompanying story.

The sun was sinking towards the west. From the loudspeaker of a nearby minaret, a cleric was asking Zamana to never forget Napoleon's defeat, to never forget how the Mongols had overrun Muslim lands in the thirteenth century.

He finished reading and sat looking out at the city's rooftops.

He hadn't had a home for a long period, and it meant that he was outside almost everything.

He went down a back staircase that was filled with defunct hospital equipment. His iPod was charging at a socket in an alcove and he stopped to retrieve it. Unlocking a heavy door with a key from his rucksack, he emerged into a corridor. He was passing nurses, doctors and patients now, the various medicinal smells. A cat flashed across the doorway of a ward with something in its mouth. There were two patients to a bed in there, lying head to foot. One of the doctors was in a niqab and she was taking the pulse of a patient who was also in a niqab.

Arriving on the ground floor, he approached the reception and told the girl behind the desk that he wished to speak to the person in charge of blood transfusions.

'Do you wish to make a donation?'

'No. I gave blood to someone here not long ago. I would like to know their address.'

The girl looked at him. 'I am sorry but it would be against our policy to share that information with you.'

'I was hoping you would make an exception.'

'God will reward you for what you did,' she said. 'Both in this life and the next. Please rest assured.'

'It was the man who was killed by the American, just along the road out there.' He held up the newspaper.

The girl's face took on a solemn expression. 'It was a tragedy and a crime,' she said. 'But I am sorry, we don't give out personal information. Now I must get back to work.'

The call to evening prayer had begun, and while writing in her ledger the girl said, 'Peace be upon him,' quietly to herself every time Muhammad's name was mentioned in the call.

'It says here the couple lived in Badami Bagh. Can you at least tell me if Badami Bagh is far?'

She put down her pen reluctantly. 'It's half an hour away, forty minutes maximum,' she said. 'Turn left outside this door and keep walking until you come to the nuclear mountain. Ask someone there.'

'Thank you,' he said and turned to go. 'Do almonds still grow there?'

'I don't think so,' she replied. 'But I've never been that way.'

He was in the lane between the two cinemas in thirty minutes, and in the shop-lined square with the massive banyan tree a few minutes after that. A passerby telling him to look for a large blue house facing a mosque. He reinserted the earbud he had taken out to ask for directions. He liked the fact that the Urdu word *mausiqi* and its English equivalent 'music' sounded somewhat similar. The story was that Musa, Moses, lost in the desert, had been commanded by God to strike a rock with his cane, causing twelve springs of water to appear, each producing a different tune as it flowed. And God had said, 'Ya Musa, qiyy!' O Moses, keep!

Mausiqi. Music.

One of God's blessings.

Nargis was in the study, stitching a page into *That They Might Know Each Other*. The pages that had been repaired were stiff and warped from the gleaming thread. The seams running in different directions on different pages, no two alike.

When the doorbell sounded she went out and discovered that Helen had already answered it. She was standing listening to someone out there in the lane. When Nargis approached, Helen stepped aside to reveal a stranger.

'*Khala-jaan*, my name is Imran,' the boy said towards Nargis. 'You don't know me, but I donated blood for your husband that day . . .'

'I hope you don't mind my visiting you. I don't really know why I am here.'

Nargis had invited him into the kitchen, and he stood looking at the pink wall with the bird wings.

'I was there when your husband received the bullet,' he said. 'You arrived and caught him when he was about to fall. At that moment I was moving forward to do the same, from a little farther away.'

'I don't seem to have many clear memories of the incident,' Nargis told him. 'Most things feel out of sequence.'

He looked towards Helen. There was no electricity and the lamplight barely reached her where she stood in the corner, her arms crossed as though somewhat hesitant to accept the situation.

'Where are you from, Imran?' Nargis asked.

He answered – but not immediately, Helen noticed.

'I am from Islamabad. Unfortunately I missed my train today. The next one is at noon the day after tomorrow.'

But it was not clear whether Nargis had heard him: her attention was on something else now. She had asked the question mechanically in any case. He had begun to roll up the sleeves of his shirt because of the heat and Nargis was looking at the small point on the inside of the right elbow, where the needle had gone in that morning when he donated the blood.

She came forward and touched the place gingerly. It was healed, and he was surprised that she could even see it. The lamp was beside him on the table, the light flaring onto both their faces. 'Thank you,' Nargis said in a low voice, lifting her fingers from his skin. And then she leaned down into the light and kissed him on the forehead. 'Would you stay and eat with us?'

He glanced at Helen. 'Yes, if you're sure.'

'Of course.'

When Nargis stepped out of the kitchen, he stood up and approached the pink wall. As though seeking permission he looked in Helen's direction before taking down the wings of the golden eagle. He opened them to their full seven-foot span – the shadows swinging up to the ceiling, agape. Folding them again with care he hooked them back in place, beside a small green pair, each the size of a leaf from a lemon tree.

'There is no noon train to Islamabad from Zamana.'

He did not turn around at first.

'I meant approximately. I have to be at the station by noon.'

'There are no trains to Islamabad,' she said. 'Islamabad doesn't have a train station.'

104

'I meant Rawalpindi. You take the train to Rawalpindi and change to the Islamabad bus.'

She took her weight from the wall and stood upright.

'Who are you?'

'What do you mean? I told you who I am.'

She pointed towards the door where Nargis had gone. 'Please don't deceive or hurt her. Just try to imagine how terrible it has all been for her.'

She came towards the table and stopped on the other side of the lamp.

'I don't want anything from her,' he said, leaning down to pick up his rucksack. The face had tensed, like a nerve firing, the briefest glimpse of an independent spirit. 'I'll leave.'

'I didn't say that,' Helen said. Realising in a panic that she wanted him to stay, that she needed him to be an honest person. 'She is grateful for what you did for Massud, as am I. But remember that she's in great pain.'

He was looking directly at her with his glass-like eyes and after a while he seemed to come to a decision.

'My name is Imran,' he said. 'I told you that. Imran Tarigami. My parents and brother used to call me Moscow. That is my nickname. And I am from Kashmir.' He hesitated and stopped altogether for some moments but then decided to continue. 'I came to Pakistan last year to receive training as a guerrilla fighter, but I walked away from the training camp and its people some time ago, and am now just drifting.'

Suddenly the room had altered around her. He seemed to have uttered the words in a dreamlike state. The workings of some truth serum inside him.

'Those are the facts about me,' he said. 'I lied about the train because I didn't want to go out into the night. I am tired, and I was hoping you would offer me some food.'

*

105

Dinner was in electric light; the current was back in the wires after an absence of seven hours.

'Why is there a mark on some of the houses here in Badami Bagh?' he asked. 'A small circle of white paint.'

Nargis and Helen looked at each other, the girl giving a shrug.

'Yes, a white circle. It's outside your front door too. I got lost on the way to this house and went down the wrong lanes several times. Eventually I began to notice the marks.'

They left the kitchen and Nargis unlocked the front door and he pointed to the circle at the base of the doorframe.

'It's recent,' Helen said. 'A day old, two at most.' She bent down to touch it and the paint was dry.

He indicated another house to his left, and then another to his right, saying that they both carried the circle.

There was no explanation that they could think of.

They returned to the kitchen where he continued to lie to Nargis about himself, avoiding Helen's eye.

It was only when they were clearing the table that Helen turned to Nargis with a frown and said, 'I think the mark is there only on the Muslim houses.'

He left ten or so minutes later, telling Nargis that he was staying with a friend not too far away.

The following evening when Helen entered the kitchen she was surprised to see him there, talking to Nargis. She didn't know that yesterday Nargis had asked him to come back because she wished to give him some of Massud's shirts, if such a gift would be acceptable to him. Helen walked with him to Nargis and Massud's car, to bring back Massud's cream-coloured linen jacket that was on the back seat. It was a five-minute walk: they had to go out of the gate at the bottom of the garden and then along a curved path along the riverbank. The lane at the front was far too narrow for the vehicle so they had constructed a garage at the back.

'Your nickname is Moscow, as in the city?' Helen said.

'Yes. As in the capital of Russia.'

'Your parents were Communists?'

'They sided with the weak,' he said. 'And in the place where they lived, during the time they lived there, that meant being a Communist.'

At 11 p.m., she was with him in the garden. The three of them had talked for far too long over dinner and now Nargis had asked him to spend the night, telling him that the bed in the study was comfortable and much loved, in spite of its appearance.

The garden was dark but he and Helen were standing next to the large window of the study. They could see Nargis tidying the bed in there and she could see them.

He was wearing Massud's shirt.

'Are you really from Kashmir?'

A smile appeared on his face. 'I am trying to think why it should be so difficult to believe.'

'Maybe the ease with which you told it to me.'

'Yes, I am from Kashmir, from the banks of one of its vast lakes. And when I said my nickname is Moscow, I meant it *was* Moscow. My mother and brother, my grandfather and two uncles were the ones who would call me that. My grandfather doesn't remember anything any more, and the other four are gone.'

'I am sorry.'

'Thank you.'

On one level she liked the fact that there was no false courtesy in him. When he looked at her he looked at her openly.

She glanced at the sky. 'I am not sure how much I know about Kashmir, beyond the obvious things in the newspapers.

Six hundred thousand soldiers sent in by the Indian government to suppress the insurgency . . . A soldier every sixty metres in the city of Srinagar . . . Can you hear the river out there? That flows out of Kashmir.'

'I know.'

Nargis had finished in there and was waving at them, and so Helen led him into the corridor, towards the study. When she took her leave at the entrance, he said, 'I promise I'll leave in the morning.'

She imagined a sister for him, a fierce young woman surrounded by the fabled mountains, the mournful willows at the water's edge.

All next day Helen wondered if he would return. There was no train for him to catch, after all. There were several faint layers of unease when she thought of him. What if he wasn't who he said he was? But it seemed just as bad if he had been telling the truth – that he was someone who had had associations with armed militancy.

In any case, he did not appear and she had to consider the possibility that he never would again.

13

Helen took Nargis to the bazaar to buy new linens for the summer.

'We won't buy anything with a vivid pattern,' Helen said. 'You didn't get anything last year either. What you have on is looking quite worn out.'

There were more than a dozen fabric sellers that they visited at various times of the year. They were known to the sellers, and as soon as they entered a shop they were brought tea or cold drinks. The shops were of various sizes, and fabrics were unwound from bolts in great lengths before them. Two and a half yards of material were required for a kameez. Two and a half yards for a shalwar. The dupattas were bought white and taken to dyers, who were given a swatch of the shalwar-kameez fabric, which they would attach with a safety pin to the dupatta. In a week they would have created a colour that matched the swatch, using tiny spoons to mix pigments, sodas, salts and other chemicals, and would have coloured the dupatta with it.

'This is the second time I have brought back this veil,' a customer was saying to the dyer's apprentice when Helen and Nargis arrived. 'It still doesn't match.'

'I'll do it right this time,' said the uneven-toothed teenager. 'Leave it to me.'

'Are you saying it'll be done right this time?'

'Inshallah.'

'Is that a yes or a no?'

'It's an inshallah,' he said, making sure his employer wasn't nearby to witness the insolence.

The customer sighed. 'It's not even mine, it's my aunt's.'

'Tell her to come herself,' he suggested, waving a blue hand her way.

'She is eighty years old.'

'She cares a lot about colours for someone that age.'

The radio was on. It was one o'clock, and the news told them that the mother of one of the motorcyclists who were shot by the American man had died. The battery acid she had ingested as a protest against the American's probable release had finally killed her.

Nargis and Helen handed their dupattas to the dyer and walked back to Nargis's car. After Nargis drove away Helen went towards Urdu Bazaar, and as she walked she was aware of examining the backs of certain young men, wondering if they might be Imran, something in the hair or some aspect of the physique reminding her of him. Once she even slowed down at the thought that she had glimpsed him in a shop on the other side of the bazaar. She thought about crossing over – perhaps some hint of his true identity would be revealed if she watched him – but then she dismissed the thought and continued towards her appointment.

At the age of eight, Helen had begun to publish Badami Bagh's only newspaper. The *Daily Monthly*. It came out once a month and consisted of four 11 x 7 inch sheets in full colour. The ideas for the stories, the reporting and the writing of them, and the accompanying photographs, were her responsibility. Her editors were Nargis and Massud, who also did the typing, layout and printing.

Now, once every two or three weeks, she visited the offices of one of Zamana's current affairs magazines – the monthly *Tilla Jogian*. Between the ages of twelve and sixteen she had contributed thirty short sketches to its children's section. And six months ago she had begun to write for its adult book pages.

Sitting in his plastic chair beside the glass door, the guard recognised her and nodded. The magazine had received threats regarding some of its content, and his AK-47 was resting across his lap.

'I love this country.' A girl Helen knew came down a staircase with a sheet of paper in her hands. She held it up for Helen to see. 'This advertisement just came in, for next month's issue.'

It was for a department store and was made to look like a Missing Persons notice, carrying the photograph of a handsome young man.

Our Dearest Romeo – Please return home.
We, your loving family, have decided to accept both *your demands.*
You can *marry Juliet.*
And your wedding clothes will *be purchased from*
The Samarqand Department Store.

Helen and the girl held each other's eye for a moment, gave a smile, and in unison uttered the two sentences that had been repeated so many times over the years:

'There is no lack of talent in this country. All we lack is decent leaders.'

Monkeys dressed in satin frocks dancing to Hindi film songs; twelve people sharing a car; a backwoods teenager attaining one of the highest grades in an international university entrance exam; poems that made the reader feel the poet had sent his soul into the world through his pen – the two sentences could be employed on any number of diverse occasions.

The girl asked Helen if she knew where she might have passport photographs taken, and she told her there was a place next to McDonald's in Soldiers' Bazaar, ten minutes away.

When Helen entered the main office, it was a quarter to two. Black and white portraits of Wamaq Saleem and Fyodor Dostoevsky were thumb-tacked to the wall above the literary editor's desk. The cubicles were emptying because the magazine's editorial meeting was about to begin, fourteen staff members slowly making their way towards a door at the back – carrying cups of tea and notebooks, balancing open laptops, pens gripped between teeth – and Helen agreed when she was asked if she would like to sit in. Ten minutes later the guard at the door was overpowered by six hooded men. They forced him to go through the glass entrance at gunpoint and there one of them shot him in the stomach and proceeded to decapitate him while he was still alive.

The men and women in the meeting room heard the shots but they thought it was a firecracker.

When the gunmen walked into the meeting, one of them was carrying the severed head of the guard. Helen was not there: just a few moments earlier she had entered the adjoining utility room to prepare a cup of tea for herself.

After the initial screams had died down, Helen heard a voice call out the name of the magazine's editor, asking him to identify himself. The door between the two rooms was ajar and the only way out was through the meeting room; she was trapped. She stood still as she listened, not knowing how many intruders there were. Hearing just the voices.

'So you are the editor?'

'Yes, I am.'

'You are responsible for everything that is published in this magazine, am I right?'

'Yes.'

'Ultimately it is you who decides whether an article will or will not appear in the pages? Am I correct? Nothing can be published in the magazine without your being aware of it?'

'Yes, you are right.'

'Do you see all the letters and messages the magazine receives from readers?'

'If they are important they are shown to me.'

'If they are important?'

'Yes.'

'Would a letter about the true and false nourishments of the soul, as outlined by the verses of the Holy Koran, be considered important enough to be shown to you?'

'I don't know what you mean, but I imagine it would be.'

'You don't know what I mean when I refer to the verses of the Holy Koran?'

'That's not what I said.'

'OK. I'll be precise. Would a letter asking you to print a strongly worded editorial in condemnation of the disgraceful French and Danish cartoons of Prophet Muhammad, peace be upon him, be considered important enough to be seen by you?'

'Yes, it would.'

'Do you remember receiving such a letter seven months ago?'

'I think I do.'

'Good. A man must know the precise reasons for his death. And do you remember turning down a *paid* advertisement from a group of religiously concerned persons that condemned those blasphemous cartoons? That was three months ago. After you refused to act on the first letter, and several others that followed it, it was decided that we could buy a page in your magazine to express our grief and outrage at the cartoons.'

'I turned down that advertisement. Because it didn't match the overall nature of our magazine.'

'What does match the overall nature of your magazine? You can print pictures of near-naked women, print lessons on lust and greed. You can write that history has to be understood as a result of human actions rather than the will of God. You can print an advertisement from a phone company before Mother's Day that reads, "Because God couldn't be everywhere, He created mothers," without realising how shockingly disrespectful it is to suggest that God is not omnipotent. All because a phone company wants to generate more money for its foreign owners. Tell me, did you know that it was in France in the year 1095 that the First Crusade was declared by Pope Urban II?'

'Yes, I did.'

'Good. You see, I am not one of those uneducated Muslims you have to share this country with, and who you can look down on with ease and pride. Have you ever been to France?'

'No.'

'Well, I have. I lived as an immigrant in a number of Western countries. You have no idea how your beloved secular world treats our fellow Muslims. My wife was spat on by men on three separate occasions because she wore a burqa. We are treated like scum all across the Western countries, worse than dogs, and when we complain we are told we are *inventing* grievances, that what we have is scars without wounds.'

'What exactly is the meaning of all this? What do you want?'

'You don't know what we want?'

'No, I don't.'

'Every time a true Muslim carries out a revenge attack against the injustices done to him and his fellow Muslims, half the world throws up its hands and asks, "Why are they doing it?" The attackers leave handwritten messages, they record statements in front of video cameras, outlining their *precise* reasons. And yet the world insists on saying, "We don't know why they are doing it, we don't understand why they are doing it." Do you know what such people are *really* asking?'

114

'No.'

'They are asking, "Why aren't they ignoring the injustices done to those they love?" They are asking, "Why aren't they ignoring – the way *we* are – the fact that this world has become a Hell for everyone who lives here?" That is what they are really asking.

'Our magnificent brother in Boston lay wounded in a boat after carrying out the marathon bombing, while the American policemen searched for him everywhere, and he wrote messages on the walls of the boat with blood – his own blood. *Get out of Iraq*, he wrote. *Get out of Afghanistan. All this will stop when you stop killing and humiliating Muslims.* But what did America and the world say afterwards? "If only we knew why he did it!" They say they can insult our beloved Prophet, peace be upon him, because they have the right to say what they want. But their right to drink wine does not mean I have to let them empty their bladders on me an hour later. Does it?'

'No, it doesn't.'

'What is this thing called freedom of speech? Can anyone call the queen of England a filthy name? If the president of France was standing there with his mother one day and I walked up and called her a disgusting name, once, twice, three times – again and again – would the president get angry? Would he be justified in hitting me?'

'He wouldn't.'

'Yes he absolutely *would* be justified! He should rip out my tongue. You would say he is a civilised man, that as a civilised man he would just ignore me. Really? If I followed him and his mother and abused her constantly, for a day, two days, three days, a year, two years, a decade, two decades, a century – how long would his civility last? Would he eventually turn around and hit me? Then why is it all right to constantly abuse our Prophet, peace be upon him, whom we love more than our mothers and fathers, more than life itself?'

'If you followed someone around for two decades, abusing them, that would make you a madman.'

'There you go! See? See? You are not stupid after all. They are *mad*. They are mad. You are absolutely right. Power and privilege have made them mad – they think they can abuse us without consequence.'

'I still don't see what you want from us.'

'I want you to tell me what your magazine's cover story is this month.'

'It's a story about Pakistan's blasphemy laws.'

'It's a story about Pakistan's blasphemy laws and how you think they should be repealed.'

'The laws are being misused. You can go to a police station and say I heard my neighbour say something rude about God or Muhammad, peace be upon him, and the police arrest the neighbour and you can move into his house. Innocent people are dead or in jail because of that law. Entire Christian neighbourhoods have been reduced to ashes by mobs accusing Christians of blasphemy. Just last week a Christian couple was thrown into the furnace of a brick kiln by a mob, for blasphemy.'

'That has nothing to do with the blasphemy law.'

'Yes, it does. People think they have the support of the state, they feel emboldened.'

In the next room Helen made herself take the first step towards her phone. She was trying hard to remember how far away the nearest police station was.

'It doesn't mean that the blasphemy law should be repealed, that you can call it "a black law". That just means people who misuse the law should be held accountable. Now, I will test your intelligence and knowledge with a simple question before showing you and the rest of the people in this room what we want. Tell me, do you know the name Amir Abdur Rehman Cheema?'

'No, I don't.'

'I thought so. Amir Abdur Rehman Cheema, may God grant him entry into Paradise, was born on 4 December 1977 and died twenty-eight years later on 3 May 2006. His death anniversary will be next month. May God grant him entry into Paradise, as I said. He went to study textile engineering in Germany, and one day he walked into the offices of the German newspaper *Die Welt* with a large knife and attempted to murder one of the editors, Roger Köppel, for reprinting the blasphemous Norwegian cartoons of our Prophet Muhammad, peace be upon him. He was arrested and, on 3 May 2006, while awaiting trial, he was found dead in his prison cell. The Germans said they found a suicide note but there should be no doubt in any true Muslim heart that he was tortured to death. Initially Germany refused to hand over his body but when there was outrage from the people of Pakistan the body was returned to us.'

'I do remember the incident now, yes, I had just forgotten his precise name. We wrote about it.'

'What did you write?'

For the next few moments there was silence. Helen had sent a text message to the girl who had gone to Soldiers' Bazaar and was waiting for her reply.

'What did you write? Would I be right in thinking that you condemned Amir Abdur Rehman Cheema's actions?'

'I don't see what you hope to accomplish by any of this.'

'Would I be right in thinking that you condemned Amir Abdur Rehman Cheema's actions, you son of a dog? First of all, the fact that you didn't immediately know who he was says something about you. One hundred thousand Pakistanis attended his funeral in fifty-degree heat, but I am absolutely sure that every single person in this room looked down on those hundred thousand people, calling them morons or terrorist-sympathisers – they who each had a living conscience.

You belittled him in your pages, don't think I don't know. Some months later his parents were invited onto a television show, and you ridiculed the hostess for breaking into tears and kissing their hands and seeking their blessings, lauding them for being the parents of such a great man. The fact that you can print interviews with Indian actors and actresses without caring how India brutalises our Kashmiri brothers and sisters, without caring how India and Israel plotted to bomb Pakistan's nuclear assets in the 1980s – that says something about you. The fact that you can ridicule the idea of djinns, when djinns are in fact mentioned unequivocally in the Holy Koran as one of God's creations – that says something about you. And it's something I don't like. Now say your prayers and die, you infidel.'

In the stillness that followed the gunfire and the screams Helen heard sobbing and laboured breathing.

'Tell me, who finances your atheism?'

'We are not atheists.'

'No?'

'No.'

'Of course, you are not atheists. You'd call yourselves "moderate Muslims", I'm sure. Well, let me tell you something, you revolting Godless bastard, we are not the kind of ridiculous Muslims who say Islam is compatible with the modern world. No. There is only one place where Islam and the modern world can meet – and that's the battlefield. The modern world forces women to behave like prostitutes and forces men into avarice, into unreasonable acts. Look around you – there is no justice in Pakistan, no food for our people, no clean water, no medicine. Is it Islam's fault? No, it's the fault of the modern world, and the corrupt swine who preside over it, both here and in the West. Under Islam everyone will be fed, everyone will be provided for, everyone will have protection. So when Islam says thieves must have their hands cut off, Islam is right, because under Islam no one will have any real need to become a thief. Only the wicked will turn to theft – and they will be taught a lesson.'

The girl had texted back to say that she had contacted the police, just as Helen heard gunfire from the room again. The cries of fear were much more subdued now – they were those of people who had accepted their fate, gone into deep shock. Or perhaps there were too few people left.

'This unjust and cruel world calls Muhammad, peace be upon him, a bad man, he who said, "A labourer must be paid his wages before the sweat on his body has evaporated." Does that sound like a bad man to you, a man unworthy of respect?'

'No.'

'Ali, the glorious companion of our Prophet, peace be upon him, said, "If a hungry man steals, do not cut off his hand – cut off the hand of the ruler of his country." Does that sound like a bad thing to you?'

'No.'

'Who wrote the cover story?'

'I did.'

Gunfire.

'We have nothing but our God and our Prophet, peace be upon him, and you want to take that away from us too? Which accursed wretch came up with the term "a black law"?'

'I did.'

Gunfire again.

'Who . . .'

The man stopped speaking and for the next few moments there was absolute silence, and then Helen saw the door to her room slowly begin to open wider. She saw the barrel of the rifle that was being used to push it. The man holding the rifle took a few steps and came into view. His eyes were downcast – Helen looked and saw the trickle of blood advancing slowly along the floor. It had come out of the other room and had been passing through the door towards her without her knowing. Finally drawing their attention to the room. She and the man raised their eyes at the same time and stood looking at each other, the phone clutched in her hands. Though only his eyes were visible, he seemed possessed.

14

Lily parked the rickshaw and hurried towards Nargis who stood in her doorway. His mouth was open though no sound came, the entire face distorted as if in a grimace of wild pain. 'She's fine,' Nargis said and moved aside. He entered the house at speed, almost stumbling on an imperfection in the floor as he ran towards the veranda. 'Lily, she's unharmed,' Nargis said again. He crossed between the arches before realising he didn't know which room his daughter was in. He looked back over his shoulder at Nargis who was following him. She pointed to her bedroom. He went in and she heard both their voices from in there.

15

In *Paradise Lost*, Adam was shown Zamana from Eden, as one of the finest cities his sons and daughters would create on earth, the glory of mankind.

> *His eye might there command wherever stood*
> *City of old or modern fame, the seat*
> *Of mightiest empire, from the destined walls*
> *Of Cambalu, seat of Cathaian Can,*
> *And Samarcand by Oxus, Temir's throne,*
> *To Paquin of Sinaean Kings, and thence*
> *To Agra and Zamana of Great Mughal . . .*

Helen turned her face towards the sky. A new day was breaking, and she wished to look at the light, not what it fell on. She was standing on the bank of the Vela River behind Nargis's house. Entering from the north, the Vela spread out into the city of thirteen medieval gates. For a few moments at sunrise the water looked like blood flowing in the city's veins, bringing it richly to life. The sky would begin to brighten, the slow and clean opening of the day, and the touch of the air would change, things would feel awakened.

They had asked her her name and had immediately connected it with the piece of writing in which the djinns were mentioned without due reverence.

They had asked her what she thought she was doing in Zamana, what she thought she was doing in Pakistan. 'You should go and live in a Christian country. This is a country for Muslims.'

In that red room they would have ended her life had the police not arrived.

It happened four days ago and she had gained enough courage only now to step out of Nargis's house, and that too at the back, a sense of safety in the secluded area.

She turned and walked back into the house, shedding her shoes as she crossed the grass, wishing there were dewdrops against the soles of her feet, thinking of Massud who had loved that sensation. She went into the staircase and emerged onto the roof, feeling surrounded by her river and her city, her land. This was where Lily and Nargis were, where Grace and Massud were – she thought of them as presences. One day this would be the city of her children.

She had told them she would never leave.

III

MOSCOW

16

Imran was sitting high above the ground, on a bough of the tallest tree in the vicinity, his legs suspended in the foliage. The day was ending and points of yellow light were winking mirage-like in the distance. Evening in the city.

He climbed down into the long grass of the garden. It was an abandoned cinema on the southern edge of the city. The overgrown garden was located at the front of the great building, though narrower strips of it continued along the other three sides. Both the garden and the cinema were enclosed by a deteriorating ten-foot wall, the top of it studded with shards of glass in different colours, embedded in cement. In places the outlines of the cypresses had fused together due to years of unchecked growth. The roses and the henna plants had returned to a wild state. He walked a complete circle around the building, going past monumental billboards that leaned against a back wall. Film advertisements from the past, the faded canvas detaching itself from the wooden frames. The ghost of a woman, who had raised her pearl necklace to her lips, was looking at him. A man stood behind another beautiful woman, his hand resting on her shoulder.

He was here because yesterday he had almost been seen by people he had no wish to encounter. Two men from the training camp he had attended. The group of militants he had walked away from, having sabotaged one of their missions. Fortunately they didn't see him and so he had fled to this abandoned building. The training camp was located in a small town beyond the eastern edge of Zamana. The money he had, almost finished now, was from the sale of the motorcycle he had used to drive away from them. It was the camp's property. As was the gun in his rucksack.

He went up to the roof of the cinema, moving through the building with his torch, along passageways and stairs. He thought of Massud and his wife, the architects. So this building was in someone's head at one point? His beam flashed into the darkness and illuminated galleries that were like drawers pulled out of the walls, one above the other. The inclined floor of the main hall with its rows of descending seats. The stained cloth of the screen.

He emerged onto the vast roof and sat down on a ledge. Were he younger, nothing would have stopped him and his brother from setting up a cricket game here.

He had ripped up a foam seat yesterday evening and he lay down with it under his head and closed his eyes. It was too late now but tomorrow he would visit Nargis and the girl in Badami Bagh. He thought of the mistrust in the girl's eyes – it was faint but it was there – and he could understand that.

The gun inside the rucksack was a 9mm Stoeger. He had taken it out of its owner's hand just as the trigger was about to be pulled for the second time. Imran and three others had entered Zamana that evening and moved towards a coffeehouse where young people gathered, a communal space where there were performances of music in the evenings, poetry recitals and readings of prose. The walls displayed framed works of art by young artists, which could be purchased.

When asked by a journalist to explain the difference between women who danced in the brothels of Zamana and the women who came to take dance lessons at his coffeehouse, the owner of the coffeehouse had said, 'The women in the brothels dance to please men. These women dance to please themselves.'

One of the slogans painted on the backs of trucks, buses and rickshaws on Pakistan's roads was DON'T GET TOO CLOSE,

OR LOVE WILL RESULT. And the owner of the coffeehouse had turned it into GET CLOSE, LET LOVE RESULT. The words hung above the door of his establishment, painted in neon colours, and they appeared on the cups and plates inside. There, at the Get Close Coffeehouse, a celebration had been held on St Valentine's Day, despite the city's clerics denouncing it as a Western custom that promoted lewdness, debauchery and secularism among Pakistanis.

It was said that the music performances at the coffeehouse were not halted when the call to prayer sounded from the nearby minarets.

The evening after St Valentine's Day, Imran was told at the training camp to accompany someone into Zamana on a motorcycle. In no way was it an unusual request or an uncommon excursion: they often went into the city for meetings or shopping, to attend religious gatherings. There would be three motorcycles that evening and four men, including Imran. He was the only one who had a passenger: the man riding pillion was a mild-mannered engineering graduate from the Zamana University of Sciences and Technology.

At a set of traffic lights less than 200 metres to the north of Get Close Coffeehouse, Imran was told by the pillion rider to ride up alongside a specific car, a black Suzuki AWH 541. He weaved through the stalled traffic, without knowing that the car belonged to the owner of the coffeehouse. Perhaps the pillion rider had seen an acquaintance, he thought as he moved the motorcycle towards the Suzuki. He would only learn of the car driver's identity in the coming days, from various news sources, learning also that his pillion rider had received training in Waziristan from the deputy head of al-Qaeda in Pakistan, a man who had been killed in an American drone strike only the previous week.

Imran brought the motorcycle next to the driver's window of the Suzuki. He then saw the gun moving towards the car window. It fired and because of the evening darkness the leap of light was visible for a split second at the muzzle, but the bullet did not hit the target: Imran had tilted the motorcycle between his legs just in time, in the direction away from the car, the gun arm swinging upwards, the shot entering the sky.

An attack on an American academic who taught at a college in Zamana; bank robberies to finance the purchasing of weapons and vehicles; grenade attacks on schools where boys and girls studied together – Imran had heard that his training camp was involved in various violent activities, but he had never witnessed anything himself until now.

In the early years of the insurgency in Kashmir – when Imran was still an infant, when one of his uncles was thinking of coming to Pakistan to receive training – the Pakistanis had no objection to training guerrillas who were not religious. It did not matter whether a man believed in Allah or Muhammad, he was welcome as long as he wanted to fight Indian soldiers in Kashmir, was willing to smuggle weapons and ammunition from Pakistan into Kashmir, was willing to go and bring back more young men for training. But soon enough the Pakistanis financed the training of only Islamists. So much so that the Islamist guerrillas sometimes murdered the irreligious ones, brutally, either here in Pakistan or back home in Kashmir. The longer Imran stayed at the camp, the more he was certain that that was what would have happened to his uncle had he come here, he who was not a believer in any sense that the Islamists would have recognised. Imran himself was having to be careful about what he said and did.

Before that evening Imran had thought several times of leaving the camp, of somehow making his way back to Kashmir on his own, or just disappearing into Zamana, becoming one of its ten million souls. Whether or not he would have acted on those impulses, he did not know. But that was what he did now: after the black Suzuki sped away into the night, and

his dislodged pillion rider – lying on the road in the thick exhaust fumes of the surrounding vehicles – was raising his gun
towards him in fury, Imran twisted the weapon free from his
fingers and launched his motorcycle into the oncoming traffic,
dodging the hundred headlights as he went. There was a noise
and he looked back over his shoulder and saw a five-metre
plume of sparks on the road: one of the other motorcycles had
decided to give chase and had been struck by a car coming
from the side.

The following month, as Imran was living the life of a vag-
abond in Zamana, there was another assassination attempt
on the owner of the coffeehouse. A successful one this time.
Even if the gun and the motorcycle were not taken into account, Imran could be said to be in debt to the training camp.
They spent about $330 on each recruit who undertook the ba-
sic course, the *Daura-e-Aam*, and about $1,700 each on those
who went onto the advanced three-month course, the *Daura-
e-Khaas*. Imran had taken both, was only a fortnight away
from completing the second.

And in all likelihood had he not saved the life of the coffeehouse owner that evening, he would have gone back to Kashmir by now.

Nargis opened the door to him in Badami Bagh the next evening, and he told her that he had returned from Islamabad.

He noticed that she had lost weight.

At dusk he talked to Helen in the garden, sitting under
the dense branches, listening to her voice telling him about
the occurrence at *Tilla Jogian*, something he had been entirely
unaware of. He waited for her to ask whether the militant
group he had trained with might be involved in this attack. She
didn't ask, but yet again he noticed her suspicion towards him.

Occasionally he got up and walked around, leaning towards something on the ground or on a nearby stem, his attention shifting away from her to a moving line of ants or a blot left on the wood by fungus.

'The bamboo is referred to as one of the Four Gentlemen by the Chinese,' he said. 'Plum blossom, orchid and chrysanthemum are the other three.'

'I didn't know that,' she said, and after a while asked: 'What were you doing before you came to Pakistan?'

'I was studying biology. The idea was that I would eventually become a doctor.'

'You can still become one.'

'Perhaps.'

Nargis was sitting in the kitchen, smoking her after-dinner cigarette, a glass of wine in the other hand. He had helped with the food, following Nargis's instructions as they prepared one of Massud's favourite dishes. 'Many of Massud's sleeves were singed because he liked to cook,' she had said to Imran, pointing to the shirt he was wearing.

Now, when Imran didn't say anything for a while, Helen looked in his direction and saw that he had fallen asleep in the grass, his knees drawn up to his chest – beside the sandstone sculpture of what the earth would look like if the oceans were drained.

'Ivy League or Oxbridge, young lady,' Massud would say to Helen, only half-joking, as she did her schoolwork. 'We will accept nothing less. And full scholarship!' In high school when children began to be separated into groups according to their abilities – those who would go abroad for higher education, those who would stay in Pakistan – she was among the first group, but she had informed Lily, Nargis and Massud that she would prefer to stay here, would not go away to another land at the age of eighteen. Grace had died recently and she wanted to be with the three of them for the time being, until she was older. 'I will go later, for my master's or a PhD.' Every few months Massud asked her to reconsider, more or less begging her at times. And it was the only subject over which his tone ever became firm with her, and hers with him; but she had refused to change her answer. 'You two studied here, didn't you?' 'Yes, but we never had an opportunity as clear as this.' Last year when the results came and she stood first in the entire city, the heated discussion between them continued late into the night, Lily and Nargis removing themselves to the garden, looking at each other in dismay.

At midnight Imran lay in the study once again, drifting towards sleep. He had entered an empty house as an intruder three weeks ago. That was the last bed he had slept in before this one. Now as he fell asleep he could scarcely believe the comfort in his muscles and bones. The girl was the first stranger in weeks – in months – to whom he had revealed the truth about himself, suddenly feeling tired of lying, inventing names on a whim. The thoughts of his brother appeared now, the beauty and sweetness of childhood. The stag antlers they brought home from hunting trips – in the dense forests of walnut, chinar and almond – would be soaked in the water of the running stream for some days, and then cut into slips as rims for the saddles of ponies. Thinking of the pink wall in this house, he remembered the cranes in the marshes and the hundred pelicans of the lake. The swans, geese and gulls. The black bears were fond of hawthorn berries, and would raid the apple orchards at the time of harvest, arriving soon after sunset. The musk deer of Kashmir, standing alert in the glowing birch woods. His grandfather had a bow and a quiver full of hunting arrows, enormous and ancient. Somehow they had escaped confiscation by Indian soldiers. And with these they would row out as near as possible to the game, he, his brother, and their grandfather, all three lying flat at the bottom of the boat that advanced through lotus and other water plants, the grandfather rowing with his hand over the side, gently taking them forward. When the winter ended, the birds took their departure northwards, going over the uppermost elevated ridges of the Himalayas. It was said that they would skim the summits of the mountains so closely that in some passes people hid and knocked them down by throwing sticks.

And I dream of the day when I shall wander about the Himalayas. Nehru, who had loved Kashmir, had written this in his autobiography.

In the comfort of the bed he felt his breathing deepen.

He was lying on his left side. When carrying his rucksack he favoured his left shoulder too. There was a slight imperfection in the line that joined his right elbow to the wrist, noticeable only to him. Twenty-three years ago, his mother was in the ninth month of the pregnancy when she had demanded to know the whereabouts of her missing husband from Indian soldiers. They had beaten her so savagely that Imran was born three days later with a broken arm.

Helen closed the book she had been reading and placed it on the bedside table. She reached out to switch off the light. Her hand brushed the vase of flowers, almost dislodging it. As she lay in the darkness waiting for sleep, she remembered how difficult it used to be to convince her mother to throw away flowers once they had lost their freshness. She smiled – almost laughing. Grace would carefully go through every stem in a dead bouquet, coming up with a single bud or blossom that she felt was deserving of clemency – to be allowed a further day or two's life in their midst. She would look for a smaller vase, or place it in her hair, or keep it on the kitchen counter beside her as she cooked.

She saw the throwing away of a good blossom not so much as extravagance as heartlessness. Unfair. There was sentiment to her protest. It was there in Lily too and Helen realised that she had inherited it from them.

Lily was with Aysha in her room, nothing but darkness around them. He used the light in his phone to obtain momentary glimpses of her, of the love and need in her face. The living, unuttered thought within the eyes. This – their desire for each other – was the simplest thing in the world, and what outraged her was not that the world could deny her something, what outraged her was that it could deny her something so small, so basic. It was there in the daily indignations of her son too.

When they heard a harsh noise echoing through the neighbourhood's air, they were both startled. Some clerics and muezzins were in the habit of blowing into the microphone before beginning the call to prayer, to clear away the dust. So before the beautiful song of faith there was that discordant sandy growl. But this was night, and no prayer was called at this hour. The minaret – it was situated more or less directly above Aysha's room – began to speak. The message was brief, and it was repeated once. The loudspeaker informed the listeners that the cleric's daughter Aysha had developed a sinful, immoral and criminal association with Lily Masih, the Christian. And that he had been blasphemously entering the mosque for their night-time trysts.

It was as though they had woken up in a boat full of blood. They heard nothing much after the minaret fell silent. Her son had given a slight unformed moan when the message began, seemingly on the verge of waking, but he had remained asleep.

Lily hadn't told Aysha but the first time he came to her room, he had had an ice pick with him, dropping from the balcony with it in his hand.

Now everything was dark, but then suddenly lights were being switched on and there were shouts and the sound of feet running. Aysha looked out and saw a knife in the moonlight.

Something brought Helen out of sleep, and after a few moments as she lay there half-awake she understood that it was a sound – and that it was still continuing, was sustained. It was in fact a voice. Someone was speaking very close to her. Soon she had comprehended that the words were being broadcast through the mosque's loudspeaker. She identified a few words and almost fell asleep again, mistaking it all for a dream, not connecting it with her life in any way. Perhaps she did fall asleep. But then suddenly she was fully awake and sitting up.

How long ago did the minaret fall silent? She did not know.

She switched on the light and reached for her phone. She saw that it was almost four o'clock. There was no answer when she called Lily. Not knowing what to do beyond that, she got up and went out to wake Nargis, pressing Lily's number again.

In the corridor, coming towards her, was Nargis.

'Did you hear?' Helen asked.

'Yes. Is it true?'

'I am not sure. I have had a faint suspicion for a while.'

'I just called his number, there was no answer.'

They both turned when the door to the study opened and their night guest emerged, brushing at his eyes.

'Is everything OK?'

'I don't know,' Nargis said. 'I am sorry if we woke you.'

Imran shook his head.

'Let's stay calm and see what happens,' Nargis said. She re-

136

membered Massud: when reading something he had written he would move patiently from one illegible scrawl to the next, waiting until he alighted on something that he *could* read, that one word making him grasp all the previous ones, making sense of the entire sentence.

She stepped into the dark lane. She had decided to go and see if Lily was at home, leaving the boy and Helen behind. She had denied Helen's wish to accompany her. It was a firm no, but inwardly she was irresolute about leaving her alone with the stranger. But she wasn't sure what she would find at Lily's house. She wanted to spare her the worst. Stepping into the mosque: in a country where Christians were in prison for drinking water from a Muslim's glass.

Across the lane, the door of the mosque was shut, the silence pervasive.

Keeping to her side, she went towards Lily's house, the beam of the torch moving ahead of her. She looked back and caught a movement in a doorway, various fears arising as she came to a halt, but then to her relief she saw that it was a movement in a flour-sack curtain draped across a door.

As she entered Lily's house with her key the torch illuminated the rickshaw under the almond tree. She spoke his name as she advanced, without raising her voice, but there was no answer.

She could not recall the last time she had come here. It was a small house, the rickshaw and the almond tree took up one quarter of the courtyard. Of the two rooms the bigger measured twelve feet by twelve. In the kitchen she was startled when the circle of her light passed over Bishop Solomon's portrait. She withdrew and walked to the back of the house, where the giant phone tower stood among the night shadows, and she called out to Lily again.

She realised that the noise she had been hearing for a while had got louder, the cause of it moving nearer. When she returned to the courtyard it was obvious that a crowd had assembled outside the house. There was a knock on the metal gate so loud that she almost cried out, and now several voices were shouting simultaneously.

She had switched off the torch but not in time.

It felt strange to think this about a place that could be so violent, but most of the time there was a deep desire to avoid confrontation in Pakistan. Ordinary people wished to be left alone, and wished to leave others alone, finding pockets of love and comfort within the strict laws that governed them. They had been owned and abused so often that at the most basic level ownership and abuse meant nothing at all. It did also mean, however, that the loud, belligerent individuals and groups could remain unchallenged.

'You have two minutes before we set fire to the house,' someone said.

She unbolted the gate and was in the process of pulling it open when several pairs of hands reached for her through the widening gap. But then everyone saw who it was, and in a shallow curve the crowd of fifty or so men went back into the lane, leaving one figure isolated in its wake – Babur.

There were lamps, torches and lanterns.

'Tell him to come out,' Babur said.

'Lily is not here. What is the meaning of this?'

'You know very well,' Babur replied. 'That man defiled the mosque with his presence.'

'That is merely gossip and mischief. We all know that not everything announced by the minarets has been true.'

'We have proof,' Babur said. Gently he pushed Nargis aside and entered the house, his shadow preceding him. 'Just now the cleric gave me this. It was found on the mosque floor.' He was holding a small crucifix on a chain.

He had gone to stand beside the rickshaw. The other men however were still outside in the lane, observing through the open gate.

'I respect you, Nargis, so I advise you to leave. I cannot guarantee your safety. This is a matter of the dignity of Islam.' And with that he waved the indignant crowd into the house, adding, 'No one can stop us from avenging this insult.'

He turned to the bedrooms and shouted, 'Are you hiding in there?'

'If you don't leave at once I shall call the police,' Nargis said.

'Don't worry,' Babur said, not even deigning to glance at her, still waving the men in. 'He'll have to deal with the police soon enough. First thing in the morning I will register a case against him.'

The men were coming in and now he shouted to them: 'Bring down that phone tower.' He was pointing the way to the back of the house. Five or six men with coils of ropes and chains on their shoulders went past Nargis. Several men were brandishing sledgehammers, onto the metal heads of which terms like THE WRATH OF ALLAH had been painted in impeccable white calligraphy.

Nargis stood surrounded. 'We don't know if that is Lily's crucifix,' she said.

'Ask that ugly black dog to show himself and tell us the crucifix isn't his,' Babur said. 'Where is his daughter?'

'I will not have you terrorise that defenceless father and daughter,' Nargis said, feeling herself shake with rage. She was frightened, but for only one moment out of a few.

But no one was listening to her. Two large canisters had been brought into the house, and she watched as one of them was opened and the petrol it contained began to be poured onto the rickshaw, the man leaning into the interior and drenching the seat, as she had seen Lily do with water when he washed the vehicle out in the lane. There came sounds of loud metallic blows from the tower at the back.

The men were raising fists. 'Let's burn down every Christian house before daybreak.'

'No.' Babur – visibly concerned – squared his shoulders in a full display of vigour. 'We mustn't harm anyone else, just the man who lives here.'

He needed to make money from the Christians, by letting them live in the houses he owned, by finding work for them.

'Every other Christian in Badami Bagh is decent and law-abiding and knows his limits. They are our brothers.' His tone was a mixture of command and cajolery.

'They are not fit to be touched,' someone muttered.

Nargis was aghast at what Babur said next.

'The Holy Book says, *And you will find that the nearest in love towards the believers are those who say, "We are Christians."* Chapter, "The Table", verse 82.'

He had memorised it.

There was nothing but movement around Nargis now, a surge of energy with an elemental aspect to it. Men were moving past and suddenly one of them turned and lifted his AK-47 and pressed the end of it to the base of her neck. She was forced back against the Hanged Mutineer's tree. His gaze unwavering, the man stood there as though in the process of forming an opinion. It was clear that her willingness to confront them all had offended him. For the first time she was no longer just afraid, she was afraid as a woman, suddenly aware of her body inside her clothes, the feel of the kameez against the skin of her waist, the shalwar against her thighs. Then the attention he was paying her came to an end and he took the rifle away and pointed with it to the gate, once, twice, until she detached herself from the tree's bark and turned and made her way towards the gate. Just as she went through it there was a faint sucking noise behind her and everything was brushed with yellow light. She turned and

140

saw the rickshaw engulfed in flames, writhing like flags, the heat and the smell rushing at her.

As she ran to the house she saw that the mosque door had been opened. The lights were on in the courtyard and the crowd it contained was greater than the one she had encountered at Lily's house.

A figure with a prayer mark on his forehead appeared in the mosque's twenty-foot tall door and stood looking at Nargis.

'Is he in there?' he shouted towards her. 'In your house?'

She turned to face him. 'Who?'

She wondered if anyone had ever looked at her with so much hatred for so long.

'You know who I mean. He who dared touch a martyr's widow with his filthy hands.'

'I hope no one will mistreat Aysha,' Helen said to herself.

Her phone was in her hands and she pressed Lily's number every few minutes without thinking. The killer of a blasphemer became a hero to a vast number of Pakistani Muslims. His prison cell was said to smell of roses. The weapon with which he killed would be auctioned off as a holy instrument.

Nargis had returned and was phoning the police – in another section of the house, away from Helen, not wishing for her to hear what she had witnessed. Imran had climbed up onto the roof, Nargis telling him to be careful and where to stand so he would remain unseen from the outside, one of those pieces of knowledge only women possessed.

Helen could sense the smoke in the air, hear the noises. In the predawn darkness, the call to the day's first prayer began, but after the prayer had been said and the sun began to rise the minaret came to life again, the speaker delivering a kind of sermon.

'Verse 51 of the Chapter named "The Table" says *O Believers, take not Jews and Christians for allies; they are allies one of another. Whoso among you takes them as allies is counted as their number.*'

The voice spoke for fifteen minutes, and afterwards the noise of the crowd seemed to increase. There was gunfire and screams, the sun rising onto burning buildings. Those small circles painted on the doors that Imran had pointed out to them: it was obvious now that they had planned it all for some days, if not weeks. They had been waiting for an excuse and nothing would have stopped them from inventing one. But now they had it. There were hundreds of men out there in the lanes and alleys, brought in by the men with the prayer-stained brows. They wanted to drive Christians out of Badami Bagh, kill as many of them as possible in the dead-end streets. Babur would resist but he would be pushed aside.

In the study Imran was kneeling on the floor. His hand entered the rucksack and, pushing aside the mass of keys, brought out the handgun. He made sure it was loaded and then stood up and reached under his shirt and concealed it at his waistband. He stood listening in the centre of the room whose full astonishing beauty was apparent only in the clear light of day. He climbed up onto a towering bookshelf – as he had done several times in the previous hour – and looked out at the lane, achieving a partial view through the skylight in the inclined ceiling. Up here he was face to face with the two hanging models of the Córdoba Mosque and the Hagia Sofia. Nargis had explained to him that they were their winter work-spaces. He grabbed a beam above his head and swung his body onto the roof of the Hagia Sophia. He crouched there beside the dome and examined the lane, his gaze completely free of obstructions.

The black smoke was beginning to thin out and disperse but neither Nargis nor Helen had any desire to answer the doorbell when it sounded. It was followed by impatient knocks that grew increasingly loud, and then the house telephone rang and the superintendent of police said that he and his men were at the door. It was nine in the morning.

The catastrophe out there had almost ended and now they had appeared.

'Are you Helen Masih?' the superintendent asked when he came in, followed by three of his men in their charcoal shirts and khaki trousers, each with a pistol in a leather holster at the right hip.

'Yes,' Helen said. She was standing beside Nargis on the veranda, facing them. The superintendent was in his late forties and the raggedness of the holes in his trouser belt marked the progress of his corpulence, the stomach ballooning with the years.

'You are under arrest for blasphemy,' he said.

'Haven't you come to stop the crimes being committed out there?' Nargis asked.

Helen felt the blood drain from her head but she was steadied by Nargis's presence beside her.

'I am here to arrest this girl for doubting the existence of djinns. She has been under investigation since the massacre at the *Tilla Jogian* magazine. In an article she wrote she cast doubt upon the existence of the djinn and therefore doubted the truth of the Koran.'

143

'Where is the arrest warrant?' Helen said.

The superintendent was visibly shocked. He ignored the question but his whole face had clenched fist-like. 'I understand your father is responsible for the mayhem out there,' he said. 'Why won't you infidels let us live in peace? Why are you people so shameless?'

Nargis was about to ask to see the warrant but stopped.

One of his subordinates handed the superintendent several sheets of paper and he extended them towards Nargis. 'The warrant. She dismissed the words and acts of Allah.'

'I did no such thing,' said Helen.

'She is right,' Nargis said. 'I have seen the article you are referring to.'

'Well, she can prove it in court. For now, she's coming with me.'

A narrow plume of smoke was entering the garden through the western wall and drifting slowly, opening out; something was burning nearby. By this time of the morning, at this time of the year, it was not uncommon to begin to feel the purity and full force of the sun. But today it felt as though the heat was caused by the flames out there.

'That father of yours deliberately placed a crucifix inside the mosque,' the superintendent said to Helen.

'Has anyone been killed in Badami Bagh?' Nargis asked.

'We'll know later in the day,' one of the men said. 'It'll be somewhere between ten to fifteen dead, I should think.'

'Seventy or eighty injured,' added one of the others, nodding.

Nargis finished reading the warrant and folded it and the superintendent reached out and held Helen by the wrist. She felt an acute all-consuming awareness of time, the future hurtling towards her, looming but undeterminable.

'Let's go,' he said.

The girl took a step back. The crime carried the death pen-

144

alty. Even now, one of the policemen could barely contain himself as he looked at her. But when the sound of a shot came from the direction of the study, the superintendent let go of her.

'Who's in that room?' he said just as the gun fired again.

Nargis had flinched both times. 'No one,' she said. 'It might be a rioter who has broken in.' She tried to picture what might be happening inside. And then she and Helen watched the men go down the corridor towards the study.

Helen saw Imran climb out of the window at the back of the house. By the time she drew Nargis's attention to him, Imran was looking at them and beckoning with a movement of his head.

Within thirty seconds the three of them were under the trees of the garden, walking towards the back gate. To Helen it seemed that there was no element of distress or hurry in either Nargis's or Imran's footsteps. Just a measured advance. In her own mind there was nothing but the willingness to follow them. At some point he had opened the gate and now he led them through it, almost escorting them. He had taken the car out of the garage on the riverbank, and it stood with its door open at the end of the path.

17

He sat up in the long grass where he had been sleeping and looked at the late afternoon sky. He remembered reading somewhere that the moon smelled of gunpowder. He gazed at the abandoned cinema where the three of them had hidden and slept for most of the day. He listened for any sound from beyond the crumbling brick wall that formed the garden's boundary. No sound. No hint of the world out there where it seemed Cain was eternally pitched against Abel. Though at times it would have been more accurate to say Cain against Cain.

He stood up and saw that Helen and Nargis were still asleep in the back of the car, a few feet away from him. Finding the driver's seat uncomfortable, he had opened the door quietly and stretched out onto the ground, the rucksack under his head. A handkerchief on his face against the insects. Like theirs, his body was exhausted and he had quickly fallen into hazardously deep sleep.

There were flecks of ash on his skin and clothes. He walked to the garden's dead fountain, pushed aside the moss and dipped his hands in the clear rainwater collected underneath and wiped his face. Afterwards he walked to the rusting front gate whose chain and padlock he had broken earlier in the day to drive the car in. There he stood examining the deserted lane for several minutes. Like the garden it seemed seldom visited, the branches hanging low almost to the ground along the edges. He knew this place, of course, but was now having to reassess every aspect of it. He was no longer alone, and must consider the safety of the other two also.

When he glanced back towards the garden, Helen was standing beside the car, looking at him, and he realised a few moments later that she was looking specifically at the gun in his hand. He reached back and returned it to the rucksack and walked towards her. She was holding her phone. As he neared he pointed to the fountain in the distance and she gave a slight nod.

Inside the car Nargis still had her eyes closed.

'Are you sure there isn't anyone you and Nargis can stay with?' he asked, approaching and sitting down on the fountain's concrete rim, three or so feet away from Helen.

She did not react immediately to the question.

'I'd rather not involve anyone else in this, as I said. And Nargis-*apa* feels the same way too. You know that.'

'I just wanted to be absolutely sure. We are less tired now so I thought you might have come to another decision.'

It was strange how the mind worked. He realised that her voice was familiar to him already, that he would recognise it among those of strangers.

'It's a dangerous matter,' she said after a while. The words seemed to come from far away. 'I would like you to leave too.'

He shook his head.

'They would be searching just for the two of us. No one knows about you.'

'I am not leaving.'

She was drying her wet face on her dupatta. When she finished she said, 'What's wrong with your right arm?'

Reflexively, he replied with a 'Nothing.' But then said: 'You noticed?'

'It's imperceptible. But you are protective of it.'

'We can talk about it later if you wish. But for now, tell me, do either of you have any money?'

'I don't.'

'I have a little,' he said. 'There is a shop nearby. I'll go and get water and something to eat and then we'll decide what to do.'

To get to the shop he cut through a bamboo grove that was at least half a mile wide. A green leaf-hall of thirty hectares. At one point he sat down on a stone, a papery rustle coming to him as the wind passed through the branches overhead, and took out his wallet and counted the rupees. Apart from the money there was a photograph of his parents and brother. Another one of his two maternal uncles and grandfather. He thought about the day the Indian soldiers had arrived at their home, up there by his Kashmir lake, wishing to know the whereabouts of the gemstones the insurgents had stolen recently, to finance their operations. The soldiers suspected that Imran's mother and grandfather could lead them to the precious stones. Imran's father had disappeared before Imran's birth; and just a month ago, both of Imran's uncles too had been picked up for questioning regarding the insurgency. One of the uncles, an engineering graduate who had been unemployed for two years, was thinking of going to Pakistan to train as a guerrilla, and the other was a young politician who had been tortured by the police and soldiers for standing in opposition to the candidate approved by the Indian government.

Neither of the two men had returned after being taken away for questioning, just as Imran's father hadn't years ago.

When the Indian soldiers came to ask about the gemstones, Imran was perhaps eight years old, his brother nine. The two boys and their mother and grandfather were told to remain in the small kitchen. His mother's face expressionless as she continued with her cooking. The Indian soldiers had searched her person as soon as they came in, tearing her clothes in two places, her body becoming visible through the long gaps in the fabric, through which the men had inserted their hands and made contact with her skin, and they had ordered the boys and the grandfather to strip. Striking the old man when he refused, his white beard slowly turning red where the wooden end of the rifle had connected with the chin. Naked, the grandfather attempted to conceal his genitals behind his hands but they told him to stand with his arms raised.

One soldier was in the kitchen with them and the others were elsewhere in the house, toppling cupboards, turning the beds upside down, forcing open the trunks. They looked for hiding places behind photographs and samples of calligraphy. During all this Imran's mother continued with her cooking. She sat in her torn clothes and added pinches of various spices and salt to the pan, throwing in onions and chopped vegetables and garlic. The expression on her face did not change when fear made Imran's brother lose control of his bladder, when the Indian soldier roughly pushed her aside and tasted what she was cooking, with the ladle he wrenched from her hand. The rest of the Indian soldiers came in soon afterwards, and searched the kitchen in the same manner as the rest of the house. Gold-rimmed drinking glasses, that were used only when the guests came, were allowed to fall and shatter on the floor. Bins of rice and grain were upended.

She was the most beautiful woman Imran and his brother had ever seen, and when one day the cleric at the mosque had told the children that Allah loved them seventy times more than their mothers did, it had been impossible for Imran to imagine the amount.

Now they could not understand why and how she was allowing the Indian soldiers to mistreat her, tolerating their screams inches away from her face, from her children's faces, from that of her father. Only a few hours earlier, she had bristled into an argument in the bazaar, on hearing someone say that women were inferior to men, telling him that Allah made Eve from Adam's rib not Adam's foot.

After the Indian soldiers were gone she silently helped the boys to get dressed, and tended to her father's wound – he had fled with his nakedness and bright red beard and had returned fully clothed. She cleared a space on the veranda, pushing aside all the broken things, and spread a cloth there for the four of them to sit down and eat. Arranging bowls and spoons in the middle. She shared out portions of the food she had been cooking. As she was returning from the kitchen with the water jug, Imran found an emerald among the vegetables on his plate, the sound of astonishment escaping his mouth.

She looked at him and extended her hand and he placed the gently steaming jewel onto the palm.

Just then his brother discovered a ruby in his plate. Within the next few minutes there were two more rubies, a small diamond, a sapphire and three emeralds on the edges of their plates – on the rims where they would ordinarily put the bones of a fish or pits from the fruit during a meal.

He emerged from the bamboo grove and went towards the solitary shop in the distance, and bought a carton of milk, some oranges, a packet of biscuits, and two bottles of water. He requested a single Gold Flake cigarette and placed it behind his ear. Helen's phone had run out of battery. He was about to ask if the shopkeeper had a charger, but then realised that the shop was too basic.

A newspaper lay beside the shopkeeper and he picked it up but it contained nothing about Badami Bagh.

He was on his way out when he stopped and bought a palm-sized bottle of Dettol for the small cut he had glimpsed on Helen's ankle.

The shopkeeper laughed as he was selecting a ten-rupee note to include in Imran's change. The words *My life, I'll wait at Charagar's mausoleum at noon tomorrow* had been written along one edge of the note with a ballpoint pen. 'I hope they managed to meet,' said the man.

Imran tried to imagine the story attached to the message on the banknote, its complexities and pathways. He could see how some people might consider coming into the possession of this banknote a sign of good luck, but he himself did not have a mind that inclined towards such things.

The shopkeeper waved a whisk at the bees coming in and landing on the open sack of sugar.

'Are you new here?' he asked just as Imran was about to leave.

'Yes.'

'I thought I hadn't seen you before. Where are you staying?'

Imran raised his hand in farewell. 'I'll tell you next time, brother,' he said and quickly walked out, looking at his watch and shaking his head miserably as a pretence for hurrying.

'What do you think happened to my father?' Helen asked Nargis.

They were sitting with the car doors open, the long branches of the various trees arcing through the air above the vehicle, many almost touching the roof. She looked out at the cinema, the paint destroyed by the sun and the monsoons.

'I don't know.'

'Do you think he's been—'

'Don't say that.'

There was the sound of a small creature nearby, the clatter of wings in the branches.

'The police will be searching for this car,' Helen said. From time to time both of them turned towards the gate, anticipating Imran.

Nargis nodded.

'I must charge my phone in case he's trying to contact me.'

The gate opened with a rusty screech and they saw Imran come in, finishing a cigarette, a full plastic bag in his other hand. The rucksack was on his back.

'I want to go back to Badami Bagh,' he said when Nargis and Helen were eating. He had told them he himself wasn't hungry.

Helen and Nargis both shook their heads.

'You tell me where you keep the money for the household expenses and I'll bring it back.'

'No,' Nargis said emphatically.

'They'll know this car,' Helen added.

'I won't take the car. I'll walk to the nearest road out there and get transport – a rickshaw or a minivan or a qingqi – to the nuclear mountain on the Grand Trunk Road. From there I'll walk to Badami Bagh. I think I have enough for the fare. Just.'

Nargis was about to speak but he interrupted:

'I'll be fine.'

'I don't want you to get involved in this,' Nargis said. 'I am sure the house will have policemen outside it. Possibly even soldiers.'

'Then I'll just come back. No one knows me there.' For a while he watched them eat and then asked:

'Why would there be soldiers?'

Nargis did not reply immediately. 'The government wants something from me.' She pointed to his elbow where she had seen the mark of the needle. 'I am supposed to be in court in a few days, to forgive the American man.'

'In that case it's not wise for either Helen or you to use your phones. Do you have yours with you?'

'I've never really owned one.'

Silence, then Nargis made an assenting noise, her face full of resignation.

'The money is kept in the green cupboard in my bedroom,' she said. 'In the top section, in a box with Massud's tie-pins. There you'll also find a set of six keys on a black cord – bring that too.'

He turned to Helen. 'Give me your father's phone number. I'll call him from a public phone.'

'What are the keys to?' Helen asked Nargis.

'I think I know where we can go, where we will be safe,' Nargis said. 'And, Imran, on my bed you'll find a large damaged book, and a pile of its sliced-up pages. There is a spool of gold thread. I would like you to retrieve that too.'

Daylight was fading by the time the rickshaw brought him to the fibreglass mountain on the Grand Trunk Road. The lights inside had been switched on and the slopes were glowing against the quickly darkening sky.

He got out and crossed the road. As in India, as in Kashmir, every third shop here in Pakistan was named Regal or Majestic, Royal or Imperial, Crown, Palace, Empire – a reminder of the recent past. He walked through the alley between the two cinemas and came to the square with the banyan tree. A teenager lay on his back under the branches, playing a double-flute held vertically at his mouth. Beyond the square was Badami Bagh and he hesitated to enter, the time needed for the spirit to steel itself. When he did walk in he encountered an intense smell of smoke.

The houses with the white circles were the only ones unaffected. The rest were charred, the fires having consumed the windows and doors, allowing him views of the gutted and blackened interiors, a figure or two moving in some of them, the soot even on their teeth when they grimaced at residues of heat, on the whites of their eyes, a woman or a man or a child collecting singed objects into piles. His mind tried to calculate the ratio between the thousand or more armed attackers and the defenders.

The surface of the lane ahead of him was black. It was surprising therefore to discover that his foot was about to land on a perfect fresh rose petal. He altered his gait just in time. Red with a yellow-white streak at the point where the petal had been attached to the centre of the blossom.

Now he stopped altogether, because a ripple of petals was descending from the sky towards the earth, five yards ahead of him. A vertical red curtain, undulating. He looked up just as another current of them appeared out of the air, some of them landing on his shoulders and face, the others continuing to fall towards the burnt earth, flickering. There was fragrance. And then he connected it all to the small aeroplane he had been hearing for a while. The air around him had by now filled up with a mass of broken blossoms, thousands upon thousands of the petals falling and twisting around him in the half-light, to lie on the ash and blackness at his feet. He looked up and saw the long banner attached to the tail of the plane, bearing the name of the politician who had hired it. The shower of petals was his way of celebrating the blessed deed that had taken place at Badami Bagh.

The plane disappeared but returned after a few minutes for another sortie.

All around him, people were standing in the roofless ruins of their houses, the red raining on them, the petals gathering in the folds of their clothes.

He went past Nargis's house without slowing down because a policeman was stationed outside, sitting in a chair he recognised as being from the kitchen. The man looked at him in the act of raising a handful of petals towards his nose. The house seemed intact, from the few glances he was able to cast towards it. He looked at the mosque and at the house behind the mosque, and for a moment he felt a deep sense of compassion towards the cleric's daughter. In addition to everything else, it was possible that this burnt rubble was a terrible reminder of the conflagration in which she had lost her husband and mother-in-law, miles away in the desert. The broken and depleted child must remember it too.

Helen and Lily's house was little more than embers, but he had seen much of the damage from the roof during the night, the large canopy of the courtyard tree disintegrating into cinders before his eyes, leaving nothing but the trunk. The phone tower had vanished from view as he stood watching last night. Now when he went past he saw that the great heat had warped the metal gate. The skeleton of the rickshaw was lying on its side, parts of it melted.

And everything was overlaid with the rose petals.

He thought about entering but then looked over his shoulder and saw that the policeman was watching him, the hand still cupped before his face.

He continued along the lane and found a cramped alleyway that doubled back and brought him to the rear of Nargis's house. The gate through which the three of them had left in the morning.

There was another policeman but it was too late for Imran to retreat.

'Come here.'

'Me?'

'Yes, you. What are you doing here?'

'I am just passing through.'

'Do you have a light?' the man said. 'What's in the bag?'

'It's just my books. And, no, I don't have a light.'

'I said come here.'

155

The call to evening prayer began from the minaret as he was walking towards him. He raised a finger and said, 'I must go and say my prayers.'

'It'll be a while before everyone arrives. Put your bag down here and open it.'

He began to take off the rucksack. 'I missed the last prayer, you see. So I was hoping to go in and offer the compensatory prayer before everyone arrived.'

The policeman seemed to think for a moment. Then he took his eyes off Imran and his hand reached down to pick up a petal.

'What do you have in your pockets?'

Imran brought out his rupees and handed them to him.

'You can go,' he said. 'But, first' – and here he extended his right foot – 'tie this shoelace.'

At the entrance to the mosque a man was distributing leaflets from a large sheaf in his hands. Imran was given one and he glanced at it as he walked into the building. It bore two photographs, one of Helen and one of her father. A reward was promised for information leading to their capture.

Inside, he listened. There was a row of taps in the bathroom, for men to wash themselves before prayer, and as he waited for his turn he began to acquire information about the fires, and then heard more out in the courtyard where the prayer mats were strewn with the rose petals.

'What happened?' he asked. 'Why are all the buildings burned?'

Lily was ultimately held responsible for the deaths of eleven Christians and of the hundred or so injured, Lily the blasphemer, who deserved the death penalty, and his daughter too. They said Helen had managed to escape, but there were contradictory reports about Lily, some saying that he had been killed, others that he had absconded, that he had been hanged from the almond tree in his courtyard, strung up from the phone tower.

'We Muslims are being murdered and insulted and persecuted everywhere, in Kashmir, Burma, Palestine, Chechnya . . .'

There were many dozens of men – some of them as young as Imran – with prayer marks on their foreheads. And he saw them go down the rows of worshippers, pushing everyone's head down firmly onto the ground as they bowed, with something resembling aggression.

The matter of how he would get into Massud and Nargis's house was resolved when he saw the policeman he had spoken to earlier enter the mosque. The man had come in to say his prayers, and was studying the leaflet with Helen and Lily's photographs, a petal held delicately in the fingers of the other hand.

He scaled the unguarded gate at the back of the house and dropped into the garden without sound, and he was out of there in twelve minutes with the money, the set of keys, and the large book with its mutilated pages. Twenty-four hours ago he had been in that garden talking to Helen, he thought this as he made his way out of Badami Bagh. Emerging onto the Grand Trunk Road with its sudden clamour and dust and lights he went into an electronics store and used the payphone to call Lily, taking out the scrap of paper on which Helen had written down his number. But there was no answer. Next door there was a shop selling Chinese food and he ordered a plate of chop suey and a bowl of 19B soup. The food brightened his senses, and he began to examine the cars parked outside. In all probability he would have to steal one quite soon. An eggshell blue ceiling fan spun above him slowly. There was a TV attached to the wall, and the news informed him that demonstrations were planned in several cities next Friday, against the prospect of freedom being granted to the American killer of three Pakistani citizens.

The next item on the news was the courts in Saudi Arabia ordering a man to be publicly beheaded for 'insulting' Islam.

As he ate, a woman leaned in from the door and asked him if he wished to have his fortune told. 'Are you sure?' she said when he shook his head. 'I predicted Benazir Bhutto's killing.' And she released a sigh before moving on reluctantly. 'If only I had had a way of reaching her before that suicide bomber did.'

He sat under the blue fan and ate.

The first dead body he ever saw was of a young man named Haq, who grew orchids that looked like vertebrae. When Haq went out his mother prayed for his safety. 'O Allah, I swear by Your compassion, and I swear by Muhammad's Night Journey, and I swear by Yusuf's beauty, and I swear by the breath of Christ, and I swear by Zainab's veil, and I swear by the milk of Halima, and I swear by the sword arm of Hyder, and I swear by the mane of Zuljana . . .' One day he was shot by an Indian soldier in the centre of his chest despite her prayers. She believed she would see him again. The destination was the same even if the paths were different – and his was just quicker, that's all.

The acrid smell of smoke was still in his head as he ate. He was experiencing a rising sense of anger. There were times when life seemed little more than a pitiless joke to him. There was an insurgency in Kashmir, a cruel occupation and a guerrilla war, and so frequently he had come across sights like the ones he just saw in Badami Bagh. But this, here, in Pakistan, was meant to be peace. Pakistan claimed that it wished to help Kashmiris in their struggle against Indian injustices, but this was how Pakistan treated Pakistanis. What a joke. What a *behenchod* joke.

And if the Christians were to take up arms, they would be called traitors. The way Kashmiris were called traitors by Indians for refusing to be treated unjustly by India.

Eleven lives lost.

The second dead body he saw was a young man who seldom uttered a sentence that did not include the words Allah or Muhammad, and who farmed honey in a village high in the hills of Kashmir. He was cornered in a mosque during Friday prayers and dragged away by the back of the collar by Indian soldiers, riddled with bullets. Something went awry with his wife's mind from then on and she went into the garden and watered plants in the rain. His laughter was always like a spark leaping from a flint. In their bedroom, a bit of his shirt could be seen where he had closed the cupboard door carelessly, before leaving the house for prayers that Friday. She let it remain like that over the coming years. Some of his blood stayed unnoticed for several months among the roses painted on the mosque wall.

After eating Imran went into the electronics shop to ring Lily's number again but there was still no reply. He was looking for a rickshaw to take him back to the abandoned cinema when he glimpsed Helen's face in an alley on the other side of the road. The traffic was too thick to cross over so he had to walk to a pedestrian overpass – and there he waited to let a shepherd come down the stairs with his thirty-strong flock of sheep. He went into the alley and stood looking at the poster. The glue was still wet to the touch. He took a step sideways and saw that one entire wall nearby was covered with the images, a row of white rectangles stretching away into the distance, her face multiplied dozens of times.

This was when he saw them. Three men from the training camp he had attended, the militants he had walked away from. Here, near Badami Bagh, he would have thought he was safe from ever encountering them. But fortunately, though they

159

were passing less than five yards from him, they did not notice him.

'I think we should spend the night here,' Nargis said, looking at the six keys he had brought. 'We'll leave in the morning.'

They had climbed onto the roof of the cinema. The thick overgrown trees surrounding the building kept them hidden from any eyes out there. There was a seemingly instantaneous flicker of moths whenever Nargis switched on the torch and looked towards Helen, who was lying on a ledge on the opposite side of the wide roof.

'What are these keys to?' he asked.

'On the other side of the city, at the farthest possible edge, there is a small island in the river. There is a building on it, designed by Massud and me. It's closed up. But being here reminded me of it as a possibility. Early in the morning we'll leave the car here and make our way to the island. We'll probably have to catch a bus.'

'Whose is it, the island?'

'It's very small,' she said. 'It was Massud's inheritance. More than a century ago, in the spring of 1910, his great-uncle and grandfather would walk out of Zamana each evening. They'd row to the island and climb the tallest tree there, to watch the progress of a tailed star in the sky. Their explanations and calculations upset their family and the clerics, who said that the star was a portent or message from Allah.'

'1910,' he said. 'Halley's Comet.'

'Yes. But, listen.' Nargis switched on the light. 'I really don't want you to come with us. It doesn't feel right to involve you in this. You can have some of the money you've brought and leave. Helen has told me who you are, and your life seems difficult enough.'

160

But he had begun to shake his head even before she had finished speaking. 'I am not leaving,' he said firmly.

The air was still dark when the sound of the girl at the fountain woke him. It was just before the sun began to rise. Above him was suspended the fantastic architecture of clouds, the wind constructing monumental palaces in the darkness.

He had opened the car door and stretched out on the grass again during the night, and a little while later she had passed him her dupatta through the window, to cover his body against insects, breathing through the thin gauze of the fabric.

Now she came towards him from the fountain. 'Can I talk to you?' Her voice quiet, mindful of the hour.

He sat up and handed her the dupatta. He switched on the light on his wristwatch to see the time. They could not disturb Nargis's rest, but he wondered if the girl would hesitate to accompany him if he suggested they go elsewhere, and so waited to be guided by her. They went to the beautiful gate with its curves and scrollwork and then he followed her out into the lane. To the east was the gelatinous colour of the dawn, the red energies seeping through a razor slit, rearranging themselves every few seconds. Soon there would be the hazy disc of the sun, but the west was still in blue-black darkness.

'Our house is completely gone?'

'Yes.'

'And they said my father is . . .'

'*Some* people said that. I told you. Others said he had managed to make good his escape.'

'What happened to Aysha?'

'I didn't know how to ask about her, I'm sorry. It seemed inappropriate.'

'I understand.' And after a few moments she said, 'Thank

you for going there, for bringing back the things we need.'

They were entering the bamboo grove – moving into the slowly breathing shadows of the leaves, the measured inhalation and exhalation. The place felt as though it were alive, full of minute decisive activity. It seemed believable that bamboo could grow three feet in a day under certain circumstances.

They moved through the grove and he could eventually see the grey road he had taken to go to the shop late in the afternoon.

They would have continued and walked out of the grove and onto the road, but she had stopped, having heard the sound of a vehicle on the road, approaching from their left. Its headlights were on and it was coming around the curve. She took a few steps back, where the interior of the grove was darker. She saw that the vehicle was a police van.

Imran too was retreating, one hand held protectively towards her.

The van was coming closer, and now, much to their relief, it had gone past the point where the two of them were, crouching behind a tussock of new growth. It continued on its way, but then it did stop.

'Did they follow me?' he whispered to himself and reached under his shirt. 'They couldn't have followed me.'

She was utterly still. She had covered most of her face with her dupatta, just her eyes visible, with a terrified light in them.

Three policemen disembarked and one of them unlocked the back door of the van. They were so close that Helen and Imran could hear one of them give a cough. A man appeared in the back door, shuffling forward, and, because he was wearing handcuffs and manacles, the policemen almost lifted him out onto the surface of the road. Two more policemen now jumped out of the back of the van.

The chained man stood between the five of them with his knees slightly bent, and now one of the policemen was bending down to unlock the manacles. Another was twisting the key to release the handcuffs. The prisoner and the policemen formed a tight little group in the brightening dawn. Helen could hear the low whimper of the prisoner, though he was standing with his face and back turned away from her and Imran. He was trying to put his handcuffed wrists out of the reach of the policeman who was trying to open the cuffs.

Eventually however the key was turned and his hands were freed. And with them he was reaching down to prevent the manacles from being undone, not wishing to be released.

The whimpering was getting louder, had almost become cries.

When one of the policemen looked first to his right and then to his left, perhaps making sure that the road was empty on either side, both Helen and Imran felt his glance pass over their bodies.

Imran looked behind him, into the darker central portions of the grove. Here, near the edge, it was really just the six-foot tussock that concealed them. If it were somehow magicked away they would be seen.

Once the manacles were removed, one of the policemen pushed the prisoner out of the little huddle. He shouted something at him. The man's pleading was loud and he was struck in the face and told to be quiet, without effect. In addition, he was now clinging to one of the policemen. 'Run,' the policeman shouted, trying to push him away. 'Go. You're free.'

Imran turned to Helen with a finger raised to his lips. Making her realise that she was giving out a small sound of distress, her breathing skewed. 'They are about to kill him,' she whispered.

The man was on his knees, touching the feet of the policemen beseechingly, and three of them were pummelling him about the shoulders, telling him he was free, telling him to run. One policeman had walked to the side of the road – coming closer to Helen and Imran by a few feet – and was standing there, stretching and yawning.

The prisoner was frozen in fear on his knees, and then suddenly he did break into a kind of run, on his hands and feet for a few yards, the way an animal would run. Then he straightened and hurried down the road, parallel to the grove. Behind him three of the policemen were raising their guns and taking aim.

'Help him,' Helen said.

'Quiet.'

'You have a gun. Help him.'

'We can't.'

She grabbed his sleeve. In another moment, in another two moments, it would be too late. 'Please help him.'

When the guns were fired the beginning of a cry escaped her, but he was quick enough to clamp his hand onto her mouth, cutting off the sound. The prisoner fell on his face on the tarmac and was in a spasm. Two policemen went forward at a lope and shot him several times in the back, one of them placing his boot at the base of the neck to still him.

It was Helen who saw all this. Imran was looking at the policeman who had been yawning, whose gaze seemed fixed in their direction. There was no way of knowing if he had heard her noise of anguish or was just looking without a specific reason. They had to wait and see. The wind seethed in the leaves above them and she was lifeless against him, his hand still on her mouth.

The murdered prisoner was dragged by his legs to the van, the doors slammed shut once he had been thrown inside.

She took his hand from her face a minute or so after the van had driven off, the hand wet from her tears of rage. She stood up and turned and took a few unsteady steps, moving deeper into the grove. He remained where he was, now looking in her direction, now towards the long sweep of blood on the road.

'I will not end up a prisoner,' she said. 'Do you understand?'

She was sitting on a stone, the shafts of light falling all around her from the roof of leaves, the flames of the sun surging at the eastern horizon.

'I will not let them do – *that* – to me,' she said, looking directly at him.

'You mustn't think like that.'

He listened to her breathing. His own heart was awash with adrenaline, convulsing.

'I'm not going to jail, not even for an hour. Not even for ten minutes.'

'I am really sorry but we couldn't have done anything,' he said. 'I hope you see that. We had no way to help him.'

'I know.' She nodded after a while, and then said, 'We should go back. Nargis-*apa* will be wondering.'

Neither of them wanted to say out loud that at first they had both thought the prisoner was Lily – before he turned around and they saw that he wasn't.

She stood up and together they began to walk towards the cinema, feeling stray touches of each other's clothes occasionally.

'They'll claim he tried to escape,' she said quietly just as they emerged into open sunlight. 'I wonder who he was, what his crime was.'

'Who knows,' Imran said, as he looked back. 'He was just poor. He couldn't bribe them.'

IV

THE ISLAND

18

The island was tear-shaped, wider and rounder at one end than the other. According to legend it was formed in AD 620, when the soil caught in the hoof of a winged horse-like creature was dislodged and fell to earth, landing in the river. The creature was named Buraq and at the time it was carrying Muhammad on its back, taking him to meet Allah in the heavens. Going there and returning before the chain on Muhammad's door had stopped swaying. An event known as the Night Journey.

Nargis stood at the island's rim and looked at the water flowing beneath the layer of sunlight. There was the noise of the current, and then a thick gust of river wind caused the trees around her to toss their branches. She turned and went up the incline towards the house, her bare feet landing on the stones of the path, feeling an unseen spider strand break across her face. The back door was open and she came into the kitchen to see the girl repairing a page of the damaged book, her head bent in concentration. This was their second day here. At the very centre of the island stood a mosque designed by Massud and Nargis, and it was considered by many to be the most beautiful modern building in the whole of Pakistan.

*

Upon arrival they had crossed the river on a half-fragmented bridge. A wall stood along most of island's circumference. At the other end of the bridge they were met by a door in this wall. Nargis had led them through it by using one of the six keys, and had then locked it behind her.

From an upstairs window Nargis could see Imran appear and disappear through the colonnades at the rear of the mosque, the grass up to his waist in places. Sparrows had built nests in the minaret's loudspeakers.

The mosque had four entrances. When she and Massud decided to build it, it was with the idea that people belonging to all four sects of Islam would come to worship here, entering through different doors but converging at a common prayer hall at the centre. Four clerics would take turns to lead the prayers. And at four points around the mosque they had placed four small homes, one for each of these clerics.

Nargis and Helen had spent the night in one of these homes. Imran had walked away towards the neighbouring one, three minutes away through the foliage.

An hour after arrival he had stepped off the island, using the bridge, to orient himself, to go and find a shop, returning some time later with a sackful of provisions from the nearby bazaar. Apart from food, he brought back a gas canister for cooking and a small transistor radio. Four kerosene lanterns. Candles. Newspapers.

Nargis saw him bending under a tree now, to pick up dropped fruit where it lay rotting, fermenting into the soil. One wire from his iPod disappeared into his ear, the other hanging loose.

Ten with shells, ten with stones, and ten that had neither shell nor stone. According to some traditions of Islam, when Adam was expelled from Eden he was given thirty kinds of fruit to take with him to earth. She and Massud had planted as many of these in the grounds of the mosque as they could, laying out an Islamic Paradise garden on the island, and now – these years later – there was an untamed profusion of them around her. Almond, walnut, pistachio, soapnut and sesame seeds were in the first category; peach, apricot, plum, date and jujube were in the second; and mulberry, apple, pear, fig and lemon were in the third.

The mosque lay abandoned because a murder had occurred here soon after it opened, a night of terrible violence. The four sects lived in mutual mistrust and resentment, in prejudice and ignorance, and were always accusing each other of being heretics, infidels and innovators. 'These so-called holy men!' Massud had said once. 'Never mind accepting other faiths, I sometimes fear that a Muslim cleric would declare *himself* an apostate if he ever read his own words under another cleric's name.'

These years later, things were even worse. Certain sects were openly bombing others' gatherings. Even funerals were not spared.

Imran entered the mosque and went along a corridor where the plaster had come away in a curved line due to gunfire, the bullets chipping away even the bricks underneath. He opened doors to rooms where the darkness seemed immune to light. In a cupboard he found a tin of rock-hard dates, a fistful of which he placed in his pocket. A cleric's dusty robe hung from a hook. It too had been designed by Nargis and Massud. He stopped at the entrance to the prayer hall. For such a vast space there were no echoes. It was filled from ceiling to floor with the webs of a family of spiders. It was as though lengths of muslin had been pinned from one wall to another, from top to bottom, at all angles. They were strong, and bent when touched. Slants of sunlight coming in through the skylights and ventilation holes complicated the sight even further. It made him aware of the volume of the hall.

He imagined cutting through them with a knife, imagined hiding behind the veils in an emergency.

He would have to be vigilant but he would be safe here. The small town where he had received training as a fighter was even further away from the island than it was from Badami Bagh.

Helen had told him about the Hanged Mutineer, who was sometimes seen in their courtyard tree by the wine-drinkers, and during the night Imran had dreamt of her father climbing into the almond branches while the rioters looked for him in the alleys of Badami Bagh: in the dream they came into his house and ignored him completely while they searched for him. Thinking he was the ghost.

His feet were in dust as he had removed his shoes. He cracked a date in half and looked at the tiny insect eggs inside, blowing them away, and then placing the toughened flesh of the fruit in his mouth. He stood chewing, the sugar emerging in his mouth.

From a shelf he took two healing bowls for use in the kitchen, verses of the Koran written inside them, from which the drinker imbibed the power of sacred letters.

Behind the mosque Helen climbed the stairs that led to the library. She stood looking at the dusty books. They were mainly Islamic texts. Commentaries on the Koran. Biographies of Muhammad and his companions. Histories of Christianity and Judaism, and books on the various sects and interpretations. Books of journeys. Details from some of which belonged in the book by Massud's father. In the fourteenth century the Moroccan Ibn Batuta had heard a verse of Saadi in China, sung on the river at Hangzhou. And in nearby Fuzhou he encountered a man from Cueta, a day's journey from his own home town of Tangiers. In Granada, he met natives of Anatolia, Central Asia and India.

The world in flux.

The word 'Pakistan' meant 'Land of the Pure'. She thought of the Silk Road, imagined branches of it entering this land. She thought of the pets and arena animals being carried along it, wools from Kashmir, the prized spinach of Nepal, elixirs of immortality (which often shortened, rather than extended, life), the knowledge of poisons, wines and olive oil, carnelians and other quartzes, indigo, Tyrian purple, Baltic amber, asbestos, opium, cardamom, turmeric, realgar that was believed to convert copper into gold, flowers including peonies, roses and camellias, stirrups, the knowledge of sages and prophets, the use of coal for fuels, architectural styles and devices, human beings – acrobats, Central Asian jugglers and musicians, grooms, dwarves, household slaves and South Sea Island pearl divers. And so it was that there was no absolute purity anywhere on the planet.

The Land of the Pure did not exist.

Occasionally the shelves carried something surprising, though the collection had been chosen by Nargis and Massud so the surprise was only momentary. A seven-volume edition of *The History of the Decline and Fall of the Roman Empire*. The entire spine of the first volume was occupied by the image of a Roman architectural column, thick and robust; that of the second depicted the same column but with a few small cracks here and there; in the third the cracks had grown longer and also a few pieces of stone had crumbled away; and so on, until the seventh volume which showed the column reduced to a battered stump half its original size. All seven volumes next to each other – it almost looked like an animation.

They had taken great care. There were no images of living things in any of the books. The streets were empty, the houses without occupants, the gardens bird- and insect-less, even though in full bloom.

She remembered coming to the island as a child with Massud, when the mosque was being constructed. Since the mosque was shut down, the staff at Zamana's architecture school had requested its keys from Nargis and Massud on a number of occasions, to show the building to students. When it was in a better condition, photographers too would come. But Helen couldn't remember the last time she had thought of it, the place having more or less slipped out of her memory. And yet here it was still, existing. For many months after Grace's death, she had experienced moments when she would think her mother was being held somewhere against her will, or that she was trapped somewhere. It was her first real experience of death, and for a few brief seconds her mind would trick her into thinking that she had to journey to some physical place and bring back her mother.

She went to the window and looked out and for a moment did not see anyone, and so she felt as though she had stepped into one of the illustrations from the books behind her.

The breeze and afternoon heat came off the river. She looked towards the house Imran was occupying. He had walked out to the bazaar again, though with four houses to choose from – all four of which had been vacated in a hurry after the murder, a murder committed by members of the sect sponsored by Saudi Arabia – they had almost everything they needed. There were pans, towels, sheets and mattresses. He had even returned from one of the other houses carrying a large box of mosquito-repellent coils.

He wore a string of Kashmiri apple seeds around his neck, the only thing he had brought with him from his homeland.

'Imran is the name of Mary's father in Islam,' Nargis had said to him yesterday.

'He is Joachim in Christianity,' Helen had added.

19

Helen came out of her room and lit a candle in the darkness of the kitchen. There was a plate with a garlic bulb on the table and beside it the damaged book was lying open, her eyes passing over it. An image of the mosque that had once stood within the Parthenon. She lowered herself into a chair and crossed her arms on the table's surface.

She wondered what happened during the fires to the toads that lived in the cracked earth behind the almond tree.

Was her father really dead? One of Lily's friends was a Muslim who had converted to Christianity some years ago and was now lost somewhere in Pakistan, fleeing both the police and his own family. His own brothers and father were searching for him in the towns and cities in order to kill him. To aid a convert was as shocking as being one, but Lily and Grace had helped their friend, hiding him in the house for almost two weeks. Later he paid a human smuggler to take him to Europe, where he hoped to seek asylum, moving from Pakistan to Turkey to Greece to Italy and then Germany. In the sea near Italy he had almost drowned; he was detained in Greece; and lived on the streets in Hamburg. His asylum application remained in an indeterminate state, and so he eventually returned to Pakistan, missing his wife and four-year-old boy, having been away from Pakistan for twenty months. His wife had gone to live with her parents in his absence. A month later their son had died, poisoned, everyone suspected, for being the child of an apostate, by someone in her family. Such was the abhorrence.

The candle flickered and she looked up and saw Imran standing in the door.

*

He had been lying on the roof of Nargis and Helen's house, the smoke from the cigarette keeping the insects away in the darkness, when he heard her in the kitchen.

He had calculated that there was power in the iPod only for half a dozen songs tonight. During his trip into the bazaar tomorrow, he would charge it at a shop. Tonight he would have to be judicious – listening to precisely forty-five seconds of a song and then turning it off, letting it continue in his head.

He got up when he heard her and went downstairs and stood in the door, moving only when she became aware of him. He filled a glass with water and placed it next to the moth-swirled candle.

He lifted a chair instead of pulling it out, to avoid the scrape, and sat down facing her.

The deeper the sorrow, the quieter it was. He recognised her shell-shocked state, having seen it countless times in his own ravaged land.

'I am fine now,' she said. At first she had been unaware of the tears.

He nodded, watching her drink.

'What were you listening to?'

'A song called "Blue Bell Knoll".'

She placed the empty glass on the table. 'I love her voice.'

'Me too. Would you like to hear it?'

'Later.'

He leaned closer. 'You mustn't worry, Helen. There has to be a way out of all this. Just let yourself rest and recover here for a few days.' Having said that he produced a guarded smile. 'As a last resort you can come to Kashmir.'

'I would love to visit Kashmir,' she said, 'but not like this.'

'I understand.'

176

She was looking at him directly now. 'I will not let anyone force me out of my country.'

His eyes seemed formed of splinters of glass in various shades of blue and grey.

'You grew up in an occupation,' she said. 'I can't imagine your childhood.'

'I can't imagine yours.'

Two of them in the half-dark room. His skin and hair were much paler than hers, the inside of the forearms almost milky, the greenish veins like a river on a map.

She broke the faint hold of the wax on the table and picked up the candle.

'Please, stay,' he said, startling even himself by the request. 'Don't go just yet. Please.'

She stood hesitating.

'Stay until the candle has burned down.'

She shook her head and placed the tip of her index finger a third of the way down the candle.

And he – shaking his own head – placed a fingertip two-thirds of the way down, looking at her till she nodded.

But once she had sat down he seemed at a loss for something to say.

'Tell me more about Joachim,' he said eventually.

'Joachim? Well. Joachim was Mary's father. According to tradition, St Anne was married to Joachim and they lived in Jerusalem. She was unable to conceive a child, so the high priest rejected him, rejected his sacrifice. His wife's infertility was taken to be a sign of divine displeasure. He withdrew to the desert and did penance for forty days and one day an angel appeared, to him in the desert and simultaneously to St Anne in the city, promising them a child.'

'Thank you,' he smiled, his eyes glittering, and for a brief moment it seemed an astonishment to her that she was doubtful about his origins – surely the Kashmiris alone had such eyes.

177

'When Joachim returned from the desert, she came to the city limit and they embraced. There are many paintings of that moment, the couple in each other's arms at the Golden Gate.'

After she left he climbed back up to the roof.

I can't imagine your childhood.

In his mind he began to talk to her. Back in Badami Bagh she had said that she knew the basic facts about Kashmir. The war the guerrillas had waged since 1990 against the Indian presence in Kashmir. The more than 80,000 civilians, guerrillas, Indian soldiers and policemen who had died. India and Pakistan fighting two wars over Kashmir in 1948 and 1965, and coming very close to a nuclear exchange in 1990 and 2002.

And so now he told her about personal things, painting the details of his life against that vast and violent backdrop.

'When I was a child I used to think magnets had souls . . .

'As teenagers my brother and I spent hours practising parkour in the ruined pavilion of a minor Mughal prince near our home, studying the techniques and movements every time we accessed the internet, the videos uploaded by people our age in Paris, New York, Kabul, the Gaza Strip . . .

'A few years earlier, as a schoolchild, I had helped smuggle ammunition for the freedom fighters, in the carrying case of my musical instrument . . .

'I never knew my father. After he was taken away by Indian soldiers, my mother came to live with her father and brothers. They were the four permanent adults in the life of my brother and me, before the uncles too were taken away to be questioned by Indian soldiers . . .

'They called me Moscow . . .'

*

The musical instrument he played was the ancient santoor. Its seventy-two strings were struck with two light mallets. They were stretched over a trapezoidal box made out of walnut and maple woods, and he would sit cross-legged on the floor with this sensitive and magical object half in his lap, and he would tenderly strike the strings, his intentions flowing from his mind, down into his arms and hands, and then like a mild electric current pass through the mallets into those seventy-two threads of steel, grouped in units of three or four. His head would be bent with a serious expression. The chimney of the lamp beside him illuminating the room.

An instrument of the Sufis.

When the santoor needed maintenance he went with his grandfather to the nearest town, on the other side of their lake, taking a boat through the reeds with the autumn mist coiling around them. Now and then they caught glimpses of ripe apples in the orchards, the boughs loaded down with the weight, ladders propped up against some trunks.

When they returned they encountered a procession of women, children and aged men, filing out of the village. Indian soldiers had arrived in their absence and asked everyone to vacate their homes. The few young men that there were in the village were being kept back, while everyone else had been told to leave. Answers and confessions were to be extracted from the young men. Who had fired on a passing convoy of soldiers? Who had attacked the police station last week with grenades and rockets? Who had daubed INDIAN DOGS GO HOME on the bridge?

How many guerrillas were there in the village?

After the attack on the police station, the enraged policemen had burned down the entire bazaar, pouring drums of kerosene into the shops. Some of the remains were still smouldering.

Imran's mother and brother were among the people who

were making their way out of the village at the soldiers' command, and he and his grandfather joined them, climbing into the surrounding hills with the santoor, to sit under the cold sky and wait for the soldiers to depart.

'We rowed past a swamp and there was a heronry,' Imran told his brother Laal. He was anxious to get home and consult his grandfather's encyclopaedia, to discover where Mesopotamia was, because the man who repaired the santoor had said a primitive ancestor of the instrument was invented in Mesopotamia around 1000 BC.

When the wind changed direction, they heard sounds from the mouths of young men who were being questioned down there in the village.

Around them were insects feeding on fallen berries, and on their second afternoon on the hill they saw flames and smoke rising from the thatch and paper-birch roofs of several village houses.

During that night, while Imran and his brother and the other children slept, the women and the elderly men were visited by guerrillas, who brought them news and items of food. What the men needed were the crates of bullets buried in the orchard owned by Imran's grandfather. The Indian soldiers gave no sign of leaving the village – they had in fact set up a kind of base in one of the houses, a headquarters and checkpoint – but it was of the utmost importance that a way be found to retrieve the buried ammunition.

'They will kill them with their questions down there, or they'll get them to talk. We need the bullets to mount an attack and free them.'

Swallows were gathering in flocks ready to migrate, audible even in darkness. And old women held daisies next to the faces of children suffering in the cold air, the yellow centres giving off a light that was believed to control difficult breathing.

In the morning Imran's mother went down to the village

and presented herself at the soldiers' checkpoint. She was accompanied by Imran and Laal. Their grandfather couldn't come because he lay shivering, his chest constricted as though in a vice, he said.

'I would like to go and tend to my orchard,' she told the Indian soldier. She was carrying the santoor. 'These last days before the harvest are very important.'

'Where is your husband?'

'He has left me.' Kashmir was full of widows and orphans.

The Indian soldier was sitting in a metal chair, his rifle between his legs. Another three soldiers were engaged in various activities behind him in the wood cabin. One of them, upon arrival in the village yesterday, had announced: 'We Indians care about Kashmir's land, not Kashmir's people.'

'Are these your sons? How old are they?'

'Ten and eleven. I would like permission to go and work in my orchard.'

'They'll be men soon. I hope they won't be any trouble to us.'

'I would like permission to go and work in my orchard.'

'Impossible. Go back to the hill.'

When they were walking away he said, 'What's in the box?'

'It's a santoor. This one likes to play in the orchard while I work.' She was telling the truth.

'Why can't he carry it himself?'

'One of his arms is weak. It was broken. But, please, I would like permission to go and work in my orchard.'

'How was it broken?'

'It wasn't his fault. Please give me permission to go and work in my orchard.'

'As his mother you should have looked after him properly.'

She nodded at the statement, and then the man asked Imran to come to him with the box. He plucked a string with a fingernail – the sound like a speck of bright voltage in the air – and

181

after that he told Imran to play something for him. Having sought his mother's permission with a glance, Imran removed the hammers from the groove in which they lay and began to play a melody composed by his grandfather, the soldiers gathering around him in that small room to listen.

Taaza aashub-e-fagan andar bahisht
Yak nawa mastana zan andar bahisht

When he finished, the soldier touched the beautiful grains of the santoor admiringly. 'You can go but leave the instrument.'

'Please, I would like permission to go and work in my orchard.'

'Go back to the hills, I said.'

As they left the village they heard an unmilked cow screaming in someone's shed.

The rumour was that the Indian soldiers had decided to stay because the superintendent of police, who wept at Urdu poetry but was known to employ electric drills during interrogations, and had painted GRAB THEIR TESTICLES AND THEIR HEARTS AND MINDS WILL FOLLOW on the facade of his station, had been blown up in his jeep by a roadside bomb. It was said that his eyes were never found.

It rained that night and again the next when the guerrillas appeared once more. They said they had seen the Indian soldiers carry three bodies wrapped in sheets into the forested hills and return without them two hours later. The fighters had searched the vicinity and discovered the shallow graves, had identified the buried men by the clothes they wore. One of the bodies was headless. The faces of the other two were without skin, all flesh torn away to prevent identification. One of these was still alive when they dug him up though he died soon afterwards.

'We need the bullets in the orchard,' the fighters had insisted in the darkness.

With three dead, twenty young men were at the Indian soldiers' mercy. As an adult Imran would learn their names, along with the full details of those nights.

The fighters went away promising to send medicines through a shepherd or woodcutter the following day, for the people who had caught fevers in the chilled downpours.

Once more their mother arrived at the checkpoint in the morning, he and Laal holding her hands on either side, climbing down the slopes where meadowsweets bloomed in their thousands. The insects their smell attracted were eaten by toads with copper-coloured eyes.

'The entire crop will be wasted,' she said. 'You have to allow me to visit my orchard, or we'll starve to death this winter.'

The santoor was there in its box on the table, and Imran was asked to play it for the soldiers, and afterwards – perhaps made placid and serene by the melodies – they gave her permission to enter the orchard, even allowing Imran to carry away the santoor.

The three of them did the weeding and performed the myriad other tasks – propping up the branches, mending a fence, examining the bark for indications of disease – and Imran would occasionally break off to remove the santoor from its case and play, the soldiers coming down the lane to look in on them, a few times, but leaving them alone on the whole. Under one apple tree, in the confined grass-filled space, a snake had mistaken its tail for a separate creature and bitten into it, and begun to swallow. The circle was smaller with each passing minute, twitching tighter as the two children watched.

Late in the afternoon the three of them went past the checkpoint, on their way back to the hillside. The santoor case was now filled with a quarter of the bullets that a buried ammunition crate had contained. The santoor itself lay under the soil of the orchard, inside that crate.

Next morning the fear was that the soldiers would ask

Imran to play for them when they arrived at the checkpoint with the empty case. But they waved them through.

The mountains that stood above the village watched the woman and her two sons from the far distance. At dawn the snow on the mountains was violet, Imran knew, and it was a pale blue at noon. After that it would move from bronze to rose to pink to yellow, and just before the sun disappeared, it was green against the blood-red sky.

At noon, having checked that the lane and all pathways leading to the orchard were deserted, their mother began to unearth the ammunition crate. Imran stood with the santoor case open, ready to be filled once again with the bullets.

When they lifted the rough wooden lid, there was no santoor underneath.

There was nothing but bullets inside the crate. Just then they heard the instrument being played from somewhere nearby, the most terrifying sound Imran had ever heard. The Indian soldiers appeared in the orchard during the next few moments, one of them holding the little hammers with which the strings were struck.

After that day Imran and Laal never saw their mother again.

When the soldiers left, the villagers managed to inform a journalist in Srinagar of the three bodies in the shallow graves in the hills. The day after the story appeared in the newspaper, the journalist's corpse was discovered by the roadside.

20

Nargis reached down and picked up a porcupine quill from the island's surface.

The length of the island could be traversed in twenty-five minutes, the width in twenty.

Around her were the foundations of a church and a Hindu temple. That had been the original idea, the ideal. A mosque, a temple, and a church – standing close to each other. But the murder at the mosque meant that all future plans for the island had to be abandoned.

She stood with the morning wind in her hair. Certain Hindu temples were built in the image of the human body. The construction would begin with the burial of a pot of seed. The temple was said to rise from this implanted germ, in the manner of a human being. And the different sections of the temple were named after different parts of the body. The two sides were wings or hands, the *hasta*. A pillar was a foot, *pada*, and the roof was the head, the *sikhara*. The innermost and darkest sanctum of the temple, the shrine, was the 'womb house', the *garbhagrha*.

She traced the outline of the temple's foundations with her eyes, the primordial blueprint of humans in brick and cement. The low brickwork was visible here and there but was mostly lost to heaped-up earth and the wild plants. What looked like fallen ruins were in fact arrested foundations.

As always her first thought upon waking was Massud, calculating how many days it had been since his death. A sal tree grew outside her window here on the island and she recalled that when the Buddha had died in the grove of sal trees their yellow blossoms had turned white.

She walked towards the island's centre. A band of calligraphy ran along the top of their mosque, verses from the Koran that Gabriel had dictated to Muhammad. The building was a white cube. At some level both Nargis and Massud had been thinking of the Kaaba in Mecca. Also, during their visit to Antarctica, Massud had taken a photograph of a towering iceberg that was a perfect cube, their dinghy circling its four faultlessly square sides, glowing against the impossible blue of the sea and sky.

The mosque stood at the highest place in the middle of the island, and the archangel's words were the sole decoration. The audible made visible.

She could hear the river.

May was about to begin. In May 1857, when the Mutiny against the British broke out, the soldiers of the 26th Native Infantry Regiment stationed in Zamana had attacked their British officers. Afterwards they had fled towards this island, pursued by police and the British officers, who killed 150 of them during the flight. Another fifty were hunted down and executed here on the island – after they had surrendered. An example had to be made of them. The remaining 280 entered the river and began to swim back towards the city but were captured on the other bank. The deputy commissioner, Mr Cooper, invited the people of Zamana to witness the executions three days later, the Mutineers brought out in batches of ten and publicly butchered, 237 in all. Those remaining were locked up in a cell without windows and no air to breathe: after they had died of suffocation their bodies were brought out and tied to cannons near the Zamana Fort and blown up. Another forty-two members of the 26th Infantry were captured and blown up from cannons later, alive. The entire incident had spread terror in Zamana and its environs – the people frightened into submission, the loyalty of princes and landlords towards the British guaranteed.

Nargis could see Imran on one of the mosque's high balconies, and the girl was standing under the mulberry tree, looking up perhaps at the fruit, perhaps at the white paradise flycatcher that Nargis had seen disappear into the branches earlier, trailing its two-foot-long tail feathers.

Generations do not age. Every youth of any period, any civilisation, has the same possibilities as always.

She thought of Imran and Helen and was suddenly filled with blind rage. A feeling of contempt rose in her for the lands in which they were born, these places ruled by the wicked who didn't recognise and honour their youth and brightness and purity, their intelligence and abilities. She thought of the boy thrown into the cauldron of war, the girl beset by various bigotries, her life in danger, and saw how unjust it all was, her fury limitless for a few moments. And she felt a sense of shame, something akin to accusation from them towards her and her generation, for not having constructed a better world to welcome and contain their beauty, to house their spirit.

She thought of the world she herself had been born into – those early years. Who had prepared the ground for her over decades and centuries? Which God or Gods had built that world?

When she was a child, during the monsoons she and her sister Seraphina would lie on the roof and look up at the sky, full of clouds like flying maps.

There was Solomon, who would sometimes chew Margaret's meat to soften it and pass it into her mouth.

In winter the cold penetrated deep, even into the pages of closed books.

The church they lived beside, in the city of Lyallpur, where Solomon was a priest, had two storeys with a staircase of acacia wood. She could recall their texture even now, the way they bent slightly under an adult's weight. The church was surrounded by jacaranda trees and the bright reality of them was almost unbearable – always, in all lights. Solomon would not use anything to kill insects in his garden. He said, 'If you want butterflies, you have to put up with mosquitoes.'

Over the years Nargis had been to see the small church: it was still there, though Solomon – as the bishop – now lived beside the great church in Lyallpur. Some of the stained glass, that had shone with vigour in her childhood days, had fallen out of the old church's windows and lay in shattered fragments in the grass. He wore a Muslim woman's burqa when he moved among his beehives, smoke issuing from a pipe in his hands, Margaret and Seraphina operating the bellows at a distance.

In his study he sat with his books while the two girls unfolded charts and diagrams the size of prayer rugs around his feet – though on the whole he preferred to be alone when he thought, the tiniest of scrapes or whispers disagreeable to him. Looking at a picture of Christ in a book, she thought she saw Arabic writing in a strip of brocade, on the right shoulder of Christ's tunic. Many years later she would come across the same image in the book by Massud's father, *That They Might Know Each Other*. It was a painting by Giotto, a fresco to be found at the Arena Chapel in Padua, and Massud's father's book would explain to her that Arabic script had been put to ornamental use by Giotto, Fra Angelico and Fra Lippo Lippi, among others. Appearing on the sleeves of the Virgin, on the robes and ribbons of the angels.

That was how one continent poured itself into another. How one person carried the answer through his life until he met the person who was carrying the question.

*

Seraphina was two years older than Margaret. As they got older the sisters would pretend their pencils were cigarettes, holding them between two fingers. And, having seen an actress light a cigarette with a bank note on a film poster in the bazaar, they would rip pages from their notebooks or old newspapers to re-enact that moment.

'The earth weighs 5×10^{24} kg,' Seraphina said when she was fourteen and yet another bad report-card arrived from school. 'That is 5 with 24 zeros after it. At that scale there is no difference between a human being and a speck of dust.'

One day she would discover the terrifying ways the world had of reminding a human being of her true insignificance.

What led to Margaret becoming Nargis was a series of small coincidences when she was fourteen years old. From the city of Lyallpur she came to Zamana to participate in the annual All Provinces Schools Debate. It would be a three-day event, and she would be staying at a hotel. She had been asked to replace another student at the last minute: this other girl was a Muslim, and had managed to persuade her parents to let her go to Zamana for the debate. But she was one of the handful of girls at the school who were already engaged to be married, and the day before she was to leave for Zamana, her future in-laws heard about it and sent an alarmed message to her parents, forbidding her to go. Her name was Nargis. During recess she would sit and embroider the pillowcases and bed-sheets that would, one day soon, become part of her dowry.

Margaret took her place, representing her school in Zamana.

The second coincidence was that the teacher who was

accompanying her to Zamana fell ill during the bus journey. She lay in the hotel room and Margaret arrived at the venue of the debates in a rickshaw by herself. She was late and the organisers sent her directly onto the stage with the others. The moderator referred to her as Nargis, and in the heat of the event she thought it too trivial a matter to correct him. There were more pressing issues up there on the stage. Arguments to articulate or counter. Making sure she remained coherent and unintimidated in front of an audience of hundreds. Later in the day, and during the rest of the brief stay in Zamana, she went along with it deliberately, thinking of it as playacting, only mildly fraudulent, a dare. The idea presented itself and was accepted. But it was as though she had just arrived in a new country. She was a child, and it thrilled her when on the second day she realised that she didn't necessarily have to carry her own glass, cup and spoon with her. No one said she smelled faintly of sewage. No one asked her when she intended to convert to the Only True Religion. Nor did anyone cut her off during the debate. Instead, her opinions were listened to with due courtesy. With each passing hour she felt as though she mattered in the wider world. She felt her inhibitions disappearing.

When she returned to Lyallpur from the debate she was Margaret again, of course, but now she became angry when for vaccination the doctor used a different syringe for her than he used for Muslims. The older Muslim boys did not make as many coarse remarks about Muslim girls as they did about her, she noticed anew. They did not think they could waylay Muslim girls as they could her, to demand certain favours. The Muslim girls held each other's hands; they borrowed each other's veils and sweaters. She had suffered from cramps throughout her life because she was forbidden from using the bathrooms at school and had to wait till she got home; now the pain was mixed with anger.

By the time she was seventeen she had pretended to be Nargis on several occasions in Lyallpur, for small durations, wherever she could. Even when there was no advantage to be gained from it. She felt it imparted a sense of triumph to her spirit, kept her mind sharp. She retained that name as a talisman, though the girl she had taken it from disappeared from school in her fifteenth year.

Seraphina was nineteen years old then, and working in the jewellery section of a department store. She stood at a glass counter, her beautiful hands resting on it, and there were mirrors behind the glass shelves and also on the ceiling. In 1966, the French fashion designer Pierre Cardin had designed the uniform for the air hostesses of Pakistan International Airlines. Seraphina had had four copies of them tailored for herself, and she wore them to work every day. An elegant A-line tunic that had pockets at the hip bones, the sleeves reaching only halfway down the forearms. It was worn with slim trousers. Green in winter, beige during the hotter months. For Margaret it was a thrill to watch her sister stride out of the house in the morning.

One evening she did not come home at the usual time. Solomon and Margaret waited for a while and then visited a neighbour's house and asked to use the telephone. They rang the department store and were told that certain irregularities had been discovered in the store's finances, that the police had been called in: members of staff with access to cash registers had been questioned, a number of them taken to the police station.

By now it was half past seven. Solomon went to the police station and was told to wait. Over the coming hours he watched as one by one the other cashiers were released. At midnight only Seraphina remained in detention. It did not escape his notice that she was the only Christian. With his head leaning against a pillar he slept for small periods of time through the night. At 5 a.m. he woke at the call of the muezzin from a nearby minaret and went to find a washroom, to splash water onto his face. He sat at a roadside teahouse among the truck drivers and drank a strong cup of tea. When he returned he was told that Seraphina had been released and had left the station in his absence.

Margaret met him at the door to the house, puzzled as to why he was returning alone.

'Where is Seraphina?'

'Isn't she here?'

'No.'

Solomon returned to the police station, intending to learn whether Seraphina had left accompanied by someone, whether she had hired a rickshaw or a tonga.

He was told that there had been a mistake. Seraphina hadn't been released, but had been transferred to another station for further questioning, the one in Civil Lines.

At the station in Civil Lines, he was told that they had no knowledge of an individual named Seraphina. When he asked to use the telephone he was told that they could not allow him to touch the instrument.

On his way back to the original police station, Solomon stopped the rickshaw outside Seraphina's department store and went in briefly and spoke to the manager. 'But the missing money has already been accounted for,' the man said. 'It was all resolved by eleven o'clock yesterday evening. We had made a mistake and we informed the police. They told us all staff members had been released.'

Seraphina was among the three staff who hadn't appeared for work that day, and the manager had just assumed that they were in need of rest, after a late and tiring day.

When Solomon arrived at the police station he was told yet again that Seraphina had gone home in his absence. The policeman behind the desk denied ever sending him to Civil

Lines. Solomon raised his voice and demanded to speak to the station house officer. The policeman reached across the desk and struck his face with great force. There was a jug of water and the man lifted it and rinsed his hand with it, letting the water fall onto the floor beside his chair.

When she appeared at home the next day, there were marks on Seraphina's face and neck. Her hair was dishevelled and the Pierre Cardin tunic was torn at the shoulder. Margaret observed the absence of life in her face. In the bathroom she let herself be manipulated like a doll by Margaret. As she began to bathe her sister, it took Margaret a few moments to fully understand what the lines drawn with a marker pen on the small of her back meant. Four vertical lines bisected by a diagonal one. There were six sets of these. Thirty lines in all.

The tally.

What had infuriated them, what had prolonged it, was that she had fought back.

That year Margaret came to Zamana to attend college and, having thought about it for weeks beforehand, she decided to present herself as Nargis from her first day there. At times it seemed as though she was thinking of little else. She practised saying and writing her new name. She acquired little books and pamphlets about the correct manner of saying one's prayers, the basic stories from the lives of Muhammad. She told herself to always say, 'Peace be upon him' after his name. In her grief-stricken mind, to pretend to be Nargis would be expedient while in Zamana, the deception freeing her from the daily aggressions of Muslims.

She had carefully forged a copy of every document she possessed, every single form or card or piece of paper she needed for her life in Zamana, erasing the path she had emerged from. She lived in a hostel for the first two years, and life in a new city meant that there were myriad other adjustments to be made. Her lie seemed just another aspect of the new reality, a problem she had to master. She feared someone from her life in Lyallpur would recognise her in Zamana, but no one did.

Each time Nargis went home she found her sister to be increasingly withdrawn from the world, more and more querulous and insulting with the few people she did come into contact with, more and more specific about the household. She never ventured out of the house now, living a life hidden in the shadows. She would release a sigh and get up and turn a vase around, because it hadn't been put there in the correct manner – she liked the motif on the other side better. She became enraged when the newspaper was ten minutes late, when she caught an eye infection, when the electricity disappeared. The door had to be closed. The door had to be open. The fan was spinning at too high a speed. The fan was spinning at too low a speed. At other times she was overly quiet, or Margaret would enter a room and find her sitting in the dark.

'Do you ever think about the Afterlife?'

'Not really . . . Well, sometimes,' Nargis said.

'What if there is a Hell but no Heaven?'

'You mean we'll be punished for our sins but not rewarded for our good deeds?'

'Yes.'

'What kind of God would do that?'

'The kind that made this world.'

'Don't say things like that.'

'This world doesn't make sense, why should the next?'

'I said don't say things like that.'

*

She was walking around the white cube of the mosque, looking up at the walls, when she rounded a corner and met Imran and Helen.

They told her they had found prints in the mud and Nargis identified them as the feet of mongoose.

The three of them moved together through pockets of foliage where the daylight was entirely hidden from them.

'Wasn't there an island where all the wounds are healed?' Imran asked.

'The one King Arthur was taken to,' Nargis said.

'Yes, Avalon.'

21

From a fistful of keys in the rucksack, Imran had assembled a chime to hang outside his window. Helen could hear its set of small noises, suddenly thrown in her direction when the wind changed. It was early afternoon and Nargis was asleep.

She stood against a pillar on the high balcony. Insects were few at this hour but in the evenings great waves of them arrived from the muddy edges of the island, forcing them to retreat into the rooms, burning the mosquito repellents just outside the front door to thwart their entry.

There was a coil of rope on the balcony, long enough for a noose or a swing.

She wished she could transport the miniature Hagia Sophia and the Córdoba Mosque from the study in Badami Bagh. Plant them in the long grasses here on the island and read inside one of them all evening, undisturbed by midges. The carved wooden bird on the Hagia Sofia's roof would be joined by real crows and mynahs. She remembered resting her elbows on the small windows, and looking out into the study, then beyond that into the garden. In her edition of *Alice's Adventures in Wonderland*, there was a drawing of Alice moments after magic had caused her to grow too tall, her head almost against the ceiling. That was what she had felt like in one of those two miniature buildings.

My dream is to build – in the woods that I already own – a house to plant roses, to give orders that I will receive no one, and to write short stories.

This line was written by Anton Chekhov in a letter.

Suddenly she felt she was being watched. She looked up and

heard someone call out her name, recognised Lily's voice. Now she could see him, down there in the middle distance, looking up at her. He was wearing the same clothes he did the last time she saw him, there was his head full of curls.

'Helen.'

She turned and rushed into the staircase and she was outside the house in less than fifteen seconds. Because of all the uncontrolled growth she could not move in a direct line towards where she had seen him. By the time she arrived he had moved away, gone elsewhere. She stood searching with her eyes and then called out to him. 'Baba!' Two of the four clerics' houses lay empty and the idea came to her that he must be in one of them. She moved towards the nearest of the two, now shouting out 'Baba!', now 'Lily!' Finding the two houses unoccupied she went to the door in the wall that guarded the island, the door that gave onto the bridge. With great urgency she turned the key that lived in the lock. Above the door was an arch from which a vine tumbled down, several branches and woody tendrils almost reaching the ground. Imran was always having to push them aside when he used the door. Now she did the same and went out onto the fragmenting bridge.

Imran came out of the water, near the pointed tip of the island. He had slipped out through a gap in the wall, turning his body sideways, and entered the river cooled by the branches. His clothes lay on the grass and he was reaching for them when he heard Helen's voice. He stilled himself and waited for it to come again, to establish the direction, and then went towards it, his shirt held at his groin. Nothing but silence. He stood looking around, taking a few steps now and then, frowning, wiping away drops of water from his eyebrows with the heel of his thumb.

When he located her in the distance – she was about to disappear through the door – he began to put on the shirt and ran back to get his trousers and shoes. He went onto the veranda, taking only alternate steps on the small staircase. He was on the bridge in next to no time and yet she was nowhere. Pieces of the bridge had fallen away over the years and through the gaps at his feet he could see the Vela flowing twenty-five feet below him. He parted the small banyans and the giant-leafed castor plants that had taken root all along the bridge. It had become more a band of vegetation than a bridge, and he saw that a small swatch from her sleeve was caught on a thorn at the other end. He looked down the secluded road that curved out of sight in the distance and led to the bazaar. About to break into a run, he stopped, not sure whether he should turn and go back onto the island first. His mind calculating the time it would take him to journey to the rucksack under his bed and return with it over his shoulder, not stopping to unzip the pocket and take just the gun. Three minutes. He decided against it and was hurrying towards the bazaar now, the torn bit of fabric held in his fingers.

'Not today,' he said to himself, his heart slamming.

It was the first day of the new month. And after the Friday prayers at the bazaar mosque, a rally was planned, against the prospect of freedom being granted to the American killer from the Grand Trunk Road, against the blasphemous images of Muhammad in France and Denmark. People were also carrying placards against the rumours that the ban on YouTube was about to be lifted in Pakistan, the ban that was imposed after the trailer of an American film, crudely slanderous towards Muslims, was uploaded onto the site. There was also mention of the American pastor who was threatening to burn the Koran publicly, in Florida. And there were a number of banners with photographs of Lily and Helen Masih on them.

When she entered the bazaar and saw the hundreds of men ahead of her she turned back. But, during the few moments it took her to come to the decision, to recover her senses, two policemen had cordoned off the bazaar entrance behind her. One of them now raised his cane and told her to continue into the demonstration and then make a U-turn via an alley. She had covered her face with her dupatta, leaving just her eyes visible, and she stood looking at her image on the banners ahead of her. The policeman raised his cane again, this time briskly, almost whipping the air with it to indicate that he wanted her gone. Both tips of the cane were reinforced with steel caps.

More than half the men had brows discoloured by prayers. She stayed at the edge of them, the shouted slogans and wafts of intense perfumes, the rosaries of day-glo plastic or of real pearls, of tiger's eye beads, swinging from fingers. She felt as if in the waters of a delta, all the various tributaries swirling around her. Soon she was no longer sure of her direction, her view obscured. The sound of so many feet on the ground, the din of so many tongues, the separate and collective motions of the limbs. A man all in white, with a heavy densely black moustache, raised a finger to forbid her when she tried to move forwards through a gap among the male bodies. She ignored him and persisted and so he held her firmly at the shoulders and moved her aside, her dupatta almost coming off. She was terrified and backed into a doorway. In there was a corridor full of pallid light and when her eyes adjusted she saw that a woman was looking down from the top of the concrete staircase located at the other end.

'My way is blocked,' Helen said.

The woman lifted her hand, waving her up. Hesitating before raising each foot, she began to climb, looking back one last time to see if the crowd in the street had thinned, but seeing the endless flow of men going by the building.

'Come and join the Rally Widows,' one of the women in the room at the top of stairs said to her when she entered. 'Has your husband decided to join the demonstration too?'

There were five of them in the room, all middle-aged, sitting on their haunches around a mat spread out on the floor, some cross-legged, others with one knee upright and the second flat. At the centre of the mat was a basket of vegetables which they were peeling and cutting up into heaps.

'Come and sit down. Make room for her, Zeenat.'

Helen looked back towards the staircase and then went forward and sat down, her face still covered. The small room was stifling despite the fact that the ceiling fan seemed to be spinning at maximum speed, the blades invisible around the central disc.

'You can uncover your face,' one of the women said. She was chewing betel leaf with a sideways thrust of her mouth. 'The men are all out.'

Helen shook her head.

'Rihana, her husband must be stricter than yours,' the woman laughed. 'She refuses to uncover herself even in the presence of women.'

They were all bareheaded due to the heat, the dupattas discarded in a heap on a chair. A tea-coloured gecko hung upside down from the ceiling.

One of the women handed Helen a knife and sent a handful of potatoes rolling towards her. 'Listen,' she said, 'don't pay too much attention to men. Do you know why a man is like a Coca-Cola bottle? No? He is empty from the neck up.'

The women hooted at this.

Helen realised that she was no longer trembling. She

hooked a finger and loosened her dupatta a little, exposing her nose but not the mouth. The air entering her lungs freely.

'Lazy to boot,' Zeenat said. 'Mine thinks he's helping me with housework by lifting his feet when I am sweeping the floor.'

One of the others now turned to Helen. 'What's your name?'

'Aysha.'

'I am Tasneem. And listen, I want you to ignore everything Zeenat says. Men have their uses, if you know what I am referring to.' She jabbed Zeenat in the ribs and shouted down the shocked laughter of others. 'No, no, I am not a saint like some of you. Hell, even the ear begins to itch for a matchstick after a month.'

'Tasneem, have some shame. We are sitting just across the road from a mosque, on such a pious day.'

Tasneem flicked a hand towards the door – including in her dismissal the crowd of men outside, the alive and importunate sound of the speeches, and perhaps even the mosque. 'Protesting against the West, ha! When are they planning to demonstrate against everything that's wrong in Pakistan? Some fool draws a few pictures in the West and they have to take to the streets like it's the end of the world. Their feelings are hurt, my foot. Why are these feelings unhurt at all the degradation and cruelty in this country?'

'Aysha, where are you from?'

'I live nearby.'

'Nearby where? I know the whole area.' And when Helen shook her head, the woman stopped slicing the tomatoes and looked at her carefully:

'I don't think you are married. You haven't run away from home, have you?'

'No, nothing like that.'

'Show me all your face.' Her expression was unkind, the eyes ready and forensic. Her hair was a deep orange with henna.

201

Either there was a religious reason behind it – Muhammad was said to have used henna to dye his beard – or a scientific one – she was allergic to chemical dyes.

Helen did as she was asked.

'Shamim, will you leave the poor girl alone. She probably has a dragon of a mother-in-law who accuses her of wanton-ness if she even raises her eyelids, the way mine used to do, may she rest in peace until I get up there to seek revenge.'

They could hear the speeches being made on the road out-side. 'That's my husband,' Tasneem shouted now, raising a finger. She listened and then shook her head. 'What makes him think he is qualified to talk about jihad when he is afraid of cockroaches himself, Aysha?'

Helen was trying not to glance towards Shamim, the wo-man with the red hair. She looked up now and saw her staring at her thoughtfully.

'How did you tear your sleeve, girl?'

'Treachery,' Tasneem said. 'Now he's talking about treach-ery! What happened to the diamond necklace he promised me on our wedding night, may I ask?'

The man with the loudspeaker – standing in an elevated place, on the topmost step in front of a shop – was speaking about the duplicitous nature of Christians and Jews, of the Western world, of non-Muslims in general. People shouted furiously every time he paused, a wave of noise that advanced and receded. He reminded everyone how for five centuries the wealth of the Muslim world had poured into Baghdad. How the Caliphs had lavished it on palaces, mosques, schools, gar-dens and public fountains. And how, in addition to meeting the needs of its Muslim majority, the city had served as the re-ligious centre for many Christians, who had been allowed to erect churches among the teeming bazaars, and it was a cultural centre for Jews too, who had built numerous synagogues and Hebrew schools. But when in November 1257 the Mongol warlord Halaku Khan arrived, Christian spies slipped back and forth between the city and the encircling Mongol camp, bringing vital reconnaissance to Halaku Khan, in the hope of future reward . . .

The crowd was like a trick of mirrors, spreading without dimensions, flowing, bodiless. Having investigated various alleys and colonnades, Imran was out of breath, being jostled by the demonstrators. *STOP UNJUSTICENESS OF USA* read a placard. Around him there were several banners that expressed sympathy and outrage at the suffering of Muslims in Kashmir. And he could see at least five large photographs of Helen and Lily.

In addition to Helen's safety, there was concern in him that he would be seen here by someone from his former training camp.

People were weeping as they listened to the speech. Every now and then the crowd would ask in unison for blasphemers to be torn limb from limb. People were screaming – the young who wished to prove their manhood, the old who wished they had.

On the other side of the city, Imran knew from the newspapers, the Communists had organised a small rally today to commemorate the Chicago Haymarket killings of May 1886.

'And so on 5 February 1258, when the Mongols broke through Baghdad's city walls and the bloodshed of Muslims commenced, the Christians joined in to loot and slaughter. Over seventeen days several hundred thousand citizens met their deaths. Centuries of hidden hatred spilled out of the Christians, who defiled and destroyed mosques, turning many of them into churches. And joyful celebration spread in Christian lands near and far at the news of the destruction of Islam's fabled city . . .'

There was the sound of footsteps on the staircase and another woman came into the room. She wore a jewel in her nostril, and her face was heart-shaped, a fact emphasised by the burqa that framed it tightly. She unbuttoned the burqa and took it off before sitting down.

'What a crowd,' she said. 'My Allah.'

'This is my daughter,' Rihana said to Helen. 'She's as clever as a computer. Her husband has just returned from three months' jihad in Afghanistan. Allah be praised. And, Samina, this here is Aysha. Aysha's husband is at the demonstration out there too. Left the poor girl to wander around the shops, so I asked her to come up and join us.'

Helen had supplied none of this information.

The girl looked at Helen and was about to sit down opposite her when she paused – having noticed the growing horror on Shamim's face, the henna-haired woman.

Shamim now rose from the mat, swiftly. Helen's first thought was that the gecko had fallen to the floor. 'My Allah, a suicide bomber,' the woman whispered in disbelief. The cold speculation in her gaze had come to an end.

'No,' Helen flinched, and shook her head desperately. 'No.'

Rihana screamed and threw herself away from Helen, her outflung feet disturbing the heap of vegetables. There was no time to hesitate or wonder. The other women too were reacting, aghast and outraged, one of them dashing towards the door in terror, going through it with continual shouts of 'Help!'

'Raise your hands,' Shamim commanded, extending her knife towards Helen, its proportions suddenly frightening as it neared her body.

She obeyed. 'Why would I be a suicide bomber?' she said, knowing fully the futility of her question, logical thinking having little use in a land that seemed at times to be full of conspiracy theories. She wanted to disappear into the wall she stood against.

Shamim, who looked as though she had turned a stone to discover a scorpion underneath, reached out and grabbed Helen's dupatta and roughly pulled it off her head. She was examining the lines of Helen's body for something she might be wearing under her kameez, and then she began to walk backwards to the door. The other women had already left, following the first one out of the room as though filaments connected them all, and they were screaming on their way down the stairs, calling out for a policeman, attracting the attention of the men moving past the door, anyone within the radius of their voices. Her knife raised, Shamim went out of the room and then Helen heard the door being bolted from the other side.

Suddenly the crowd around Imran contracted backwards, the bodies tightening around him with terrific speed, probably making way for something he couldn't see. Then he heard the words 'suicide bomber' being spoken repeatedly and then a panic spread. His ribs were being pressed from all sides. He tilted with the crowd, a slow wave that brought him back to an upright position after a few seconds, his mind lurching. Appeals of help to Allah and Muhammad were raised, the placards and banners leaning awry around him. There had been no explosion and soon enough he learned that a young woman wearing a suicide belt had been trapped on the first floor of the building across the road. That was when he saw the policeman holding Helen's dupatta.

The women were screaming, their distress compounded by the fact that they had left their dupattas in the room and were now shamefully bareheaded before the entire bazaar. Eight policemen, their pistols and rifles at the ready, stood in a group at the door to the building the women had emerged from. 'You and you,' the most superior one of them commanded a pair of policemen, 'go to the back and watch the window.'

'There is no window back there,' Imran said, drawing closer with a sudden wild hope.

The policeman looked at him. 'One of the women said there was.'

Imran shook his head. 'This is my aunt's house, I should know.'

The two policemen had set off but were now called back.

'No need. Boy from the family says there is no window.'

He went towards the back, ready to identify the rear window by counting the buildings as he moved down the alley, wondering if it might have the same colour of paint as the door at the front. But when he neared he discovered Helen standing at the base of the rosewood tree that grew outside the window. The sight had the same feature of unreality as everything else during the previous hour.

The moment he locked the door to the island and turned around, she placed her arms around his neck, her mouth against the side of his face. He clasped her at the waist and they stood there against the door. The branches of the old woody vine, hanging down from the arch, partially concealed them.

She was still but he was shaking.

'All I kept thinking was she can't die because I haven't asked her so many things yet.' He was speaking with his eyes closed. 'Tell me something. Speak to me.'

She shook her head.

'Speak to me. I want you to be my friend.'

'There is a moth in Madagascar that frequents sleeping birds at night to drink their tears,' she said eventually, her tone drowsy.

'Tell me something personal.'

'I want to see this place in the rain. There are some places, a building or a garden or a landscape, that you have the urge to see in the rain. You can't help but imagine how the falling water and the changed light and the wet wind would alter it. Most of all I want to be on this island in the rain.'

He tightened his hold on her. 'Let's stay here till the monsoon.'

'Our money would have run out long before then.'

'I'll find work on a construction site.'

'Will you make me a chime?'

'That one is for you. I didn't know how to give it to you.'

'Earlier, up on the balcony, I was thinking about dying – about destroying myself, I mean. But not now, don't worry.'

They stood for several minutes until finally she said, 'We should go in. Nargis-*apa* might be wondering.'

'Yes,' he said, 'in a little while.'

Towards midnight, after she and Nargis had withdrawn to their bedrooms, she was standing at the table beside her bed, threading the needle, when she saw his shadow appear on the floor. He was at the door, which she had left open. She did not look up as he came towards her and stopped beside her, their bodies almost in contact, the heat of his face being received by her own face. During this whole time she was looking down at the stitches she was making, a minute series of papery sounds being emitted by the page. He thought he would lose his mind. She turned her head sideways and looked into his eyes eventually. 'What?' he said, barely audible. She was smiling with her lips against his, breathing the shared air. He had been unaware but she had lifted the tail of her shirt and stitched it onto his sleeve, and had then sewn both of these onto the page. She secured the final knot now and broke the thread.

When the candle on the table died during the night, their two shirts hung empty from the page onto which they had been stitched, where he and she had carefully slipped out of them. It was as though two names from the book had come alive and entered the world.

22

There were crows numberless as flies around Lily. He got up from where he had spent the night with a group of homeless people – under the high curve of a concrete flyover – and went along the road. A small boy slept using the belly of a sleeping dog as a pillow. There was a large piece of Styrofoam under the head of a woman, an eighty-year-old who sold combs at traffic lights past midnight, a thousand wrinkles on her face.

He counted and decided that today would be the seventh day since the burning of Badami Bagh, though his mind was acutely fatigued and he couldn't be sure of the calculation. Wasn't it the eighth day?

That night Aysha had persuaded him to leave her room without her, telling him she would deny everything to her father and to the men with the prayer-marked foreheads. He had insisted that she and Billu come with him but she had refused. 'Go and be safe somewhere for now. If they catch you here they'll know the announcement is true.' Perhaps 'persuaded' was the wrong word. There was not much time for reasoning things with each other or weighing the options: they could hear the men climbing the stairs towards her room. He had hurried out and they actually had passed a few feet away from where he hid in an unlit corner. He realised he had left his phone in her room but it was too late.

He should never have left. He should have stayed with her.

Trembling, he sat down on the edge of the road.

He was hungry but the money he had in his pocket that first night had run out the day before yesterday.

He had disappeared from Badami Bagh, and a few hours

later at a teashop on the Grand Trunk Road had learned that almost every Christian house there had been set alight. It was all said to be the fault of a man named Lily Masih, whom the police were looking for now. Someone said the fire started because the traitorous Christians had been burning the Pakistani flag. A little later, from a pile of second-hand clothes being sold at a footpath, he had bought a T-shirt and a pair of corduroy trousers moulted at the knees, throwing away the shalwar-kameez he had been wearing. He had his hair cut down to a bristle, in the hope of further altering his appearance, the moustache and small beard also gone. Helen had gone to spend the night at Nargis's house, so he was certain of her relative safety. However, while he was paying the street barber for shearing off his hair, he saw Helen's face on a poster across the road. He stood looking at it before walking up to it, not knowing what the words said. Recognising only her name. The passerby whose arm he grabbed in a panicked daze and asked to read the poster for him, put on his glasses and told him what it said, followed by a string of obscenities towards the blasphemer.

'Why do you want to know? Do you know her?'

'No.'

Later he had phoned Nargis's house, a male voice answering on the third try, and demanding he identify himself, asking roughly why he wished to know where Nargis was. And it was a male voice, a different one, that answered when he called Aysha. Clearly Shakeel, her brother-in-law, had taken away her phone.

He rang his own number but it was unresponsive.

One day two months ago, while talking about the danger of what they had embarked upon, Aysha had said, 'My marriage, and the end of my marriage, has taught me something. Now when I do something out of the ordinary, I tell myself, "I know the consequences of this. I know the repercussions." I make myself say it clearly and out loud. I make myself hear it. Later, if and when things go wrong, I don't blame fate or Allah or luck. I remember that it had been my *choice*. Do you understand?' And when he had nodded she had said, firmly, 'It doesn't mean that the consequences don't hurt, or hurt less. I just know how it came to pass.'

Now, this morning, sitting on the edge of the road, the realisation came to Lily once again that he had to return to Badami Bagh, to discover what had happened to her, and to Helen and Nargis. They to whom he was not replaceable, as they were not to him.

He looked up into the branches of the tree he was sitting under, the sun ascending in the sky. Some trees felt like daughters to him, some like sons. The almond in the courtyard of his house had always been a wise and slow personage – a grandfather or great-uncle – who knew everything about him whenever he lay down underneath it, knew his memories and thoughts. The twisting of the branches was as familiar to him as the letters of his name, of Helen and Grace.

He stood up and began to walk. He hadn't eaten for twenty-four hours and knew he had to find work today.

He felt a momentary sense of rage, and he knew that if something had happened to his daughter or to Aysha he would spend the rest of his life hunting down the perpetrators.

He turned back on seeing a pair of policemen ten yards ahead of him and entered an alley he had gone past earlier, breaking into a run until he was halfway along it.

There was a tap and he splashed water onto his face and then began to drink deeply – gulp after gulp as fast as he could. This hurry was the result of an ever-present fear. If someone were to discover he was a Christian, he could be accused of polluting the water. As a child he had had numerous beatings.

During an evening of conversation some months ago, he

and seven of his friends had realised that there wasn't a single street in the entire city where they or their wives and children hadn't been abused for being Christians.

Not a single one.

At the other end of the alley there was a tandoor, and he watched the man as he made kulchas, the smell of the hot bread maddening to him.

He stood there and watched, mesmerised.

The man dusted flour onto a wooden surface, set a ball of dough the size of an orange onto it and rolled it flat. He sprinkled the dough with sesame seed. With the tips of his eight fingers held in a row, he made more than fifty indentations in the dough, covering the entire surface very rapidly, in little more than a second. Then he smoothed this prepared circle of dough onto a cushion he had lightly coated with water-thinned milk. Finally he reached down into the tandoor's mouth and slapped it onto the hot wall, withdrawing his arm and the cushion very quickly. He used two yard-long rods of steel – the tip of one flattened into a small spatula, of the other bent at a right angle – to prise off and then lift out the baked kulcha. It made a stiff cardboard sound when he dropped it onto the others.

Lily needed to eat.

'Is there anywhere I can find work?'

The tandoor-wallah looked up but his hands continued forming the bread. 'The day labourers gather on the next crossroads at this hour. Bricklayers. House painters.'

'The crossroads in which direction?' His eyes were on the pile of kulchas.

'Or you could help me with the deliveries. My apprentice won't be here this morning. I can't pay you much though.'

'I just need a meal.'

'What's your name, brother?'

'Nicholas.'

The man didn't raise his eyes. 'As I said, the labourers gather on the next crossroads. On the left.'

The labourers sat outside a teashop. It had no shutters or doors because it never closed. It was full of truck drivers, as well as drivers of rickshaws, buses, wagons, qingqis, and tongas. The labourers squatted on their haunches on the ground before the establishment – some had paint brushes with them, and ladders, pickaxes and spades, others had just their muscles and bones to offer. Yesterday's paint was on some sleeves and wrists. People who wished to engage them were stopping their cars and vans, and the men were getting up in groups, haggling, and then disappearing into the vast day of the city, to work until nightfall.

Lily asked if he might wait with them for an opportunity to be employed.

The waiter from the teashop – a thirteen-year-old in a stained vest, with a chintz rag on his shoulder – was bringing out cups and bowls of tea for the labourers. The television bracketed to the far wall was showing the talent competition 'Pakistan Idol'. A young man with a beautiful voice was in trouble because he was illiterate and could not read the lyrics of the songs he had to sing. The judges were quarrelling over whether or not to eliminate him from the contest.

Lily pretended the sun was in his eyes and turned to sit the other way when a pair of police constables appeared at the teashop. They had ordered tea and were looking at the glass cabinet full of yellow fruit-buns, pastries and loaves of sliced bread.

The waiter approached Lily and the man next to him: 'So what do you two think of Kareena Kapoor?' He nodded over his shoulder at the poster pinned to the wall of the teashop. 'I am telling you,' he grinned, 'the next time Pakistan and India are at war, India should just get its movie heroines to stand in a line in front of its soldiers. We Pakistani men would lose our senses and would be easy prey.' He laughed and wiped the sweat on his forehead with his rag. 'Shall I bring two teas here?'

'Not for me,' Lily said. 'I have no money this morning.'

'You can start an account,' the boy said. 'What's your name?'

'Sadiq Munawar.'

With a laugh the man beside him patted Lily on his shoulder and said to the boy, 'Bring him a cup, he's named after our chief minister, our prime minister's own brother.' He let his hand remain on the shoulder. 'You can pay me tomorrow.' Then waving to the other men around them, he said, 'Do you know this joke? A man was shouting at a crossroads, "The prime minister is a bigger idiot than a donkey, the prime minister is a bigger idiot than a donkey!" A policeman walking by grabbed him by the scruff of his neck and said, "You're under arrest for calling the prime minister a bigger idiot than a donkey." "No, no," the man cried out, suddenly afraid, "I didn't mean the prime minister of Pakistan, I meant the prime minister of France." And the policeman, incensed, said, "Now you're definitely under arrest, for thinking I don't know which country's prime minister is a bigger idiot than a donkey."'

Everyone laughed.

'Lots of sugar,' Lily shouted to the waiter, and turning to the man said, 'That's very kind of you.'

The constables were walking away, he saw, but in the same glance he noticed a group of four men walking in his direction. One of them was dragging the twenty-foot length of bamboo used for cleaning blockages in sewers. They were sent down into the underground darkness through the manholes on the surface. The supple bamboo was trailing behind the sanitation workers, raising dust, and Lily recognised them. Cyril, Hector,

Harper and Jacob. They were from Badami Bagh. Two of them his childhood friends.

He whipped his head back, and tried to think fast about what he should do. Should he raise his hand partway? But here in the seated crowd there was no discreet way of doing anything.

From the corner of his eye he watched them approach at a steady pace and go past him and the other labourers.

The boy brought them the tea, Lily taking the first sweet gulp and almost gasping, not only because he had burned his tongue, but with gratitude too.

Cyril, Hector, Harper and Jacob meanwhile had moved on and the trailing end of the bamboo had drawn up to Lily. One bamboo stem was split in four lengthwise, and these lengths were bound together end to end – becoming four times the height of the tree. If it met something obstinate in the sewer, a man or child would then have to climb down into the darkness. He remembered being bitten by rats down there when he was nine or ten.

He had managed to catch Jacob's eye as they went by, perhaps; he wasn't sure.

'Good tea, chief minister?' the man beside him said, giving a little laugh.

'Yes,' Lily replied, swallowing the liquid in great scalding sips, blowing on it, more to cherish it than to lower the temperature.

He placed the half-full cup on the ground and stood up, ready to walk after them now. He was about to turn around when he fell forward from a blow to the back of his head, a savage shimmer appearing before his eyes as he landed on the ground and hit his head. 'You son of a bitch!' He was on his stomach and someone had climbed onto his back and was strangling him from behind. 'I will kill you, you motherfucking son of a bitch!' Lily managed to loosen the fingers on his throat and shook off the assailant and rolled himself onto his back. It was Hector.

Hector came at his neck again, his deadliness undeviated.

'My Martha is gone because of you. I will kill you, you motherfucker. I will drink your blood.' As he screamed these words spittle was flying out of his mouth, the hard bones of his fingers closing around Lily's throat, choking him.

'My baby girl was burnt alive because of you.'

Lily freed himself but failed to overpower the grief-stricken man who struck his face heavily with his fist twice. Harper, Jacob and Cyril had arrived now, running, and were pulling Hector away, trying to contain him, his panting curses. Jacob was frowning at Lily's altered appearance, saying, 'Lily, is that you?'

The squatting labourers had got out of the way when Hector's assault began and were now standing in a circle around the five of them.

'Lily?' the teashop's proprietor shouted. 'No, no, no,' he rang his ladle against the samovar and pointed to the waiter and then to Lily's cup of tea. 'Pick that up and bring it back. They must bring their own cup, they have to bring their own cup.'

Lily touched his mouth and the fingers came away covered with blood and he saw that the constables had stopped and were looking towards the scuffle from not too far away. Hector was weeping in Jacob's arms, uttering Martha's name repeatedly, held back when he tried to lunge at Lily again. He was back at work only a week after his child's death. Lily knew how poor he was. The plan was that when the money from the mobile-phone tower began to come in, he would buy a rickshaw for Hector.

Martha. Whom Helen had made a gift of a mechanical bird last Christmas.

Lily stood with his head down in the morning light, breathing heavily. He was doing what he always did to quell a shock, reciting Helen's childhood story to himself in his mind, stroking one wrist with the other hand, comforting himself, absently at first, then deliberately.

He looked up. He knew the danger was not over, was in all probability just beginning.

The man who had bought him tea, and had put his arm around his shoulder, was staring at him. 'Pretending to be a Muslim, you black bastard!' Lily at that moment was the visible justification of his fears, too deep, too imagined. It was a fine, fatal blade. In a paroxysm of wrath and enraged disgust, he approached and pushed Lily away with such force that Lily stumbled onto the road. Straightening just in time to miss an oncoming bus by a few inches, the sun swerving off the tons of steel and glass, the slaying weight. The raised grit had a stinging component, and the horn sounded grimly.

'Look at him . . . Just look at the dirty bastard looking at me with his eyes, with his Goddamned Christian eyes!'

He raised his elbows to protect his face from the rocks and other missiles the labourers had begun to throw at him, one of them – one quarter of a whole brick – catching him on the temple, sending him onto the road again. He spun and saw that the two constables were running in this direction. There was a wall across the road. Scaling it under the hail of stones and fragments of brick, he looked down over the other side and without hesitation plunged towards the garbage heap that lay twenty feet below.

He fell asleep or perhaps lost consciousness and woke with the details of a dream. He was in the waters of a dark translucent lake with Grace and Helen, and Aysha. There was a certain haste to their movements, and he understood that they were pilgrims who had to be present at a sacred site at a specific hour on a certain day. As they swam a fragile light played on the lake's surface, illuminating the thousands of books that were floating in the water, some submerged partially, others fully, with the pages turning slowly to offer glimpses of beasts and legendary loves and rescues, poems and prayers that were mankind's deepest silences made visible. They swam among the books, the four of them, soon realising that the ink on some of the pages was poisonous, dissolving and entering the water to seep strength and motivation from their muscles, causing blindness, and a corrosion of the mind. There was a city on the far side of the lake and in the dream he understood that that was where their pilgrimage ended, that eventually all four of them would climb ashore, though he was not asleep long enough to see it happen.

He found himself on the back veranda of a small building. At the front there had been a hand-painted sign he couldn't read, in the rounded Urdu script and the more rectangular English. There was a small car with peeling paint nearby. He had taken off his T-shirt and now held it against the wound just below the hairline. The fabric was black so the blood wasn't apparent, just as it didn't show well on his own dark skin, now or in the past.

He opened the back door and looked into the dim high-ceilinged interior. A progression of glass-fronted cupboards stood along three sides of the room, containing coloured objects. The windows of the room were closed – the only light came from the ventilation holes near the top of the walls. The centre of the room was occupied by what he took to be tables but which turned out to be – when he went in and advanced towards them with silent treads – display cases. Under the panes of glass lay dozens of coloured flowers and leaves. They were made of plastic, the material pulled or bent or moulded into details – the curved foliage, the bead-like berries. Next to each plastic plant there was a white piece of card with elegant writing on it. The cupboards against the walls too were full of these false blossoms and branches, he saw now.

There was so much to see, his eyes constantly adjusting.

A sound came from the veranda and made him sprint to the corner, where he folded himself into the space at the side of a desk, the top stacked with books and paperwork.

He heard the scrape of feet on the black and white tiles and over the next few minutes heard the windows being unlatched with sharp metallic sounds, sensing the light increase around him.

The man wore half-moon glasses and had greying hair. He opened the door to an adjoining room and disappeared through it, engaging in some activity in there, nothing but the occasional sound of him clearing his throat, once a sneeze. When he returned to the room Lily was in, to retrieve the teacup he had forgotten on a windowsill, he was holding a fountain pen.

He was approximately the same age as Nargis and Massud. And it seemed that just like them he walked around in the mornings not singing snatches of songs to himself, the way everyone else did, but melodiously quoting Urdu poetry.

Lily could not leave because he would have to go past the open door to the other room. Ten minutes later, perhaps a quarter of an hour, the man came out and spent some time examining the contents of one of the cupboards very close to Lily, writing something in a notebook. He went away but re-turned with a cup of tea and a kulcha on a plate and set them on the windowsill. Lily could see the steam rising from the tea, twisting in the sunlight. He angled his head and saw the man's back. With a magnifying glass he was studying a large spray from a pomegranate tree.

'That food is for you.'

Lily stilled himself. Had he left the fog of breath on the glass when he leaned down to look at the contents of a display case? But no, that only happened in winter, and even then it would have disappeared by now.

'I can see you, you are reflected in the pane in front of me,' the man said without turning around.

Lily stood up slowly, being mimicked by his ghostly image caught in the glass, not sure whether to move towards the food or towards the door. All around the vast room the flowers shone in the clear light, the colour murmuring in them like the breath of life.

'Where is your daughter?' He had turned around to face Lily.

'I don't know what you mean.'

'Yes, you do.'

'I don't have a daughter.'

'Yes you do. You are Lily Masih. You're wanted for blasphemy on half the walls in this city. As is your daughter, Helen. Where is she?'

Lily took a step towards the exit.

'Is she hiding here, like you?' The man looked around. 'And you can leave after you have eaten, if you wish.'

'I don't know what you're talking about.'

'Lily,' the man said firmly. 'Where is Helen?'

'I don't know where she is.'

'What happened to your head?' The man was about to say something further but stopped because Lily had begun to move towards the food.

Lily tore a bite out of the kulcha and chewed, lifting the cup to his full fast-moving mouth, his eye on the door to the outside.

'Come into the other room and sit down, there is more food there. My name is Farid Alvie. I manage this museum. We are

220

closed today so no one should disturb us.'

'A museum for plastic flowers?'

He came and took Lily's cup because only one of Lily's hands was free, the other staunching the blood on the temple. 'You obviously didn't see the sign out there.'

'I saw it, I just can't read.'

'It says, "The Museum of Glass Flowers".'

He bandaged Lily's wound and went upstairs and returned with a new shirt for him. After eating his fill, Lily helped him with a number of tasks – replacing the cracked pane in one of the cupboards, relining the dusty interior of several cabinets with new linen, holding the fabric in place with tiny pins. This plant life – there was glass fruit too, apples, grapes, apricots – had been made in Germany in the 1920s, the man said. Almost a hundred years ago. A nawab had had them brought over to educate the younger members of his family. There were nearly five hundred specimens – representing all continents of the planet. Lily held them carefully in his hands. The markings on them were like spots and threads of ink. He could see now that they were glass because wherever the material was thin the morning light shone through, even making the shadow of that part coloured. The man named Farid said that he had been engaged by the heirs of the nawab to run the place.

Late in the afternoon Lily expressed the wish to depart. Farid had fed him lunch too, but he didn't wish to endanger him by being there for too long.

'I live upstairs,' Farid said. 'I'll make a bed on a cot. You can stay until you are better. But you'll have to be careful. The building next door is the headquarters of a militant organisation.'

But Lily insisted on leaving. Farid told him he could return if he ever wished, told him what hours of the day would be safer for him to arrive, the activity in the neighbouring building at a minimum.

'What about your family?'

'My son in doing his PhD in the USA, and my daughter is studying at a university in China. My wife died five years ago.'

It was late in the evening when he left, Farid having persuaded him to stay and eat dinner with him.

'My son hates Pakistan,' he had said to Lily as they finished eating and walked out. 'He actually used the word the last time he visited. He said it was a rotten and barbaric place. Full of liars, fools, and brutes. He said he *hated* it, and that he would never ever return to live here.'

'And you? What do you think?'

He was silent for a while, as though collecting his thoughts. His small car with the old paint had a dent in the side that was twenty years old, he had told Lily earlier, from the day he had bumped into the poet Wamaq Saleem's car, the damage he hadn't wanted to have repaired.

'What I am about to say does not apply to you,' he said in answer to Lily's question, 'because you have been wronged every day of your life by this country, I am absolutely sure. So I am only speaking for myself when I say that despair has to be earned. I personally have not yet done all I can to change things. I haven't yet earned the right to despair.' He looked at Lily and smiled. 'That is what I think of Pakistan.'

At 2 a.m., he was walking towards Badami Bagh.

Getting nearer he entered the river and swam to the back

of his house. In the darkness he climbed into the long grasses that grew on the bank like the pelt of a wild animal. The phone tower was gone and an intense smell came from the charred things as he went into his courtyard, disturbing a piece of debris with every step, flinching at the small sounds. It had taken him three hours to walk to this part of the city.

He opened the warped gate and looked out carefully. A policeman was sitting outside Nargis and Massud's home, the light above the door shining on him. Lily looked towards the house behind the mosque, and then he retreated and walked to the grass at the back of his house once more, following the Vela upstream until he arrived at the rear door of a house. The very old man who answered it, Samuel, expressed his disbelief in a loud whisper.

'Lily, my son! Are you alive or dead?'

He was a friend. He was carrying a lantern in whose light Lily saw the burnt condition of the door he had knocked on. The old man embraced him and they crossed a small courtyard piled with singed and twisted objects; the bent, melted belongings. In the bedroom Samuel's wife Diana fell into Lily's arms. She carried the smell of smoke like her husband.

'Where is Helen?' the woman asked, going to the bedroom door and looking out. 'Isn't she with you?'

'I was hoping you would tell me where she is?'

He felt weak without the energy he used to obtain from his daughter's presence, the awareness of her close to him.

'There is no news of either her or Nargis. The policeman outside the house waved us away when I tried to ask why he was there. Sometimes the soldiers arrive and talk to the policeman or go into the house.'

'Why are all the windows in the cleric's house boarded up? Where is Aysha? Has anything happened to her and Billu?'

'No one has seen her. Maybe she's been sent away.'

'What about the boy? Doesn't he go to school?'

'No one has seen him either.'

Sitting under the ceiling full of holes he begged forgiveness for visiting them and putting them in danger by being there.

They told him about the scores of people injured and the twelve deaths, eleven on the night, one later. Samuel went out into the night and brought more and more people, some of them offering consolation, kissing him for being alive, others accusing him, one woman striking his face. Her son had been attacked with an axe during the riot but had survived the night. However there was no money for the medicines he needed in the coming days so he had succumbed to his injuries, becoming the twelfth death.

Just before dawn he walked out of Badami Bagh. He was lying under a railway bridge when the sun rose and a street dog came and lay down next to him, arranging his spine against his.

Twelve deaths.

23

Two months into their marriage, Lily had asked Grace what food she wished she could eat. He was nineteen years old, and she was seventeen. It was a casual question but she had revealed the answer shyly, giving him the name as though she considered the food item to be something above her station. Prepared to be laughed at by him. The next day he came home early and asked her to get ready. With great formality she had bathed and dressed herself. There was lipstick on her mouth and she wore high-heeled shoes that had silver interiors and silver soles. She made sure his own clothing was impeccable, his hair combed. He had rented a bicycle and she climbed onto the bar and they rode out of Badami Bagh. A spring afternoon thick with flying grass seed. His arms enclosed her as she sat before him on the bar of the bicycle. In a country where public displays of affection between couples were frowned upon, he had always loved seeing a man and a woman on a bicycle, their bodies in free and open contact. Just as good were women sitting pillion on scooters or motorcycles, their arms around the men's waists.

He stopped to buy a string of jasmine from a roadside garland seller for her to tie at her wrist and then continued.

He left her in the Mughal garden that had been built by Bahadur Shah Zafar, the emperor who claimed he could transform himself into a gnat and enter other countries in order to spy.

Lily was gone for twenty minutes, returning with a paper bag. He took out the cardboard box that contained the beef burger, and with great tenderness he spread a paper napkin on her lap and placed it there. She had pinched her lips between her teeth, to avoid grinning with pleasure, her eyes glittering. Too overcome. Finally she composed herself and opened the lid ceremoniously. She had been working as a servant girl since she was seven years old, and had always wanted to eat this exotic fare she had seen the children of the rich eat in the houses she cleaned. Lifting the burger she began to take small bites out of it, looking at his face now and then, dabbing her lips with the luxury of a second napkin. Halfway through she had sufficiently mastered her awe to remove the top half of the bun and examine the meat and the slices of vegetable lying underneath. He himself did not take his eyes off her for a single moment. A boy in love with a girl.

V

THE AVOIDED MIRROR

24

Each night Helen emerged with the lamp and waited on the veranda. Between this house and the house Imran had chosen for himself there lay a stretch of darkness that she found too disconcerting to cross unaccompanied, though it was only three minutes away. He would see her light from the distance and came towards her – as did the moths, making her think he himself was one such creature – and he led her through the trees and vines, the ground uneven, forced up here and there by roots. Going past the half-shattered boat they entered the house. Sometimes he was without a shirt in the hot May nights.

One morning he walked smiling into their kitchen carrying a *rohu* carp he had caught in the river, Nargis sending him to the bazaar to buy the tamarind and gram flour they would need to prepare it.

One after another the days were burning. There was no movement in the air but then suddenly there was a breeze, composed of sensations. In the afternoons he and Helen lay in one of the interiors, the hours stunned by the heat, the giant leaves of a creeper, shaped like footprints of prehistoric creatures, hanging just outside the screen in his bedroom. Falling asleep he told her that the third chapter of the Koran was named Imran – the word meaning 'the family of Mary'. He told her how the chapter spoke of the angels throwing down their quills when it was being determined which one of them would get to care for Mary, be her guardian. 'There was a quarrel!'

Or they sat with Nargis and matched the damaged pages from her book, placing them on tables and counters and other surfaces of the kitchen, resting small stones on them as paperweights.

She told them of the legend whereby the island was formed when a bit of earth fell out of the hoof of the Buraq. 'Many features in Ibn-ul-Arabi's description of Hell, Paradise, and the Beatific Vision', Helen read out from a triangular piece of the book's page 653, 'are to be found in Dante's *The Divine Comedy*.'

Nargis, sitting alone in the kitchen, looked up at a noise.

She didn't know what the outcome of her flight would be. The consequences. They could track her down to the island somehow. There could be a solid knock on the door in the wall tomorrow, or the day after, or within the next hour. With each day she was absent, she imagined that man's fury increasing.

And she was constantly trying to think where Lily might be.

He was alone and helpless out there.

She went out through the trees but stopped when she saw Helen and Imran by the fractured moss-covered boat. It was late morning and she stood fully clothed while he poured water from a bowl over her head. Their feet in the mud and grass. She retreated to allow them their privacy.

She heard muffled laughter behind her, the strong splash of water on the ground. This time last year she and Massud were visiting Qasr Amra in Jordan. The frescoes in the rooms surrounding the caldarium depicted gardens and lovers, scenes of hunting or performances on musical instruments. It was the advice of medieval Arab physicians, who believed that baths drained the spirits of the bathers. The paintings were there to revive the three vital principles of the body – the animal, the spiritual, and the natural.

'All rickshaw drivers in Zamana, including my father,' Helen said to Imran, 'drive barefoot. Their slippers placed alongside the pedals.'

During the nights the two of them talked to each other in low voices, their bodies lit by a small flame. At dawn on the windowsills the ants threw inches-long shadows in the angled light, and the bees swarmed in the vicinity of a guava in bloom.

She had told Nargis about all this immediately.

'You will be careful, won't you?'

'Yes.'

'Don't hurt him, and don't get hurt,' Nargis said. She thought for a long time before continuing, as though wishing to grasp what she wanted to say and to then express it correctly. 'The beginning, the middle, and the end of love – they all have their rules. Both of you must act with dignity and honour towards each other during these stages.'

That was all she thought she needed to convey, the only advice she imparted. And Helen was grateful to be treated with such comforting seriousness.

The first chair to enter China, Imran read in a fragmented page, *must have come from the borders of the Roman or Byzantine Empire. The Chinese called it the* hu chuang, *'the barbarian bed'* . . .

In a teashop at the bazaar, while his iPod was charging, he sat and drank tea and watched television. One day there was

231

a program on which there was a live conversion of a Christian man to Islam, the teashop owner and most of the other customers murmuring 'Praise be to Allah!' as they watched. During the commercial break, when there was a public health announcement about mosquitoes, almost everyone around him agreed that Dengue fever was a CIA conspiracy to decimate Muslim populations. They were deeply convinced, and it didn't matter whether such accusations were true: what mattered was that they *felt* true. Trying not to laugh, the young man sitting beside Imran leaned towards him and whispered, 'If Isaac Newton was Pakistani, he would have said, when the apple fell on his head, "This is all the CIA's doing."' Another day he watched a Turkish drama serial, the bare legs of the heroine pixellated for Pakistani sensibilities.

A dog the colour of the sphinx had come to recognise him and sometimes padded alongside him for a while.

He bought the newspapers every day and took them back to the island, all of them carrying articles about the abuses and disappearances in Kashmir. In India itself, not far from Delhi, a mob of Hindu militants had beaten to death a Muslim man whom they claimed had eaten beef. The announcement of his crime had been made from a temple loudspeaker. Following the lynching, the police had sent the meat in the man's fridge to a laboratory for analysis, to ascertain whether or not it really was beef.

'When did you decide to come to Pakistan?'

It was past 2 a.m. and they were awake, stretched out beside each other under the mosquito netting.

'How did your brother die?' she asked. 'Tell me.'

'It was after his death that I came to Pakistan.'

By temperament he liked being alone. After a few days in

the company of people, he delighted in being solitary for a period, noticed how his thought-patterns changed, how his mind slowly rewired itself. 'Hello, friend!' he would say, recognising his profounder, perhaps truer, self. But now he waited for Helen to walk into every room, the eye searching for her in every view.

He began to speak about his lake, his home on its shore. The distant mountains and glaciers where the second coldest place on earth after Siberia was located.

Shortly before he was born his father – who was twenty-eight years old at that time – was taken away. Within hours it was clear that it was a case of mistaken identity. His name was Naeem Ahmed Tarigami and the Indian soldiers were looking for Naeem Ahmed Ahangar. But the weeks went by and he did not return.

As children he and his brother Laal had approached the fountain in the garden one day and seen the reflection of the guerrillas hiding in the branches overhead. 'There is a djinn in the water,' Imran had told his mother.

As the years passed, their mother continued her search for her husband, for her two missing brothers, travelling to numerous jails in India, sometimes taking Imran and Laal with her, sometimes asking her father to accompany her. To Meerut, to Varanasi, to Rajasthan. To Delhi's Tihar. Following every possible lead.

'If only they had given him a different name,' she would say at times.

'If only the Indian soldiers hadn't come here,' her father would reply, every single time.

The Indian soldiers who had taken him away – Captain Kumar and two others – were the only ones who knew of his fate, and they were protected by others in the hierarchy of the military and civilian government. So there was never any categorical answer. The same was true when it came to her missing brothers. Tens of thousands of Muslims had been killed, tortured, raped or been made to disappear by Indian soldiers since 1990, and a precedent could not be set of making a soldier answerable for something. Again and again she was asked why she wouldn't just accept the 'compensation' – 100,000 rupees – and let the authorities conclude the matter.

'Because we live in a time when human beings are not for sale,' Imran remembered her shouting back one day.

Neither Naeem Ahmed Tarigami, nor his two brothers-in-law, were among the ten bodies that turned up in a rice field one day. She and her father had gone and examined the faces and bodies of the corpses. And then she too was taken away, the day in the apple orchard when she dug up the crate with the bullets and discovered that the santoor they had left in it was gone.

The two boys were now with their grandfather, whose memory deteriorated over the years. At first he was capable and firmly anchored within himself, with an occasional minor lapse, but by the time the two boys were teenagers he was experiencing long periods of confusion and forgetfulness. By then, both Imran and Laal had themselves spent several nights at the Indian soldiers' interrogation centre.

Early one morning – Imran must have been about seventeen – his grandfather shook him awake. 'What is it?' he asked, sitting up in the clear plain silence of the hour. Laal was asleep in the bed next to him. The aged man did not speak but Imran could see that he was attempting to. The expression on his face was that of a musician searching for a sound.

'What is it?'

The floor of the room was littered with keys. The walled orchard had been closed since the day Imran's mother was taken away. The Indian soldiers had dug it up, searching for buried ammunition, and afterwards had placed a heavy padlock at the gate. His grandfather had begun to collect and make keys with the intention of letting himself in one night – to see if his daughter was working in there.

His own father – Imran's great-grandfather – had disliked the softness of Sufi Islam that pervaded Kashmir. It had turned Muslims into docile slaves, he had claimed. He wanted Muslims to be robust, vigorous men who fought against fate and destiny. He had been sent to the penal colony in the Andaman Islands, for making a speech against the Hindu ruler of Kashmir.

Imran wondered whether he should rouse Laal. Finally, the grandfather said, 'When your father was taken away, he was wearing the green coat you've seen in his photographs.'

'Baba, I already know. You and Mother told us to keep a lookout for that coat when we were children.'

Imran's grandfather shook his head at the interruption. 'In the pocket was a twist of newspaper. In it there were flower bulbs. He had just bought them and they were in his pocket.' He placed his hand on the boy's shoulder and looked directly at him. 'Moscow, I will draw you and Laal a picture of the flowers that come out of those bulbs. I don't know the name. I want you to search for them in the hills, and in the fields and forests. If they have buried him in a shallow grave, the bulbs will germinate and let us know where he is.'

None of this meant anything, but the boy didn't say anything, just nodding in assent. A night of sleepless fears had led to the old man's words and with the daylight he might see the inconsistencies himself. Perhaps.

'He bought the bulbs from a shepherd named Munir,' his grandfather said, his mind and eyes far away. 'Munir was killed a year later. The Indian soldiers mistook him for a fighter in the hills. We all knew him.' The grandfather sat in silence after these words, Imran waiting to see whether he would leave or say something further. The old man looked at him eventually. 'When Munir was a child someone had asked him if he knew what the soul was, and he had replied, "Yes, the soul is a pock-et, in which you carry the names of those you love.'"

The mass graves of Kashmiris, who had been killed and buried in secret by Indian soldiers, were beginning to be discovered by then, and thousands of young men were missing – either murdered, or crossing the border into Pakistan for guerrilla training. The grandfather began to advise everyone to carry bulbs and seeds in their pockets, and to inform their family and friends what specific plant each was carrying upon their person, in order that they would know what flowers to look for after the Indian soldiers had tortured them to death.

The keys were how the guerrillas around Imran's valley passed along messages now. 'Brother, did you drop this key?' 'Good aunt, is that your key lying there on the ground?' If the answer was yes, then that was the person to whom the message had to be delivered, the piece of paper furtively pressed into the palm of the hand. A burqa-clad woman would embrace a man in a burqa and the gun would be transferred from one to the other, a collaborator shot with it an hour later. 'No, son, this is not my key. Why don't you put it next to that pillar, so its owner can find it easily.' And behind the pillar would be the package of medicines needed by the guerrillas in the mountains.

By the time Imran was eighteen years old, and Laal nineteen, they had taken up the search for their father and uncles, in addition to the search for their mother. They had gone to the

Home Ministry in Delhi, and tried to move the High Court through a petition so that the soldiers who had taken their parents and uncles could be made accountable for their fates. But they were told that Captain Kumar now had cancer and could not travel, and that the soldier who had taken custody of their mother, Singh, too was suffering from the same illness. As were the soldiers who had taken away the uncles. 'And in any case,' an official told the brothers, 'the Home Ministry's sanction is required to proceed with the matter, and the ministry has lost the files. All four of them.'

Imran was attending college in Srinagar when by accident he heard a young woman mention the name of the army major in her home village, and how he had a long scar on his right cheek, dipping under the chin. It was as though Imran had received an electric shock. He asked the young woman if it was possible at all for her to describe the man further.

It took Imran and Laal two and a half months to reach her village. It was a journey which under normal circumstances would have taken just a few days. But there were army checkpoints and minefields to avoid, going the long way up the slopes and cliffs, fording icy rivers and entering night forests, waiting for days for curfews to be lifted in a zone so they could move forward by a few streets, hiding in orchards while Indian soldiers passed so close they could smell the soap they washed their faces with. They dodged timber-smugglers who had been brought into the forests by the soldiers, the trucks full of logs protected by them for a cut of the profits. One village was under curfew because an Indian commander had wished to marry a beautiful local woman and had massacred her family for refusing his wishes. One dawn an enraged wild creature growled at them from a ravine, and they were sure it was because it had never seen a human being before. Descending into gullies they would leave a trail of keys if they were unsure of a path, to be able to work their way back.

After more than sixty days of that life – it had stopped being a journey by then, had become their existence – both of them were gaunt and weak. One day they stopped by a cobalt mountain stream to eat the last of the food they had collected from a village they passed through.

When he finished eating Laal got up and went around a granite boulder, and from there a minute later Imran heard his faint groan followed by a whimpering, then a shriek behind locked teeth. Imran found him leaning against the curved granite, his right hand at his groin. The air was bitterly cold and his urine was steaming on the ground.

'Didn't you say you had recovered?' Imran said. He moved his brother's hand away from the groin and did up the buttons of the trousers.

'I thought I had, but I was wrong,' Laal said when he was able to speak, in a weakened voice.

He was weeping with pain, his breathing shallow.

'I thought I had, but I was wrong,' he repeated.

'When was the last time you saw Dr Aalam?'

'Just after he turned up in a shallow grave.'

It had always been a pleasure to argue with the doctor. When he heard the cleric talk about the Koran from the minaret, he had said, 'I refuse to believe that this degenerate fool has read a 400-page book.' He called Indian soldiers in Kashmir 'vultures and murderers, all 700,000 of them'. He said, 'And Pakistan can go fuck itself too.'

'They killed Dr Aalam?'

'The soldiers took him away for questioning. Just like they did me and you. Maybe we're dead too.'

Imran remembered the terror-filled hours of interrogation.

A new wave of pain came and Laal could barely stand up,

Imran reaching forward to prop him up, his head limp on Imran's shoulder. Like this he walked him back to where they had been sitting.

After a while, with Laal's eyes still closed, Imran said quietly, 'I read about Japanese baseball in a magazine not long ago. Do you remember?'

The shared pleasure between brothers. He had been the first companion of Imran's life.

'How did we ever get into that?' Laal said without opening his eyes. 'Masanori Murakami. Sadaharu Oh. The old venerable ones.' He gave a faint laugh. 'Hideki Okajima of the Yomiura Giants. I can't believe I still know the names.'

'Yes? What year did Kazuo Matsui make his debut for the Seibu Lions?'

But Laal had fallen asleep in his arms. While Imran was away at the Srinagar college, the soldiers had chased a band of guerrillas into the village graveyard. Surrounding that plot of earth, they had laid siege for two days, firing into the cypress trees, allowing the bullets to fragment the green headstones and the mounds. On the second day they employed people of the village as human shields, firing over their shoulders. 'We are doing this for your own good,' they repeated again and again, referring to their fight against the insurgency. 'If Kashmir broke away from India, every Muslim in India would be butchered by the Hindus in revenge.' There was no way out of the graveyard, and so eventually when the guerrillas stopped responding it was assumed that they had all been killed. Perhaps they had run out of ammunition. At dawn the soldiers decided to enter, walking under the bullet-shredded trees, along the paths between the damaged mounds, the spent cartridges rattling under their feet. They found no trace of the guerrillas. There was no blood. No one was breathing his last breath in the tall grass. Laal had told Imran how the soldiers had then walked with a loudhailer through the streets and asked the villagers to gather at the cemetery with every possible digging implement they possessed. They had convinced themselves that there was an underground passage in the cemetery, and so everyone was made to dig down for the rest of the day, Laal and his grandfather and the others, the women and the children, made to submit with rifle butts when they refused, the bones of the dead becoming exposed through the soil in due course. By nightfall they were moving with lanterns in a hell of churned-up earth and the spent bullets, the skeletons and the ripped-up yellow irises, the plant of martyrs.

Laal woke ten minutes later and stood up with steely determination. He took a loud breath, and exhaled just as noisily. 'Let's go,' he said to Imran, his voice bright.

'Are you sure you can walk? I was thinking of building a fire and staying.'

'No.' Laal reached into his rucksack and pulled out the gun. He looked at it and then put it back. 'Let's go,' he said. 'I want to find that man and ask him where my mother is.'

On the last day of their journey to the village they saw Imam Bibi and Nasima Bibi. They knew instantly who they were. The ancient women who sold toys and magic tricks. They had painted their donkey with black and white stripes to make it look like a zebra for the children. They moved from village to village, a timeless sight in the hills and on the wooden bridges, with children clamouring around them. How to shatter glass with your glance. How to start a fire by spitting.

Along with toys, they carried weapons, food and medicines for the freedom fighters in the forests. And now both of them lay facedown in the water where the stream widened into a pool. There was the print of a boot between each of their shoulders. Where the 'zebkey' was, the brothers couldn't see. Their sons had been gunned down years ago, having returned from Pakistan as guerrillas.

The brothers stood on the dark hillside and looked at the village in the valley below. The journey was over and they were crazed with hunger and fatigue. But they had been there since noon the previous day, and no opportunity to go down into the village had presented itself – to go and ask someone if they had dropped a key. They were very close to the border with Pakistan, and the presence of Indian soldiers was obvious. The uniformed figures appeared and disappeared through the mists down there, bits of them lost in the swaying vapour.

They spent another night shivering in the cold. Out of the darkness came the muezzin's call for the predawn prayer, and in the first hints of dawn they followed the smell of warm bread into the village. Later it would seem unbelievable that they had done that; it would seem unbelievable that they had just walked in and asked the baker if this key was his, and when he had said no, they had asked him to give them some sesame rolls out of charity, and then Laal had openly asked the location of the Indian Army base. The man waved them away but they had refused to move, whispering that they needed help. Eventually, the astonished man handed them two pieces of bread and motioned them towards the door at the back of his shop, barely interrupting what he was doing, not meeting their eyes.

He came to them as soon as he could where they stood chewing. He had locked the outside door of his shop, and he now grabbed Imran by the throat with one hand and struck him with the flat of the other. Then he spun around and did the same to Laal. They still hadn't recovered when he reached down, removed his shoe, and began to land blows on the two of them with the heel, Imran and Laal curling up on the floor, protecting their heads with their arms. 'Are you trying to get me killed?' he said again and again as he hit them, ignoring their pleas of 'Uncle, please!', 'Uncle, listen!' Only when he was exhausted did he stand back, looking at them where they lay sobbing. He refused to believe how they had managed to make their months'-long journey through Allah's desolations out there. Wilderness aside, how had they remained uncaught by the soldiers? The countless roadblocks. The contemptuous Indian soldiers aiming their AK-56s at you and demanding to see identity cards, demanding to know where you were going and why. And even if you were blameless, they would not allow you to pass without a bribe. Buses were stopped and their passengers told to disembark and line up for interrogation. 'People need permission just to have a wedding,' he said. 'The guest list has to be approved by the soldiers.' And beyond everything else, there was a bunker full of soldiers just at the end of that very street! He thought they might be collaborators and it took them more than an hour to convince him otherwise.

In the end he told them that the soldier they had come to meet had been killed the week before by freedom fighters.

And he offered to hide them for as long as they wished. The previous year a tear-gas shell fired by the Indian soldiers had hit his daughter in the face and she had fallen backwards. Over the course of the next half hour, she slowly drowned in her own blood while he watched her from a window. She lay in full view in the street but no one could help her, the soldiers reacting with bullets to the smallest of movements. She was fourteen years old, and emaciated after three months of curfew.

They accepted his hospitality for a few hours, until it grew dark when they would slip away again. Imran was brought out of sleep by the sound of gunfire a few hours later. The afternoon was ending. Laal had woken up ten minutes earlier and gone downstairs. There he had seen two Indian soldiers move past the bakery and had recognised one of them and had gone out and walked up to him and shot him point blank in the heart. He was the one who had interrogated Imran and Laal in their village, hanging them from the ceiling by their wrists and applying electric shocks to their bodies, pouring lighter fluid onto Laal's genitals and setting them on fire. The long beginning of pain. 'Couldn't you have convinced us of your innocence earlier?' he had said as he unchained them from the hooks in the blood-spattered ceiling. 'It would have been much easier for you.'

'Things being as bad as they are,' the baker had said to the two brothers earlier, 'this world won't last for much longer.'

'I've got worse news for you, uncle,' Laal had replied. 'The world will survive forever, with everything staying exactly as it is now.'

His brother was gunned down outside the baker's shop, the corpse dragged through the streets behind a military vehicle over the coming days, until nothing remained at the end of the rope. Imran managed to disappear and began another long journey, this time towards Pakistan, with twenty-two other young men.

25

Nargis was counting the number of pages that had been repaired.

In the damaged book there was a story about a boy abandoned on an uninhabited island, who was reared by gazelles. Growing up alone, he was not a child of the wilderness but rather a soul chosen for perfection. Free from the temptations of the world and the flesh, he attained wisdom through what was inborn. Through observation and thought.

It was a romance written by the Andalusian mystic Ibn Tufail, published in 1175. *Hayy ibn Yaqzan.* Ibn Tufail discovered the seed of the story in an allegory by Avicenna, and some of its elements probably derived from the Ramayana – the same elements from the Ramayana that Boccaccio used in his *Decameron.*

Through various translations in Europe, Ibn Tufail's story eventually fed into Daniel Defoe's *Robinson Crusoe* in 1719.

From the stitches Nargis could tell who had mended which page. Imran's sewing was surprisingly neat, the threads parallel to each other, placed equidistantly. A sound of frustration escaped him whenever he thought he had made a mistake. Her own and Helen's repairs were much less even. She realised Massud's would have been the finest.

Nargis reached forward and bit off the excess thread issuing from a knot, making the seam neat.

The volume was divided into twenty-one sections. And the

very last section was named The Book of Warning. It was printed on black pages in black ink, and it had to be held at a
certain angle to be read. It catalogued some of mankind's dis-
astrous encounters, outlining what happened when a people
failed to value others, ignoring their right to dignity. The mistrust. The deceptions. The disregard.

*In a letter to Catherine the Great of Russia in November
1771, Voltaire expressed hope that other powers would
join her to 'exterminate, under your auspices, the two
great scourges of the earth – the plague and the Turks . . .*

Here is what Ibn Batuta (1304–1377) said in his book, A
Gift to Those Who Contemplate the Wonders of Cities
and the Marvels of Travelling. *He was describing the
Quwat-ul-Islam mosque in Delhi: "At the Eastern Gate
there are two enormous idols of brass, prostrate on the
ground and held in place by stone. Everyone entering or
leaving the mosque treads on them. The site was formerly
occupied by a temple and was converted into a mosque
upon conquest . . ."*

*The headquarters of the East India Company in Leaden-
hall Street in London had a portico that depicted
Britannia, holding out her hand to a kneeling India who
offered her treasures. When the British landed in India, it
contained twenty per cent of the known world's wealth.
When they left 200 years later in 1947, only three per cent
of the known world's wealth remained . . .*

Nargis looked at the photograph of a statue, that of the Holy
Roman Emperor Charles V of Spain, his foot trampling the de-
mon of religious war.

What was it that made one group suspicious of another? she
wondered. Once during an air journey, she and Massud had
fallen into conversation with a Tunisian air steward, who had

245

said, 'There are a lot of Italian visitors in my country.' And when Nargis had asked him to explain, he replied, 'It is due to the Punic Wars. They haven't left yet.' Nargis had to look up the details of the Punic Wars. They had taken place between 264 BC and 146 BC.

A survivor of the Hiroshima atomic bomb, Shigeki Tanaka, won the 1951 Boston Marathon. The crowd was silent.

26

Imran was passing outside Nargis's room when he heard her voice. He stopped and took out his iPod and searched for the ghazal she was half-singing half-humming, and knocked on the door.

He handed her the device and she inserted its little speakers into her ears, the white wires disappearing into her hair, and sat listening on the bed.

'I am old enough to remember being amazed by the fact that this little thing contains hundreds of songs,' she said when the ghazal ended. 'We carried around cassette players, then CD players. A cassette had ninety minutes of music at most, if I remember correctly.'

Imran was scrolling through the screen. 'I want you to listen to a live recording of that ghazal. Performed in 1976 in Karachi. It is phenomenally good.'

Nargis sang to herself in a low voice.

> *Let the breeze pour colours*
> *Into the waiting blossoms.*
> *Oh love, now return,*
> *So the promised springtime may at last begin.*

Helen entered the room just as Imran was saying, 'This may sound strange coming from someone who grew up playing the santoor, but I avoid ghazals if I can.'

Nargis looked at Helen and shook her head in consternation.

'I know,' said Helen. 'I couldn't believe it either when he told me.'

It was dusk and the room was getting dark. Helen lit the lamp before coming to sit on the bed beside Nargis.

'They are too melancholy,' he said with a defensive look. 'They are needlessly and wilfully sad. I listen to just one and the rest of the day is poisoned.'

'That's a sign of their power.'

'They make you miss the lover you never lost, make you praise the God you don't believe in.'

'As I said, that's a sign of their power.'

He pretended to grab at his heart. 'Oh the wounded heart, oh the self-pity . . .'

'Helen, I forbid you from ever marrying this philistine.'

'Nargis-*apa*!' Helen said, mortified.

He looked at the girl and grinned.

Nargis resumed her singing, Imran joining in for a phrase halfway.

> *My heart is poor, it needs no reminding,*
> *But it holds all the wealth of longing.*
> *On hearing your name I'll always return,*
> *Once again become the one to share your sorrows.*

'I didn't exactly say I dislike them,' he said, made somewhat languid by the words. 'I just like to ration them carefully.'

'Too late,' said Nargis. 'We insist you and your Cheetah brand shoes leave this room.'

'What's wrong with my shoes?' He looked down at them, lifting a foot and turning the ankle to get a sideways look.

'Nothing,' Helen said, laughing. 'I have a pair myself at home. But if you were a Pakistani you would know their un-official claim to fame.'

'Which is?'

'Mullah Omar was wearing Cheetah shoes when he escaped capture by the Americans in 2001.'

'I wish we had wine,' Nargis said.

'Me too.'

'I shall make some discreet enquiries in the bazaar tomorrow,' Imran said.

Nargis leaned towards him. 'The French jewel merchant John Baptista Tavernier, who passed through our city in 1664, wrote in his *Travels*, "One can obtain wine in Zamana."'

'Drinking alcohol in a Muslim city?' Imran shook his fists with mock outrage.

'I know,' Nargis said. 'Is that why Omar Khayyam, Ghalib and Wamaq Saleem wrote those beautiful verses about milk?'

Imran began to sing lines from a ghazal by Mir.

> *Who lies buried at the horizon*
> *With his heart still on fire?*
> *Each dawn a flame sets the sky ablaze.*

Helen went to the window and looked out at the river and then back at the two of them, lost as they were in the music. She was smiling, watching these brief moments of pleasure, the delight in each other's company. He was singing as she watched him. She had noticed that when she sang a song to herself, she sang it slightly faster than the original singer. She moved through the verses, whereas the singer *inhabited* each word for a little while. The singer explored the word's possibilities, its emotional potential, before continuing to the adjoining word. He considered whether or not to bend or stretch the current one, according to – or in defiance of – the rules he had been taught.

'Each moment can be temporarily permanent for the artist,' Massud had said once.

And so she wanted to stay here, in this room, this island with its great white cube, with them, waiting for her father to reach here somehow.

Nargis had switched on their little transistor radio and was trying to find a classical music station. When she found one, she recognised the raag immediately.

'Bare Ghulam Ali sahib!' Imran exclaimed with delight, identifying the voice.

And with her eyes closed, Nargis said, 'Everything Bare Ghulam Ali sahib saw, heard or uttered was in musical terms. Once, looking at a fish flitting from one corner of its aquarium to another, he said, "Look, it's darting as though in time to the raag Todi . . ."'

Two nights later, and Imran and Nargis were sitting in the kitchen, the bottle of wine on the table. Helen was asleep on the long seat against the wall on the left, the back of one hand pressed into her cheek, her legs drawn up.

'Is your grandfather still alive in Kashmir?'

'He is being looked after by a family friend there. I email now and then.'

It was past 1 a.m., and there were six stars in the window. The moths fluttered around the candle.

'Would you go back one day?'

'It's a dangerous journey. Indian and Pakistani soldiers shoot at each other overhead while you try to cross the gorges . . .' He trailed off. 'I don't want to think about it.'

'I am sorry, I shouldn't have asked.'

'Don't worry.' He was looking out of the window, the empty glass in his hand. The tall cypresses were swaying in the breeze outside, the sound distinct from the flowing of the river, the dark slithering mirrors.

'Helen tells me we are staying here till the monsoons at the very least. You're getting a job as a woodcutter.'

He gave a laugh and looked at her deeply, trying to read her character.

She looked away.

'It would have been nice if I had got to know you both under other circumstances.'

'You have no idea, dear boy,' Nargis said.

At that moment Helen stirred and sat up and stretched her body. She raised her arm towards him and he went to her.

'I'd say he has no idea,' Helen smiled. 'Me, my mother and Nargis-*apa* – sometimes the three of us drove my poor father and Massud-*chacha* mad.'

'I am sure they liked it,' he said.

After the two of them had walked out into the night, Nargis carried the candle up to her room, the house dark behind her.

The rains were too far away.

She thought of Massud.

After her sister had been brutalised by the policemen, Margaret had come to university in Zamana and become Nargis. In Zamana, she realised that she knew more about Islam than some of the Muslim students. She had forced herself to learn the various intricacies of their religion, but they themselves could just shrug if they made a mistake about a fact or ritual, saying they weren't really 'that religious'. Twice she became furious at a Muslim for saying a person could get by perfectly fine without Islam in Pakistan. They didn't know how privileged they were, and being ignorant of privilege was part of that privilege. She also saw that her fury was partly directed at herself, for even entertaining the thought that they might be right. But what if they *were* right? If she had arrived in Zamana as Margaret would she be any different now?

She was getting older by then, was no longer a teenager, and the pretence became too much at times, her mind – evolving into new ways of thinking, processing new experiences – was beginning to accuse her. There was complexity in the situation where she had only expected simplicity. Solomon and Seraphina in Lyallpur were the mirror she was avoiding. She told herself she was a deceitful person on the whole, that she was dishonourable and a liar in all aspects of her life. She never allowed anything to interfere with her studies but all other activities seemed to exhaust her.

On a winter morning, as she was dozing in the room she rented in Anarkali, she felt touched by a sense of well-being. It was joy, perhaps even a mild form of euphoria. She worked her way back through the topics she had been thinking about, trying to isolate the one thing that had caused the gladness, and she was apprehensive when she arrived at Massud, the young man she had been introduced to a fortnight or so earlier. A party at the house of a renowned architect that she had forced herself to attend, after more than two months of isolation. She had encountered him on a few occasions since the party, and had had a brief exchange of words about a project – all without realising that anything significant was occurring until that morning.

One of the reasons she disliked going to parties and gatherings was that she knew she would never be able to accept or offer love. She wanted temptations kept to a minimum, because they could lead to wretchedness later, moments of depression in her room. Many people she knew had become couples, but any time a young man came too close to her she would wind down their acquaintance.

She was dazzled by Massud, the attractiveness of his character, his body. He belonged to a family that had produced individuals of great distinction – orators and essayists, a granduncle who wrote an opera about the Russo-Japanese War in the late 1900s, another who was an editor of an Urdu newspaper in the 1910s. And in the 1950s, when the Communist Party was banned in Pakistan, Massud's mother and father had met for the first time, while they were both in hiding.

Massud visited her in her room, his presence stirring up its staid air. He had gathered Persian lilacs for her. They were not considered something to be brought indoors and no flower seller would have stocked them. The tree was too commonly found, its leaves and berries poisonous. And yet he was carrying a large mass of them and the magnificent sight caused an intake of breath, the smell talcum-like and exquisite. There was no foliage.

He lifted one of the three dozen or so large envelopes from the table in her room, absentmindedly turning it in his hands. She noticed his fingers, the clear moons in the pink fingernails, the generous hairs on the wrist.

'What is inside all these envelopes?'

The full extent of her loneliness became apparent to her with that question, the need for a companion, the need for *him*.

She took it from him and opened it and carefully removed the thick folded layers of paper. Then she shook her head, too distressed and saddened. What she held in her hands was a building – a landmark of a kind in Zamana, the yellow-coloured private house with six doors on Nisbet Road – that she had reconstructed in ordinary paper, as tall as she was. It lay collapsed within the envelope but could be unfolded and made to stand at the centre of the room – there were thin cords attached to its roof and they could be fastened to the small hooks she had fed into the ceiling. The city of paper – this was what she did when other young people were delighting in each other's company, seeking comfort from life's various confusions and fears.

She replaced the Nisbet Road house in the envelope and returned it to the stack and asked him to leave. He stayed away for three weeks, a period during which she was afraid that she would never see him again, and also afraid that she would hear him walking up the stairs to her room any second now. And one afternoon, he did.

She was twenty-two years old now, no longer a child. *Would she carry her deceit into her relationship with him?* she asked herself. And eventually that was precisely what took place, precisely what she allowed to take place. After their marriage she disliked being photographed; her hair, which had always been short, she now let grow till it hung down to her waist. She did not know what Solomon had told his friends and acquaintances about her disappearance from Lyallpur. What he had told her own old school friends.

Through all this, and beyond, there was the matter of deceiving Massud, of not disclosing the truth to him. She had used the grain of truth about her parents' death, telling him she was an orphan, but after that everything was succinct fiction, a few quick and brief sentences. The orphanages she did not wish to think of. The handful of distant relatives she did not wish to see and who did not wish to see her. Occasionally, and especially in the beginning, she was appalled at herself. *What else will I see myself do?* The few times she planned to tell him the truth during those early years, there was the evidence yet again of his goodness. His moral and emotional integrity. The fact of the matter was that she did not want to lose him, could not bear to have the last thing she loved in this world be taken away from her. She was coming out of years upon years of loneliness and had been given this gift.

What would such a person think of Nargis's deceit and pretence? As the years passed, she played out various scenarios in her mind. He would become upset and leave her. No; he would be hurt but remain with her, but he would begin to doubt everything else about her from then on. She did not wish to injure him, be the cause of disquiet in his mind. There was that too. So she let the matter lie. But eventually, once she learned enough about his character, she realised what the most likely outcome would be if she told him: after a period of consideration he would be sympathetic – he would come to understand why she had done what she had done, and he would tell her that she could have trusted him from the beginning. But would he then wish her to re-establish contact with Solomon, to reawaken Solomon's pain and grief?

Every year around the anniversary of Seraphina's death she would become disconsolate, though managing to hide it successfully; and about a decade into their marriage, as the date of Seraphina's death approached one year, she decided to tell everything to Massud. She waited for several days for the opportunity and the required courage, but when she walked into the study decisively one afternoon, she found him standing there ashen-faced with the receiver of the telephone in his hand. He gave her an overwhelmed look that made her panic. He replaced the receiver and slowly came towards her.

'Majid has a second wife.'

'Majid? Our Majid?' This was all she could think of to say. He was the husband of Massud's sister Zarina, and he was a dear member of the family – Zarina and he had been married for fifteen years.

'Yes. I just spoke to Zarina. She just found out.' He had sat down on the sofa and she went and lowered herself beside him. 'There is a second wife and two children in Karachi,' he continued. 'He's been married to her for seven years.'

Massud had never needed Nargis more, it seemed, than he did over the coming days and weeks. No one had ever suspected anything of Majid, and the pain Zarina was suffering was difficult to witness. Months later Zarina asked for a divorce and eventually she moved abroad, and Massud had clung to Nargis for certainty and support in the face of the betrayal – needing her fidelity and reassurance, holding onto something he could trust. It was a long time before he managed to recover.

And in this way everything had remained how it had been at the beginning.

Nargis knew she did not deserve any sympathy for what she had done, but it was also true that she had never caused any pain to Massud during all other aspects of their shared life, which was the central thing in her existence. The years had passed and, yes, she did live through moments of anxiety – it would lose intensity and then strengthen, then weaken again. And then one April morning he was lying in her arms on the edge of the Grand Trunk Road, his blood on both their clothes.

27

The man from the military-intelligence agency, Major Burhan, arrived with five companions at Nargis and Massud's house in Badami Bagh.

The policeman sitting beside the door, on the chair from the kitchen, knew the major by now and he stood up respectfully, apprehensively. He unlocked the door for them and stepped aside. Major Burhan did not acknowledge him. He walked into the house, preceded by the five lieutenants, one of whom fastened the door bolt behind him.

Major Burhan went into the couple's bedroom. Systematically over the past week they had been examining the contents of the house, trying to understand where Nargis could have disappeared to. The clue, the essential detail, was here somewhere. The rooms were in disarray, the drawers upended onto the floors, folders and document boxes and portfolios opened on any available surface. Almost everyone the couple had known had been visited by the intelligence agents. The most intimate friends had been identified and their movements and houses were being watched in case Nargis contacted them, and some of the landlines and mobile phones had been bugged.

Whichever room they happened to be in, they dropped their cigarettes on the floor after they had finished smoking them, putting them out with their boots. The house was littered with the flattened ends.

This morning two of them were investigating the contents of the wardrobe in the room that had been Helen's. It stood open with the hangers stripped, and they were placing all similar items in separate piles on the bed.

One of the lieutenants walked in from the study, holding a large-format book entitled *100+1 Architects and Their Creations* and handed it to Major Burhan. The book was a decade and a half old. Major Burhan looked at the table of contents and turned the pages until he came to the entry on Nargis and Massud. There were photographs of a number of houses they had designed – some of which Major Burhan or his men had in fact visited over the past few days. Isolated in large letters amid all the smaller ones, there was a quote from Massud about a mosque the couple hoped to build on an island in the Vela River one day.

Major Burhan finished reading the pages and closed the book, his index finger marking the place. He looked around the room, at the ammonites and the brain coral set on the windowsills, the skull of a cobra with the wide flaring bones of the hood underneath, the photographs on the wall, the long rows of white-spined journals and magazines.

The American man was languishing in jail, facing a triple murder charge. He had been separated from the rest of the prisoners, and the guards around him did not carry weapons, a concession for his safety that American officials had managed to extract from the prison staff. The United States Consulate in Zamana had negotiated another safeguard: a team of dogs was tasting his food in case it was poisoned.

Pakistan had hoped that the US government would tell them immediately what they already suspected, that the man was not a diplomat, that he was working for the CIA. They expected that a deal would be made as quickly and as soon as possible: the USA would admit the truth privately, and with immaculate stealth the killer would be spirited out of the country, never to return again. Pakistan could extract certain favours and advantages immediately, or it could be leverage for the future. But everyone was astonished when the Americans insisted, and continued to insist, that he was not with the CIA and had to be released on the grounds that he was a foreign diplomat with immunity from local laws, even those prohibiting murder. Perhaps they feared that if they admitted he was a spy, the Pakistanis would kill him in jail.

More than two weeks after the shootings on the Grand Trunk Road, the American president had offered his first comments about the affair. The matter was simple, the president said in a news conference, 'our diplomat in Pakistan' should be immediately released under the 'very simple principle' of diplomatic immunity.

'The president neglected to explain what kind of diplomat carries a loaded gun,' Major Burhan had said to the chief of Pakistan's military-intelligence agency, General——.

Major Burhan came from a military family and the general was his maternal uncle.

The general had in fact spoken privately by phone to the director of the CIA within hours of the murders, and he was furious when the director lied to him:

'No, he's not one of ours,' the director had said, emphatically.

The general, whose team had already begun to approach the relatives of the victims, to inform them that they would be required to pardon the American man very soon, now decided to leave the killer's fate in the hands of the judges in Zamana.

'The United States has just lost its chance to quickly end this dispute,' he said to Major Burhan, incensed. The general had a hard hawk-like patrician nose, and the skin around his eyes was very dark. He was a chain smoker and once, during a ten-hour meeting that had continued later than expected and still showed no sign of ending, he had asked the peons to hand over their packs of cheap K2 cigarettes. In 1998, when al-Qaeda had bombed US embassies in Kenya and Tanzania, the general had worked with the CIA in setting up a sixty-person commando team that was trained in the United States, and whose aim was to find and capture Osama bin Laden. In May 1990, when tensions between India and Pakistan rose over the issue of Kashmir, and the Deputy Director of the CIA was sent to both countries to quieten things, the general had listened silently to the deputy director, who had said that the USA had war-gamed the matter and calculated that Pakistan would lose any war with India, that Indian soldiers would end up occupying Pakistani territory.

Now he felt even more insulted, the sense of betrayal immense.

Soon after the death of the woman who had swallowed battery acid, the Americans confessed the truth to the Pakistanis, spymaster to spymaster.

It was a week before the general's rage died down. Then he told the Americans how they should resolve the situation, what he had planned all along: under Sharia Law, a killer could pay the relatives of his victim 'blood money' and walk away a free man.

'No one would dare object,' he had smiled at his nephew. 'We'll have them hauled into court for blasphemy. The Islamists want this man hanged, but they also want Sharia Law. They have been asking for it since the inception of the country.'

In Nargis and Massud's study, one of the lieutenants opened a large envelope and pulled out the layered thickness of paper it contained. With a degree of care that increased with each passing moment, he began to unfold it. It was large and rectangular like a cluster of kites, unfurling and spreading from his hands. When he started to comprehend that it was in fact a building constructed out of paper, he went out into the garden with it. One of the other lieutenants joined him and together they erected the structure on the grass, suspending it under the trees. Lengths of string had been glued to the paper roof, and they reached up and tied them to the branches. The floor had to be weighed down with small stones. It was a copy of the Charagar mausoleum, and it was large enough to step inside, just.

The two of them went in and brought out armfuls of other envelopes, sending them spinning to all possible corners of the garden, like distributing seeds. For the rest of the day, whenever they needed relief from the monotony of their task, the two lieutenants appeared in the garden and put up one of the buildings. The paper was glowing in the sunlight, the texture of pulp visible. They moved around this paper city, something one could take in at a glance, the grass on the ground resembling avenues or streets.

One of the lieutenants approached Major Burhan in Nargis's bedroom, and handed him a small black-and-white photograph, of a man with two little girls.

At the back there was the stamp of the photographer's studio, located in the city of Lyallpur, and there were the words *Me and my sister and my uncle.*

The small envelope from which the photograph had been extracted contained a letter too, which Major Burhan now took out.

It was an ordinary letter, from an adult to a young girl, who seemed to be attending a boarding school. The words offered advice, passed on everyday news. It was addressed to someone named Margaret, and had been written by a man named Solomon.

'Who is this "me" in the photograph?' the lieutenant said, looking at the back of the image.

'I think we should find this Solomon in Lyallpur,' Major Burhan told him. 'From the letter he appears to be some sort of priest.' He returned the photograph and the letter to the envelope and handed them to the lieutenant. 'It's probably nothing, but still, I want you to contact the people we know in the Christian community in Lyallpur.'

Major Burhan opened the book of architects again. There was no photograph of Nargis but there was one of a young Massud. He resembled his dead brother a good deal.

Major Burhan had familiarised himself with the details of the young journalist's death.

A decade ago, when the world learned that Pakistani nuclear scientists had been selling atomic secrets to Iran, Libya and North Korea, the chief nuclear physicist A. Q. Khan was dismissed from his post, and he was made to appear on national TV to declare that he was guilty of transferring nuclear technology and knowhow to Iran between 1989 and 1991, and to North Korea and Libya between 1991 and 1997. The man's daughter however had managed to fly out of Pakistan with documents that could prove that the senior military and government officials had always been in charge of the covert nuclear-sales programme.

The general knew that the woman had to be stopped.

From Pakistan she had gone to Dubai, but there she made the mistake of calling Islamabad. The phone call was traced but by the time the general's men broke into the Dubai apartment, she had moved on to England. The general's team turned the place upside down looking for the dossier but could not locate it. Upon arrival in London she was debriefed by MI5, who were keen to know what secrets she had brought with her. It was her father's affidavit, and its contents were hidden from the world to this day.

But Major Burhan could guess what they were. A thirty-year network, involving thousands of scientists, middlemen, agents, suppliers, importers and exporters. Pakistan's nuclear secrets were scattered all across the planet – documents thrown into disused South African gold mines; files drained from the hard drives of hotel guests in Shanghai. It was precisely one of these secrets – the name of a military-intelligence officer who was involved in the nuclear proliferation – that Massud's brother had uncovered.

A secret for which he paid with his life.

In addition there was the matter of him having refused to write stories in favour of the military-intelligence agency. The very attractive financial incentives he had been offered failing to sway him.

It was seven o'clock in the evening when Major Burhan and his lieutenants left the house, summoning the policeman to carry away the armfuls of books, files and paperwork they needed. He in turn waved over any passerby he could see.

The paper city remained in the garden. No one saw the thin walls begin to vibrate gently at midnight a day later, the air pressure changing. The grass blades thrashing where they stood fixed to the ground, like the needles of a measuring instrument. They were the first few hints of the dust storm that soon arrived over the city. Even if someone had been there and had run out, they could not have untied the strings from the branches fast enough now, their eyes and skin attacked by the dust. It went into the paper buildings through the doors and windows or it ripped open the fragile roofs and poured itself in through there. It was as though the city were attempting to become airborne. The walls came apart within five minutes and twisted away on the currents, and when the storm died down fifteen minutes later nothing remained but tatters that hung from the branches.

28

Helen was in the library, surrounded by the smell of sun-heated paper. She placed her lantern on a shelf and took out a stack of books and carried them to the window.

Termites and white ants had marked most of them. The holes they had bored through the thickness of a book appeared as though a bird's long beak had pierced the covers, in order to extract words, as a beak would reach into a tree's bark and pull out insects or caterpillars.

She opened one and carefully tore out the two endpapers, from the front and back. The thick blank pages appeared yellow in the lantern's flame.

She picked up the next book and then the ones after that, ripping out the two blank pages from each.

She walked out of the library with the sheaf of these and went along the night trees into the kitchen. Over the next hour she stitched all the small pages into one single sheet. A perforation here and there by a creature – she found those pleasing too. She rolled up the sheet and went out onto the veranda with it. As a child, she had been unable to believe her good fortune when she discovered this phenomenon of endpapers: there they were in the thousands of books in Nargis and Massud's study, their whiteness even as milk. She had managed to amass a thick pile of them one afternoon before she was discovered by Grace.

Imran saw her lamp from the distance and appeared beside her. He was naked, the clean lines of his body wet from the river, his hair drenched flat. She walked with him to his house through the grass.

Her dreams in this place were rich in comprehension.

During the night she lifted the mosquito netting and got out of bed and lit the lamp. She unrolled the large gold-sewn sheet and began to draw his sleeping form onto it. She moved with skill, the mind combining its existence with the hand. The only sound was the pencil and her fingers scraping faintly against the paper. She was collecting clues to his character and personality through his physical features. Remembering the curl of irritability on the lips when the ghazals became too much for him. 'I hate to break it to Urdu poets but the bulbul does not visit the rosebush because it is in love with the rose. It wants to eat the aphids.' There were the muscles along the back which tightened when he was above her during lovemaking. The marks of Indian soldiers' torture on his back, shoulders and legs, the welts of beatings on the soles of his feet. The two lines of anguish that appeared between the eyebrows when he told her about the origin of each set of marks. It was all there, this information, inscribed on his body.

What she longed for were a few hours when her mind was free of other considerations, so she could think about him and nothing else. She felt a little selfish in wishing for this. But she wasn't sure what was occurring between them, whether she was being her best self. She was trying to be. But these conditions were not normal. The chimes needed free movement in the air in order to sing. Placed on the floor, they were silenced by gravity.

She was old enough to know that neither of them was old enough yet to know what they felt. Perhaps he would disagree. Perhaps she herself would disagree with this later.

She looked at him.

This would suffice for now. For the rest she would have to wait patiently and see.

*

Towards dawn he got up and turned the sheet over and began to draw her on the other side. When the sun rose he went out and held the sheet up to the light, to see where the lines on either side crossed and overlapped.

VI

THE DESIRE PATH

29

Helen and Moscow went into the city.

She had woken him and told him to get ready, not revealing the surprise, not telling him why they were leaving the island.

He did not wish to tell her that he would rather not go into certain areas of the city, did not wish to add to her anxieties and disquiet.

'Just give me a hint of where we are going.'

'No. And don't worry, I'll be safe.' She covered the lower half of her face with her dupatta.

'OK.'

Later when he came into the kitchen of the two women, Nargis did not divulge any details either. Smiling, Helen led him to the double-height door in the island's wall and they went out through its arch, Nargis just telling them to be careful. They walked to the bazaar and entered a rickshaw.

Many decades ago, the poet Wamaq Saleem, a young man at the time, had walked for eighteen miles to the house of the woman he loved, to declare his feelings for her – a journey that took him from one end of Zamana to the other.

The roads he had taken were now considered a single thoroughfare and it was named after him and the beloved woman, a continuous line running through the city. And Helen had decided to journey along it with Imran.

An hour later Nargis too left the island. They hadn't taken the keys with them so she wondered how they would get back in, in her absence. She wrote a note on one of the endpapers Helen had left lying around on a shelf and pinned it to the door, informing them the keys were under the large rock beside the frame. Telling them she would return late at night, to not be anxious about her.

From the bazaar she went to the Daewoo coach station and bought a return ticket to Lyallpur.

At fifty-two, she could still evoke the colours of the fountain pens she had owned as a young girl. There was the pink one, a faded blue one, and a deep green. With the logo stamped in gold along the shaft. Eagle, or Bahadur, or Dollar. Seraphina was two years older, and was required to write with fountain pens before Nargis. (It was possible that her first – the blue Bahadur – was a hand-me-down from Seraphina. Or was it Solomon's?) Nargis remembered being impatient, unable to wait until she was older, to jettison pencils. In her mind the fountain pens conferred a form of distinction. To be trusted with the large dangerously spillable inkpot. A bladder, like a thin deflated balloon, lived inside the pen's body. She would dip the nib into the ink and first depress and then release that bladder, to draw the ink into it.

Nargis.

Margaret.

A preoccupation of medieval Christian scholars was attempting to solve the Riddles of the Queen of Sheba, not specified in the Bible. Depicted in medieval tapestries of the time, one popular riddle was Sheba presenting Solomon with two identical-seeming flowers and asking him to identify which was genuine. The wise King had had some bees brought in and they had flown to the real one.

*

On the coach to Lyallpur, she sat beside the window, the focus of her eyes moving from the landscape to her own reflection in the pane.

Just the other day she had been thinking about her grand-father's mind becoming confused in old age, how he would draw a cross on his hand. 'This way I know who I am.' But now a new detail came to her:

One day, in a moment of mischievousness, Seraphina had rubbed off the mark as he slept and drawn one on her own skin. When the ancient man awoke and saw her hand he had looked utterly confounded. 'But if you are me, who am I?' he had asked.

In Lyallpur, Nargis hired a horse-drawn tonga that traversed the bazaars with her in the back seat, facing away from the dir-ection she was travelling in.

The hooves sounded on the tarmac and the driver kept up a conversation with someone on his mobile phone throughout. She had arrived at the hour when the heat was at its highest, though the crowds still bustled. The bazaars and streets were more or less as she remembered from six years ago, which was the last time she had paid a surreptitious visit. It was a smaller city than Zamana, the manners and clothing subtly different. Things required for the day-to-day living could be bought here within a smaller radius of shops than in Zamana. She sat look-ing out from under the khaki hood of the horse carriage. The large churning mass of uniformed children released from the gate of a school was like something pouring from a torn box. A pair of sewage workers disappeared underground through a manhole, their dhotis hitched up above the knees, their thin, ribbed torsos bare. The photographer's studio was still there at the edge of the bazaar, a small peepal tree sprouting in a crack in its wall, the ruin of a temple abandoned by Hindus in 1947 standing beside it. Oxen in pairs were pulling carts with cloth sides as high as a boat's sails, filled cruelly with hay all the way to the top.

She decided to visit the Christian graveyard before going to Solomon's house.

She pulled up some of the grass blades with her hands from Seraphina's grave, though on the whole it looked well tended. She lifted a small clump of soil and enclosed it in her palm. Its outer layers crumbled eagerly but the centre was firm. She ran her fingers along the carved letters on the headstone. The shadows within the indentations moved with the sun as she sat there. Though her hair was like a schoolgirl's – two braids that trailed over her shoulders – Seraphina was twenty-three years old when she died. She was utterly withdrawn and remote during that period, speaking only when spoken to, sometimes not even then.

To the west of the church – along a curved path that emerged from Solomon's house at the time – there was a luminous green pond. Water buffaloes entered its shallower edges and emerged with the sequin-like weeds stuck to their hides, the teeth moving under the rubbery muzzles as they chewed the cud. Seraphina had asked Solomon to bring her a handful of lotuses from there, with the thought of transplanting them in their small garden pool. She herself would not step out of the house even for that small a distance. She had always loved the lotus, the curves forming a blossom eight inches in diameter, and the seedpods that resembled the spouts of watering cans. In winter they would be detectably warmer than the air, maintaining a high temperature to attract cold-blooded insects.

Solomon had gone out to the pond with a plastic tub and brought back three leaves and the rhizomes trailing muddy roots. There were two large flowerbuds, enclosed as though in overlapping scales, reminiscent of an artichoke or a pangolin. She and Solomon dropped them into their pool but as the weeks passed it was obvious that they had failed to take. What occurred next was surprising: one day Seraphina walked out to the pond on her own, in order to bring back more of the rhizomes. Leaving the house for the first time in four years.

Other than Solomon, she had not spoken to a man for more than seven months.

He told Nargis later that he had watched her from the window as she took the first hesitant steps beyond the gate, fearfully looking back. Margaret had just visited from Zamana the previous week, and he thought she had finally convinced her sister to venture out.

She disappeared from his view. Still at the window, he imagined her walking down the curved path towards the pond, towards the location on its edge where the lotus leaves emerged from the water. He went downstairs some minutes later, imagining he would see her returning with the plants she had pulled up, the toes and the soles of her feet covered in mud.

But she was not there. He went along the path and described a circle around the pond, eventually calling out to her. The buffaloes were in the water at one place, submerged up to their necks, looking at him with open curiosity as they always did with humans, the spines and hipbones jutting out like archipelagos. He felt panic rising in himself, a wave of nausea. There were scattered clumps of water hyacinth on the surface. Looking for the colour and pattern of her shalwar kameez, he went away from the pond and walked to the road.

It was only after the funeral – after the mud-covered body had been brought out of the water – that Margaret revealed the part she had played in the death.

Stupefied by the turn of events, she told Solomon that she had been pretending to be a Muslim in Zamana.

He seemed not to understand. She had expected the

beginning of disgust and revulsion, but all she saw was confusion in his features.

'What do you mean? What are you saying?'

'At college in Zamana I pretend to be a Muslim. Everyone there thinks my name is Nargis.'

'Are you telling me you have converted?'

'I just pretend. I began to do it when I was fourteen—'

'What does that have to do with Seraphina? She drowned trying to pull up a rhizome.'

He was looking at her the way he sometimes looked at his own father, after his confusing acts and statements, the mind fissured by dementia.

'During my last visit I told her what I've just told you.'

It was all so recent: some of the gifts she had brought on that visit were still unwrapped, still in the bags. The bottles of ink Solomon liked from Zamana's Urdu Bazaar. The tin of habshi-halwa a friend from Karachi had brought for her and which she had saved for Seraphina.

'And I told her that someone was threatening to expose me. That I might even go to prison, be questioned by police. I have been receiving anonymous letters of late, someone saying that they know I have an unforgivable secret. They don't specify anything. I told her the police would probably come here to talk to the two of you.'

There was the beginning of comprehension at last, the facts sinking down inside him. Margaret had got up and come towards him and placed her arms around him where he stood, all indulgence having drained away from his features. She pressed herself against him, asking – challenging – him to return the embrace, more and more desperate when he didn't, almost burrowing into him. She felt as though she had murdered her sister, and he was behaving as though that was indeed the case.

For months, years, she continued to expect a letter from

him, a telephone call reproaching her, or a visit from him, demanding a complete explanation. So much so that during the initial months of her marriage she had thought of Massud as a temporary presence in her life, someone who would be taken away from her once the truth about her was revealed by Solomon. But none of it had transpired. Solomon had turned away from her, his fury unreleased. He was protecting and punishing her at the same time.

As she stood there embracing him that day, it was some time before his bewildered hands had pushed her away. It was an act as simple as it was final, his head averted and eyes pinched shut as though she had just struck him.

She asked the tonga-wallah to take the road that passed between the church and the bishop's house. Telling him to make the horse slow down when they neared the two buildings. There was no one that she could see, no presence in any window. The past sealed up. The churchyard, and the balcony on the first floor of the house, with its grille forged in a paisley pattern, were both empty. She had visited this location in exactly this manner – that is to say, secretly – on a number of occasions over the years. She had seen the curtains change, had seen that grille replace the older wooden one. The last time she had asked the tonga-wallah to stop and had got out and paid him. She had opened the gate and advanced into the garden. *And why take ye thought for raiment? Consider the lilies of the field, how they grow . . .* She would remember his voice, she was certain. In her mind's eye she had observed tranquillity on his face. She'd stood there, as if waiting for someone to appear beside her. Only when she was about to knock had she stopped, feeling she had no right to disturb his peace, to remind him of everything at his age. She had glimpsed a medicine bottle on the windowsill and the fact that she didn't know what it was for seemed momentous. Although she was here, the distance was deceptive, like distances on a map where a few inches could represent hundreds or thousands of miles. And perhaps it was like a mirror, a realm only an inch away that could never be entered.

There was the grief. After what had occurred at the police station, he had become closer to Seraphina, strengthening a bond that had been weak in the earlier years. All this had happened while Margaret was away in Zamana.

Now, just as she was about to ask the tonga-wallah to stop the carriage and let her out, she saw Solomon come out of the back door of his house, accompanied by the man from the military-intelligence agency.

They were talking, the old man's head bent, as they came through the garden towards the road where her tonga was passing.

She raised the edge of her dupatta and covered half her face, the hooves of the horse continuing their clip-clopping. He had aged since the last time she saw him, sitting at the back of the church during his sermon six years ago.

Neither the soldier-spy nor Solomon looked towards her carriage and it carried her to the end of the road and took her away.

How had they found him? How long ago? It was the photograph from the house in Badami Bagh, she was sure. And her mind was too numb to think what they could be asking him, what they were threatening him with.

*

It was 2 a.m. when she arrived back on the island, Helen and Moscow coming with a lantern to let her in.

'Where did you go?'

'I'll tell you, later . . . I'll tell you one day . . .'

In one's twenties there was the confusion and activity of constructing a life. Being in one's fifties was trying to understand what it all meant.

In her room she lit a candle and lay down on the bed. What were they threatening him with?

Years later Nargis was to find out that the anonymous letters had been written by someone in Massud's family and were caused by romantic jealousy. A young cousin who was in love with Massud, who correctly suspected Nargis of having begun a physical relationship with him. That was the indefensible secret referred to in the letters. It was a sin and also a criminal offence, then as now.

In the mornings when Helen walked back from Imran's house, she went along the line of flattened grass that their feet had by now created between the two houses. There was a stone path that she could have taken. It had a curve to it that added no more than thirty seconds to the journey. The path flattened through the grass, however, was a straight line and she preferred that. She had encountered such shortcuts in many places around the city, people forgoing the official route in favour of a quicker informal one. Massud had told her once that such a path was known as 'the desire path'.

If she lived in a colder province she would wait for the first snow and study the patterns of people's feet through parks, gardens and hills. The lines that had the highest number of impressions, that was where she would lay down paths.

Helen emerged from the staircase and entered the kitchen, where Nargis and Imran were preparing lunch.

She was smiling and holding the small radio. She approached and touched Nargis's shoulder.

'I know where my father will be two evenings from today.'

Nargis turned and saw her delighted face.

'He will be at the Charagar mausoleum on Thursday evening.'

Nargis lowered the heat under the pan. Imran was washing the fenugreek leaves in a bowl and he stopped too, looking now at Nargis, now at the girl.

'The annual celebration,' Nargis said. 'The saint's death anniversary. Lily and Grace always attended.'

After Grace was gone Lily had continued to attend by himself.

'I don't remember them ever missing it,' Helen said. 'They went and placed three roses on the grave. It's a week-long celebration but he always went on the first day.'

Nargis approached a chair and sat down, thinking.

'There will be thousands of people there. Pilgrims from all over Pakistan,' she said. 'And it's a vast complex.'

'I know.' Helen was grinning. 'But he will be there.'

Imran was smiling at the happiness on Helen's face. She turned to him:

'He *will* be there.'

Imran knew about the saint, had known about him even in Kashmir. He was fabled and loved. Hindus, Sikhs, Christians and Muslims of many sects came to him in search of blessing. Female, male, and hijra. People prayed or just sang and danced, reciting the Koran as well as the saint's own poetry. And the sect sponsored by Saudi Arabia loathed him and his mausoleum for that reason.

He nodded. 'If that is what you want. We'll have to be careful, but we should go.'

The location of the mausoleum was where the saint had lived in the eleventh century, beside a small mosque he had built with his own hands, dying there in the year 1066.

Helen went to stand beside Nargis.

'There will be thousands there and it's a huge building, but there is only one grave, and I will sit by it all evening. Till midnight and beyond. At some point he'll appear.'

It was Vitruvius who had advised that libraries should face the east, to catch the morning light and reduce the humidity that might damage books. There was a stack of books on Nargis's bedside table that she had carried into her room from the mosque's library. There were also the steadily multiplying reams of newspapers that Imran brought back from the bazaar each day. She read these for a while by the light of the lamp before falling asleep.

Though sleep tonight was difficult yet again. Twenty-four hours had gone by, and she still didn't know what to do about seeing Bishop Solomon in the company of the man from military intelligence.

The previous hours had been too full of Helen's excitement, and her own guarded version of it; the prospect that they might encounter Lily the day after tomorrow and bring him to this place of relative safety on the river.

As she fell asleep – it was almost 3 a.m. – her last thoughts were about Solomon. She told herself that she would decide what to do about him on Friday, with Lily here with them.

32

Aysha – in the house behind the mosque in Badami Bagh, all its windows boarded up – was trying to think of a way to visit the Charagar mausoleum.

It was Wednesday evening, and tomorrow the annual celebration would begin, marking the day and hour of his death, according to the various chronograms and chronicles. She would often walk across the green onyx courtyards of the mausoleum with her father to say a prayer at the saint's grave. Almost four months ago on a visit there, she had asked Charagar for reassurance that her son would not suffer too greatly in life due to his injuries. That very night Billu had appeared in her dream – while his real self lay asleep near her. He was standing beside a personage she understood to be Charagar. Both of his legs were intact and he was smiling and in the morning she took that to be the reassurance she had sought, and she vowed to visit the saint's mausoleum on his next death anniversary.

From the shelf she picked up the oil with which she massaged Billu's thighs before sleep each night.

He was sitting propped up against the pillow, wearing a singlet and his underwear because of the heat, the artificial legs removed and dropped onto the floor. He had told her that on the whole he liked the boarding up, that he felt safe and protected. She poured some oil into the cup of her hand and rubbed it between both palms.

'I'll be quick.'

'Alligator Bear Cormorant Duck Elk Frog Gull Heron Iguana Jackal Kangaroo Lark Moose Newt Ostrich Pelican

Quail Rhinoceros Stork Turtle Urial Vole Weasel Xray-fish Yak Zebra.'

'You are a clown.'

'Mama?'

'Yes, darling.'

'I wish we had a TV.'

'It'll upset your grandfather. We can't hurt his feelings, can we?'

'You said you watched TV when you were my age.'

'I didn't grow up in this house. I grew up in another city. And anyway, aren't the programs you watch at Farzana's house enough?'

He grinned. 'I have never ever watched TV at Farzana's house or Tariq's house or Simon's house.'

'One day your tongue will turn black from all the lies you tell.'

'Audi Bentley Cadillac Dodge Equus Ferrari Golf Honda In-victa Jaguar Kia Lexus Mercedes Nissan Oldsmobile Porsche Qingqi Rolls-Royce Suzuki Toyota Ultima Volvo Wiesmann Xedos Yamaha Zenvo.'

'As I said, a clown.'

'Mama. I will have a computer when I am ten, yes? You promised.'

'Of course. I have already started saving.'

'With an internet connection?'

'Yes, you'll need it to do your homework, to look things up for your essays, to know how to apply to which university.'

He was smiling hugely and mischievously to himself as he listened.

'What?'

'Nothing.' He was trying not to laugh.

'Tell me this instant or I'll tickle.'

A squeal of pleasure from him at the threat.

'OK, OK. But you can watch TV on a computer if you have

an internet connection. You and grandfather will think I am doing my homework, but I'll be watching cartoons.'

'You rascal.'

As her fingers worked she watched his expression intently, to note how he reacted to the varying pressure. 'How does the oil feel?'

'Tingly. Like drinking hot tea after eating a spicy samosa. But on the legs not on the tongue.'

Ten times an hour she marvelled at his resilience in the face of what the world had done to him. At one point he had made the neighbourhood children believe that the missile from the American drone was just a rumour he and his family had spread. 'The real reason for my missing legs is that I had wings growing on my ankles and was able to fly.' The magical legs, apparently, had been put away for safekeeping because a sorcerer wanted possession of them. 'My mother and I have come to Zamana to hide from him for a little while.'

The room was suffocating in the May heat, because of the windows and the absence of electricity.

'America Belgium Cameroon Denmark England France Ghana Hungary Iceland Japan Kazakhstan Libya Malta Norway Oman Pakistaaaaaaaaaaaaaaaaaaaaaaaaaaaaaaaaaaaaaaan Qatar Russia Sweden Turkey Uzbekistan Vietnam Wales Yemen Zimbabwe.'

'I am finished.' She kissed the air twice where each knee would have been, and he slid himself lower on the bed.

He crossed his arms on his chest and gave a sigh. 'I wish I was ten.'

'What else do you wish?' She was arranging the pillow under his head.

'I wish Uncle Shakeel would go away.'

'What did I say about respecting your elders?'

He closed his eyes and turned his back to her. 'I am hot. Would you fan me, please?'

As he fell asleep she sat beside him with the hand fan, making sure the draughts she created did not extinguish the candle, and then she picked up his limbs from the floor. With the passing of years she would need to find money for the increasingly larger prosthetics he would require. The bones of his spine would have to be monitored carefully as he grew, any misalignment prevented. She was hoarding a coin at a time for all this. He hated using crutches, the marks left by the friction and the pressure at the armpits. In addition he felt ashamed of the empty space between his knees and the ground.

With disinfectant she wiped the cups in which the stumps were housed, and then she embraced both false legs tightly to herself. At times, to pretend to be courageous was difficult. She felt like someone held within lightning.

The awfulness of being responsible for the deaths here in Badami Bagh that night, for the destruction of homes and the injuries to bodies and limbs – it never really left her, and the smell of smoke was constant in her head to this day, merging with the smell of smoke she had brought with her to Zamana from Waziristan. Her existence had become a question to her and she felt she needed to go and stand at the head of the saint's grave, to ask him how best to proceed with the rest of her life.

She hadn't been allowed to step out of the house since the night the minaret revealed her relationship with Lily. She had not been allowed to communicate with anyone but her father, her son and Shakeel. He had demanded to see her mobile phone. But she had destroyed it in time, knowing Lily's number was in the address book and the call log. Later she had found Lily's phone in her room and smashed that too, burying the pieces in the garden.

The child had been taken out of school and was being educated by her at home. She had resisted this initially, had demanded the boy continue with his schooling, but Shakeel had threatened that he would send him away to a madrassa in Waziristan.

While her father and Shakeel were questioning her that night, Billu had woken up in the next room and she had gone to him. They followed her in to continue with their questions as she and the boy clung to each other on the bed. Suddenly it had occurred to her brother-in-law to ask the child.

'Does your mother ever meet a man, a stranger?'

She had tightened her grip on him, to restrict any sound or movement he might make, his face pressed into her clothing.

He had asked again and then managed to wrench the child away from her and walked away with him, holding him under one arm, the stumps flailing. Locking her in the room when she attempted to follow. Half an hour later the door opened and the cleric brought the boy in, his small weight a visible strain on the old body.

'Would you like some milk?' she asked Billu, once the sense of tranquillity returned to him, reassured by her presence. He didn't answer straight away. She had heard him being threatened.

'Yes. With crushed ice and Rooh Afza in it.'

'What did he ask you?' she said as he was drinking, a pink moustache forming on his upper lip.

'He said, "Does anyone come to the room?"'

'And what did you say?'

'I told him the truth.'

She got up and began to fold and put away the clothes she had washed earlier that day.

'And what is the truth?'

'I said, "Yes, the ghost of the Hanged Mutineer comes."'

She looked at his sleeping eyes now, the thick black eyelashes, the mind behind them busy with dreams and muddles. The lids were not fully closed, leaving perhaps a quarter or fifth of the eye visible. As though he remained on guard even in sleep. There was a point, earlier, when he used to wake up in panic, saying, 'I'm disappearing, my legs are gone.' Sometimes he threw a tantrum, demanding to know why he should still remember how to knot his shoelaces.

Shakeel wouldn't want her to leave the house, and he certainly wouldn't want her to visit the Charagar mausoleum. To him and his sect the place was an abomination. A den of heretics, innovators, and blasphemers.

Their idea of limits was fierce and fearsome. They said life had to be pure, while the saint had said it was the process of purification.

She looked up when her father came into the room, his small hands carrying the encyclopaedia of sins and the rosary.

She reached forward and smoothed his long white beard, its liquid-seeming waves. He would sit with her for a while before sleep.

In the shadow of the mosque, the domes against which angels reclined to rest in the evenings, she had lied to him that night about the minaret's announcement, saying that it was all slander, the work of mischief-makers. There was no way to prove that the crucifix discovered in the mosque belonged to Lily.

To save a life you could violate every commandment of Allah, she knew that. He himself had said it to her.

She opened the book of sins now and turned its ancient pages without really looking. She had known it all her life, and as always it deposited a combination of smells on her hands, of paper, dead petals, and worn leather. It was pleasant but with a clear-cut note of seriousness – what she would imagine as a child the breath of something like a leopard to be.

They sat beside each other without words. It was really quiet with the fan off.

'What are you thinking?' he said.

She shook her head, but then found the energy to speak.

'One day,' she said, 'when I was a child I saw you break a lock without much effort. It was a tiny lock, one of those Made-in-China things, and I'm sure I could break one myself now. The key had gone missing, so you just twisted the lock off the hasp, not even gritting your teeth. And I saw how weak a lock could be in reality. It's the *idea* of a lock that signals "out of reach" and "impossible".' She smiled at him. 'It's the suggestion of a lock that is strong, not the lock.'

A little while later, after the cleric had retired to his room and she too had extinguished the candle, she understood that with that memory she had made up her mind to walk out of the house tomorrow evening and go to Charagar.

She lay awake in the darkness and waited. She had never realised how completely alone women were in the world.

At dawn the light spread over the pilgrims sleeping in the green courtyards of the mausoleum. The river flowed outside the onyx building in a metallic curve. Some people had stayed awake, reading the Koran all night or meditating among the arches. *Na-qisaan ra pir-e-kamil* was what they said in Persian about him. 'The imperfect finds the perfect teacher.'

The preparations were being made – at a flexible pace in the morning, with the full pleasures of slowness, and then with a certain degree of promptness into the afternoon and late afternoon. Men climbed onto the central dome, stringing bunting and coloured lights from the tip of the finial to various corners above the courtyards. There was the hammering together of a podium for the Qawali singers. A truck brought firewood for the cooking, and sacks of rice and flour arrived along with cartfuls of vegetables, and sheep and goat carcasses with the kidneys still attached from the city's slaughterhouses.

Nargis, Helen and Imran were there by 4 p.m. Passing

through the metal detectors, Helen led them determinedly through the veranda towards the basement shrine, where the grave was located, a staircase spiralling down to that level. Near the top step, a woman stood perfectly still, singing a rest-ful *naat*, the words reassuring the listeners that the powerful and the dominant were not the measure of all things. There were ten entrances to the complex and Helen had asked the rickshaw-wallah to drop them at the one nearest to the base-ment. The lower half of her face was concealed behind her dupatta, as was Nargis's.

As the sun set, the crowd thickened, seemingly with each passing minute, on the ground floor of the building as well as in the shrine where Helen and Nargis had settled cross-legged in a corner. There was an energy in their silence.

It was strange for the senses to be among so many people, amid such cacophony, after the days on the island, its weed meadow and its insects making soundless rings on the water-filled ditches, the germinating stones of dropped fruit.

The saint had roamed from the Indus to the Caspian Sea, Azerbaijan, Damascus, Ramallah, Bistam. In the centuries that followed his death, wandering thinkers and storytellers had arrived to meditate at his grave, before spreading into the subcontinent to establish their own Sufi orders. Aspiring to a new beginning for humanity. This evening devotees had come from India, Bangladesh, Nepal, and from England as well as from the Pakistani neighbourhoods in other Western countries. Little Pakistan in Brooklyn. Little Karachi in Oslo. Pakcelona.

To begin with Imran stayed with them, in a state of hyper-vigilance, going up to the courtyard now and then but returning very quickly, despite Nargis reassuring him that they were out of harm's way here. Eventually he was comfortable enough to stay away from the basement for thirty minutes – to stand shoulder to shoulder with supplicants and beggars and officiates, the overworked and the unemployed, and say his prayers in the courtyard. They could not afford a pilgrimage to Mecca, so they had come here and asked the saint to intercede with Allah and Muhammad on their behalf. There were doctors who treated the sick without charge during the celebration, as a form of devotion. There was a distinct trace of marijuana in one section of the arches, and underneath the dome the wasps were enlarging their houses, chamber by chamber. The helicopter of a politician landed a street away and soon every space became even more congested, indoors as well as out, because various lanes and pathways and corridors were blocked by his security team. 'The Koran says, "When kings enter a city, they ruin it"', someone said to Imran when the politician's helicopter left.

He bought bottles of water and took them to Nargis and Helen. Back up on the ground floor he fell into various brief conversations. The descendants of the saint, the men and wo-men who controlled the mausoleum and the saint's legacy, were avaricious and more than a few could even be described as charlatans, Imran knew. Kidnappers were said to work the premises too, and there were gangs of pickpockets managed by the police.

The cauldrons of food had been cooking for most of the day, and people were buying them now and having them distributed to the poor and the pilgrims, to show gratitude for the various boons the saint had granted them: a son, a job, recovery from an illness, desired outcome in a court case, visa to a Western or Gulf country. Chappatis were stacked a metre high, and a camel was slaughtered and its meat fitted into twelve cauldrons. At eight thirty he stood in the queue and was given a plastic shopping bag of pilau rice. Nargis remained by the grave while Helen came up to eat with him, both of them scooping small amounts out of the bag. Afterwards she went down and Nargis appeared and took her meal.

Lily was on his way towards the grave in the basement when he was seen by Aysha. She wore a black burqa and he was about to go past her.

'Lily.'

His immediate reaction was panic, but then he recognised the voice, the eyes and the burqa, and turned and reached out for her hand. He had come in for ten minutes – had calculated the use of each one of the ten precisely. Telling himself he would use the entrance nearest to the tomb and walk directly to the basement with his head down, and afterwards walk straight out. He had not wanted to come, had managed to resist it up until now, but ultimately the pull had been too strong. He was wearing the baseball cap given to him by that man Farid Alvie that day, hoping its bill would obscure part of his face.

She touched the bandage on his temple. 'What happened here?'

He began to lead her to some corner, away from the press of people. She had intended to defy Shakeel, but late in the morning, and suddenly, with urgency, he and his friends had left Badami Bagh, informing her that she should not prepare food for them that evening, as they would be absent till quite late at night.

'Where have you been?' she asked Lily when they sat down beside each other, next to a large whitewashed column.

Lily shook his head. 'If he has touched you I will kill him.'

She removed the dark cloth from the lower half of her face. 'I am fine.'

She wished for seclusion and his own hands and eyes

seemed eager. Sufi mausoleums allowed free access to women and it wasn't unusual to see couples sitting together, the way they were now, but a certain decorum and distance had to be observed. Still he quickly raised her fingers to his mouth.

In unison they said: 'How is Billu?' 'Where is Helen?'

'I don't know where she is.'

'Billu lost another milk tooth, you can imagine the conversations I am having with him about a new one growing in its place eventually.' She looked at him. 'I don't have much time. What are we going to do – have you thought of something?'

'I don't know. I sleep on the streets, I am using fake names. There's an election later in the year so all the politicians are clamouring to put a bounty on a blasphemer . . . No, don't cry . . . I'm sorry . . .'

'Where will we go?' she said. 'I can't leave my father. Arthritis in the fingers means he has difficulty even pushing a tablet out of its foil strip now. It takes him five minutes to do up the buttons of his kameez.'

Qawali singers in green velvet caps were performing in the distance, garlands of marigolds on their wrists, their ecstatic song drifting to the two of them. A policeman passed by behind them at a leisurely pace, Lily becoming still until he had disappeared into a corridor in the near distance.

'Can you meet me here in a week?' Lily said.

She nodded. 'Of course.'

'I'll think of something.' He was aware that his words sounded more like a prayer than a promise.

During the early days when they were falling in love, he had doubted the wisdom of what they were doing. 'We belong to two different worlds,' he had said to her in desperation. She had dismissed his comment. 'Different worlds? Next you'll be telling me God has no connection with humans, because we are down here and He lives all the way up there.'

'Have you been down to the grave?' he asked her now.

291

'No.'

'Let's go and pay our respects.'

'I would like to wash my face first.'

He stood up but she did not rise. Suddenly she seemed furious. He heard her breathing loudly to herself as she sat there. *'This* is a mosque,' she said in a fit of instinctual wrath. 'I don't see any sign of Allah's anger about you being here. I could drop a dozen crucifixes here and no one would care.'

Though she was gentle most of the time, there were moments when being with her made him think that he had befriended a hawk. Or a wolf.

'Allah, damn the Saudi royal family,' she said through gritted teeth. 'Damn them all to Hell! Damn the Americans and damn this whole country too!'

He sat down. She had buried her face in her hands, and he pulled at them but she would not allow it, her wrists becoming rigid. He stopped trying and sat beside her passively until eventually she uncovered her face and reached for his hands, clasping his fingers into her own, and they remained there like that for some minutes.

When at last she was ready they walked back into the multitude of people.

It came to him that he should tell her to meet him at the Museum of Glass Flowers instead of here. He hadn't been back there, so as not to endanger Farid, but perhaps he should seek his help. He took her aside and told her about Farid, told her on which road his museum was located. Telling her to make sure her brother-in-law did not follow her there. Then he watched her disappear towards the women's washroom. Everywhere there were large moths like those pieces of celluloid that were found under the collar buttons of new shirts. He was watching their beautiful flight, as they arced every which way, when he felt enveloped in a blaze of light, the thunderous hurting sound arriving in his ears a few seconds later.

The first of the two suicide bombers entered the mausoleum through Entrance 5 at 9.34 p.m. He wore a vest containing approximately twenty kilograms of explosives, packed with ball bearings. He was in his twenties and he was carrying a bag full of hand grenades. As he passed through the metal detector, the alarm went off, but he managed to avoid the hands grappling for him and dashed into the crowded courtyard.

When he detonated his vest, the impact of the blast ripped open the courtyard.

The second attacker, a teenager wearing a similar vest, came in through the same entrance five minutes later, at 9.39 p.m., unchallenged amid the horror and confusion, the smoke, the fires, and the screaming, and he disappeared towards the basement where he exploded himself.

They were foot soldiers. Over the past two decades, the leader of the militant party they belonged to had been personally accused of killing more than fifty people across all four provinces of the country. There were many court cases pending in many cities but no one dared set a date. During one particular hearing the frightened judge had attempted to conceal his identity behind a screen, but the militant had mockingly recited the names of the judge's children and the schools they attended. The case was abandoned. He had been a cigarette-seller and a thief in his youth, but had then taken up religion in his twenties, every inch of his forehead now black with the prayer stain, not just the middle. The US government had placed a $5 million bounty on his capture, and he was said to have been one of the men present in a 'control room' in Karachi from where terrorist commanders had phoned in instructions to the attackers in Mumbai in November 2008. He had sent thousands of passionate killers to their deaths in various jihadi battlefields in Bosnia, Kashmir, Afghanistan, Iraq and Syria, but was himself still here. 'The gun lasts longer than the bullet,' he was reported to have said.

His militant party had a 'martyr ratio', telling people, 'If you have four sons, then you must give us one. If you have six, give us two.'

The marble staircase into the basement was shattered, so Nargis and Helen – and the other survivors, some of them badly injured – had to wait for ladders to be lowered through the smoke. They stood amid the tangled prayer rugs and the torn Korans, the bodies and body parts of men, women and children. A woman was picking beads of her rosary off the floor as though plucking spines from a cactus. Imran was waiting to meet Nargis and Helen at the top, and then he and a group of other men went down the ladders and began to carry the wounded up to the surface on their backs. Outside the mausoleum, the police had resorted to firing into the air and were throwing rocks to disperse people who wanted to come into the complex and find their loved ones. Torches were being shone into the crevices of the nearby fibreglass replica of the nuclear mountain, in case a miscreant was hiding in there.

Once Nargis and Helen had recovered their senses, they went forward to see if they could be of help, their faces as numb as those of the people around them. Beside Entrance 7, at the northern end of the complex, there were two store-rooms with blue doors, and Imran was sent to get a bundle of sheets from one of them, that could be torn for bandages and tourniquets. He had just entered when there were raised voices behind him, and then someone from outside quickly shut the door, locking him and a dozen or so other people inside. It appeared that there was a third suicide bomber still at large in the complex, and someone had seen him running in the direction of the two storerooms. This information was shouted at the occupants through the blue door by a policeman.

Everyone in the room looked at each other, with the madness and unreason of fear. A woman braced herself against a far wall, her eyes shut tightly and a low scream emerging from her open mouth, the process of comprehension slowing down. The police were shouting threats outside, warning the bomber to give himself up. There seemed to be more and more of them gathering out there with opinions and decisions, wondering whether they should blow up the doors, go in behind a spray of bullets.

'There is no bomber here,' Imran shouted eventually, and he repeated himself with a firm banging of his fists on the door until he was heard. 'Let us out.' The men in the room had lifted their shirts to show each other that there was no suicide vest underneath.

The people in the next room too were informing the policemen of the same thing. Imran could hear their shouts through the wall.

It took almost forty minutes for the men out there to decide what to do. They were convinced that no Muslim could or would ever carry out such an attack on his fellow Muslims. So it had to be the work either of India or the CIA. Of non-Muslims.

They were in a rage. 'And we had been congratulating ourselves that April was the first month in three years when there had been no suicide bombings in Pakistan.'

They told the occupants of the two rooms that, with their guns at the ready, they would open the door and the occupants would step out one at a time, their arms raised. The women would be allowed to walk away – the third bomber was said to be a male, like the other two – but the men would have to open their trousers for inspection. If he was circumcised the man would go free, but if uncircumcised he would be detained for further questioning at the police station.

Imran was the first to step out of his room. There were six policemen with their rifles trained on him. And they stood about seven or eight metres away from the door, obviously taking that to be the safe distance, beyond the blast radius, should he try to detonate a device upon stepping out.

'Stay where you are and remove your shirt. If you take a single step forward we will shoot you.'

He did as he was told. Once they saw that he was not wearing a suicide vest under his shirt, one of the policemen pointed with his gun to the wall on the left.

Imran moved in that direction, the barrels of the rifles shifting with him, and a policeman began to walk towards him.

'State your name.'

'Imran.'

The policeman arrived and looked at him with contempt.

'That's what you're telling me but I'll soon find out the truth. You think you can bomb the light of God and get away with it, you son of an infidel bitch?'

'Sir-ji, we're in a mosque,' one of his shocked subordinates said.

But he was ignored.

'When I get you back to the station I will rip your motherfucking skin off.'

Roughly he unfastened the drawstring of Imran's shalwar and let the shalwar fall to his feet and then pulled down the underwear.

Once he had looked, however, his manner changed entirely. He asked Imran to lower his hands, referring to him as 'my son', and motioned for him to pull up his shalwar, to pick up his shirt.

Imran began to get dressed and the policeman walked back to his colleagues. 'Next,' he shouted.

There were eleven people in the second room, Lily among them. He stood stock still in the corner farthest away from the door, watching it open every other minute and a person go out. The room emptying around him.

33

Imran lay in the tall grass of the island. The trees threw the shadows of their branches onto everything, the roofs and the walls, his own body. Perhaps he should trace them with paint, fixing in place forever these days and nights he had been given with Helen, their sorrows and their joy.

On the damp moss-stained wood of the boat beside him, there was wax from the many candles they had burned, sitting outside in the breeze on the hot evenings, the goldbugs falling through the air.

Last night after returning from the mausoleum, they had listened to the radio until 2 a.m. Now he switched it on again, waiting for the news.

It was almost six in the morning.

With his fingertip he followed the line of a branch upwards on a wall, slowing down when the wind moved the shadow, allowing it to settle. Helen was still asleep. Her father remained lost in the city, out there somewhere. One evening here on the island she had said, 'If I was home now I would be alert to the sound of my father's rickshaw arriving outside the house.' She would open the metal gate so Lily could drive into the courtyard. He would step out of the vehicle, sometimes so exhausted he would leave the keys in the ignition, his skin and clothing covered in the day's dust, his eyes red from the smoke and the terrible fumes because the trucks and buses used petrol mixed with kerosene. She would reach in and take out the keys herself.

Imran stood listening to the news bulletin.

Forty-nine people had died, and over 200 had been injured.

And the mausoleum was closed for the very first time in centuries.

Nargis was sitting on the step of the library with today's newspapers in her lap. She stood up and let them fall to the ground and walked away from them.

Kill non-Muslims for not being Muslims. Kill Muslims for not being the right kind of Muslims.

A bomb in Peshawar had killed 130 people in 2009, and the suspect Sayar Khan was caught in Sardinia, hiding in the large Pakistani community there, in a town called Olbia.

Another story for the black pages of her father-in-law's book.

She remembered the Maccabees from her childhood. How King Antiochus, in order to promote Greek customs throughout his kingdom, had erected a statue of Zeus in the temple at Judea.

It came to pass also that seven brethren with their mother were taken, and compelled by the king against the law to eat swine's flesh, and were tormented with scourges and whips . . . The mother was marvellous above all, and worthy of honourable memory – for when she saw her seven sons slain within the space of one day, she bore it with good courage . . . Last of all after the sons the mother died.

She watched as a small sunbird rose out of the foliage before her and crossed the roof, dropping into the canopies on the other side. Migratory birds, they wintered in southern Sindh and southern Baluchistan, arriving in Zamana about the first week of March and beginning to build nests between the 15th and 20th of the month. She and Massud had been watching them in their garden for almost ten years now. Aysha's father would leave the trimmings from his beard on the ground for them to use as nesting material. In August they would disappear back towards Sindh and Baluchistan.

She saw Helen walking towards the house and went down to meet her. There was something she admired in the girl's character, something she perhaps herself did not have at that age. One day, in answer to the question, 'Who are you?' put to her by Lily, Helen had answered, without any thought at all, it seemed:

'I am my father's daughter, I am my mother's daughter, I am Nargis's niece, I am Massud's niece, I am my friend's friend, I am my neighbour's neighbour. If I had a brother I would be his sister, if I had a sister I would be her sister, and one day I shall be my husband's wife . . .'

Nargis had found this somewhat disconcerting, the idea that the girl did not put herself at the centre, that she began with others and worked her way towards herself. Did it mean that she did not wish to be an individual? Nargis thought of a series of glass plates, each with part of an image painted on it. When they were all placed one on top of another the complete image appeared. Helen.

And the fact that she questioned it had shamed Nargis a little. She remembered the summer she had decided to become Nargis, how she would look at the other Christians and become somewhat angry and dumbfounded by their conviction that life would be good to them. In later years she would put that down to the callousness of youth. But perhaps that was slander. Not all young people were callow, and so it was that Helen hadn't learned to be good much earlier than Nargis had – she had always been good.

She entered the kitchen and found her there. Helen turned and looked at Nargis, her eyes tired and far away.

*

Helen lay in her room, her head resting on a dark pillow, the chime of keys hanging from the window frame. She had wondered if he had brought the keys with him from Kashmir, but he said he had collected them during his time in Pakistan, a habit he had fallen into, of picking up any key he could.

Moscow.

'Moscow of white stone,' Pushkin had written. 'Market of the fiancées.'

She felt Massud's absence. 'How did Tolstoy find out about Pushkin's death?' she had asked and he had interrupted whatever he was doing and the pair of them had spent the next hours consulting the various biographies in the study, had searched the internet.

'In 1837, Dostoevsky was sixteen, so he must have remembered receiving the news that Pushkin had died. Turgenev too, who was nineteen. Tolstoy however was nine . . .'

The radio lay on the pillow beside her head. Zamana was close enough to the border with India for Indian transmissions to be received here. The news of the attack had spread to India more or less with the same speed at which it spread through Pakistan, and along with expressions of horror and sympathy there was a note of vindication, if not exactly celebration. 'Pakistan is getting a taste of the violence it has inflicted on India and the rest of the world through its jihadi monsters . . .' 'The seed sewn by Pakistan in Mumbai on 26 November 2008 has produced a deadly fruit . . .' 'This is called chickens coming home to roost . . .'

She got up and went to the window. The island belonged to Massud's family but they had made a gift of it to Pakistan. Before the mosque was built this was a fertile piece of land, cows and water buffaloes would be brought on barges and left here to graze for weeks, the milkmen arriving each day to milk them, taking away the pitchers. Whenever she thought of Massud she thought of his almost mythical awareness of what needed to be done, for the good of Pakistan. Soon after Grace's death, a despairing Helen had asked Massud if things would ever change in Pakistan. 'Pakistan was born in 1947,' Massud had said. 'Look at the USA and see what that was like when it was just sixty-five years old. Germany, England, France, Sweden. We can't lose heart, and we can't lose focus in trying to make things better.' Right or wrong – she saw that it was the only answer he was capable of giving.

She breathed the river air, bringing the Vela deep into her lungs. Lily was out there somewhere. As was the man who had killed Grace – free. She looked at the sky for signs of clouds. She remembered Lily's compilation CD of monsoon songs, kept in a compartment in the rickshaw next to the handlebars. *Saavan kay jhoolay paray* and *Kahan se aye badra* and *Aye abr-e-karam* and *Rim-jhim giray saavan* and *O sajna, barkha bahar aae* and *Saavan aye, saavan jaye.* As he drove around Zamana during July and August he would listen to them with the volume turned high, a thrill for the customers too. He would lean back in his seat, steering with one finger. At nine years old he had split open the head of an older Muslim boy, who had grabbed him by the hair and slammed his head repeatedly into the wall: 'Convert! Convert!' But in the rains there was never any glimpse of any kind of harshness in him. 'That *has* to be the noisiest man God created,' Nargis would say next door, hearing him sing in the morning at the top of his voice. He'd come home with his clothes drenched in the monsoon, holding a bottle of wine, his skin showing through the wet fabric, and ask Helen and Grace and the ghost of the Hanged Mutineer to dance with him, and they would.

Aysha remembered her father telling her that every memory of every human being began in Eden.

She was in the kitchen preparing dinner, and looking occasionally at the bathroom door, alert to any untoward sound from in there. Her father was bathing and at that age it was always a fear that he would slip on the wet cement floor.

She was making mung daal, cutting up the onions and tomatoes that would form the base. When Adam was expelled from Eden and came to live on earth, he was wearing a crown of leaves, fashioned from the trees in Eden. When they eventually dried up and fell off his head, from them sprouted many of the foods that are found today on earth. This legend came from a book named *Tareekh-e-Tabari*, which was increasingly under attack from today's militants because it seemed to be a gloss on the Koran, an extrapolation of the received text. The Saudi Arabian rulers and the Saudi-sponsored sects wanted it eradicated, even though it had been freely published and read in Pakistan and India for generations.

She went to the kitchen door and stood listening, head bent towards the bathroom.

'Only one wooden lion is left at the shop in the square,' Billu said from the bed when she looked in the room where he had been taking his afternoon nap.

'How do you know?' She went in and picked up his legs. There were times when he woke and forgot about his condition and tried to get out of bed and fell. But they were becoming rare.

'Steven and Bradley told me, on the doorstep this morning.'

'Don't you love our Prophet, peace be upon him?'

'I do.'

'Is this too tight?'

'Steven said the tails of lizards grow back if they are cut off. And the antlers of deer.'

'I asked, "Is this too tight?"'

'No.'

He put his hands under his thigh and lifted the other stump in her direction.

'Thank you. We must learn to do this together. What three things did Jinnah say would make Pakistan into a great country? Faith, Discipline and—?'

'Unity.'

'Yes. Unity.'

There was a sound and she turned and saw that Shakeel had appeared in the door behind her. He had come to take Billu to the mosque for prayers. He had been in bad humour for the previous two hours, when he had overheard a group of youths mockingly refer to him and Aysha's deceased husband as the 'drone brothers'. He had been pushing the forehead of one of the youths into the ground while he prayed – and tempers had flared.

Prior to that, all day there had been excitement and delight from him and his companions, at the Charagar bombings. The pleasure was immense that the mausoleum was forced to close down, though there was disappointment at the rumour that it would reopen as early as next week. She listened to them commend the two suicide bombers, saying how they were the true heroes of Islam, that the forty-nine people who had died were not to be mourned because they were not real Muslims; and later she listened to him give a sermon over the loudspeaker, telling everyone that the bombings had been carried out by the Americans who were 'no longer content in just killing us with drones, but want to kill us openly on our streets – as one of them did last month right here in Zamana – *and* in our sacred houses of worship – as they have now done with the Charagar mausoleum'.

One day her father had said he would be interested in seeing what Allah did with such a man.

There were times when she thought of her father and saw the utter inadequacy of his virtues, of his selflessness and patience.

She watched Billu walk unsteadily alongside Shakeel, moving towards the door that opened into the mosque. His gait was a series of small labours, his posture that of someone walking through knee-high mud.

'What did I say to you about talking to infidel children?' she heard him say to the boy just as they disappeared through the door. 'It was their kind that took away your legs, your father and grandmother.'

She wished she could follow them but beyond the door lay the men's part of the building.

She picked up a glass from the shelf and hurled it with all her might at the door, where it exploded.

She watched as the door opened and he came out. He strode across the floor towards her and stopped a yard or so away, maintaining eye-contact throughout.

'Listen to me carefully, you whore. He is my brother's son. It would take me less than a day to have myself declared his legal guardian, and have you and the old fool who thinks he's a Muslim thrown out of this mosque.' He was shaking with frenzied rage. 'I'm sure you would like that. You would be free to degrade yourself with anyone you wanted out in the alleyways of Zamana – living or ghost, believer or infidel.'

His good eye was still on her face, daring her to speak. She had never ever seen a woman, of any age, with a forehead stained by prayers – that certificate of piety that men like him carried around. Not even a woman who had been praying for decades, who had never missed even one prayer in her life.

He turned and began to walk away. He had taken off his shoes after going into the mosque and had emerged on bare feet – his stride unbroken as he stepped on shattered glass here and there, leaving a small smear of blood in each place.

'It's all very well abusing women and children and those who are weaker than you,' she said. 'And, yes, the Americans took away your brother, mother and Billu's legs, but it's the Pakistani military and the intelligence agencies who secretly gave them permission to fly their drones above Waziristan. In return for rewards and weapons and money. Nargis and Massud's house is visited by people from the military almost every other day. Why don't you go and take this matter up with them?' She took several steps towards him. 'Or are they too powerful?'

He had stopped but hadn't turned around.

'Yes, I look out into the lane and see those soldiers come and go,' she said, past caring now. 'If nails can be driven in they can also be wrenched out.'

She waited as he stood there, perfectly still. A coin-sized amount of blood collecting at his left foot.

'You sent the old fool, as you call him, to talk to Nargis, to tell her not to forgive the American thug who killed Massud, but why not talk directly to the army officer who was asking her to forgive?'

She didn't wait to see what he would do. She turned away and went to pick up the broom in order to sweep away the glass shards.

When she came back he was gone.

She had been unable to locate Lily in the chaos after the bombings. The police funnelling the crowds every which way. The hour becoming later and later so that there was the fearful urgency of wanting to get back home too. It was past 1 a.m. when she left the mausoleum and found a tonga to bring her back to Badami Bagh. Shakeel had returned home by that time. Frantic with worry, because the news of the bombing had spread into the city, her father had told him where she had gone. Shakeel and his companions were getting ready to go to the mausoleum and look for her when she arrived.

Today she had scrutinised the names of the dead and the injured – a partial list had appeared in the newspaper, the numbers still rising by the time the newspaper went to press – but Lily's name was not among them. Not that that meant anything. He was using counterfeit names, as he'd told her. The only consolation was that they had planned to meet in seven days – six now – at the Museum of Glass Flowers. Perhaps in the coming days she should slip out of the house and leave a message for him there.

She returned to the kitchen and washed the onions under the tap. Afterwards, as she dried her hands she looked down at the newspaper that lay folded into a quarter on the table. There was a list of all the suicide bombings in Pakistan over the last ten years – only a fraction of it was visible to her, facing upwards, and she promised herself that she would not look away until she had read it all.

On 13 October 2012, a suicide bomber exploded his
vehicle in Dara Adam Khel and killed 16 and injured 40.
On 17 February 2012, in Parachinar there was a suicide
bombing and 41 people were killed, 24 wounded.
On 19 August 2011 in the Jama Mosque in Jamrood, a
suicide bomber blew himself up, killing 57 worshippers.
On 26 May 2011 in Hungu, at the police station near the
DCO's office, there was a suicide bomb attack in which 39
people died . . .

She looked away from the newspaper, unable to go on. There were hundreds upon hundreds of entries. But as she read she felt as though she were underwater, unable to breathe, desperately searching for the surface.

On 3 April 2011 in Dera Ghazi Khan, two suicide
bombers blew themselves up outside the shrine of the saint
Sakhi Sarvar, killing 51 people and injuring 92 . . .

No.
It was impossible to continue.
She was the mother of a child mutilated by the Americans, a child who was collateral damage, the daughter-in-law of a

woman who was killed because she happened to be near the enemy when the hour struck. And this – here in the newspaper – was the other side: people claiming to retaliate against the West's influence and crimes, by killing Pakistanis.

It was time to resume her work. She moved towards the bowl on the windowsill. The mung daal had been soaking in water since the morning. She had checked it for fragments of stones, dead insects, and chaff beforehand. Each small seed was swollen to almost twice its original size now and the dark green husk on each had come away a little. She rubbed them between her hands to separate them fully. It took her almost ten minutes to remove and wash away all the husks. The kitchen was filled with the various sounds of water, the clinking of her bangles against the bowl.

She was relieved when she heard the bathroom door open and her father emerged, drying his beard on the towel.

'It's time for your pills,' she called to him. 'Shall I bring them with lime water or lassi?'

'With tea,' he answered, slowly on his way to his room. 'And I know you were listening.'

'I wasn't.'

'I am not an invalid.'

'I never said you were. How will you swallow the pills with hot tea?'

'I'll wait for it to cool down.'

'All right, I'm coming,' she said.

VII

THE SOUL AND BODY OF SOLOMON

34

A few hours before his death, Bishop Solomon woke up with the desire to pray.

He sat up in bed and brought his feet to the ground and felt for his slippers with them. He remained sitting in that position for several minutes, his eyes closed, his hands resting on the edge of the bed. In winter there would be the quilt on his back, moulded against his shoulders and spine as he sat there, and the shape would stay there when he eventually stood up. He remembered the laughter of Seraphina and Margaret, when they were children, at the upright ghostly contour he left behind. In the months before her death, Seraphina began to find the sight disquieting, so he always turned around and flattened the quilt before walking away from the bed.

He was seventy years old and had been deaf in the right ear for over a decade, unable to hear raindrops, consonants and whispers on that side, but since last December he had also been experiencing 'musical hallucinations' – a faint choir-like singing in his ears. It was a form of tinnitus, the doctor told him, saying that the music the sufferer heard was quite often from his childhood. It pleased Bishop Solomon that a Muslim friend of his with the same affliction – a cleric at a nearby mosque – had been hearing Qawalis instead of a choir. Both were songs of praise.

The bishop's house was white, inside and out, standing across the road from Lyallpur's largest church. He got dressed: a hinge of the wardrobe door was broken and had been temporarily mended with a strong safety pin, so it had to be opened tactfully. The clothes lay folded on a shelf inside, ironed by the housekeeper Alice, who knew he liked a layer of talcum powder on his handkerchief. Each stack of garments was so neat it appeared to be housed in a transparent box. She referred to the protective spray for his suede boots as the 'medicine' for his shoes, and often reminded him that she had placed his 'hearing' in the trouser pocket, referring to the hearing aid.

Bishop Solomon went to the window and looked out at his garden. May was the month of Mary.

Now and then, over the years, he had seen the face of Margaret in the crowd at the church. Perhaps she had come to see him, perhaps it was just his imagination, for he had seen the face of Seraphina too on occasion, and she was without doubt absent from earth, he knew. Nor did he know what Margaret looked like, the face she grew into as the years passed. Just once in a while the conviction was there that a certain woman in the gathering was Margaret.

The garden he was looking at was planted for Mary and there were the gulmohar trees – their petals were the substance of which ghosts and prophets were made – and the hanging almost-grape-like bunches of the laburnum, the air currents carrying the dusty smell of the thirty cypresses towards him.

In the kitchen Alice was preparing tea for him. There were always drops of water on her blue apron, appearing like stains.

'You should not have got up,' Bishop Solomon said. 'Did I wake you?'

She shook her head but did not say anything. Then she came forward and took his right hand and pressed it to her mouth, her eyes inert and lifeless.

'I can manage perfectly well for now,' he said. 'You should go to your room and rest.' Her husband had 'liked' a disrespectful comment about Muhammad on Facebook five years ago, and had been arrested for blasphemy. The case finally came to court this month and he was sentenced to death. He was found hanged less than an hour after he arrived back in his cell after the verdict. The wardens said it was suicide, but couldn't explain why he was still handcuffed.

The judge had said to Alice's husband, 'You claim to respect and honour Muhammad, peace be upon him. Then why don't you convert to Islam?'

Bishop Solomon walked with Alice to the kitchen door. She was still holding his hand to her lips. The dead man was named Sebastian, and Bishop Solomon remembered that St Sebastian had served as an officer for one reason only. It meant he could have access to Christians he saw being tortured, to be able to strengthen their resolve when it began to weaken.

After Alice left, Bishop Solomon returned to the kitchen table. He took a sip from the tea and discovered that she had forgotten the sugar and he looked for the sugar bowl.

Bishop Solomon carried the cup of tea back to his bedroom. Having locked the door behind him, he lifted the pillow on his bed. He pulled up the corner of the counterpane and then the corner of the thin mattress underneath. The revolver lay exposed on the woven ropes of the bed and he stood looking at it. Finally he decided to pick it up and placed it in his pocket. He looked at his wristwatch. It was still very early. At noon the judge who had sentenced Alice's husband to death had a session at the court.

Bishop Solomon felt very tired. He sat down on the bed and drank his tea. He could not remember why he had risen so early. He picked up his Bible and looked at the torn binding. It had been given to him by Juan Alonso, a former principal of Lyallpur's Church School, a friend who had come to live in Pakistan from Madrid and had fought in the Spanish Civil War. He should repair the book at the earliest opportunity to prevent the damage from spreading. The signatures would have to be re-sewn with waxed- or quilting-thread. He had no binder's tape, but he remembered seeing a roll of fabric medical tape in one of the drawers that looked strong enough. There was a pot of glue, and there was a jumble of rubber bands somewhere in the house – the precise location escaped him for now – with which he would hold the repaired book firmly in place while the glue dried, rendering it immovable.

Now he recalled why he was out of bed at this hour. He placed the tea on the chair and concealed the weapon back under the dark-pink mattress and made his way out of the house through the back door, taking the eight-inch-long key that hung from the nail on the wall. The rich smell from the soil and that from the plants mingled with his memories as he walked across the garden towards the church. As Bishop Solomon's gaze took in the early flowers, the feeling was close to music, and he thought of Sophocles. *No one loves living as a man growing old.*

At the centre of the church garden was a cross of red sandstone, taller than two men, believed by some to be the original one from the very first church that had been established in the city of Zamana during the reign of Emperor Shah Jahan. Though that claim was shared by a number of crosses in Pakistan.

Coming out of his garden, past the beehives, Bishop Solomon saw that the grey car was parked once again under the gulmohar tree. The driver looking at him openly. Bishop Solomon could tell from the broken foliage on the roof that the vehicle had been there all night.

It was from the military-intelligence agency, he knew. A major named Burhan had visited him a while ago. Wishing to know the names and whereabouts of his nieces. After the first visit he had returned twice, and each time Bishop Solomon had responded as evasively as possible. *Seraphina was dead and Margaret had converted to Islam as a young woman and broken all contact with him. The last he heard she had moved abroad. Australia, Canada, Singapore – he couldn't be sure.* The man went away, seemingly satisfied, but not long after the most recent visit the bishop's house was broken into. They tore the doors off cupboards and wardrobes, destroyed cushions and book bindings. A sheaf of certificates and other papers related to his family was taken. Among the photographs that were now missing from the house was one of Bishop Solomon with Seraphina and Margaret as children, taken at a Bhwana Bazaar studio here in Lyallpur – Seraphina looking out of it for all eternity.

He had been unable to bury her in consecrated ground because she had committed suicide.

Bishop Solomon stood among the plants now, watching the driver in the grey car.

He crossed the road and unlocked the sacristy door and went into the church, stepping over the marble flagstones that had come from a ruined Mughal pavilion. The statue of the Virgin and the glass saints glowing dimly in the windows brought a measure of peace to his mind. The smell of the candle wax, the touch of the communion rail. On the other side of the nave were plaques commemorating the men of the Punjab Regiment who had fallen in Mesopotamia during the Great War.

When he emerged again into the open, half an hour later, the sun was fully up and his uncertainties had somewhat receded and he felt the possibility of dignity in suffering and sacrifice. There were times when he believed that he had been lonely most of his life. But now there was a crystalline inner awareness of the majesty of existence. Of course Bishop Solomon had known doubt – fighting the hours of solitary combat. *That religion is inappropriate for the overwhelming majority of people, and therefore cannot be called the religion of love, that he had come only for the chosen, for the strong and mighty, and that those who suffer his cross will not find anything that has been promised . . .*

Did Bishop Solomon love God or did he simply wish to be associated with Him? The phenomenon of Him, as opposed to Him. The scientists said the earth had lain empty for millions of years, the sun rising and the moon rising on no creature, no man. The stars revolved above vacant deserts and the expectant stillness of rocks. The ghost moon was there during the day, just as the heat of the sun was emitted from the ground during the night. Bishop Solomon could delight in that vision. Its logic lay inside the boundaries of his understanding. The winds surged with energy along fields of snow, raising clouds of pollen above cliffs, carrying particles of dust, finite but countless. But within his concentrated and intense mental life, what he loved most was an idea that was brought to the world by Christ. It was the idea that man was a brother to man. It was not there before Christ. Humans had loved each other before him, of course. There was kindness and generosity and compassion, but it was all done for other reasons – other valuable, cherishable, good reasons. But the idea that one man had to be good to another because he was his *brother* was not there before. The kinship of humanity was what Christ brought into the world. This insight was the great achievement of Bishop Solomon's thinking life. It was the equivalent of a scientific breakthrough, the result of many decades of questioning, observing and reading. *I love you not because you are my neighbour but because you are my brother . . . I love you not because you offer me guidance and food but because you are my brother . . .*

The bishop's great-grandfather had been a sweeper who captured *sahna* lizards. He remembered his father and grandfather telling him about this ancestor, his waist-belt strung with slain lizards whose oil he sold for lighting purposes at the same price as clarified butter, the lizards' flesh being his family's staple food. There was no photograph of him, of course, but Bishop Solomon had been able to imagine the skirt of reptiles.

It was his great-grandfather and his great-grandfather's twin sister who had alerted him to the possibility. They had become preachers in their old age, half-blind and almost deaf, and their open arms – raised towards the sky or towards him and others as a call to embrace – were one of the abiding memories from his childhood. What was now known as Bell's Palsy meant that the woman had never been able to marry, and the man was a widower, and those arms had heaved baskets of human and animal excrement onto their heads all their lives, had been doing so since they were children. They claimed that the waste had touched every part of them, their legs, armpits, tongues, eyes, sexes – even their hearts, livers and kidneys, they believed, everything except their souls. And that nugget of purity was what they took out and held in their impure hands when they preached. The nearest church was far away, on the other side of the city, and among them were people who had never seen a priest or a Bible. And so once a month everyone gathered before Solomon's great-grandfather and grand-aunt wherever it was possible, in someone's courtyard or roof, in a cowshed while the water buffaloes were at the pond, or in the cemetery among the dead. The space would be lit by the two souls held in the dirty fingertips and they talked sometimes in unison and sometimes separately. They were interested neither in sin nor Paradise. The listeners knew themselves to be nothing but flesh, knew that the dirty and dirtied feet, hearts, hands, knees, hair, navels, fingernails were all they had, that they possessed nothing as clear and uncontaminated as what the two ancient people before them held aloft in their fingertips, or put on the ground next to them when they needed both hands to emphasise and animate what they were saying. But by the end of the hour each one of them had located a shining fragment of their own somewhere within themselves, a brilliant splinter in the meat or bone. The brother and sister insisted they feel for it upon their persons, insisted the women help the men find it, and insisted the men help the women find it. Men searched for it in other men, women in women, and it was done sometimes in groups and sometimes singly. 'Help your neighbours, your sisters, your brothers and your sons and your daughters . . .' And always there was laughter or tears of disbelief when it was eventually discovered, the amount of light in the space increasing slowly.

Bishop Solomon stood in the deep doorway of the sacristy, with the great black key in his right hand, looking at the car with its roof covered with the gulmohar litter.

He knew Major Burhan would visit him again, soon. He had been looking into the man's background – a soldier, the son of a soldier. And this being the Pakistani military, there was story upon story of corruption and criminality, of brutal meanness. Someone told him about the general whipping a subordinate in a garden with a live snake that happened to be passing.

Bishop Solomon crossed the garden and went back into his house and took out the gun from its hiding place and put it in his pocket again. The pillows were embroidered by Seraphina.

The room was small. It was where he withdrew to write and read, to think. His sermons and Easter letters arranged in boxes in one corner by Alice. This morning he would be unwilling to approach the newspapers, he knew. The bishop of a city in the north had been accused of embezzling the aid and compensation money that had come in following the Islamist suicide bombing of a church last year.

Bishop Solomon took down a volume from the shelf and opened it. *Milton loved me in childhood and showed me his face. Ezra came with Isaiah the Prophet, but Shakespeare in riper years gave me his hand . . .* The details of William Blake's boyhood as described by him in the year 1800. Bishop Solomon remembered reading these sentences out loud to Margaret and Seraphina. *Paracelsus and Behmen appeared to me, terrors appeared in the Heavens above and in Hell beneath, and a mighty and awful change threatened the Earth. The American War began. All its dark horrors . . .*

As he was mending the Bible torn by Major Burhan's thieves, Bishop Solomon looked at his wristwatch. It was a quarter past ten, then a half past, then twenty to eleven. It would take him twenty minutes in a rickshaw to reach the courts. Alice had emerged from her room an hour ago to give him breakfast and despite his protestations gone out to the bazaar to buy vegetables and the weekly fruit.

Since the year of Seraphina's death, he had often thought about going to the city of Zamana. He imagined a house, imagined himself standing outside it, waiting, hoping Margaret would emerge. But even in his mind he had always withdrawn. A feeling of trespass in him. Not wishing to interfere with the lie she had constructed for herself, the place of safety she thought she needed in this life. Perhaps it was better that way. After all, he hadn't been able to protect her sister.

When the doorbell rang he put down the Bible and the scissors.

'I have been expecting you,' he said, bringing Major Burhan into the kitchen.

The man sat down but immediately stood up again. 'I don't

think I should have done that. I always forget what the protocol is . . . Your Holiness.'

Bishop Solomon raised his hand towards him. 'There is no protocol. Do you know how to behave in the presence of a seventy-year-old Muslim cleric?'

'I think so.'

'Let's begin there. You might even forgo the "cleric" bit. I am just a seventy-year-old man.'

Major Burhan took a seat. Bishop Solomon sat down on the other side of the kitchen table, pushing aside the broken book.

Major Burhan reached into his pocket and brought out two copies of the studio photograph and placed them on the table. One he had taken from here; the other he must have discovered at Margaret's house in Zamana.

'Where is your niece? Nargis. Margaret.'

'I told you she moved to another country a long time ago. To the best of my knowledge.'

'She lives in Zamana.'

'I wouldn't know. I didn't even know she had named herself Nargis.'

'She hasn't contacted you?'

'No.'

'Can I trust you?'

'Can you trust a Muslim holy man?'

The man gave a small laugh. 'The way things are, that's the last person I would trust.'

Bishop Solomon smiled. 'You clearly haven't been associating with the right ones. But, yes, some people when they are brought to the spring of God proceed to gargle with the water, instead of drinking it.'

'You did lie to me during the previous visits. You denied even writing the letter. You said the little girls in the photograph were just the children of friends.'

Bishop Solomon nodded. 'Yes, there is that.'

320

'We need to find her.'

'I don't know any more now than I did during your other visits.'

'It's a matter of national importance. Of an international importance too, but I don't care about that.'

'Major, you didn't ask me if I trust you.'

'You can trust the fact that I am a patriot, Your Holiness. I would do anything for Pakistan.'

'For the Pakistani state, perhaps. Not the Pakistani people.'

For the next few moments there was silence.

Bishop Solomon realised that he no longer believed in the existence of evil. To him 'evil' was now just another word for stupidity, for not knowing what really mattered in life – in your own and in the lives of others.

'Are you sure you would be able to get her to cooperate?' the bishop asked, glancing at the clock.

He could feel the weight of the weapon in his pocket.

Major Burhan stood up. 'She will cooperate, Your Holiness. I'm sure. She will have to. There is no record of her ever having converted. Her life in Zamana is based on forgeries, we know. If we expose her, she'll face very serious charges. Pretending to be a Muslim, etcetera etcetera.' He walked to the door and turned around. 'Incidentally, I wonder if the charges could extend to you too. It is my opinion that you knew about her deception, her unconscionable duping of innocent Muslims, and yet you did nothing to inform the authorities.'

Only after the man was gone did Bishop Solomon think that he should have asked for his photograph back. He finished mending the Bible and secured it with elastic bands and placed it on a high kitchen shelf, a place of evenly distributed heat, away from the direct sun which might result in warping. He would like to see the photograph again and he believed that he would. Over the years he had become aware of the fact that he had neglected the two children. He had always been solitary and back then there had been disappointment in love. He had been rejected, had made a mistake, and they were the years of absolute sorrow for him, and perhaps that had led to him discovering his vocation. To an extent, yes. Preferring order and silence, he hadn't really known how to adjust when the two orphan girls arrived in his life. He saw it now as one of the occasions he had failed in life. He was distant with the two children and, perhaps, authoritarian after the few initial days of politeness and consideration. The mind of his father had been deteriorating fast, and now a permanent housekeeper had to be employed for the little girls. He remembered the daily series of annoyances that resulted from having three new people in the small house. The demands and problems of his congregation were immense, saving sometimes their souls, sometimes their bodies, and it must be said that he had come to see even his own needs as selfish. When he wasn't reflecting on a series of holy words, or wasn't devising a solution to the problems of a soul in crisis out there, he asked very little from life for himself and he was sure now that he had expected the people in his household to do the same. His clothes were threadbare, his food basic, and he had never felt ashamed of his solitude.

Margaret proved to be a gifted student so he had enrolled her in a school in the foothills of the Himalayas, hundreds of miles away from the sister she loved. The letter he wrote to her while she was there was now in the possession of Major Burhan. She had saved it from that time; he hadn't known that.

Seraphina could be heard weeping in her room at night after Margaret was sent away. 'Why is she behaving in this manner?' Solomon had asked the housekeeper one day, feeling lost to a certain extent.

'Father, she's upset because she misses her sister,' the woman had replied, quietly.

And when he had said, 'I fail to see what there is to be upset about? Margaret will be here during all the holidays, and she will get a first-rate education at that school,' the housekeeper had tilted her head and spoken to him in an exasperated manner for the only time:

'Forgive me, Father, but I didn't say *I* was upset.'

At the end of the first month the nuns in the Himalayas telephoned him in Lyallpur, telling him that Margaret had disappeared. They had searched everywhere, the hills and the surrounding forest, the ravines. There was the fear of leopards.

It was raining gently when Solomon arrived the next day, having set off upon receiving the message. The valley was covered as though with a lid of thick grey clouds. And in these clouds there was one small circle of light, a smudged amber glow. And Solomon had raised his finger towards it.

'That's my niece up there,' he said to the nuns. 'That's Margaret.'

Although the mountain village was far away from any sea or lake, every house in it owned at least one net. It remained rolled up for most of the year, but early on a spring morning each of them was unrolled and then spread out on the roof, its edges allowed to fall off the sides of the house, draping it. Each house looked as though it had been fished out of water. After this was done, women and children walked along the streets with lengths of rope, connecting all the many nets to make a single enormous one. It was like stitching pieces of cloth together. The men now went to the outskirts of the village and positioned themselves there, spreading out evenly – surrounding the village in a loose circle. Then they bent down and attached long ropes to the giant net that lay over their village. And at the signal from the minaret at the centre of the valley, they shouldered these ropes and began to walk upwards into the hills, the tops of which were lost in the clouds.

As the men climbed, the vast net stirred in all directions – squares becoming trapezoids, triangles narrowing to spikes – and then suddenly it was lifted above the houses, moving higher and higher until it disappeared into the clouds.

The men walked up the slopes, the heaviness of the net pulling at them. Injury was not unheard of during this annual journey into the sky. Near the top of the hills, the men would have to enter the clouds and continue more or less blindly, their eyes aching. Finally, up there, they would tie the ropes to the trunks of the pines and cedars. The net was now sandwiched between the clouds that floated above the village.

The ropes would begin to absorb the moisture from the clouds, and eventually it would fall as rain on the village. This process could take a day or thirty-six hours to begin.

Without the colossal net the clouds would simply drift away without releasing rain. It was something to do with the pattern of winds and the shape of the hills. Or perhaps it was divine punishment, as the elders believed. Generations ago someone in the village had refused a drink of water to a mendicant.

Something else occurred up there on the cloud-hidden net.

During the soft week-long drizzle, the laughter the people occasionally heard in the air was lovers trysting, high above the fields and orchards. Their feet balanced on wet ropes. Finding each other by the storm-lamps they held in their hands. The cloud entering their lungs and their eyes. An hour of joy. A gift. But it had never occurred to the nuns at the school that a homesick child might dare to vanish up there.

Now Solomon walked up the hills with the group of holy women, a procession of silent figures moving among the granite outcrops. They had brought torches – canes wrapped with pitch-coated cloth at one end – and the flames lit the paths, and they were occasionally swung from side to side to keep the possibility of wild creatures at bay. Holding these fires in their hands they all stepped onto the net. They wandered along the long paths of rope, calling out the girl's name in the low visibility, telling her that he had come to take her back to Seraphina. To never be separated again. Down in the valley the villagers looked up at the distant meandering points of light. At last one of the nuns saw her, sitting in the vapour with a lantern, her legs plunged into the sky. Back in Lyallpur, it was many weeks before she spoke to him again.

Yes, it was egregious. Yes, over the years he had blamed her, blamed her for removing herself from the difficulties of her life as Margaret, for finding personal happiness as Nargis. He would have preferred it had she used her life as a way of bettering the lives of others *collectively*.

But then who was he to pass such a judgement?

He remembered St Sebastian again, who stood watching two brothers who were about to be beheaded for their faith. They were from one of the noblest families, and their parents visited them to persuade them to relent, to revert to idol worship so that their lives might be spared. 'Here is a novel way of dying,' said the weeping mother, 'when the victim begs the executioner to strike.' Sebastian stepped forward just as the hearts of the brothers were beginning to soften. 'Most valiant soldiers of Christ, do not let these appeals rob you of your eternal crown.' And turning to the parents he had said, 'Do not fear, they will not be separated from you. They are going before you to prepare you a dwelling among the stars.'

It was time to leave. Bishop Solomon touched the weapon in his pocket once more and emerged from his house. He crossed the garden and stood looking at the church and then went along the road. He glanced over his shoulder to find the grey car following him at a steady distance. The green Pakistani flag with its crescent and star hung from a pole outside the school at the corner. A portion of the flag was white to acknowledge and celebrate the nation's non-Muslim citizens. Perspiration was forming on his temples due to the heat and he took out his handkerchief and wiped his face. At the crossroads an intense smell was issuing from the tar that the heat of May had partially melted. He had forgotten to bring along his spectacles and could not see into the far distance. He raised his hand in anticipation of a rickshaw but none appeared, so he waited there on the footpath, beside a man selling second-hand clothes from Western countries. They were donated by charities and were meant to be free, but in Pakistan due to corruption they had to be bought. He decided to walk to the next crossroads and halfway there a beggar with a red beard asked him for a rupee in the name of Allah, pointing to his mouth, then pointing to his stomach, then pointing to the sky, and Bishop Solomon stopped and gave him a few rupees from his pocket. He realised that a vein in his temple was pulsing and that he was looking at everything keenly, all his senses alert. A fruit shop displayed half its products on the footpath, placed in baskets that had been placed on crates and tins, lined with fresh lucerne foliage. It was like a cornucopia tilted beside him as he stood with a raised hand, all the colours and bright flavours of the Punjab. On the other side there was a group of girls playing hopscotch under a tree, and boys were hunched over glass marbles. There was graffiti on the wall beside him – the word 'Denmark' crossed out emphatically.

He was at the courts just before noon, his rickshaw followed by the car from the military-intelligence agency. The car's driver did not get out when they arrived, pulling up and beginning his wait, for Bishop Solomon to emerge again, perhaps noting down the time of arrival. Bishop Solomon walked along the corridors, in that palace of wisdom and judgement, passing lawyers, magistrates and petitioners, the policemen leading prisoners in chains, the relatives, the witnesses.

The door to the courtroom was closed and there was a peon outside. Bishop Solomon sat down on the bench outside and brought out his pocket Bible.

When the door opened fifty minutes later and people began to emerge, Bishop Solomon went in, walking down the central aisle towards the judge who was collecting his things. People in the large room were getting up – what was the word to describe them, the 'audience'? Bishop Solomon wondered. He stopped halfway up the aisle.

'Judge!'

Bishop Solomon had been loud enough for almost everyone else to stop and listen. As the judge looked at him, Bishop Solomon put his hand into his pocket and brought out the pistol. The little finger of his right hand was somewhat crooked from having healed badly. He had broken it when he pressed his hand into the gap between a doorframe and a door – this was the hand with which he had wished to strike Margaret after she had revealed her betrayal, during the days after Seraphina's death.

He heard the beginning of panicked screams in the courtroom, people flinching away to safety. Becoming a part of the world's past in a single instant, Bishop Solomon pressed the barrel to his chest and shot himself in the heart while the judge watched.

35

An exile returned to his homeland in the guise of a pilgrim. He wished to dig up the treasure he had left buried when he fled. He had gone to France and from there moved to Italy and then Germany. His forefathers were Christian but had been Muslim prior to that – and it was thought that he himself was still loyal to Islam, still tainted with it. All this was in Spain. After 1492, the Muslims who remained in Spain were compelled to convert to Christianity, but the sincerity of most of these conversions had remained in doubt. And many *did* hold on to Islam. These people – they were known as Moriscos – could be denounced simply because they rejected an invitation to dinner during Ramadan. There were battles over the dead, the Church insisting the dying Moriscos receive extreme unction.

The man who had returned disguised as a pilgrim was named Ricote. As he neared his village he recognised his former neighbour and sat down with him in a poplar grove.

'And now it's my intention, Sancho, to dig up the treasure I left buried, and since it's outside the village I'll be able to do so safely, and then write or go myself from Valencia to Algiers, where I know my wife and daughter are . . .'

Nargis was mending the page about Ricote Morisco, the character in *Don Quixote*. She had read from these chapters when she was a young woman, a student in Zamana. It was late at night, the end of a party at the house of Zamana's great architect, everyone drunk or drowsy, slouching wherever possible.

Someone had performed a soliloquy, another person read a poem. And she had opened the large book she had taken down from a shelf. In her own room in Anarkali she had that book, borrowed from the college library. Now she began to read from it.

'*Later in the novel, a Spanish ship is attacked by the Turks at sea. The Turkish captain is captured and brought to the viceroy, with a rope around his neck, awaiting death.*

'*The viceroy looked at him and, on seeing him so handsome there, and so elegant, and so submissive, such beauty was like a letter of recommendation and he felt the desire to save the young man, and asked:*

'"*Tell me, Captain, are you a Turk, or a Moor, or a renegade?*"

'*To which the boy replied, "I am neither a Turk, nor a Moor, nor a renegade."*

'"*What are you then?*" *the viceroy asked.*

'"*I am a Christian woman," said the boy.*'

She was in fact the daughter of Ricote. She declared that she was a genuine Christian, but had been taken to Barbary by her Morisco aunt and uncle against her will, settling in Algiers, 'which was the same as settling in hell', she said. She was returning to Spain to dig up the family treasure.

After Nargis finished reading, a young man at the party approached her and said that the book she had read from was written by his father. *That They Might Know Each Other.*

'My name is Massud.'

'My name is . . .' She hesitated the way she had never done with anyone else during her years in Zamana.

'Nargis. I know. I overheard earlier.'

Helen was upstairs, changing the sheets in the bedroom when the sound of something shattering in the kitchen reached her.

It was evening. They had eaten their meal and the first candles had been lit. When she went down she saw Nargis with a broken plate at her feet. The radio was on and Nargis stood still, staring at it as she would at a person who was giving her terrible news.

'Bishop Solomon has killed himself,' she said to Helen.

The newscaster was reading the details of the incident. The protest of despair. They listened and when the voice moved on to another item, Nargis switched off the radio.

'Are you all right?' she asked Helen, remembering the photograph of the bishop hanging in Lily's house, knowing how important he was to the Christians.

'Yes. But it's shocking,' Helen replied. 'Poor man.' She was holding the clean sheet she had brought with her downstairs without thinking, and now she sat down on the last step of the staircase, the cloth bunched up on her lap.

Her movements measured, Nargis collected the pieces of the broken plate – not sure for an instant what to do with them, appearing as though she were holding a cut-up page from the book. After disposing of them, she murmured something to herself. Then she turned to Helen and said quietly:

'You must always behave with honour.'

The girl nodded. 'I know. You have taught me that.'

'You mustn't do anything foolhardy.'

'What's wrong? Why are you talking like that?'

'I was so young,' Nargis said.

One of the few occasions Helen had witnessed Massud and Nargis in argument was when she decided to forgo – to postpone – studying abroad. 'She's a child, she must stay with us if she wishes,' Nargis had said; to which Massud had replied, 'She's eighteen!' 'Precisely, she's a child,' Nargis had said, 'she can go when she's older. For now she has to be with us.' 'On the one hand you are saying she is a child,' Massud had said, 'but on the other you think she should be allowed to make this important decision.' Helen had sighed and muttered something about them both being insane and had walked out of the room.

Now she got up, placed the sheet on the table, and went towards Nargis. She did not wish to press but clearly there was something Nargis wished to say. She brought Nargis to the chair and made her sit down, Nargis letting herself be guided.

'What's wrong?'

'During the early years, I was afraid Massud would leave me if he learned the truth. He deserved to know but I was too weak.'

Helen was filling a glass with water.

'I have no idea what you are talking about. Here, drink this. And then begin at the beginning.'

Nargis took a few sips. 'Where is Moscow?'

'He was climbing a tree the last time I saw, pulling a lantern behind him on a rope.' All day he had been building an eyrie, like the one he imagined Massud's grandfather must have made here on the island in 1910 to view Halley's Comet.

'I knew Bishop Solomon . . .' Nargis said, part-eagerness, part-anxiety.

Imran came through the midnight darkness when he saw Helen's lamp. But when he approached she asked him to sit down next to her on the veranda, instead of coming away with him.

For the past three hours she had been unwinding Nargis's story out of her, waiting while she paused, nodding when she asked if she should continue, going into the kitchen to bring back tea. She was afraid of Helen's judgement. Afraid of being condemned by her.

Now the girl sat beside Imran.

'I have to stay with her tonight,' she said. 'I don't think she should be alone.'

He gave a nod.

'She wants to go to Lyallpur tomorrow to see the body.'

'I'll take her. But I don't want you to be here alone.'

'I'm too drained to think.' She lifted her head and looked up at Nargis's window, the faint flicker of the light in there. 'I should go up.'

'How are you feeling?'

'I don't know. I don't think clearly enough fast enough. It'll take some time for me to know how I feel – days, weeks.'

'I'll look for your lamp.'

She nodded. 'But let me tell you something about her – a small detail, something Massud-*chacha* and I used to laugh at sometimes. After giving a party, she would write thank-you notes to the guests for coming.' She stood up. 'I am what I am partly because of her,' she said. 'I don't think I will ever be able to find any fault in her behaviour towards me. The lessons she learnt silently from her mistake, she taught them to me. So I myself don't have to make those mistakes.'

He lay down on the cracked tiles of the veranda, looking up towards the window from time to time, his gaze swinging from the sky to that square of dull yellow. Breeze and night creatures passed through the slanting grass of the island as he went in and out of sleep. Bandicoots. Mice. Something with mirrored eyes. Flying beetles. A few days ago Nargis said she had seen a turkey in the foliage, escaped from someone's home and living in the wild, devouring the fruits with a sweet hunger.

Helen woke him early in the morning, his eyes skewed against the sunlight. 'Nargis-*apa* is leaving for Lyallpur. She says she'll take the Daewoo coach and will be fine on her own.'

He took the mug of tea from her hand and swallowed a gulp and handed it back.

'Maybe we should both go with her.'

'She doesn't want either of us to come,' Helen said. 'She would like to be alone.'

'I'll take her to the coach station at least.'

36

Nargis stood looking at the large crowd outside the church, and the all-white house across the road from it. Loneliness was such a terrible thing, it was said, it made even God cry out to man. She went into the garden and sat down on a bench under the rosewood tree, at the back of the house where there was the set of beehives. A window close to her was broken, mended with tape. Among the many small replicas at the house in Badami Bagh in Zamana, there was one of this white building. One of the many 'dollhouses' Helen dragged from place to place when she was a child.

For a while Seraphina and Margaret had thought all burqa-clad women they saw on the streets were actually honey farmers. Due to Solomon and his burqa when he harvested honey. Each of the hives gave eight to ten kilograms of comb in a good year, she remembered.

St Margaret. She remembered reading about her in one of Solomon's books. The daughter of the patriarch of the pagans. When she reached the age of reason she was baptised, and so incurred the bitter hatred of her father. She was thrown into jail, put on the rack and beaten with rods and raked with iron spikes. 'You foolish girl,' the prefect had said, 'have pity on your beauty. Worship our gods and you will have nothing to fear.' And yet her cell was filled with miraculous radiance, while she lay there broken, praying to the Lord to reveal to her the enemy she was fighting.

It was getting towards evening. The light had diminished to a soft burn.

'Well, here you are.'

She looked up and saw the man from the military-intelligence agency, moving towards her.

'I thought you might come,' he said. 'We have been waiting.'

'I suppose you know everything about my past now.'

'Yes. So you will leave here with me, as soon as possible.'

'I have one condition.'

'I don't think you are in a position to dictate conditions.'

'Consider it a request.'

'No.'

'Let's call it a transaction, then. You can have the money the Americans will give me for forgiving my husband's killer.'

It was as though he didn't even think about it, so quick was his reply. 'What do you want?'

'I would like you to guarantee the safety of Helen and Lily Masih.'

'The rickshaw driver and his daughter.'

'Can it be done?'

He laughed derisively. 'Of course. We'll get them new identities, move them to a different city if they wish, or help them seek asylum in a Western country. There are at least half a dozen options. Where are they?'

'I don't know where the father is, but the girl is at a safe location. For the time being I'd rather not tell you where.'

And with that Nargis stood up determinedly:

'I am ready.'

She hadn't looked at him since that first glance. Now she turned to him and said, 'I also want my photograph back.'

37

On the island, smoke from the mosquito coil was in the air. Helen and Moscow were in the house enclosed by the lines of night shadow. On a windowsill there was the wing of a bulbul she had found in the grass, bringing it in here with the intention of taking it back to the house in Badami Bagh one day. He was mending a page of the book, the golden thread in his hands.

He bought an hour on the internet at a computer shop in the bazaar. YouTube was banned in Pakistan and so he used a proxy site to access it. There was a video of him, uploaded on YouTube years ago, playing the santoor at someone's wedding as a child, up there in Kashmir. He downloaded a program that allowed him to isolate and store the sound from videos. He converted it into a file, logged onto his music account, and added his performance to his iPod.

On the island he sat before Helen as she listened to him playing the beautiful strings a decade ago, hundreds of miles away from her.

The best small apples in Kashmir were found near Sopur, he had told her, half-sour, half-sweet. There was the *nabadi* which was yellow, the *jambashi* which turned red, and the *sil* which was a deep crimson. Sometimes in his sleep he cried out, still fastened by chains in the interrogation room, some lobe of his brain sealed up in the nightmare with Indian soldiers. When she shook him awake it could take him a few moments to recognise her.

In the morning they lay out in the open, the sun's heat coming to them through the bitter cold of outer space. In one corner of the mosque there stood the rolled-up lengths of straw prayer mats – some of them twenty yards long, for men to stand on side by side, in brotherhood. Imran had brought one of these lengths out of the building and folded it upon itself several times, making a soft bed for them under the trees. Suspending the mosquito netting from a branch overhead.

Something later that evening made him speak of the time he had spent at the training camp here in Pakistan. 'I left them because I didn't want the Kashmir they wanted.'

Helen knew that she wouldn't be surprised if the bombing of the Charagar mausoleum was traced back to one of the camps where guerrillas from Kashmir were also trained.

'In Kashmir we had no real idea of what the camps were like. Now I know that they are little more than gangsters. We just come here to learn to resist Indian soldiers. Not turn Kashmir into a desert caliphate.'

He had called Kashmir 'the victim of maps' once.

> *Though tyrants may command that lamps be smashed*
> *In rooms where lovers are destined to meet.*
> *We shall acknowledge their power*
> *Only if they extinguish the moon.*

These words that a poet had written in a prison cell came to Helen. Decades had gone by, and that wing of the prison was now named after him.

With the earbuds in, he hummed the devotional lyric to himself. It was morning again and she lay there listening to him. It was a piece of music she loved, as did Lily.

My master has planted a sapling inside me
By the name of Alif, the first letter of Allah . . .
The flower has blossomed
And stirred a tumult of musk in the soul . . .

Alif, the first letter of the alphabet and the first letter of the god known as Allah.

One day when she was a small child she had asked the man named Massud what was meant by the word 'reading'. She was the daughter of the servants in the house, and had been told to sit quietly in one place while the parents worked. He had thought for a while about her question and then said, 'I am thirsty.' He picked up the device he called a pen and touched the shiny end of it to a piece of paper and deposited some marks on the paper. Handing it to her. He asked her to show it to Nargis in the kitchen. Helen had done just that, and she had been stunned when Nargis sent her back to Massud with a glass of water. 'Reading is magic,' the man had declared. She herself had no memory of this incident – she was perhaps four at the time, if not younger – but Nargis, Grace, Lily and Massud had all told it to her countless times during her life, slowly creating images in her mind that felt like memory. Around that time it was decided that she would receive an education.

And the end to their time on the island, when it came, was swift. That afternoon a policeman in the bazaar felt something untoward about Imran. It was the day after Nargis had left for Lyallpur.

Some movement of his had made the man suspicious. He had gone there to buy milk and had seen the policeman and thought it prudent to slip into a shop for a few moments. He thought he had been discreet enough, had managed to evade him. Without him being aware, however, the policeman followed him for ten minutes. One day when he was a boy and was caught eating lead from a pencil, he had denied it. But his mother had asked him to open his mouth and had known the truth. She had brought a mirror and insisted his tongue had turned black for all to see because of the lie, not due to the lead.

By the time he detected the policeman's presence behind him, the policeman had already summoned one of his colleagues. Imran had memorised the layout of the bazaar during his first few days there for just such an eventuality – the alley behind the kiosk where he bought newspapers every morning, the lane alongside the shop where he acquired condoms, the path through the cemetery that coated his feet with pale dust, the three separate ways in and out of the milk-seller's compound. He had even glanced into the underground sewers, gauged the distance between one manhole and the next in each road.

He used most of these secret routes now and he thought he had freed himself from them, but they found him again on the small road that led to the island.

He sat in the roadside foliage for twenty minutes, watching them move towards the bridge. The longest minutes of his life. He revealed himself noisily, in order to distract them, and led them towards the bazaar again. He was running now – there was nothing in his mind but the moments he was living through one by one, propelling his body forwards – and they were running after him. People were looking at them, stopping to watch. Blocks of ice were being loaded onto a donkey cart outside the ice factory, the water melting off them almost making him lose his footing. There was a friend of his in Kashmir named Saif. The day after he returned from his military training in Pakistan, a soldier killed him at sunset, the chase lasting almost ten miles through the hill slopes and village streets.

He did not want to part from Helen, the months and

perhaps years he had envisaged in her presence, if she were to allow it. It took him two hours to return to the island, describing a circle a mile long, the policemen finally shaken off.

Later, in the afternoon, when the heat had silenced the birds, Helen was coming down the eighteen steps of the mosque library when she stopped on seeing the policeman at the bottom of the stairs.

'You're the girl wanted for blasphemy, aren't you?' he said. 'Is your father here too?'

She looked and saw the group of policemen by the door in the wall, too many of them, wrathful, contemptuous, careless as fire, subduing Imran where he lay on his stomach on the ground. The policeman came up the stairs and grabbed her sleeve, taking care not to touch her skin.

38

The American man was escorted into the courtroom in Zamana, his wrists cuffed in front of him. He hadn't been told what to expect. He thought the judge would officially inform him that his trial was going ahead, and then a new court date would be issued.

He was brought to an iron cage near the judge's bench, on the right-hand side, and locked in it.

The general was sitting in the back of the courtroom, sending a series of messages to the American ambassador on his mobile phone, updating him on the proceedings.

Nargis was standing in the corridor that led to the courtroom, to the left of the judge's bench, with fifteen relatives of the other victims, some of whom were openly weeping.

During the first part of the hearing, the judge announced that the American killer would be tried for murder in a Pakistani court. The statement was brief. Newspaper reporters frantically began filing their stories: it was clear that the American man would not be released from jail anytime soon.

But then the judge ordered the courtroom to be cleared, and the sixteen relatives of the victims walked in through the side entrance.

The judge announced that the civil court had now switched to a Sharia court.

Each of the family members approached the American man, some of them still with tears in their eyes, and declared that he or she forgave him.

After the last person filed past the caged white man, the general informed the ambassador that the matter was settled. The laws of Allah took precedence over the laws of humans; the American man was free.

It had all happened in Urdu, and throughout the proceeding the accused sat inside the cage with a baffled look on his face.

He looked astonished when Pakistani intelligence officers hurried him out of the courthouse through a back entrance and pushed him into a waiting car that sped towards Zamana airport. The American ambassador and several other officials were anxiously waiting for him at the airport. He had, after all, already shot dead three men he believed were threatening him. If he thought he was being taken away to be killed, he might try to make an escape, even attack the Pakistanis inside the car.

When he arrived at the airport and pulled up to the plane and saw the ambassador and the CIA men gathered there, only then did he realise that he was safe, that he was about to fly out of Pakistan.

The aged man standing beside Nargis asked her if she knew where the court mosque was, as he wished to say his prayers. Some of the fifteen people around her had referred to their dead in the present tense, she'd noticed, because a martyr never died.

People were beginning to disperse. There was a rumour that four of the forgivers were on the same plane as the killer – having asked for US citizenship instead of the money.

39

Lily's ghost walked out of the jail named after the poet. Next door was the zoo, and in the darkness the tiger turned its head, to look towards where the ghost crossed close to its cage. The birds shifted uneasily in sleep. He hadn't been dead long enough. When someone in the world of the living spoke his name, he became visible, for the duration. Other than that there was no reflection of him in the mirrors in Nargis's house, in the basin of water from which Aysha washed her face, in the panes of the display cases in the Museum of Glass Flowers. He felt simultaneously awake and asleep. On occasion, 'yesterday' and 'last year' were the same to him – time having lost all meaning. He watched Aysha wash her face, lifting water in the palms of her hands. He remembered that when he was alive one of his most cherished memories was the day Aysha had agreed to meet him for an hour in the Lions' Gate Garden. 'See what a beautiful answer God had given to your questions?' he had said to himself. Yes, the dead had memories too. The ghost remembered being in the room at Charagar's mausoleum, the evening of the suicide bombing, one of the two rooms with the blue doors. The policemen were calling people out one by one. How he managed to acquire the courage to run out of that blue door, he wouldn't have been able to say. He was the last man in the room and the policemen had grown complacent, perhaps. Men had been going out, stating their names and then having their trousers unfastened. No one had been detained. It was a storeroom of sorts, and there were no windows, and only one exit. When the policeman shouted 'Next!', he had opened the door and seen a headless man in front of him. The man

344

who had left the room before him was putting on his shirt, his head lost in the garment. Cana flowers grew in massive pots beside the door at the other end of the courtyard and he was running towards them now, the shouts of the policemen behind him. There was the sound of their guns firing. Outside, the milling crowd instinctively made way for him at first, but then – the policemen must have become visible behind him – hands began to grab for him, a grip tearing his shirt. He turned and struck a man. Muslims said that there were seven doors to their Hell, and one was reserved for the person who had raised a hand or weapon against a Muslim. When he was growing up his mother had talked to him of nothing but control. To not be provoked. To not be provoked *outwardly*. She knew she was only a human being and could not really protect him. He remembered this as he ran. Had he already been shot by that time? He wasn't sure. He did remember the pain in the ankle though, acid, cutting, electric. He fell and rose a number of times. He broke his fall by reaching out his hands and hurried like an animal along the ground, the left leg dragging behind him. A manhole appeared ahead of him, its cover stolen, sold for scrap-metal by the poor or the wicked or the city's helpless drug-addicts – and he swung his body down into it.

Beneath all the main neighbourhoods of Zamana there was the star-like confluence of eight sewers. As soon as Lily landed, up to his waist in the thick liquid, he tried to think if it was possible for him to wade his way away from the mausoleum. But before that he had to go back to Charagar, somehow, and complete his search for Aysha, to see if she was among the dead. The policemen were firing bullets, through the manhole above him. Beams of light were being shone down. He was so close to them. There were metal steps attached to the wall, leading from the manhole to the dirty water he stood in, like a series of staples half-pushed into the brickwork. But he knew the sense of disgust would not allow the men to climb down. He pressed himself against the filthy wall and decided to wait but every now and then an assault rifle would come down out of the manhole above him and release a burst of bullets in all directions, swivelling on a wrist, the flashes sometimes lasting for a minute. And now a lantern on a rope was being lowered slowly, illuminating him where he stood. He saw a doll's head float past him. At the Charagar mausoleum he had seen a policeman carrying the heads of the two suicide bombers. He began to move away, the pain in his foot unbearable when he tried to place any weight on it. He was thinking he would arrive at the next manhole along the channel and climb out. But he had not gone ten excruciating yards when a beam of vertical light appeared ahead of him, accompanied by gunfire, the water leaping in a spray where the bullets entered it. In the darkness he tried to feel along the walls, his hand sinking up to the wrist in the slime, to see if there was an opening into another channel between the two lit entrances. How long did he move through the buried stars under the city, how many days, how many hours? He was lost, he was walking with his bullet wound. He realised he had collapsed into the stinking water, into the black liquid shit, and was drowning – his body waking him up just in time. Once he found himself screaming in terror, his body trembling, the mouth letting out that roar of madness, into the pure airless heat.

He tried to think what his crime was, working his way back to earlier in the evening, earlier that day, earlier that week, the month, the year, his early adulthood, his youth, his boyhood, his childhood. The tunnels were full of echoes and he heard voices and he called out to them, but no one came because even your shadow deserted you when you were in darkness. He could hear his own childhood voice now, the fearful breathing of the eight-year-old who had been lowered into the sewer in order to clean it, and it was as though his child self lay trapped in the vast underground network, waiting for him. He saw daylight shining down from a manhole at last. A circle of pale sky in the darkness above him. He saw it grow brighter and then begin to fade again. He had been watching it for the duration of a whole day without being able to move more than a few inches towards it, too weak and too thirsty. The wound submerged in the dirty water was killing him, his leg immovable up to the knee, then up to the thigh. Infected. It would have to be cut off if he did not move quickly, he knew that much. It had happened to many. It took him several attempts to go up the slippery steps, his hands and feet losing their hold, sending him down into the black slime repeatedly. At last he emerged onto the road, the cars passing two feet away from him. He lay bent at the waist, his face pressed against the tarmac, his legs still underground. Exhausted from the effort. How long he lay there, he did not know. Did someone overcome their repugnance and drag him out fully? It was like being born. Perhaps that was what he was remembering. The policemen were dragging him out of the manhole onto the road. He was covered in fluid between his mother's legs and then someone held him with tenderness.

Where were the other dead? The ghost wandered through Zamana and sensed them but could not see them. Traces of them were present in the air of the city, on street corners, within houses, in the gardens. At this spot Grace had stood drinking milk with almond pulp beaten into it; and here was

Grace telling him about her cousin who had converted to Islam so he could have four wives; and here was Grace talking to the rich woman she had once worked for, and who had declared proudly that she had never beaten her child servants; and here was Lily carrying Grace out into the courtyard, both of them naked, so they could make love in the thrashing rain; and here was Grace's laughter suspended in the air when she told him that he was a fool like every other man on the planet, as if he didn't know; and here was the young Grace confessing her greatest fear to Lily, that he would stop loving her one day; and here was Grace, the teenaged servant girl, trying on her mistress's lipstick and jewellery; and here were the ants carting away the thousands of blossoms the *harsinghar* tree had dropped onto Grace's grave, so that the ground looked as though it were moving, or that the flowers had come alive.

The past and the present were combined now. Here was Lily buying his rickshaw and someone asking him how does it feel, and Lily replying, 'It's almost like holding a gun'; and here was Lily's mother waiting for her favourite song on the radio all week, cassette players not being common back then; and here was Lily's friend Amanullah telling him he wanted his just-born son to be the first Pakistani to play football for Barcelona; and here was the teenaged Lily dreaming of going to Dubai, to buy the mansion where his mother laboured as a servant; and here was Lily's father trying to steal the finial from the top of a mosque's dome, thinking it was made of gold, and here was his fall into the mosque courtyard, and here was the cleric who nursed him back to health without revealing his crime to anyone.

*

The policemen had pulled him out of the manhole and taken him away in a van. They had encircled him within a large room and they were coming closer and closer, without him knowing. He had been blindfolded. He was exhausted, by being born. They were converging, their weapons at the ready. They all wanted the privilege of killing the blasphemer, to have all their sins wiped out with that one act, and it had been decided that they would all stand around him in a circle and fire their guns simultaneously. At the count of three. They would bury the corpse in a shallow grave afterwards. All their lives they had lied, deceived, been envious, neglected prayers and fasts, and had disrespected their elders and brutalised innocent fellow Muslims and engaged in sordid acts, they had struck women, they had sodomised children, they had stolen from the sick and the hungry – and here was salvation, the instant guarantee of Paradise.

The ghost stood under the trees of the island where Nargis and Massud's mosque was situated, and the ghost called out Helen's name. He moved through serrated grass and the weeds. In places they came up to his shoulders. The sun was setting. Twice he had brought Massud and Nargis here, accompanied by students of architecture or photographers. There was not enough room in the car so a few people had had to get into his rickshaw. And so why had it never occurred to him to think of this place when he was alive and on the run? It was so obvious that this was where Nargis and Helen would have gone to hide. But then he had taken them to a hundred different places. Perhaps it was only obvious because he was dead. All mysteries had been solved now. He could now see the invisible paths that existed between people and what they desired. He now knew the location of the woollen hat he had lost two winters ago.

Just as he was no longer illiterate. He who had wanted to open a school in Badami Bagh! He could read everything now, exit signs, the *Once upon a time*s at the beginnings of fairytales, as well as the *happily ever after*s at the ends, the billboards advertising apartments in Dubai and London, the little stickers on fruits, the wrappers of bottle rockets the children sent into the sky. There were little words to be read under the plates and saucers and cups. There were words embossed on bars of soap, vibrating on the windows of buses and trucks. They called out to him, shouted at him. Tiny hidden words whispering to him the name of the country where an object was made; large ones telling him blasphemers should be beheaded; telling him *TALKING RELIGION AND POLITICS IS FORBIDDEN HERE.* The receipt for a safety razor from a shop owned by a devout Muslim told him, *We are selling the razor on the understanding that it will not be used to shave beards.* Carvings on tree trunks told him Sajad loves Razia while Kamran loves Meena. A man sat outside a hospital, holding a *KIDNEY FOR SALE* sign. Words. Words. Words. Every object had been talking all the time while he was alive, saying something to him, he just hadn't heard it. Now he knew what ghosts were: they spoke to you all the time but you just didn't comprehend their language.

'Helen,' he called out. He was standing on the island, scratching the area of his chest where his heart used to beat. He was under the window from which hung a wind chime made out of keys. Seeing it jostled by a fierce gust of wind, a feeling rose in him for a moment – a prompt to defend a weaker life form. 'Helen.' He remembered the red flowers whose petals Helen attached to her nails as pretend claws; and he remembered the young men and women she knew, interviewing inner-city shopkeepers for their PhDs; and he remembered Helen telling him that when Genghis Khan's forces invaded Zamana in 1221, the commander had ordered every book in the city to be burned; and he remembered the seven-year-old Helen murmuring to herself in the garden, reciting the book of childhood, the book she had become by being born; and he remembered the forest of colour unfolded by a fabric seller at Helen and Nargis's feet; and he remembered Massud telling Helen that there was not a single idea that was being thought in the world that wasn't also present in some mind in this great city. 'Nargis-*apa*?' The door did not creak when he went into the house. He laughed out loud and then buried his face in his hands with relief when he saw the mutilated book on the kitchen counter, the book Nargis had been mending in Badami Bagh all those days ago. 'Helen. Nargis-*apa*.' He was laughing as he tried to add a few stitches to a page.

Dusk found Lily on the veranda of the mosque, the air darkening fast. He got up and went into the building, free to roam. He could enter any house, any mansion, any palace he wished now; walk down any road or bridge, touch any object. He went up to the mosque roof and looked at the city in the far distance, surrounded by the moonlit river, its many channels and streams entering it, spreading out through it. His city. His river. The river reflected Grace stretching a line between two Persian lilac trees before hanging out her kameez to dry. And it reflected Lily as a teenager climbing an electricity pole to steal electricity. It reflected the steps of the mosque where destitute Mughal princes had begged for alms when the Mughal Empire ended; and it reflected a cleric giving a sermon on whether Muslims were allowed to eat mermaids; and it reflected those of Lily's rickshaw passengers who had police records and gang rivalries, and those who were thugs, extortionists, jackals, healers, seamstresses, dyers, heroes, dancers, meddlers, orators, traitors, professors, street dentists, cattle rustlers, motorcycle thieves, television repairmen, hunters of heresies, Baluchi guerrillas, seed and pesticide merchants; and it reflected the bazaar with its 6,000 shops selling lottery tickets, slabs of marble cut so thin they let in light, suit lengths, upholstery, furniture both local and from Chiniot; and it reflected Nargis's favourite sweet shop that had stood at the same spot since 1790; and it reflected Billu dreaming that he had turned into a bulbul and flown off to meet Prophet Muhammad; and it reflected unemployed young men who sat idling and full of rage in the streets, and who sometimes killed each other over a drawstring; and it reflected Nargis and Massud's serious and dignified friends who knew how to criticise religion without ridiculing religious people; and it reflected the jeweller's hands as he collected the gold dust from them at the end of a day's work; and it reflected Billu asking his grandfather if Western scientists would be rewarded by Allah for inventing the aeroplane, thus making it easier for Muslims to go to Mecca; and it reflected a man telling the youths in the street to go and stone the offices of the electricity company because the power cut was in its tenth hour; and it reflected the shock of Muslim children upon discovering that Christian holy men didn't always have beards; and it reflected a mullah declaring on television that anyone who did not refer to the marrow as the 'blessed marrow' was a blasphemer and therefore should be murdered, marrow having been one of Muhammad's favourite vegetables; and it reflected Aysha's father who gave away his pilgrimage money to someone in need, and was told later in the year by those returning from Mecca that they had seen him there, Allah having sent an angel in his guise to perform the pilgrimage for him; and it reflected rooms in moonlight in which he lay with Aysha, in which he lay with Grace, the singing of insects as he held the child Helen in his arms, the sun driving its bright spokes through the trees as he talked to Nargis, the chrome massifs of the monsoon clouds as he sought Massud's advice about something, and the rose-ringed parakeets knifing the morning air. And it was all him, it was all Lily, no matter what anyone said. It was his birthright, his self. He was Vela. He was Zamana.

'Helen.'

'Helen.'

353

VIII

THE GOLDEN LEGEND

40

It was Nargis who had selected the words that ran along the top of the mosque's white cube. And it was her hand that had calligraphed them, holding the reed pen in three fingers, the other two curving away. It was done on large sheets of paper before being transferred to the building. A continual adjustment in the direction of the hand and the pen had been required to produce the thick and thin writing.

It was pleasing to contemplate that the pen and the flute were both made from the reed, and how the breathing of the calligrapher had to have a rhythm too, just as the flute-player's did. Where the ink thinned – the dark and light shading – it was as though the pen were catching its breath, wishing to be lifted off the page for a while.

She had made the ink with the soot of burnt lamb bones. It was a greasy black powder and she had heated it in a cast iron pan with water, vinegar, and spoonfuls of oxen bile, stirring constantly, adding gum-arabic upon cooling to ensure a smooth flow, as well as a good dose of powdered saffron to make the ink jet black, finally testing it for adhesiveness and smear-resistance. Calligraphers fiercely guarded their ink recipes, but she had sought one of the best in the country and persuaded him after many months to show her how he composed his.

Above each of the four doors was a saying attributed to Muhammad. 'The believer in the mosque is like a fish in water. The hypocrite in the mosque is like a bird in a cage.'

All across the world of Islam since the seventh century, words decorated buildings – they were inscribed onto whitewash, carved in stone, baked with pigment into tiles, chiselled out of wood, and it was said that it was the largest collection of inscriptions any civilisation had ever produced.

These years later, and each July the monsoon clouds darken every space and structure on the island, its four houses and the white mosque. Lightning enters through the windows, making black shapes on the walls and floors, casting shadows on the ceilings. The bolts dart towards the earth again and again, and it is the end of the burning sunlight, and the water falls out of the sky without stopping for two or three days at a time, flowing silver through the trees. In Zamana, there are whole hours when voices cannot be heard unless raised. Earthworms emerge from the soaked soil in order to breathe, to keep from drowning, and the trees invade each other's canopies, their branches growing with such swift wildness. The air is green, choked with moths whose wings are ribbed with light, and the grass in the jamun groves is littered with the exposed pink flesh of broken fruit. A bird keeps saying *I am I am I am* . . .

Nargis watches the rains as they open rivulets in her Badami Bagh garden, the winds tearing away a fragile limb from the Persian lilacs. Farid comes along the path carrying the pail he has brought with him. In the pail a water-lily is floating, a gift from his pool to the one in this garden.

Aysha had gone to see him, seven days after the Charagar bombings, expecting to meet Lily there. She had introduced herself, but Lily hadn't come, and now Farid was a part of their lives, Billu insisting they all go to live in his museum. He wants legs made out of glass.

At night the sky is almost a hallucination as it is covered and uncovered by the glowing clouds.

A line from a poem enters Nargis's head but disappears immediately, the rain too noisy to allow the thoughts to focus. Towards dawn she hears the call to prayer from the minaret across the lane, the loudspeaker crackling in the drizzle. The Badami Bagh mosque is being run by Aysha's father once again – Aysha's brother-in-law and his friends, the young men with the bruised foreheads, having disappeared after attempting to assassinate Major Burhan. The soldier-spy had been visiting Nargis and they had ambushed him in the lane.

The rain intensifies, sounds within sounds within sounds, and from her window she watches Aysha's son leave for school in the morning, his gait steady in spite of his hurry, in spite of the mud and water. His mother is watching from the doorway and she and Nargis exchange a smile, their eyes expectant. Neither of them has any news of Lily, both of them waiting. Because of the rain the cleric's turbans are drying on a rope stretched temporarily on the mosque balcony. Billu turns in irritation and gestures for his mother to stop watching him and go inside, the water pouring off his umbrella.

Farid drops the flower with the dark heart into the pool and turns towards Aysha. This small and graceful mosque had been designed and financed in the eighteenth century by a Mughal noblewoman. At that time it stood within the dense orchard. The fact that it bore a woman's name had caused it to be abandoned on a number of occasions over the centuries, the city's clerics casting doubts on the validity of prayers offered in such a place. The building would fall into disrepair, becoming home to jackals, wild peafowl, hornbills and bats, but time would pass and the objectors would be replaced and forgotten, and the faithful would return.

Some months ago Nargis read that the American man had been arrested in Washington DC for assaulting a fellow

American over a parking space, the bail set at $15,000.

She imagines the island in the rain, the water soaking to the depths of the soil, the wind in the chime of keys outside Helen's window. In the kitchen it turns the pages of the half-mended book, scatters the various sections of the pages on the floor.

She had gone there with Major Burhan after the American man had been granted his freedom, but there was nobody on the island. Neither Helen, nor Moscow. Then the news had come that they were in police custody on the other side of Zamana. Around that time, around nightfall, a mob was gathering outside the police station. The word had spread that Helen Masih was being held there. There were more than a thousand armed men, baring their chests to the twenty policemen who were threatening to open fire if they came any further, to drag out the blasphemer from her prison cell.

When Nargis and Major Burhan got there, and once the mob had dispersed, they were told that the two young people had escaped in the tumult.

There was no way of knowing if it was the truth.

She has been unable to find the strength to revisit the island. She tells herself she should go back one day, bring back the book, bring back the hanging keys, Moscow's little music machine with its five hundred songs.

In the afternoon she enters the study of her house. The Mosque of Córdoba hangs near the ceiling but the Hagia Sophia is still here on the floor, this late in the year. She had neglected to winch it back up in February and then had become used to its presence at the centre of the room.

She walks to the corner where the system of pulleys and cranks is located, and begins to operate it. The building rises through the air but she stops its ascent when it is only halfway towards the ceiling. There on the desk that had been contained by the building – the desk that has come into view – is the book.

She lets out a sound as though bitten by something and moves towards it. And she opens it and sees that all the pages have been mended. The gold sutures run in a thousand different directions. The density of stitches has made the book one and a half times its original thickness. It is somewhat splayed open. *It is true for the first time in history all peoples on earth have a common present . . .* She reads the first words on the very first page, the epigraph. She looks up and stands listening, waiting to be approached. But there is no one, no noise or call.

In the evening she lights a candle in every room of the house and waits. The trees with their good shading leaves can be heard dripping, the rain having paused for now. An illiterate woman from the next lane had come earlier in the day to have a letter written to her mother in the city of Heer. It was only half done and the woman would return tomorrow to dictate the rest of the words to Nargis. She looks at the text now and decides to copy it out in a clearer hand. There is an awareness throughout all this, like music heard, then lost, then heard again. Towards 3 a.m. Imran whispers her name and she picks up the light and looks in the direction of the sound.

ACKNOWLEDGEMENTS

This is a work of fiction. All characters, events and organisations depicted in it are the author's creation. No resemblance is intended to any persons living or dead, to any organisations and events past or present.

I am delighted to acknowledge that the four italicised sentences on page 77 – they are from the story Helen writes at the age of seven – were written by my friend Maya Mishra in 2015, when she herself was seven years old. I thank her for allowing me to quote them here.

The italicised line on page 33 is by Velimir Khlebnikov, quoted in Raymond Cooke, *Velimir Khlebnikov: A Critical Study* (Cambridge University Press, 1987). The words the 'Waq Waq Tree' speaks to Alexander the Great, on page 82, are from *The Shahnameh* of Firdowsi. The italicised lines on page 187 are from *This Business of Living: Diary 1935–50* by Cesare Pavese (Peter Owen, 1961). The lines on page 182 are spoken by Tahir Ghani Kashmiri in Muhammad Iqbal's *Javednama* (originally published in 1932). In English the lines are: *Bring forth a melody – entrancing, bold / And let new madness rage in Paradise* (translation by Shaikh Mahmud Ahmed; published by the Institute of Islamic Culture, Lahore, 1961). Nargis's description of the architecture of Hindu temples on page 185 is based on A. K. Ramanujan's celebrated description. The details of the massacre of soldiers during the Indian Mutiny, on page 186, are from *Lahore: Tales without End* by Majid Sheikh (Sang-e-Meel

Publications, 2008). The verses Nargis sings on pages 247 and 248 are by Faiz Ahmed Faiz. The italicised lines on pages 315–16 are from Dostoevsky's *Notebooks for the Brothers Karamazov* (University of Chicago Press, 1971). Dostoevsky excised these lines from the finished novel. The lines Bishop Solomon refers to on page 319 are from *Blake: Prophet Against Empire* by David V. Erdman (Princeton University Press, 1977). The lyrics Moscow sings on pages 337 and 338 are by Sultan Bahu. The details of Islamic calligraphy on page 357 are based on descriptions found in *The Aura of Alif: The Art of Writing in Islam*, edited by Jurgen Wasim Frembgen (Prestel, 2010). The epigraph to Massud's father's book – quoted in italics on page 361 – is by Hannah Arendt.

This novel would be poorer without three books. I acknowledge my debt to their authors: Urvashi Butalia's *Speaking Peace* (Kali for Women, 2002); Ranjit Hoskote and Ilija Trojanow's *Confluences* (Yoda Press, 2012); and Mark Mazzetti's *The Way of the Knife* (Penguin Press, 2013).

While writing this book, I drew courage and conviction from Pankaj Mishra's magnificent and invaluable essays on Kashmir, originally published in the *New York Review of Books*, and collected later in his book *Temptations of the West* (Picador, 2006).

Thank you: Salman Rashid. Cathryn Collins. Martin and Federica Frishman for their love and support during the years I spent writing this book. Andrew Wylie, Sarah Chalfant and Charles Buchan. Stephen Page, Lee Brackstone and Angus Cargill in London. Meru Gokhale in New Delhi. Diana Miller and Sonny Mehta in New York.

The Blind Man's Garden

Shortlisted for the DSC Prize for South Asian Literature, 2014

Jeo and Mikal are foster-brothers in a small city in Pakistan. Jeo is a medical student who has been married for a year and Mikal is a drifter, in love with a woman he can't have.

After 9/11 as the conflict intensifies in Afghanistan, Jeo decides to secretly enter the country to help care for the wounded, and Mikal goes with him. But can their good intentions keep them out of harm's way?

Left behind is their family, and at its heart their blind father who is haunted by the death of his wife and the mistakes he has made in his life. *The Blind Man's Garden* is an evocative and powerful portrait of ordinary people torn apart by war.

'Extraordinary . . . Once or twice a year a book stuns me. *The Blind Man's Garden* has done just that.' *Independent on Sunday*

'A gripping work that goes to the heart of Muslim fanaticism and Pentagon intransigence alike. Aslam is a wonderful talent and we are lucky to have him.' *Sunday Telegraph*

'[Aslam is] an exceptionally gifted writer . . . *The Blind Man's Garden* is . . . a gripping and moving piece of storytelling that gets the calamitous first act in the "War on Terror" on to the page with grace, intelligence and rare authenticity.' *Guardian*

ff

The Wasted Vigil

Marcus Caldwell, an English widower and Muslim convert, lives in an old perfume factory in the shadow of the Tora Bora mountains in Afghanistan. Lara, a Russian woman, arrives at his home one day in search of her brother, a Soviet soldier who disappeared in the area many years previously, and who may have known Marcus's daughter. In the days that follow, further people arrive there, each seeking someone or something. The stories and histories that unfold, interweaving and overlapping, span nearly a quarter of a century and tell of the terrible afflictions that have plagued Afghanistan – and of the love that can blossom during war and conflict.

'Unforgettable . . . Tragic and beautifully written. Aslam is a major writer.' A. S. Byatt

'The richest reading experience I had this year . . . a love letter to Afghanistan and also an elegy for its casualties, human and cultural.' Adam Mars-Jones, *Observer* Books of the Year

'My favourite book of this – or any – year . . . A heartbreaking glimpse into the ravages of history . . . I can't recommend it highly enough.' Tahmima Anam, *New Statesman* Books of the Year

ff

Maps for Lost Lovers

Winner of the Kiriyama Prize and the Encore Award, and
shortlisted for the IMPAC Prize

In an unnamed English town, Jugnu and his lover Chanda
have disappeared. Rumours abound in the close-knit Pakistani
community and then, on a snow-covered January morning,
Chanda's brothers are arrested for murder. Telling the story of
the next twelve months, *Maps for Lost Lovers* opens the heart
of a family at the crossroads of culture, community, nationality
and religion.

'Thoughtful, revealing, lushly written and painful, this timely
book deserves the widest audience.' David Mitchell, *Mail on
Sunday* Books of the Year

'One of those rare novels that enters your imagination and
stays there. Its power comes from the haunting beauty of
the language and from excellent characterisation.' Helen
Dunmore, *Daily Telegraph* Books of the Year

'Aslam's vivid and tender portrait of the strict Islamic mother,
isolated by her unassailable belief, has stayed with me; as has
his metamorphosis of an English town into a poet's universe
of flowers, trees and butterflies.' Alan Hollinghurst, *Guardian*
Books of the Year

ff

Season of the Rainbirds

Winner of the Betty Trask Award, the Authors' Club First Novel Award, and shortlisted for the Whitbread First Novel Award and the John Llewellyn Rhys Prize

A sack of letters lost in a train crash nineteen years previously has mysteriously reappeared, and the inhabitants of a small village in Pakistan are waiting anxiously to see what long-buried secrets will be uncovered. Could the letters bring any information regarding the murder of the powerful and corrupt Judge Anwar? And what other interests within the community will be brought to light in the following days?

Award-winning author Nadeem Aslam has created a lush and timeless picture of daily life in Pakistan, played out against an ominous backdrop of assassinations, changing regimes, and faraway civil wars.

'A writer of singular genius.' Eileen Battersby, *Irish Times*

'A novelist of ravishing poetry and poise.' *Guardian*

'An exquisitely turned portrait of small-town life on the sub-continent: it is a real treat.' *Daily Telegraph*